D0594559

ZANE PRESENTS

PUT A RING ON IT

Dear Reader:

What can I say about Allison Hobbs other than she is phenomenal? There are very few writers that I can say that I actually admire. Allison is on the top of that list. She is a powerhouse of a writer and she keeps churning out one masterpiece after another; year after year. It is always my pleasure to personally edit her books the second they are turned in. *Put a Ring on It* continues to excite and entice my literary palate.

Lately, there has been much emphasis placed on women seeking that diamond ring; to be validated by marriage. Books, songs, movies, you name it; the controversy has exploded. Now the three women in *Put a Ring on It*: Vangie, Harlow, and Nivea, scramble to see who can make it to the altar first. But making it down the actual aisle is the least of their problems as they have to contend with baby's fathers who make disappearing acts, fiancés who get tied up with blood diamonds, and a younger sister's love interest who would rather have sex with his sister-in-law to be. Scandal, drama, lust, surprises and shockers. All the signature elements of an Allison Hobbs novel are contained herein.

Allison's next book is right behind this one; titled *Scandalicious*. What a sexy title! Make sure to check it out this fall. Also make sure that you join Allison on Wednesday nights as she conducts her weekly chat at 10 PM EST on PlanetZane.org. The topics are always sensual and on point.

As always, thanks for supporting myself and the Strebor Books family. We strive to bring you cutting-edge literature that cannot be found anyplace else. For more information on our titles, please visit Zanestore. com. My personal web site is Eroticanoir.com and my online social network is PlanetZane.org.

Blessings,

Zane

Zane
Publisher
Strebor Books

ALSO BY ALLISON HOBBS
Lipstick Hustla
Stealing Candy
The Sorceress
Pure Paradise
Disciplined
One Taste
Big Juicy Lips
The Climax
A Bona Fide Gold Digger
The Enchantress
Double Dippin'
Dangerously in Love
Insatiable
Pandora's Box

ZANE PRESENTS

ALLISON HOBBS

PUT A RING ON IT

SBI

STREBOR BOOKS

NEW YORK LONDON TORONTO SYDNEY

Strebor Books

P.O. Box 6505

Largo, MD 20792

This book is a work of fiction. Names, characters, places and incidents are products of the author's imagination or are used fictitiously. Any resemblance to actual events or locales or persons, living or dead, is entirely coincidental.

© 2011 by Allison Hobbs

All rights reserved. No part of this book may be reproduced in any form or by any means whatsoever. For information address Strebor Books, P.O. Box 6505, Largo, MD 20792.

ISBN 978-1-61129-919-9

Cover design: www.mariondesigns.com

Cover photograph: © Keith Saunders/Marion Designs

Manufactured in the United States of America

DEDICATED TO KHA'RI JOHNSON
*I love everything about you: your big beautiful smile,
the sound of your laughter, your braids, and even
your obsession with wrestling.
No one else in the world could make me
sit still and watch wrestling matches.
But I do it for you!*

ACKNOWLEDGMENTS

To my friend Daaimah S. Poole, thank you for eight years of friendship. The support you've given me is deeply appreciated.

Cairo, you are so sexy and smart. I call you the male version of Zane. So glad you're in my life. I cherish our friendship.

Nakea Murray, thanks for running all over New York with me. I couldn't have navigated the Big Apple without you. The Hudson was so magical! We have to run around Fifty-Eighth Street in our PJ's one more time!

Jason Frost, my fellow Sagittarian, premier book reviewer, and also my dear friend.

Keith Saunders, this cover takes my breath away. Thank you.

To my publicist at Simon & Schuster, Yona Deshommes, I appreciate everything that you've done for me. But I won't get mushy because I know it irks you. LOL

Charmaine Parker, I miss you! Thank God I'm going to see you in Jamaica!

Zane, I usually don't give a darn what anyone says or thinks about me...but when it comes to you...I CARE! Thank you for that matrix-like turnaround with the manuscript. You're incredible!

Karen Dempsey Hammond, thank you for helping me with numerous cover concepts, book titles, and for helping when I've written myself into a corner. You've been by my side throughout my literary journey and years before it ever started. No matter how hard I try, I could never repay you for all you've done for me.

CHAPTER 1

Call it a woman's intuition. Call it a sixth sense, but instead of driving home after work, Nivea felt an urge to swing by her fiancé's old apartment.

When she rolled up in front of the building where Eric used to live, she gave the place a smug look. Eric's former apartment building was a dump. She had no idea why he'd been so resistant to the idea of moving into her upscale townhouse.

But that was water over the bridge. She had introduced Eric to a better lifestyle and she was proud of that fact.

Nivea did a double take when she noticed the Highlander parked at the curb. Her heart rate began to accelerate when she recognized Eric's license plate. *What's he doing here? He's supposed to be working overtime.*

With the motor running, she jumped out of her Mazda and removed a couple of lawn chairs that were holding someone's nicely shoveled parking spot. Brows joined together in bafflement, she parallel parked, cut the engine, and then got out.

Nivea peered up at the second floor apartment that Eric had left six months ago when he'd moved in with her. She could see the twinkling colored lights that adorned a Christmas tree. She frowned at the Christmas tree. It was the first day of December, too soon to put up a tree in Nivea's opinion.

Eric had sublet the place to one of his unmarried friends. *Which one?* She couldn't remember. Feeling a rush of uncomfortable heat, she unbuttoned her wool coat, allowing the frigid evening air to cool her.

There had to be a good explanation for Eric being here. Something really innocent. *He didn't have to work overtime after all, and decided to stop by and visit his buddy*, she told herself.

Even though moving into Nivea's townhouse was a step up for Eric, it had been hard convincing him to give up his crappy bachelor's pad. She was so elated when she'd gotten him to agree to move in, that she hadn't bothered to question him about the details of his rental transaction.

But she was concerned now.

Carefully, Nivea climbed the icy concrete steps that led to the front door. Inside the vestibule area, another door, this one locked, prevented her from forcing her way to Eric's old apartment. She read the name that was centered above the doorbell of apartment number two: D. Alston.

Who the hell is D. Alston? She jabbed the doorbell twice, and then pressed the button without letting up.

She heard a door open on the second floor. "Stay right here. Let me handle this," Eric said gruffly.

Who the hell is Eric talking to?

Eric thumped down the stairs, causing a vibration. At the bottom of the stairs, he looked at Nivea through the large windowpane that separated them. She expected a smile of surprise, but Eric gawked at her, displeasure wrinkling his forehead.

He turned the lock, cracked the door open, and poked his head out. "Whatchu doing here, Niv?"

"I should be asking that question. You're supposed to be at work!"

"Yeah, um…" He scratched his head.

"Who's renting the place now?"

"Uh…"

Refusing to give him time to gather his thoughts, she pushed the door open, and zipped past Eric.

"You can't go up there, Niv."

"Hell if I can't!" Nivea took the stairs two at a time, the heels of her boots stomping against the wooden stairs. Eric was up to something, and she had to know what the hell was going on.

Eric raced behind her. He roughly grabbed her arm. "You outta pocket."

She yanked her arm away and spun around. "Let me go, Eric!" Eric was a big, stocky man, but she gave him such a violent shove, he fell backward, stumbling down a couple of steps.

Motivated by a suspicious mind, Nivea bolted for Eric's apartment, which was at the top of the stairs. The door was slightly ajar. She pushed it open.

A woman, who appeared to be in her early twenties, stood in the kitchen, clutching a baby. One glance told Nivea that the woman was street tough. Hardcore. She was not cute at all. Light-skinned, reed-thin with a narrow, ferret-like face. The Kool Aid red-colored weave she was rocking looked a hot Halloween mess. Anger flickered across the woman's mean, sharp-featured face.

"Who are you?" Nivea asked, hoping to hear, *I'm Eric's cousin.* Hell, she was willing to accept childhood friend, or even long lost sister. She'd happily go along with any relationship, except jumpoff. She stole a glance at the baby that was buried beneath blankets.

The skinny chick looked at Nivea like she had sprouted a second head. "How you gon' bust in here axin' me who da hell I am?" Her bad grammar and attitude confirmed Nivea's suspicion that the chick was a hood rat.

Nivea scanned the kitchen quickly. The appliances were as outdated as Nivea remembered, and the cabinetry was still old and chipped, but the room was spotlessly clean and somewhat better furnished than when Eric had lived there. Nivea took in the rather new, but cheap-looking kitchen set that had replaced Eric's old one.

The female tenant had tried to brighten up the dismal kitchen. Matching potholders and dishtowels were on display. The former dusty mini blinds that had once hung at the kitchen window had been replaced with ruffled curtains.

What is Eric doing here with this ghettofied heifer and her child?

As if she'd read Nivea's mind, the thuggish chick turned toward Nivea. Holding the baby upright, she gave Nivea a full view of the infant's face. Nivea felt her heart stop. The little boy, who looked to be around four or five months old, was a miniature replica of Eric.

"Oh, my God!" Nivea squeaked out. She grimaced at the child who was Eric's spitting image.

Okay, I'm imagining things. That child can't possibly be Eric's baby!

CHAPTER 2

Eric barreled into the apartment. Nivea suspected he had been hanging out in the hallway, trying to get his lies together.

"You need to check yourself, Nivea. You know you dead wrong for running up in the crib like this."

Nivea was stunned that Eric, her gentle teddy bear, was growling at her like a vicious grizzly bear.

Nivea stared at the baby and then at Eric. She swiped at the tears that watered her eyes. "What's going on, Eric?"

The skinny chick bit down on her lip, like she was struggling to control her temper. "I'm not with this shit, Eric. You better handle it."

Eric tugged Nivea's coat sleeve. "This ain't the time or the place, Niv."

"Have you lost your mind, Eric? You told me you were at work. I need to know what the hell is going on. Get your coat!" She motioned with her hand. "Talk to me on the way home. We're out of here!" Nivea waited for Eric to go get his coat, but he didn't budge.

The ghetto chick snickered, and then looked down at the baby. "Don't worry, Boo-Boo; Daddy ain't going nowhere."

Daddy! No way! That is not Eric's child, Nivea told herself. With a hand on her hip, she glared at Eric. "Who is this bitch? And why are you here with her?"

"My name is Dyeesha. I ain't gon' be another bitch, *bitch*. I don't know who you is, but you trespassing." The woman with the bad grammar spoke in an annoying scratchy tone, her nostrils flaring as she furiously patted her baby.

"Eric! Tell this girl who I am!" Nivea spoke through clenched teeth.

Looking like a cornered rat, Eric was at loss for words and could only come up with utterances and sputtering sounds.

"How you expect him to remember the name of e'ry hooka he done slept with while I was pregnant with his son," Dyeesha said with a sneer.

The abrasive sound of the girl's voice, her assumption that Nivea was a stripper and a prostitute, and her terrible grammar… it all grated Nivea's nerves. "For the love of God, will you please tell this ignorant-ass, ghettofied, hood chick who I am!" Nivea yelled.

As if his lips were sealed with Super Glue, Eric was mute.

"Ghettofied! You da one acting ghetto." Dyeesha contorted her lips. "For your information, I'm Eric's baby mama. In a few weeks, I'ma be his wife." Dyeesha shot a hot glance at Eric. "I can't believe you let one of your tricks run up on me like this."

"Stop calling me a trick! You're not marrying Eric. I am! Our wedding is in June," Nivea shouted.

Dyeesha grabbed the doorknob. "Keep dreaming. Now bounce, bitch. Take your trick ass back to that strip club you crawled out of."

Nivea stared at Eric. "Are you gonna just stand there while your jumpoff insults me?"

Dyeesha snorted. "You da damn jumpoff! Now take your home-wrecking activities somewhere else!" Dyeesha tried to pass the baby to Eric. "Hold your son cuz I'm 'bout to go on her trick ass!"

Nivea gasped. She wasn't expecting to get into a fistfight with a street tough thug chick.

Eric calmed Dyeesha by rubbing the length of her willowy arm. "I told you, I got this."

The gentleness in Eric's voice, the tender strokes he delivered to Dyeesha's sweater-covered arm...and the baby! It was all too much to bear. Hotly jealous, Nivea felt her anger rising like steam. She pounced on Eric, trying to claw at his face. "You lying, cheating, broke ass, no-good scumbag. I should have never got involved with a damn warehouse worker!"

Dodging Nivea's fingernails, Eric tossed her off of him, knocking her into the fridge. Too wound up and too furious to feel any pain, Nivea kept fighting, jutting her kneecap upward as she aimed for Eric's groin, which in her opinion, was the real culprit in this triangle of lies and deceit.

She missed the intended mark, but Eric grunted in pain as Nivea's kneecap rammed his inner thigh.

"Get that bitch, Eric. Fuck her up," Dyeesha goaded.

Holding the baby, Dyeesha followed Nivea and Eric as they scuffled along a short hallway, ending up in the small living room.

"Stop acting crazy!" Eric demanded as he grabbed Nivea by the shoulders and gave her a brisk shake. To Eric's credit, he hadn't actually hit Nivea; he'd merely tried to restrain her.

Nivea maneuvered out of his grasp and landed a hard slap across his face.

"Ow! Shit!" Eric rubbed his cheek.

Dyeesha sucked her teeth. "Hold the baby, Eric, so I can whoop that ass."

"I got this!" Eric insisted as he lunged for Nivea.

Swinging both hands, kicking, and scratching, Nivea was prepared to fight to the death. She wasn't leaving the premises without her groom in tow. In the midst of the squabble, Nivea noticed a series of photos in silver frames. There was one with Eric holding the baby. Another with Dyeesha and the baby, and the third silver-framed photo held a family portrait.

Feeling lightheaded, Nivea stumbled, bumping into the small

Christmas tree that sat atop a table, the one she'd seen twinkling through the window.

Three red and white stockings were thumb-tacked to the wall: Eric, Dyeesha, and Eric, Jr. was printed in glittery letters.

Nivea punched Eric in the face. His large form toppled the Christmas tree. Glass balls shattered. Mini lights crashed against the floor.

The baby screamed. Dyeesha pressed the baby against her bosom. "Bitch, I know you don't think I'ma let you fuck up my family's first Christmas together."

Eric pulled himself to his feet. "Get the baby out of here. I got this, Dyeesha," he mumbled, picking up the dwarfed tree, trying to get it to stand up straight.

"You better get this trick outta my house before I call the cops."

"Stop calling me a trick. I'm his fiancée." Nivea held up her ringed finger as proof.

Dyeesha looked at the diamond ring and snorted. "Pole dancers make lots of money. You bought that bling and put it on your own finger."

Nivea drew in a breath. The truth hurt. She had put the expensive ring on her credit card, telling herself it was okay as long as Eric made the payments, which he hadn't done at that point. And with this horrible turn of events, it wasn't likely he'd be making any payments in the future.

Eric stepped in front of Nivea. "What's wrong with you, girl? Why you tryna make me hurt you?" He drew his lips together in a threatening manner. Nivea couldn't believe her eyes or her ears. *What the hell?* Eric had been such a pushover. The way he always let her have her way had endeared him to her. Now he was threatening to hurt her.

"When were you going to tell me about your secret family? On our wedding day?"

"He ain't marrying you!" Dyeesha hissed.

"Oh, yes he is," Nivea insisted. She knew that she should have turned around and walked away the moment she saw that baby's face, but she had put so much time and effort into Eric...into her wedding, she couldn't walk away.

In an act of desperation, Nivea reached for Eric's hand. "We can discuss this at home."

Refusing the gesture, Eric placed his hands behind his back.

"I guess you didn't get the memo, trick. The only wedding that's going down is mine and Eric's." Dyeesha rolled her eyes at Nivea. "Tell her, Eric," Dyeesha coaxed.

Eric lowered his head. He stuffed his hands inside the pockets of his jeans, and began jiggling change. He spoke in a low tone. "I should have told you about Dyeesha. I can't go through with it. The wedding is cancelled, Niv."

Dyeesha puffed up with pride. "You hear that, trick! Your imaginary wedding is cancelled."

The wedding is cancelled! Nivea opened her mouth and began shrieking as if someone had thrown a pot of boiling oil in her face.

The baby screamed along with her.

"Yo, get a grip. You scaring the shit outta my son," Eric said.

"But you don't have any children," Nivea replied dumbly.

"That's my son," Eric confirmed. "I wanted to tell you but I ain't know how."

Any normal bride-to-be who was getting hit with one bombshell after another would have been lying prone on the floor, while awaiting an emergency ambulance team to rush in and recharge her heart, but Nivea didn't have time for heart failure. She appealed to Eric's sense of reasoning. "My gown, Eric. What about my wedding gown? I'm scheduled for my next fitting in a few weeks."

Eric blinked at her, held his hands up in the air.

Dyeesha's mouth was twisted, like she'd eaten something rotten. "Don't nobody care about your raggedy-ass gown. You better get your damn deposit back. Eric's not leaving me for you or any other trick-bitch."

Dyeesha's slanderous words had lost their sting. Nivea was deep in thought. Like a broken record, *the wedding is cancelled*, repeated inside her mind.

It was unbelievable that Eric had been leading a double life. Nivea tried to imagine sitting her parents down, and telling them this horror story, but it was too humiliating to ponder. She had to figure out a way to fix this awful mess.

"You gotta go, Niv," Eric told her. "You're upsetting my family."

"Fuck your family!" Finally giving into the rage that was bubbling inside, Nivea grabbed both silver-framed photographs and sent then zinging toward Eric's head.

Eric hit the floor. His eyelids fluttered as blood oozed from an open wound on the side of his head.

"Help!" Dyeesha screamed. Dyeesha raced out of the apartment and out into the hallway. Neighbors began to open their doors. "Help. There's a crazy bitch in my crib. She's tryna kill my whole family," Dyeesha's shrieked.

With the single thought of escaping punishment, Nivea left Eric moaning and bleeding on the floor, and ran out of the apartment.

"There she is. Somebody catch that trick." Dyeesha's voice climbed higher. "Don't let her get away!"

Whizzing past several puzzled neighbors, Nivea bounded down the stairs and out the set of doors.

Nivea rushed along the slushy pavement. Slip-sliding across the icy street, she jumped in her car. *A few stitches should take care of Eric's head*, she told herself. She gnawed at her bottom lip as she pulled the Mazda forward. The tires thudded against a mound of hardened snow. *Fuck!* She had to get out of the tight parking spot before the police arrived.

Suppose he's dead! Nivea grimaced. The idea of doing jail time for murder was far more distressing than being dumped six months before her wedding.

Ramming the car behind her, she forcefully gave herself room. As she zoomed away from the scene of the crime, hot tears splashed against her face. Eric deserved to be dead, but for the sake of Nivea's freedom, she needed him to live.

CHAPTER 3

If they could see me now, Harlow thought with a self-satisfied smile. According to statistics, a person with Harlow's background was not expected to get very far in life.

Harlow sprayed her neck and then each wrist with a fragrance that was touted as the world's most expensive perfume. Blissfully, she closed her eyes and inhaled the floral scent. A one-ounce, handmade crystal bottle adorned with a sparkling brilliant-cut white diamond on the collar, the perfume's container was an exquisite piece of art.

Like all of her rich possessions, the sinfully expensive fragrance was a gift from Drake Morgan. Drake rented and sold exotic cars. He owned three locations on the east coast, and had recently begun increasing his fortune with online sales. Exporting luxury vehicles overseas, primarily to African countries, had become a very lucrative endeavor.

Ever since Drake had entered Harlow's life, nothing had been the same. The past eighteen months had been like a montage of romantic movie scenes from an amazing love story.

Drake treated Harlow like a goddess, showering her with lavish gifts, and introducing her to a lifestyle that was so luxurious, she often had to pinch herself to make sure she wasn't in the midst of an incredible dream.

With her hair in place and her makeup complete, she slipped into a curve-hugging blue dress, conveniently forgetting to put on panties. Smiling slyly, she knew Drake wouldn't be able to resist such easy access to the goods.

Carrying an overnight bag, Harlow left her villa-style accommodations, and walked to the lobby of the exclusive resort.

"Good evening, Ms. Grant. Your car is waiting." Efficiently, the concierge motioned for the bellhop to relieve Harlow of the travel bag. Despite his attempt at professionalism, the young man's eyes roamed Harlow's hourglass figure.

Harlow wasn't offended. She was accustomed to male attention. Though her looks had caught Drake's eye, he told her that it was her inner beauty that had captured his heart.

She slid inside the sleek black limo and relaxed against the sumptuous leather. As the car moved smoothly into the moonlit night, Harlow stared out the window, marveling at the magnificence of St. Croix: the lush greenery, the warmth.

She made a mental note to call her girls, Vangie and Nivea, and tease them. While they were freezing their butts off in Philly, dealing with blizzards and frigid weather, Harlow was basking in a tropical paradise.

Harlow accompanied Drake on his numerous business trips to several exotic locations, but St. Croix had become her favorite spot.

The limo glided to a stop near the pier. The driver opened the door. Outside the limo, Drake's right-hand man, Alphonso, was there to greet her.

She gazed in awe at the three-story, mega-yacht that was named The Water Nymph.

Alphonso took her bag. "Drake is still in the meeting—tying up loose ends of the transaction. He wanted me to escort you onto the ship and make sure you're comfortable." Alphonso was all business; he didn't crack a smile.

"Thanks, Alphonso." Harlow fell into step with him as they headed toward the boarding ramp.

Harlow inhaled deeply, catching a whiff of the ocean breeze that carried the intoxicating scent of tropical flowers. She was far away from the squalid neighborhood where she'd grown up.

❤ ❤ ❤

Music was pumping. The party was already in full swing. Talib Chitundu, a young and very wealthy African, was the host of The Water Nymph bash.

According to Drake, Chitundu had a penchant for luxury cars and a passion for pretty women, and he had no problem throwing tons of money around.

Scanning the guests, Harlow noticed that the party girls, as well as the female staff, were all flawlessly beautiful. There appeared to be at least four skimpy-dressed women to every man. No doubt, the men aboard The Water Nymph would have their every sexual fantasy fulfilled.

Harlow was relieved that Drake didn't have a wandering eye. Drake was serious about his money, which was the only reason he was in any way affiliated with a fun-loving, ladies man like Talib Chitundu.

Carrying a tray with a variety of vividly colored drinks, a bikini-clad, blonde-haired beauty made her way to Harlow and Alphonso. Harlow took a drink from the tray.

"I'm going to wait for Drake in our cabin," she told Alphonso.

In the solitude of her cabin, she sat on the private balcony, sipping a mango mojito and enjoying the tranquil view of the dark blue, Caribbean Sea.

She had a feeling that tonight was the night that Drake was going to propose. And tonight she was going to fuck him like there was no tomorrow.

When she heard the door open, she set the drink down and excitedly sprang to her feet.

Drake entered the cabin. Tall, with a distinguished and prominently angled face, Drake had a broad and muscular build. His mocha-bronzed skin looked kissed by the sun, a nice contrast with the light-colored suit he was wearing. Mouthwateringly sexy, Drake was a gorgeous man. For Harlow, he was heaven sent.

She rushed into his arms. The mere nine hours they'd been apart seemed like weeks. Bending, Drake gave her a bear hug. "I missed you."

"Missed you more," Harlow whispered, embracing him tightly. Her fingers glided across the fabric of his jacket, itching to touch his bare skin.

"You know I'm off my square if you're not in a five-mile radius," Drake said, his words tickling her neck. His large hands wandered downward, coasting over the sheer blue fabric. Palming her ass, he pulled her closer. Harlow could feel his erection straining inside his pants.

Desire rippled between her thighs. Damn, she was hot for him. So hot, she had to restrain herself from ripping Drake's clothes off. "Do you know how much I love you?" she whispered.

"Tell me."

"I love, worship, and adore you. You got me craving you like you're a drug."

"That makes two of us. We're both sprung."

Ready for her fix, Harlow lifted her head and offered parted lips.

Drake's kiss was quick.

Confused, Harlow raised an eyebrow.

"We have to join the party, mix it up with our gracious host and his guests," Drake explained. "I just sealed a major deal with my man, and I don't want Talib to feel like he's being snubbed."

Harlow winced at the thought of mingling, making small talk, and having to share this special night with other people. "With all those half-naked women out there, I don't think Mr. Chitundu will miss us. I want a private party...just me and you," she said, her lips pouty.

"We have to at least make an appearance. Just for a little while."

Harlow made a face. Determined to get her way, she pulled up her dress, enticing Drake by showing off her private body parts.

He breathed in roughly, groping her bare ass. "Aw, now, you're not playing fair, coming at me with no panties on." His voice was coarse with yearning.

His hard-on throbbed against her stomach. Harlow touched the thick bulge. It felt hot beneath her hand.

"We'll mingle later. I need you," she told him breathily.

"I'm all yours."

Tormented by the heat that rose inside her, she tightened her hand around his rigid shaft.

Harlow reluctantly released Drake's erection, while she pulled her dress over her head. At five-foot-nine, Harlow was statuesque, giving the impression of being model thin. But out of her clothes, she was long, shapely, and surprisingly thick, especially in the hip and thigh areas. Her plump rump was another hidden bonus.

Drake's eyes lit up. He moistened his lips as he took in the magnificence of her physique. "Your body...so beautiful, baby."

Being admired by the man she loved was thrilling. But she was too hot and bothered to enjoy the caress of her lover's eyes. She wanted hands, lips, tongue. And dick. She was so horny, she could barely stand still. She hadn't been kidding when she'd told Drake that she needed him. She needed to feel every thick inch of him, pounding inside her.

With trembling fingers, she unknotted Drake's tie. Her hungry mouth kissed and licked his neck. Her breasts were full and heavy with desire. Her nipples were puckered, jutting out like thimbles.

Once the knot of his tie was undone, she yanked it from around his neck and flung it aside. Hurriedly, she began working on the buttons of his shirt.

With one arm in and the other out of its sleeve, Drake's jacket hung at his side. Ridding himself of the jacket, he shook it off his arm, letting it drop. Knowingly, his lips took in the beaded nipples of Harlow's painfully swollen breasts. "Is that better?"

She responded by pressing his head closer to her bosom, persuading him to take in a mouthful of hardened nipple and tender breast. Needing to be touched all over, she guided his hand down to another sensitive spot.

Searching for moisture, Drake's fingers threaded through the honey-soaked thatch of hair that covered her mound. He parted the silken lips of her sex.

She shivered at his touch. "Take off your pants," she urged him.

"Not yet." His voice was firm and controlled. Slowly and with tenderness, he inserted his middle digit into her heated moisture. His finger wriggled and probed, sending shock waves through her system. "Do you like that?" he asked.

"Yes," she whimpered. As if speaking for itself, her pussy muscles began to spasm, clenching around the bulged knuckle that skimmed against her delicate insides.

Harlow gasped. Getting finger-fucked was an agonizing pleasure. Heightening the sensation, Drake massaged her distended clit with the pad of his thumb. Blissfully, Harlow cried out, her hips rocking as Drake worked magic with his long, thick finger.

She didn't want to cum…not like this. Ready for the real thing, she clamped her thighs together, entrapping his hand, stilling the movement of his prodding finger.

"Drake, please." Harlow's voice was a soft plea.

He slowly extracted his finger. Bringing it to his nostrils, he drew in her scent. "Your pussy smells better than that expensive perfume."

She smiled at the compliment.

But when his tongue began to swipe at his finger, licking away her juices, she felt her knees go weak. Harlow yanked on his belt, promptly unbuckling it. She shoved his pants down, and slid her hand inside the opening of his briefs, wrapping her hand around his jutting erection.

Both naked now, Harlow and Drake came together on the bed. Lying on her back, she opened her legs.

Drake mounted her. Caging her to the bed, he pressed his naked flesh against hers. The head of his dick kissed her pussy lips. Flames erupted all over her body. Nudging past the slippery folds, he eased the smooth crown inside her, and then withdrew it, causing Harlow to twist and moan and beg for dick.

"You want some more, baby?" Drake asked; holding his heavy dick, he stared at her face.

"You know I do."

With his erection secured in his hand, Drake once again parted her slick opening with the tip that was lubricated with her juices and his own pre-cum. "How much do you want?"

"Stop torturing me, Drake."

"Tell me how much dick do you want?" His voice was low and sexy.

She bit the soft flesh inside her bottom lip. "All of it, Drake. I want it all."

Drake stared down at her. "Not yet. You gotta be patient."

Ready to protest—prepared to stand up for her rights and take the dick that was rightfully hers, Harlow tried to rise up on her elbows.

"Lay back down," he said softly.

All she could do was whimper and squirm as he steered the large crown of his dick back to the hot moisture between her legs. Her pussy made helpless little wet sounds as though crying for a hard thrust.

But Drake took his time, easing in an inch at a time and then pulling out, making her pussy pucker with need.

"Don't tease me, Drake," she said, sucking in bursts of air. "I'm begging you."

"Begging for what?"

"I'm begging for all your inches. Please. If you give me what I want…" Before she could finish the sentence, Drake reentered her, groaning as he pushed into her clutching depths. Dick embedded to the hilt, he halted his movement. Harlow became still also, savoring the sensation of their hot bodies fused together.

Resorting to begging had paid off; she had his dick right where she wanted it. Pleased with herself, she smiled.

Drake kissed the smug smile off her lips, his tongue thrusting deeply, making Harlow's sex clench.

"Fuck me, right, baby. You know how I like it."

Winding his mid-section, Drake sexed Harlow in a slow, circular fashion.

She arched her hips and widened her thighs, urging him to go deeper and faster.

Obligingly, he plunged inside her. Her tight pussy sheathed his raging hard on.

With each thrust, blinding sensations blazed through Harlow's body. "Nobody fucks me like you do!" She threw her legs around his waist, giving it back the same way she was getting it, hard and fast. Sweating, clawing, and crying, she rotated her hips wildly, panting and grunting. Then she felt little jolts of electricity coursing through her—the feeling was a precursor to a powerful orgasm.

Harlow tensed. Unable to help herself, she bit down on Drake's shoulder while her pussy walls tightened around the length of his dick.

"You ready for me, baby?" Drake's voice was gruff.

"Uh-huh," she uttered, nodding briskly.

Drake shifted the direction of his stroke, suddenly jutting upwards, expertly striking against the soft pad of her G-spot.

Incoherent murmurings spilled from her lips. Her body shook and jerked violently.

"I love you, baby," he groaned; his lips close to her ear.

Using her strong legs to pull him in closer, Harlow invited Drake to join her in orgasmic pleasure.

As though bracing himself for a tremendous eruption, he clenched the covers on the bed. Harlow fixed her gaze on Drake's face, watching his handsome features contort into a grimace as he shot out hot jets of white passion.

CHAPTER 4

It was six-forty in the evening when Vangie and her five-year-old son, Yuri, left the childcare center. The sky was already dark and brooding. So depressing. It was practically immoral to bring her son outside in the cold darkness of night.

"Where's the car, Mommy?"

Feeling burdened by single motherhood, Vangie released a disheartened sigh. "I couldn't find a spot—had to park around the corner."

Vangie and Yuri trudged through slush and navigated around mounds of snow. With the high price of childcare, it was downright criminal that the center didn't provide on-site parking.

Money worries turned down the corners of Vangie's mouth. Her salary as an administrative assistant at the local cable company wasn't cutting it. Her tight budget barely allowed for the few hours after school that Yuri spent at the childcare center.

As though trying to run from her problems, she walked faster. Instinctively, she reached for her son's hand; it was an automatic and motherly gesture.

"I'm not a baby," Yuri reminded her, stuffing his gloved hands inside the pockets of his coat. Always a prankster, Yuri slid behind a giant mound of snow. "You can't see me," he teased.

"Come on, Yuri. I'm not in the mood."

Yuri jumped out from behind the snow mound. "Here I am! You couldn't find me, Mommy!" Proud of himself, he grinned.

Even with two missing front teeth, Yuri was such a cutie. Vangie couldn't hold back a smile. "Keep it up, Yuri, and I'm going to tell Santa Claus to take everything off your list."

"No such thing as Santa Claus!" Yuri exclaimed.

She couldn't argue about that. This year, her friend, Harlow, had assumed the role of Santa, generously paying for Yuri's presents.

Though the Christmas break would raise her daycare bill from part-time to full-time, looking on the bright side, Vangie was thankful that she'd be relieved from the headache of helping Yuri with his homework.

Yuri's homework assignments were one of the reasons that Vangie spent so much money on fast food. Vangie and Yuri didn't get home until ten minutes to seven, sometimes later, depending on traffic. There wasn't any time to cook a decent meal and help with homework.

Bath time followed homework. Vangie shook her head, thinking about the disorder of the bathroom after Yuri's bath. Toys in the tub. Clothes and water on the floor. Soaking wet washcloth and towel flung haphazardly. Toothpaste stuck on the faucets and smeared on the mirror.

Being a single parent was hard. Vangie couldn't begin to imagine how a single mom with more than one child was able to manage.

Her life could be so much easier if she had some help from Yuri's father. Yuri was devilish and was getting more out of hand every day. He needed the kind of guidance that only a man could provide. And Vangie deserved regular, financial support from Yuri's father.

But expecting Shawn to co-parent was asking for the moon. Shawn had figured out how to beat the system a long time ago. A barber by trade, Shawn made his money under the table. Vangie didn't receive court-ordered child support. Shawn gave her dribs and drabs of cash as he saw fit. He hardly ever put in any quality time with their son, and the neglect of their son both infuriated and hurt Vangie to the core, turning her into a foul-mouthed, name-calling, crazy woman on the rare occasions that Shawn bothered to stop by to give Yuri a haircut.

Yuri only knew his parents as adversaries. He had no conscious memories of them being a loving couple.

Once the car was in sight, Vangie hit the keypad, unlocking the doors.

Yuri scrambled into the back.

Vangie situated herself in the driver's seat. "Seatbelt!" she said sharply.

"Can we go to McDonald's?"

"No, Wendy's is closer."

"We got food from Wendy's yesterday," he said, sulking.

"What about Subway?" Vangie asked in a cajoling tone.

"No! You promised we could go to McDonald's!"

"The roads are bad. I'm not driving all the way to McDonald's. It's Wendy's or Subway. Take your pick."

"Neither!" Yuri blurted and then started crying at a high volume.

"You can turn off those crocodile tears. Tantrums don't work with me."

She made a left turn into Wendy's drive-through lane and pulled behind a long line of cars.

"I want my daddy!" Yuri hollered when he realized that his mother was not giving in.

"You want your daddy? Okay, I could use a break." Vangie pulled out her phone, scrolled to Shawn's name. *He probably doesn't even have the same number. That bastard changes phones like the damn weather.*

"The subscriber you've called…" began an automated voice. Vangie hung up and tossed her phone inside her purse. "As usual, your father's phone is cut off."

"I want my daddy!" Yuri yelled at the top of his lungs.

Vangie felt a headache coming on. "Stop all that noise, Yuri."

Yuri cried louder.

My life sucks. I wish I was in St. Croix with Harlow, soaking up sunshine and sipping on a tropical drink.

CHAPTER 5

Nivea made it home without an encounter with the law, but she was a nervous wreck, expecting the cops to show up at any moment to arrest her.

If she called her parents to tell them about the situation, she'd have to divulge the sordid story of Eric's betrayal. *What should I do…call a lawyer? Suppose he advises me to turn myself in? Oh, fuck that!*

A rustling sound on the other side of the front door sent Nivea into a panic. Then a familiar metallic clatter told her it was Eric! The creep was alive and had the audacity to use his key, as if he still had that privilege.

Wearing a hooded jacket, Eric strode into the living room. He yanked the hood down, and arched an eyebrow toward a blood-stained, poorly wrapped bandage that surrounded his head.

Nivea stared daggers at Eric.

"Why you fuck up my head?" Eric asked.

"That's all you have to say to me?" Nivea stuck her hand out. "Give me my damn keys, get your shit, and take your ass back to that welfare to work, bitch!"

"Come on, Niv. You trippin'. It's not even like that."

"Oh, really? So, you don't have a son and a side chick taking up residence at your old place?"

"Yeah, I got a son. But that's all it is. On some real shit, ain't nothing going on between me and Dyeesha."

"You stood there and let that tramp call me every name in the book.

You took up for her and co-signed on your upcoming marriage."

"That was just talk. It's all about you and me. Ain't nothing changed."

"You were yanking me around and tussling with me, Eric!"

"You ran up in the crib all crazy. I had to restrain you."

"I discovered that my fiancé is leading a disgusting double life; how the hell was I supposed to react?"

Guiltily, Eric shifted his gaze down to the floor.

"You have a baby that I never knew existed. And according to your girlfriend, you two are getting married in a few days."

"Nah, it ain't like that!"

"Well, how is it? I deserve to know why you deceived me for so long." Arms folded, Nivea waited.

Eric didn't respond.

"Answer me! How could you be so deceitful?"

"I guess I got caught up."

"What's that supposed to mean?"

"After I found out Dyeesha was pregnant, I let her stay in the crib. I was tryna look out, you know."

"When did you find out she was pregnant?"

He rubbed his head again. "Um, that was a while back. Way before me and you got serious."

"Were you ever going to tell me?"

"Eventually. When she first came at me, I didn't really believe she was carrying my baby. It could have been anybody's kid, know what I'm saying? I met her at a bachelor party. I wasn't the only man that smashed that night."

Nivea's mouth dropped open. "She kept calling me a trick, and she's a damn ho! You raw-dogged a stripper while you were in a relationship with me."

"I was strapped up."

Nivea rolled her eyes at Eric.

"The condom broke."

"Umph," Nivea uttered with disgust.

"After she had the baby, you know, after I saw him with my own eyes and everything, there wasn't no doubt that he was my seed. I ain't even need the DNA results."

"You're a fucking moron, Eric. You're reckless and stupid."

"I'm sorry, Niv. How can I make amends?"

"You can't! You allowed some random slut to come between us and ruin the fabulous wedding I've been planning."

"We can still go through with it."

"How can I plan an elaborate ceremony when Dyeesha is threatening to force you into a shotgun wedding?"

"She knows I'm not wifing her."

"I want her completely out of the picture."

"What about my son?"

"I can't let my family and friends know about your love child. You're gonna have to keep him a secret."

"Okay."

Nivea sucked her teeth. "I can't believe you've got me in this awful position."

"I'm sorry, baby." He tried to hug her, but Nivea moved from his reach.

"How did you manage to live in two places?"

"I don't live at the apartment. I just stop through, you know, to spend time with my son."

She took a hard breath. "Eric, please stop lying. Those family photos of you and your welfare wifey speak volumes."

"They aint nothing but pictures. Some memories for my son."

"None of this would be happening if you'd never allowed that tramp to move in."

"What was I supposed to do…let my baby mom and my son live in the street?"

Indifferent, Nivea shrugged.

"I had to make sure my son had a roof over his head."

"My son, my son," Nivea said mockingly. "You worked hard to hide the fact that you had a son; now you won't shut up about him. To be honest, I'm sickened by this discussion. Seriously, Eric. Just give me my keys, and go!"

"Come on, baby. I know I messed up. But you gotta let bygones be bygones."

"How can I forget your indiscretion if you're going to be bringing up that baby every chance you get?"

"I won't bring him up anymore."

"You better fucking not."

"I promise; I won't."

Eric held her in a tight embrace. "I love you, Nivea. We can get past this," he whispered in her ear.

Nivea knew that she should be stuffing Eric's clothing and other belongings into trash bags, but she couldn't. She'd be a laughing-stock if her family and friends knew what Eric had done to her.

"We have two appointments next week," she said weakly, deciding it was in her best interests to go full speed with the wedding. "An appointment with the florist—"

"I'm there," Eric interrupted, smiling broadly. "You dig me, baby? I'm with you at that flower place; I'm there helping you pick out the invitations, going with you for all your fittings… anything you want me to do." He released a rumble of relieved laughter.

Nivea gave a sad smile. Eric was joking around as if he hadn't just taken her to the bowels of hell.

"What else you need me to do?" Eric asked.

"We need to select our cake. I'm going to set up appointments with a couple of bakeries so we can sample some cake flavors."

"Cake tasting? Bet!" He rubbed his slightly protrusive stomach. "Now that's something I can definitely get into."

Thoughts flashed in Nivea's mind. She pictured Dyeesha trying to hustle Eric off to City Hall. The image made her nervous. "Considering everything that's happened, I think we should speed up the wedding date. Cut the guest list, and invite only family and close friends."

"Whatever you say. How soon you wanna make a move?"

"As soon as possible."

"Word." He meandered toward the kitchen. Nivea followed.

Eric opened the fridge and considered the meager contents. "Ain't nothing to eat. You want to order Chinese?"

"I don't care," she muttered, unconcerned about food. She was going to have to put in a lot of extra work, downsizing her wedding. She needed to find a smaller venue, put a rush on her gown, and narrow down the number of bridesmaids.

Eric reached out for Nivea. "Do you forgive me?"

Nivea nodded. Hoping that she was making the right decision, she eased into his open arms.

CHAPTER 6

After Yuri finally went to sleep, Vangie relaxed in bed, drinking red wine as she watched a repeat episode of *Bridezillas*. She found the show disgusting and titillating at the same time. Her DVR was programmed to record *Bridezillas*, *Say Yes to the Dress*, *Amazing Wedding Cakes*, *Bridal Bootcamp*, and her most favorite guilty pleasure, *Platinum Weddings*.

With Nivea engaged and Harlow expecting Drake to pop the question any day, Vangie felt left out and desperate to find Mr. Right. She'd taken an almost fanatical interest in all TV shows that had anything do with getting married. She viewed these programs religiously, studied them as if the shows possessed a hidden clue on how to hook a husband.

In Vangie's mind, her future husband had the body of a male stripper and the sexual stamina of a porn star. Best of all, he had an oral fetish, and loved making her cum with his tongue. A connoisseur in the art of pussy eating, her imaginary lover did not gulp up her juices and then speedily stuff his dick inside. No, her future husband was a fine diner, and he savored her pussy as if it were a delectable meal.

Her flesh began to tingle, and her nipples hardened, making imprints on her nightshirt. Heeding nature's call, her hand worked its way to her panty crotch.

Bridezillas droned in the background as Vangie's experienced fingers rubbed the strip of fabric between her thighs, making her sex moisten.

Hastening her caresses, a desperate moan escaped her throat. She had to slow down and adhere to the ritual that prolonged her self-pleasuring experience. Oh, fuck that! She'd had a long, rough day and was desperate for release.

Kicking off her panties, she spread her legs, granting Mr. Right the kind of access he required. She writhed impatiently as she imagined him taking his time, his eyes riveted on the sight of her pussy that dripped and throbbed with nearly whorish desire.

Eat this pussy! she demanded in her mind, as her middle finger sliced through juices that were thickened with lust. She imagined him separating her pussy lips. With great compassion, Mr. Right attempted to calm her by blowing on the flames that raged.

Eat it, baby, she coaxed, using a gentler tone.

His lips were achingly close. She arched her body, offering a swollen clit to imaginary lips. But he ignored her inflamed flesh, and began nibbling on her pussy lips, nipping at one and then the other. "Oh!" she uttered, as she pretended that her finger was his tongue, flicking against her pink pussy lining.

Her finger inched upward, inciting her hips to dance to an inner rhythm. She gasped as she envisioned his tongue connecting with her sensitive clit. Her finger moved circularly around her pleasure hub, making it slick and stiff. Craving sexual relief, her body tensed. Her breathing became ragged. The shorter, index finger teamed with the longer one. Working in tandem, her fingers trapped the swollen flesh, squeezing it in just the right way, extracting an outpouring of honeyed nectar from her core, and unrestrained cries of pleasure.

"Oh, God! Ahhh!" An orgasm hit with the force of a lightning bolt. Ecstasy tore through her body, but her fingers kept a tight grip. Over and over, surges of electricity jolted her, as if Mr. Right had become a sadist, cruelly using his tongue like a stun gun.

The intensity of the orgasm subsided, and Vangie slowly became aware of her surroundings. She released a sigh of regret. The fantasy was over and she was back to reality. There was no fantasy man. No warm body to snuggle next to. And no husband anywhere on the horizon.

CHAPTER 7

"A toast to the man who will quench my country's thirst for luxury vehicles," said Talib Chitundu, raising his champagne flute.

With a halfhearted smile, Harlow raised her glass. It was too early in the morning for grinning and small talk. And drinking champagne for breakfast did not agree with her stomach. Last night, she'd had fallen asleep inside Drake's arms, and was rocked to sleep by the gentle motion of the waves. Now, in the morning light, and in the company of a party of fools, the waves of the ocean were making her nauseous.

Harlow doubted if Talib or any of his guests had gotten any sleep at all. The people aboard The Water Nymph were still in party mode. Talib was obviously tipsy, making the second or third toast to his business venture with Drake. Everyone at the massive table indulged him, cheering and raising their flutes as if for the first time.

Throughout breakfast, the spoiled rich boy had been monopolizing the conversation, making one toast after another…toasting to everything under the sun. Harlow didn't think she could stand to hear his slurred, heavily accented voice much longer.

Flanked by two blondes, Talib behaved lewdly, groping the breasts of one woman, while intermittently tongue-kissing the other. Neither blonde seemed to mind sharing Talib. *Money talks*, Harlow surmised disgusted. What she felt for Drake was not based on his bank account. If he lost every penny, she'd still love and adore him. Being in the presence of these fake-ass people seemed to cheapen what she and Drake shared.

She nudged Drake with her elbow, signaling him to excuse them from this disgustingly decadent breakfast.

"A few more minutes," Drake whispered.

"I'm ready to go," she whispered back.

"Soon," Drake placated.

The ship would be coming ashore in an hour or so. She preferred to spend that time on their private balcony. The blue skies and ocean backdrop formed a perfect spot for Drake to ask for her hand in marriage.

"I have to tell you a funny joke," Talib stated. All sidebar conversations ceased as the guests waited for the young billionaire to tell his joke.

Oh, God! Harlow couldn't take much more of the spoiled rich boy.

Talib's joke went on endlessly, with no predictable punchline. Waiters emerged and began refreshing the champagne flutes.

I've had it! Drake can sit here if he wants to, but I'm not allowing this jerk to hold me captive at this table any longer. Harlow stood. "I have to excuse myself, Talib. I'm feeling queasy. Seasick," she explained.

"But today is a day of great celebration," Talib said, sounding sad as though Harlow's feigned illness was ruining his breakfast bash. "Don't leave. I have a physician onboard. He can give you medication for sea sickness."

"No, I don't need medication. I just need to lie down for a while."

As waiters busied themselves refilling the champagne flutes, Harlow noticed something glittery at the bottom of her flute.

A ring! A sound of surprised delight escaped her lips.

"Feeling better?" Drake whispered with amusement in his tone.

"Much better." She sat down and picked up the flute. Mesmerized, she stared at the diamond ring that was resting at the bottom of her glass.

"Is that a diamond in your glass?" the blonde on Talib's right squealed.

"Did he propose to you?" the blonde on the host's left inquired.

Harlow gazed curiously at Drake.

"Will you marry me, Harlow?" Drake's voice was deep and serious.

She answered with a wide smile and several enthusiastic head nods.

"You're supposed to get down on bended knee," suggested another female member of Talib's entourage.

"I'm good," Drake said, laughing.

Too impatient to drink the champagne, Harlow began pouring out the bubbly into an empty glass. She retrieved the huge diamond ring, and held it in her palm. As she gazed at it, tears formed in her eyes.

Drake took the dripping ring from her hand and began wiping it with a cloth napkin.

"I love you, Harlow," he told her, as he took her hand and slipped the ring on her finger.

Harlow gave a blissful sigh. Drake's marriage proposal made up for everything. Erased her painful past, promising the happy ending that little girls dream of.

"Thank you, Drake," she murmured.

The blondes rose from their positions next to Talib and rushed over to Harlow, fawning over her large diamond.

"That's a hell of a rock," said one blonde.

"Looks like four or five carats," said the other.

"Six carats," Drake informed.

Smiling, Harlow tilted her hand, admiring the way her diamond sparkled as it captured sunlight.

Abandoned by his dates, Talib looked confused and out of his element. He was accustomed to being the center of attention, not applauding the happiness of others. Talib frowned in disapproval, his dark eyes roving from Harlow's bejeweled finger to Drake. "What are you doing, my man? I thought you were a player."

"Nah, man. I'm out of the game. I'm about to be happily married."

"Marriage is for suckers," Talib said harshly, intentionally disrupting the harmony at the table.

Reacting to Talib's anger, the blondes hurried back to their places at his side.

"A real man cannot be satisfied with only one woman." Talib grabbed the hand of the blonde to his left and placed it on his crotch. "A virile man such as I, captures women with his manhood, not a promise of matrimony."

Drake bristled at Talib's derogatory remarks.

The air was so tense, Harlow felt concerned for her and Drake's safety. "Can we go back to our cabin, celebrate in private?" she stammered.

The muscles at Drake's temples throbbed furiously. He made a steeple with his fingers as he glared at Talib. "Tell me, Talib, do you make it a practice of doing business with suckers?"

"Honey, he's drunk. That's the liquor talking," Harlow said, trying to dissuade Drake from getting into an altercation with their youthful host.

"Drunk mind, sober tongue." Drake stood up. He jabbed a finger in the host's direction. "You got a problem with me, man?"

"My problem is with bitchassness. I don't like it." In his accent, Talib pronounced the slur as *beech-ahs-ness.*

"Who you calling a bitch ass?" Drake demanded. Frowning, he tugged on the front of his suit jacket. His legs separated as he assumed a confrontational stance.

Talib's goons rushed forward. They surrounded Talib in a protective cluster, their weapons visibly jutting from their waistbands.

Drake's right-hand man, Alphonso, had been posted near the door. He now stepped forward, jaws tensed, quietly seething. His penetrating dark eyes were focused on Drake. Alphonso pulled his jacket to the side, revealing the shiny chrome butt of his gun.

Wearing a taunting grin, Talib stretched his arms out and embraced his two blonde playmates. "This is the life you're giving up. You can have all this…like me."

"I don't like the plastic blow-up doll type. I like a real woman like the one right here beside me." Drake glanced down at Harlow.

"Let's go back to the cabin, Drake," Harlow pleaded.

"Nah!" Drake brushed her off and returned his attention to Talib. "Man, you got to be crazy if you think I'm gonna sit back and let you disrespect my fiancée and me. Fuck this Water Nymph bullshit. I'm not impressed by this yacht. In fact, you can take this ship, all your little Barbie dolls, *and* the multi-million-dollar deal we just signed…you can take all of that shit and stick it all up your misogynistic, socially undeveloped, ignorant, Neanderthal ass."

The insult to the host drew a collective gasp from the female guests and glares from the thugs who called themselves a security team. The staff of waiters stood frozen in place.

The head of the security was a fierce-looking, bald African. Reaching for his waistband, he glanced at Talib. "Say the word, boss, and that foolish American will be filled with lead. The sharks will have a good time feasting on his remains."

"Yo, y'all muthafuckas ain't the only ones strapped. I dare any of you jungle bunnies to even think about pointing a weapon at Drake," Alphonso asserted as he wrapped his hand around the chrome handle. "Go for it if you want to, but I guarantee you that I'm taking Mr. Chitundu out. That rich boy's not gon' look so appealing to the ladies with a third eye in the middle of his head."

Looking petrified, Talib swallowed hard, his eyes locked on the door as though plotting to make a run for it.

Harlow was wild-eyed and frantic. *All of these men…Alphonso, Drake, and the Africans…they're all acting like blood-thirsty barbarians and somebody is going to get hurt.* She appealed to Drake, grabbing his wrist. "Baby, this is ridiculous. Tell Alphonso to chill."

Drake shook off Harlow's grasping hand. "Yo, Talib. I know you're accustomed to talking to your flunkies any way you want to. You've led a pampered life. But it took intelligence, street smarts, business sense, and a lot of hard work for me to reach my level of success. You're sadly mistaken if you think I'm gonna sit back and allow you to talk trash and attack my manhood. Your people want bloodshed? Well, let me assure you, it's going to be your blood that's going to flow, man." Drake spoke through clenched teeth. "Your blood's going to rush like a fuckin' river if you don't apologize to me and my future wife."

Harlow gasped. Had Drake lost his mind? Couldn't he see that those bloodthirsty African henchmen were eager for an opportunity to open fire?

In an abrupt change of heart, Talib waved his hand like he was waving a white flag. "Let's dispense with talk of guns and behave like civilized men. I apologize to you and Harlow. I didn't intend to give the impression that I was stirring up violence. I thought we were having an intelligent debate. You know, a discussion about our cultural differences." Suddenly sober, Talib's words came out in a steady and coherent stream.

Talib made a gesture with his hand. His bodyguards stepped away from him, reluctantly leaving him open and vulnerable.

"No more talk of bloodshed," Talib said. "Drake, my man. We're doing big business together. You can't back out on our deal."

"I can and I just did. I don't do business with disrespectful, young punks," Drake stated.

"But my people are expecting a shipment of fleets carrying luxury vehicles. My father allowed me to negotiate this deal. He'll be very disappointed if I don't deliver." Talib wiped sweat from his brow.

"Find another supplier," Drake said.

"But we have a legally binding agreement."

"Sue me!" Drake challenged.

The ship's horn sounded. Through the window, Harlow could see the dock. The ship was coming to port. *Please, God, let us get off this ship alive and unharmed.*

"Have a good day, gentlemen." Drake reached for Harlow's hand. "Come on, baby. We're out of here."

"Wait! We can renegotiate your terms," Talib shouted desperately. "I'll give you a much higher profit margin. Twenty percent! How does that sound?"

Drake paused. "Forty percent sounds better."

"Deal!" Talib shouted happily. "My lawyer will amend the contract."

"Yeah, whatever, man," Drake mumbled as he guided Harlow away from the table.

"A toast to the happy couple," the fickle host cheered. "May their union produce many sons!"

The clapping and cheering and tinkling of champagne flutes became distant sounds as Harlow, Drake, and Alphonso exited the ship's dining room.

CHAPTER 8

The house phone rang out a melody that was loud and annoying. Vangie squinted at the bedside clock. *Who the hell is calling me at six-damn-thirty on a Saturday morning?* Frowning, she peered at the caller ID. Private. *Hmph!* She pulled the covers over her head, deciding to ignore the private caller.

But the ringing persisted.

"Hello!"

"Hey. I'm downstairs. Buzz me up," Shawn said, sounding cheerful.

Wide awake now, Vangie was fuming. "I'm not buzzing shit! You have a lot of nerve, Shawn. We haven't heard from you in weeks."

"Why do I have to get cussed out every time I try to spend some time with my boy?"

"Because I'm sick of your shit, Shawn. You can't pop up whenever you get good and ready. What did you get Yuri for Christmas? Let me guess…another stupid videogame? I hope you know that your son is addicted to videogames. Wanna know why? Because he doesn't have anything else to do. His father is too busy chasing women to spend any quality time with him."

"Vangie…" Shawn spoke her name in a soft, patient tone.

"What?"

"It's freezing out here. Can we discuss this inside the crib?"

"No! I'm in bed, and Yuri is still asleep. Call later and set up an appointment."

"I won't stay long," he said humbly. "I wanna drop something off, and I'll be out. Gotta get to work by seven-thirty."

Work? Shawn was an unlicensed barber with no legitimate income. According to Shawn, he couldn't afford to pay regular child support because the chump change he made cutting hair in his mother's basement barely covered his own living expenses.

With a regular job, Shawn could finally start giving her regular child support payments. Envisioning an improvement in her cash flow, Vangie threw on a robe. She made a beeline to the living room, and hit the buzzer.

Shawn strolled inside her apartment, giving off a whiff of manly cologne. He was wearing a black, fur-trimmed, hooded leather jacket. The leather looked expensive...soft as butter. Designer shades, an oversized chrome watch, stylishly ripped jeans, and a pair of Ugg Butte boots indicated that Shawn's money was definitely up.

Vangie looked at him sideways, and sucked her teeth. *Yuri and I are barely making it, but this mofo done stepped his game up. I'm trying not to black out on this fool, so he needs to hurry up and pull out a gift card to GameStop or Toys "R" Us or somewhere!*

Vangie pictured herself grabbing a knife from the kitchen. She got an adrenaline rush from the fantasy of slashing through that butter-looking leather. His jeans could use a few more rips, too. Then she'd work her way down to his boots. She'd enjoy poking holes in those three-hundred-dollar boots, and stabbing a couple of toes while she was at it.

"You take good care of yourself, don't you, Shawn? Meanwhile, your son might get kicked out of daycare if I don't come up with some extra money." Boiling anger put a homicidal glint in Vangie's eyes.

Cautiously, Shawn started backing up a little. "I'm not trying to go through nothing with you, Vangie."

"You should be ashamed of the way you treat Yuri. It's bad

enough that I'm the only one providing for him, but he can't even pick up a phone and call you because your shit is always out of service, or the number is changed."

"That last number I gave you was on my sister's plan, and—"

Vangie motioned with her hand. "I don't want to hear it. You always have an excuse."

She noticed Shawn's remorseful expression. *Good! I struck a nerve.* "So, what's up? Why are you at my door at six-something in the morning?"

"I told you, I wanted to drop something off."

"Well!" She stared at his empty hands, wondering if he had a bike or something in the trunk of his car.

Wearing a sly expression, Shawn dug into his pocket. He pulled out neatly folded, one-hundred-dollar bills. "I've been working a lot. Didn't have time to go shopping," Shawn explained as he placed a crisp pile of bills across Vangie's palm.

The scent of new money wafted up to Vangie's nostrils, enticing her into a better mood. In fact, she felt so giddy, she had to fight back a grin. Shawn was finally doing what he was supposed to do, but he surely didn't deserve a smile from her. Vangie refused to even say thank you.

"That's thirteen hundred," Shawn piped in proudly.

"I can count!" she snarled. *Deadbeat motherfucker expecting some kind of applause just because he finally decided to step up to the plate.*

"I want my boy to have a nice Christmas."

"That's all good and everything, but Yuri is getting older. He needs a man in his life. You only come through on Christmas and birthdays, yet Yuri considers you a hero. I have to play Mommy and Daddy, twenty-four, seven…throughout the year. On top of that, I have to deal with him crying his heart out whenever he can't get in contact with you. Your son needs you, Shawn. You need to man-up and start acting like a father."

"I'm working full-time," he said. "Got a chair in this new shop on Girard Avenue. The place is real chill…kicked back vibe. Stays open twenty-four hours. Steady stream of customers around the clock."

"You finally got your barber's license?"

"Nah, not yet. I'm working on it, though."

Vangie gave a skeptical head nod. Shawn had been working on that barber's license since before Yuri was born.

"The money's good at the new shop. They let me cut all night if I want to."

"How come the owner is letting you rent a chair when you don't have a barber's license?" Vangie was thinking long-term. She didn't want to get too excited about Shawn's additional cash flow if it wasn't going to last.

"As long as I'm working under a barber who has a license, it's cool. But I'ma get mine. I want my own place. The young bull who owns the spot is making crazy loot. His name is Brad and he's only twenty-two years old, but he got a head on his shoulders. Good business sense and he got skills with the clippers."

"You have a twenty-two-year-old mentor?"

Shawn laughed. "Ain't that some shit?"

Vangie was shocked that Shawn was being so good-natured about working as an apprentice under a younger man.

"It's all good. I don't mind being the protégé. Brad's not a hot head. He doesn't carry himself like a young bull. I guess he's got an old soul. Anyway, I'm trying to get my act together. Time is moving on; my son is in school now. I want to be a better father than I've been. Maybe one day, I'll have my own shop. Something to pass on to Yuri."

Vangie was impressed. She wanted to personally shake the hand of Shawn's youthful mentor for helping him get some sense into his head.

"Anyway, Yuri won't have any trouble getting through any-more." He reached inside the pocket of his jacket, and pulled out a sleek iPhone.

"Nice phone."

"Thanks," Shawn said while tapping the luminous touch screen. "I'm calling your cell and the house phone, making sure you got my number on both phones."

"Okay," she mumbled, feeling overwhelmed by the new, responsible Shawn. She'd viewed him as a loser and the person responsible for ruining her life for so long, she was baffled by how quickly her heart was softening toward him.

"I gotta head out. So, look…uh, make sure Yuri calls me when he wakes up."

"Okay. I will."

"Aye, I'm out." Shawn sent Vangie a smile that was soft and sexy. His eyes roved over her breasts and hips, seeming to penetrate her cotton nightshirt.

Is Shawn flirting with me? Nah, there's no chemistry between us anymore. I'm trippin' because I really need to get laid.

CHAPTER 9

N ivea looked through the peephole and was shocked to see her mother standing on the other side of the door. Her mother hardly ever visited her. Nivea wasn't in the mood. She thought about tiptoeing to her bedroom, and ignoring the doorbell. But guilt made her open the door. She didn't have the heart to leave her mother standing outside in the cold.

"Hello, Mother. What brings you out in the cold?"

Looking grim, Denise Westcott stepped inside. She pulled off her knit hat, shook out shiny salt and pepper curls that gave off that fresh-from-the-hair-salon whiff.

"Your hair looks nice," Nivea mumbled.

Mrs. Westcott came out of her coat and gloves. "We have to have a serious discussion."

Oh, God! I'm going to faint if my mother knows about Eric's double life.

"I need a cup of coffee." Her mother rubbed her hands together, warming them.

"I'll make some." Nivea plodded to the kitchen wearing a bathroom and slippers. She couldn't imagine what was so important that her mother felt the need to make a personal visit.

"You're normally an early riser. Why were you still in bed?"

"I'm grown, Mother; I can get up when I please." Lips pursed in aggravation, she scooped coffee from a Starbucks bag.

"Excuse me for being a concerned parent." Mrs. Westcott took a seat at the kitchen table.

"What do you want to talk about?"

"Your wedding." Her mother's tone was morose.

Nivea took a deep breath. "I was going to tell you later on today, but since you're here...well, my wedding plans have changed."

"Don't tell me Eric has gotten cold feet!"

"No, we're still getting married. But we decided to change the date and trim down the guest list."

Mrs. Westcott shook her head woefully. "Why are you downsizing your wedding? Money troubles?"

"No. It's not about money. Eric and I decided that we want a more intimate ceremony." Her body was aching from fighting Eric. She was physically and emotionally drained from yesterday's disastrous incident. Having to cook up a story for her mother was depleting her of her last bit of strength. And sanity.

Nivea quietly poured coffee into two mugs. She wanted to collapse inside her mother's arms, and blab the whole sordid story. But she couldn't breathe a word about Eric's secret son. Too embarrassing.

"Something's not adding up," her mother said suspiciously. "When is the new date?"

"Next month."

"Why so soon?"

Her mother was acting like a detective, snooping and asking so many questions, Nivea was starting to sweat. "Why are you making such a big deal out of this? It's my wedding; I can change the date if I want to."

"Out of nowhere, you want to change your date and downsize. It doesn't make sense."

"It makes sense to Eric and me." Nivea raised her voice a notch.

"Then why are you so upset? Something's wrong. I can hear the anxiety in your voice."

"You don't hear anxiety in my voice; you hear joy!" *What a dumb lie!* Trying to cover up Eric's deception was giving Nivea a headache. She closed her eyes and rubbed her throbbing forehead.

"You can try and deceive someone that doesn't know you, but you can't fool me."

Anxious under her mother's scrutiny, Nivea's hand tightened around the handle of the coffee mug.

Mrs. Westcott leaned forward, and patted Nivea's fisted hand. "Are you pregnant, honey? Is that the reason you want to speed up the wedding?" Her mother kept a sharp eye on Nivea's face, reading her expression.

"Of course not!" A lump formed in her throat as she pictured Eric's love child. She should be the one with Eric's baby...not that trashy Dyeesha. "Mother, what do you want to talk about?"

Mrs. Westcott took a sip of coffee and then set the mug down. "Your sister is getting married, and she didn't have the heart to tell you that she has to focus on her own wedding...she can't be your maid of honor."

Courtney's getting married? It was disturbing news, but Nivea kept a straight face. "I wanted my friend, Vangie, to be my maid of honor, but I listened to you. I allowed you to pressure me into accepting Courtney."

"You're off the hook now."

"It doesn't really matter, now."

"You're right. Your father and I were waiting for the appropriate time to tell you that Courtney selected a date two weeks before your wedding."

"Two weeks before my wedding? You've got to be kidding me. That brat is always trying to upstage me."

"That isn't true."

"Mother, it's so unfair. Why would you and Daddy go along with that?"

"Well, it's water over the bridge now that you've changed your date."

"You didn't know that when you agreed with Courtney's selfish decision."

"Courtney didn't want to steal your thunder, but she and Knox have gotten pretty serious."

Nivea could feel a hot jealous flush covering her face and moving down her body. "How long has she known him…like a couple of months?"

"They're in love." Mrs. Westcott beamed like she was marrying Knox.

"This seriously sucks. My little sister takes a temp job as a receptionist at Temple's School of Podiatric Medicine. She dates one of the students. And now they're suddenly getting married! Mother, can't you see what she's doing?"

"What is she doing, besides following her heart? There's no crime in that."

"Bullshit!"

"Watch your language."

"Sorry, but—"

"Your sister and Knox say that they're in love. Your father and I believe them."

Nivea sucked her teeth in annoyance. "Courtney is an unskilled, unemployable spoiled brat who still lives at home with you and Daddy. She's only marrying this guy, Knox, to make me look bad."

"That's ridiculous."

"No, it isn't. She's been competing with me her whole life; now she's trying to make me the laughingstock."

"If you feel that you're being upstaged, then it's your own fault.

You and Eric want to downsize your wedding, so go ahead. I won't try and stop you. Courtney wants a big wedding and your father and I are going to make sure she has one."

"That's my point, Mother. I've had to work hard to be a success, but Courtney gets everything handed to her on a silver platter."

"You can't blame your sister for having the good sense to marry someone who can take care of her," her mother snidely commented.

"I can take care of myself. I don't need anyone to take care of me," Nivea shot back.

"I know you can, Nivea," her mother said in a softer tone. "There's nothing wrong with allowing a man to take care of you. It's natural for woman to desire the kind of man who can be relied on to provide for her."

Though spoken gently, her mother's words hurt deeply. "Are you going to pretend that Courtney isn't marrying that fake doctor?"

"There's nothing fake about podiatry."

"Knox is studying podiatric medicine, Mother! Oh my God, don't you realize that podiatrists are so low on the totem pole; they're not even recognized as real doctors."

"I beg to differ, young lady."

"Seriously, they don't earn—"

"He's going to earn plenty and watch your mouth."

"Bullshit! I'm grown, so don't tell me to watch my mouth. This is my house and—"

"You sound bitter, Nivea," her mother interrupted. "You sound bitter and jealous of your baby sister."

"I have no reason to be jealous of her. I'm just saying…Courtney is always trying to outdo me. And you and Daddy…you guys allow it. I can't believe you're both eager to co-sign on her decision to marry a damn foot fetishist!"

"Knox is ambitious. I'll have you know that his family's church is one hundred percent behind him. That young man's church is raising money to get him set up in private practice."

"It takes a lot more than some church donations to set up a practice."

"Knox is going to buy out one of the parishioner's practice. I've obviously overstayed my welcome." Denise set the coffee mug on the kitchen table and stood.

Nivea followed her mother into the living room. She silently watched her mother slide into her coat. "Listen, Nivea. Nobody is out to get you," Mrs. Westcott said as she pulled her hat on her head. "It's your own fault that you chose to marry that grubby, uneducated, warehouse worker."

Leaving Nivea to marinate on those last hurtful words, Denise Westcott slammed the door behind her.

CHAPTER 10

Over the phone, Harlow finished telling Vangie her account of the Water Nymph incident. "Testosterone levels were high, girl. There was all kinds of crazy on that boat. I don't ever want to be stuck in the middle of the ocean on a private yacht again."

"The way Drake defended your honor sounds extremely romantic," Vangie said dreamily.

"I couldn't even enjoy my moment. I felt like I was in a scene from a gangster flick. Those Africans were reaching for pistols, and Alphonso and Drake weren't backing down."

"Mmm. Alphonso is starting to sound real good. When are you going to hook us up? You know I love bad boys."

"I'm serious, Vangie. There was nothing funny about that situation. They were talking about spilling blood and tossing mofos to the sharks. And I couldn't talk any sense into Drake. He was so furious, he was ready to wage a war on the ship. I've honestly never seen that side of him, Vangie. He was scary."

"Scary enough to call off the wedding? I know you're not tryna take that big bling off your finger."

"Hell no!" Harlow laughed. "Oh, Vangie, can you believe it? Drake and I are engaged!"

"Congrats, girl. But you're leaving something out."

"No, I'm not."

"What else is Drake into? I wouldn't think that someone in the business of selling cars would need an armed bodyguard."

"Drake is constantly dealing with large money transactions—that's why he keeps Alphonso close by. After that frightening episode with Talib, he needs more than one guard. My baby needs to be protected by a security team."

"Don't you think you need to know a little bit more about what he's into?"

"It's not my business."

"It will be. Now that you're engaged, Drake's business is your business."

"I guess," Harlow said, sounding pensive.

"Have you set a date?"

"Not yet. We'll do that after the holidays."

"First dibs on maid of honor," Vangie blurted. "You gotta give me the sympathy vote since Nivea's getting married in six months."

"You know Niv and I aren't all that tight. She's your friend. I just put up with her. You're definitely going to be my maid of honor."

"Thanks. I'm feeling a little down, though."

"Why?"

"Nivea's engaged. You're engaged. I feel like a reject."

"You'll find someone, Vangie. It took me a lifetime of kissing frogs to find my Prince Charming."

"You're a lucky woman, Harlow. And Drake's a lucky man. You and Drake are making me want to believe that the concept of true love is more than a myth. I wish I could meet a man like Drake. Why won't you introduce me to his man, Alphonso?"

"I want you to find someone, but I'm not sure if Alphonso is the right fit for you. You're all chatty and happy go lucky. Alphonso is all about business. He hardly ever talks, and never cracks a smile."

"Sounds sexy. Come on, Harlow; introduce us. Let me be the judge of who's the right fit for me."

"Okay, I'll talk to Drake about it."

CHAPTER 11

Drake made a series of business calls while Harlow swam laps in their private pool. Exhausted, she grabbed the ledge and pulled herself out of the crystal blue water. Eyeing her with admiration, Drake reclined on a lounge chair. "You swim like a fish, baby. Lemme find out you got some mermaid blood."

Harlow laughed. "I used to fantasize about being a mermaid and living in a kingdom under the sea. But unfortunately I'm completely human. With human fears. That said, I have a question for you."

His expression impassive, Drake stroked his chin. "What's on your mind?"

"Do you have some gangster tendencies that I don't know about?"

Drake didn't answer. Looking briefly pensive, he shifted his position. His jawline tightened as he laced his fingers together.

"I thought Alphonso was your right-hand man," Harlow went on. "But now he seems more like a bodyguard."

Drake studied her for a moment, and then finally said, "I'm sorry you had to go through that this morning. But on some real shit, it wasn't about anything."

"Oh, really? The way Alphonso and Talib's security people were patting their waistbands and revealing weapons, it seemed pretty damn serious to me."

"Talib was trying me; that's all. Now that he and his goons know how I'm built, we can amend this deal to work in my favor."

"I don't trust Talib. He's a loose cannon. Do you really think it's wise to do business with someone as young and impulsive as Talib?"

With a hand motion, Drake dismissed the notion of Talib being a threat. "Talib's nothing but talk. A spoiled rich kid; that's all."

Harlow brought a towel to her head, drying her hair that had spiraled into curls. "You were awfully bold, Drake. Seemed foolish of you to deliberately antagonize men carrying guns."

"I had my piece on me."

Harlow flinched. She removed the towel from her head, and let it drape around her shoulders. "You carry a weapon?"

"Hell, yeah."

"I didn't even know that you owned a gun. I can't imagine you using one." She looked at Drake questioningly. "You're a Yale graduate…a businessman. How can you switch from being dignified and respectable to being a gun-toting thug?"

"I got some thug in me," he admitted with a quick smile.

Harlow didn't return the smile.

Drake's eyes became dark and serious. "I have to protect myself. And I have to protect you. I'm going to do what I have to do to keep us safe; even if it means pulling a trigger," he said without a trace of regret.

"I don't feel like I know you as well as I thought."

"Unfortunately, you caught a glimpse of my other side. You weren't supposed to see that. Had I known shit was gon' get ugly, I wouldn't have brought you on the ship." Drake blew out a harsh breath of air. "I didn't know that Talib couldn't hold his liquor."

"I'm still processing the fact that you carry a weapon. You're working on a strange business deal…" Harlow paused, studying Drake closely. "You **proposed** to me. You say that you want to get married."

"I do."

"There shouldn't be secrets between us," she said softly, looking away after the words came out of her mouth. She had her own secrets, and she wondered where she'd draw the strength to tell Drake the complete truth about her past.

Drake shifted his position. "To an extent, you're right. I do need to be forthcoming about certain things…like faithfulness, but I don't need to report to you about my business dealings. I don't want you worrying needlessly."

"If there's nothing to worry about, then why would I?"

"You're worrying right now. Look at you, with your pretty face all twisted up."

"Stop teasing me, Drake. If your business is legitimate, why do you need to carry a gun?"

"Now you're prying. You're expecting too much if you think I'm going to give you a rundown of every aspect of my business practices. You'll always be safe with me. I love you, Harlow, and I'll never let anything happen to you. That's all you need to know."

There was nothing Harlow could say.

Responding to Harlow's sad expression, Drake held out his arms. "Come here, baby." He folded her into a long consoling hug.

Drake had secrets, too. His refusal to tell her why he needed a bodyguard and a weapon when conducting business made her less guilty about confessing to wrong deeds that she couldn't undo.

❤ ❤ ❤

A hand touched her in the pitch-black night. Her body stiffened. Fingers brushed across her hip. Harlow gasped and jolted awake, opening her eyes to impenetrable darkness. *Oh, no!* She lay motionless, holding her breath, and fearfully biting down on her lip.

Maybe if she pretended to be asleep, he'd leave her alone and go away.

But he was already in bed with her. She could feel the heat of his body next to hers. Fear clung to every fiber of her being. As her eyes darted wildly, she could see shadows everywhere. Then her vision slowly began to adjust to the darkness. She made out the vibrant colors of tropical artwork. A soothing sea breeze wafted through lace curtains, revealing wicker chairs on the balcony. Everything within her eyesight evoked peace. *I'm safe*, she told herself as she waited for her pulse to slow down.

"Drake?" she spoke his name questioningly, as if checking to make sure it was really he and not some monster from her past lying beside her.

"What's wrong?"

Reassured by the warm and familiar sound of Drake's voice, Harlow said, "Nothing's wrong. I had a bad dream."

Drake circled his arms around Harlow's waist. Pulling her near, he kissed the back of her neck, whispering his love as he lifted her nightgown, running his hand over her bare ass. He clasped her tightly to him, and then from behind, Drake sank deeply inside her.

Harlow gritted her teeth. The tears that brimmed created a burning sensation in her eyes. She couldn't tell Drake that being pulled from sleep—being groped in the dark, terrified her. She had no way to explain that she felt no pleasure right now. What he was doing felt like an ambush. Sex that was initiated without her knowledge or permission was unsettling, and disturbingly reminiscent of the worst times of her life.

She released an agonized groan, which Drake mistook as a sound of pleasure. Tightening the grip around her waist, he drove deeper, unaware that Harlow was crying.

CHAPTER 12

Wiping tears from her eyes, Harlow stared at the ceiling. Careful not to awaken Drake, she eased off the mattress and crept out the bedroom. Inside the luxurious bathroom, she huddled in a corner. Shuddering, she covered her mouth, muffling the sound of her sobs.

Being snatched from sleep by an insistent, sexual touch was a surefire way for Harlow's past to come back to haunt her. On numerous occasions, her carefully constructed façade had unexpectedly shattered. It was an awful way to exist. Keeping up a brave front, pretending that she had it together while silently suffering inside, was challenging.

Drake was going to be her husband. He deserved to know the truth about her. But imagining his revulsion, Harlow's tears poured like rain.

Her head began to throb and she moved to the sink. Searching through the vast array of toiletries shared by her and Drake, she located a bottle of aspirin and twisted off the cap. Absently, she shook the pills into her palm. Instead of the familiar smoothness of tablets, there was a heavy and rugged texture of something foreign.

Harlow blinked in confusion at three dirt-covered rough-hewn stones that were clustered together in her cupped hand. *What the hell?* She peeked inside the plastic bottle. There were two more misshapen and filthy little pebbles. She shook those into her palm also. She inspected them with her eyes and touched them with a fingertip, yet she was unable to identify the crude objects.

❤ ❤ ❤

From the balcony outside the bedroom, Harlow gazed at the spectacular view of the ocean. Her mind was filled with troubling thoughts. She'd tossed and turned for hours last night, but had finally put two and two together. The morning light brought clarity and she now realized what those filthy stones were.

During her phone conversation with Vangie, her friend kept insisting that there was something suspicious about Drake's business activities. Vangie had questioned why a person selling cars would need a bodyguard or have a reason to carry a gun. And now Harlow had the answer.

She took a sip of the strong island coffee, but had no appetite for the beautiful display of food that had been delivered ten minutes ago.

Drake joined Harlow on the balcony. Looking dapper in a dark tailored suit, he murmured, "Good morning," and kissed her on the cheek.

"Morning," she mumbled.

Drake picked up a piece of toast. "Did you sleep well, baby?"

She nodded and poured him a cup of coffee.

"You're quiet. Is everything alright?"

Harlow took a deep breath. "I had a headache last night, and I needed…" She paused, gauging Drake's expression.

He looked at her, waiting for her to continue, and then enlightenment shone in his eyes. "You opened that bottle of aspirin?"

"Yes, what's going on, Drake? I know what those stones are." Her lips curled in anger as she thought about the children in Africa being maimed and slaughtered. "I can't believe you'd get involved in diamond smuggling."

His eyes shifted nervously. "I'm not."

"Don't lie to me!"

"I can explain."

She held up her hand. Her ring finger glittered with the promise of forever. "Is this a blood diamond, too?" she asked, her face a mask of agony.

"No! I bought it from a jeweler in New York. I have the certification."

Harlow's face crumpled. "So you're admitting that those are conflict diamonds in the bathroom."

He nodded. "I believe they are."

"How did you get involved? Do you love money so much that you'd become a part of something as heinous as that?"

"It's not what you think," Drake muttered, looking down.

"Then explain it. I know Talib has something to do with this. I guess he's not the harmless fool that I thought him to be. He's ruthless and—"

"Talib doesn't have anything to do with those stones."

"Then how'd you get them?"

"They were given to Alphonso by one of Talib's men."

"One of his bodyguards?"

"Yes, someone who's using his connection with Talib to smuggle diamonds. The individual assumed that Alphonso was as thirsty and grimy as him. I'm guessing that the man thought that Alphonso would go along with the plan to use my cars as a front."

"What are you going to do?"

"Handle it."

"How? Those people who deal with diamond smuggling are evil. They're dangerous! They kill!"

"I got this."

She looked doubtful. "You're not giving me the full story."

Drake grasped her shoulders. "Look, baby. This is serious, and

I want you to go back to the States. I'll join you in a week or so."

"No!" she shouted. "I can't leave you." When she noticed Drake staring at her with a brow raised, she realized that she was cling-ing to his shirt sleeve. Self-conscious, she released her grip.

Drake's voice softened. "I hate being away from you, Harlow. But I've got to deal with this."

Her lip began to tremble. "We promised that we would never be apart."

"I can't put you in harm's way. I need to know that you're safe."

"I want you to be safe, too."

"Don't worry about me. I'll be alright. I want you to make arrangements to fly back to New York."

"I don't want to go to New York. If I roam around that big apartment by myself, I'll lose my mind worrying."

"Do you want to go to Philly? Spend some time with your friends? I'll join you there as soon as I can."

"And what about the stones...what are you going to do with them?"

Drake shook his head. "It's a delicate situation. The less you know about it, the better," he said gloomily.

CHAPTER 13

Pretending to be in high spirits, Harlow called Vangie.

"I never thought I'd miss the cold weather in Philly, but I do."

"And…" Vangie said.

"I'm coming through!"

"You and Drake are leaving your island paradise to come to *Filthadelphia*?"

"Drake is staying in St. Croix, but I'm looking forward to seeing you and Yuri at some point during the holidays."

"At some point?"

"I'm not exactly sure when I'm flying in."

"Don't get me wrong," Vangie said. "I'm excited about seeing you, but I don't understand the sudden change in plans. You and Drake are always together. Is something wrong?"

Harlow hated lying to Vangie, but she had to. "Nothing's wrong. Drake has some last-minute business details and he has to stick around. Girl, as much as I hate the thought of being apart from Drake, I'm a little shook from that incident on the ship. I'm actually looking forward to leaving St. Croix. Hopefully, Drake will tie up his deal and join me soon."

"Aren't you nervous about Drake dealing with that crazy African?"

"No, Drake said that Talib is harmless…a spoiled rich boy. Nothing but talk."

"Rich and harmless…Hmm, maybe I should get with Talib," Vangie said, laughing.

"Girl, Talib only deals with blonde, big-titty bimbos. By the way, have you spoken to Nivea? The three of us should get together when I get to town."

"No, I haven't been able to reach her. I'm kind of worried."

"Don't worry about Niv. I'm sure she's fine," Harlow said. "You should be grateful for the break from that Bridezilla. Didn't you tell me that she's obsessed with her wedding and talks about it all the time?"

"I know. Nivea is straight trippin' over her wedding."

"You don't have to worry about me acting crazy. I'm going to be on chill mode. My wedding planner will handle everything from flowers to the glam squad that's gonna beautify me and my bridal party."

"That's so exciting. How's it feel to be rich, Harlow?"

"I'm not rich. Drake is."

"Well, how's it feel spending his money like water?" Vangie laughed.

"I love the lifestyle he's giving me. But I'm in love with Drake; not his money."

"I believe you, Harlow."

"Sometimes I get really scared, you know?"

"Of what?"

"It's irrational fear, but sometimes I feel like I don't deserve happiness…I get this feeling that I'm going to lose Drake, that it's all just a fantasy…too good to be true."

"Girl, hush. If you don't deserve happiness, then who does? Well, besides me?" Vangie laughed. "I'm getting so desperate. Hurry up and give Alphonso my number."

"I haven't had a chance to talk to Drake about it. But I will. I promise."

"Great. Oh, yeah, please don't set your wedding date close to Nivea's. She'll have a fit if she has to share her bridal limelight."

Harlow snickered. "You're right. I'll run some dates past Miss Control Freak. I don't want to steal any of her shine."

"I think she's marrying Eric because he allows her to be in control. She couldn't stand to be with somebody who is her intellectual equal or someone who makes more money than her. She needs a man she can boss around."

"It's working for her. Eric loves her and doesn't make a move without Nivea's permission," Harlow added.

"Will you be in Philly for New Year's Eve? If so, let's do something together."

"I'll let you know."

"Why are you being so secretive, Harlow?"

"I'm sorry. I don't mean to be secretive."

"Something is up with you, but I'm going to drop the subject. Give me a call the moment you touch down. Oh, by the way, you'll never guess where Yuri is?"

"With your mother?"

"That diva wouldn't dream of interrupting her life to baby sit Yuri. He's with Shawn."

"Whaaat? How'd that happen?"

"Shawn is working at a barbershop in North Philly. Full-time! And he seems to be making good money. He gave me thirteen hundred dollars out of the clear blue sky. Says he wants to be a better dad, and I'm not gonna stand in his way. Yuri is thrilled about spending time with his dad. You should have seen the big grin on his face when Shawn picked him up this morning."

"I hope Shawn doesn't disappoint Yuri. You know, get him all excited and then vanish."

"If he hurts my son, I'll fuck him up. Do you hear me, Harlow? I'll bust out all the windows of his car, I'll blow up his momma's house, and the barbershop—"

"Shut up, Vangie," Harlow said, laughing.

"I'm serious. I'm giving him one more chance to make things right with his son, and he better not fuck it up."

"For Yuri's sake, I hope it works out."

"I'm keeping my eye on Shawn. Can't let my guard down..." Vangie paused. "Do you want me to pick you up at the airport when your flight gets in?"

"No, I'm good. A car service will get me to my hotel."

"That's right; I keep forgetting that you're not regular folk anymore. Getting picked up in limos and shit must be nice."

"It's convenient. But be grateful for what you do have—your family and your health. I've never had any family...Seriously, you should be grateful for what you do have, Vangie." There was sorrow in Harlow's voice.

"You're right, Harlow. Guess I'll see you when you get here." Vangie knew that Harlow had slipped into a blue mood. Harlow had no blood relatives, no family to come home to. Once Harlow and Drake started a family, Harlow's life would finally be complete.

CHAPTER 14

"I helped Daddy at the barbershop. I made ten dollars!" Yuri excitedly pulled crumpled dollars from his pocket.

"You're rich, Yuri. You can buy our dinner tonight," Vangie said, smiling. Then she gave Shawn a questioning look. "How'd he earn it? Don't tell me you had my baby in the shop giving shape-ups," she said, laughing.

Shawn chuckled. "Nah, he helped me sweep the hair up from the floor." He ruffled Yuri's hair. "I would still be in there sweeping around my station if my lil' man hadn't pitched in."

Yuri's grin stretched wider. "Daddy's customers call me Little Shawn. Can I change my name to Shawn?"

"No, Yuri's a beautiful name. Your father and I chose it together. Didn't we, Shawn?"

Shawn nodded. "But it's cool to go by Lil' Shawn when you're at the shop with me. Okay, buddy?"

"Okay. Can I go to work with you again tomorrow?"

"Fine with me, but you gotta ask your mother." Both Shawn and Yuri stared at Vangie, waiting for a response.

Vangie shrugged. "I guess so."

"Yay!" Yuri pumped his fist in the air.

"I want you in bed early, son. You need a lot of rest if you wanna hang with me."

"What time should I go to bed, Daddy?"

Shawn looked up in thought. "Lights out by eight o'clock, son."

"Okay!"

Vangie gave Yuri a long look. "Are you serious, Yuri? I can hardly tear you away from your videogames; now you can't wait to get in the bed."

"That's my little working man," Shawn said proudly. "I'm gonna swing by and pick you up at six-thirty in the morning, so I want you to be dressed and ready to roll out."

"Okay, Daddy!"

"Isn't the shop closed on Sundays?" Vangie asked.

"I told you, Clean Cutz stays open seven days a week. I usually work at least six days; sometimes seven. I got my hustle on. Trying to get mine so I can do right by my son."

Vangie felt warmed by Shawn's fervent desire to take care of Yuri.

"Did you cook, Vangie?" Shawn asked.

Righteously indignant, Vangie's stuck her hand on her hip. "No! And whether I cook or not is none of your business."

"Yo, chill. I'm not trying to get in your business. I was only asking, in case you wanted me to run out and pick something up real quick. Dag, I'm just tryna do a good deed."

Both Yuri and Shawn glowered at her; Vangie felt like a villain. "How was I supposed to know your intentions? It's gonna take some time for me to get used to you helping out and being dependable," she explained.

Shawn asked Yuri, "What do you want to eat, man? Cheesesteak or pizza?"

"I want McDonald's!" Yuri yelled.

"Okay. Let's go get a grub on." Shawn glanced at Vangie. "Should we bring Mommy back a Happy Meal?" Shawn asked teasingly.

Yuri giggled at the idea of his mother having a kids' meal.

Vangie blushed, not sure if Shawn had made a sexual innuendo or if her imagination was going in overdrive.

"No, thanks. I've had enough McDonald's to last a lifetime," she said, shaking her head.

"What do you want? Do you still get cravings for sushi and spaghetti?" he asked, chuckling.

She smiled and shook her head. "Those crazy urges for a Japanese and Italian combo only happened while I was pregnant," she said, fondly remembering her and Shawn driving to separate eateries to satisfy her pregnancy cravings.

"What are you in the mood for?"

"KFC," she admitted. "Fried. I hate their grilled chicken."

"Dark meat, right?" Shawn smiled slyly, informing Vangie that he remembered her preferences.

His thoughtfulness moved her, but once again, Vangie wasn't sure if there was a sexual connotation in Shawn's words: *Dark meat. Umph, umph, umph.* She wanted to douse herself with cold water as she recalled the thickness of Shawn's personal dark meat.

❤ ❤ ❤

Yuri munched on his Happy Meal. Vangie and Shawn shared a bucket of chicken. Shawn went for a wing as Vangie reached for a drumstick. The accidental touch of their fingers sparked electricity.

"Sorry," they mumbled at the same time, withdrawing their hands and exchanging furtive glances.

After Yuri gobbled his last chicken nugget, Vangie looked at the clock. "It's time for bed, honey."

"Aw, Mom. I'm not ready—"

"It's bedtime, son." Shawn's deep authoritative vocal tone instantly cut off Yuri's whine. "Let's go, man." He swooped Yuri into his arms and hoisted him upon his broad shoulders.

High in the air and headed for his bedroom, Yuri waved his arms in the air and yelled, "Look at me, Mommy! I can touch the ceiling!"

Vangie couldn't help being impressed with the way Shawn and Yuri were bonding. But she was also a little disturbed by the sexual tension between her and Shawn.

Over the past five years, their love had been replaced with animosity. But there was no denying that they shared a sexual attraction. Now that she was no longer pissed with him, she was able to enjoy Shawn's appearance. He was as fine as ever with his full, luscious lips and yummy, coffee-colored skin.

She recalled how they used to be in bed. Back when they were together, Shawn had been an imaginative lover. Flashes of memories of hot sex beneath satin sheets sent a burning rush of heat between her legs.

I wonder if Shawn is seeing anyone. It doesn't matter; I just want some no-strings attached, good sex. But ex-lovers trying to raise a child together shouldn't dabble in uncommitted sex. All I really need is for Shawn to make regular child support payments and be a good father to our son.

"Yuri's tucked in and sound asleep," Shawn said when he returned to the kitchen.

"That was fast. What's your trick?"

"No tricks. I deal with Yuri, man to man. I don't baby him like you do. When I say that it's bedtime, I mean business."

Vangie raised a brow. "Are you criticizing my parenting skills?"

"Not at all. I take full responsibility for not being in Yuri's life like I should have. A child needs the right balance. He needs a mother and a father. I can't change the past, but I'm in my son's life now, and I'm going to do the best that I can to teach him to become a good man."

Deep in thought over the regrettable past, Vangie nodded absently. Why hadn't she and Shawn tried harder to work out their differences…for Yuri's sake? They'd created a life, yet they'd been too stubborn and too selfish to consider what was in Yuri's best interest.

She studied Shawn's handsome profile, and then sneakily scanned his muscular physique. He looked so damn tempting. The feelings that swirled inside of her were more of a carnal nature than a concerned co-parent. Embarrassed, she pulled her eyes away.

Shawn pulled his leather jacked off the back of the kitchen chair. "I'm about to be out. You good?"

Panic seized Vangie as she realized that she didn't want to alone. "No, I'm not alright."

"What's wrong; whatchu need?"

She closed her eyes briefly, and then against her better judgment, she softly admitted, "I need you."

CHAPTER 15

Vangie didn't have to twist Shawn's arm to get him inside her bedroom. Practically salivating, Vangie watched as Shawn shed his shirt. Every beautiful bulge and gorgeous ripple that covered his sculpted frame enticed her. God, he was making her hot. She craved an orgasm. Couldn't remember that last time she'd had one that hadn't been self-induced.

Her admiring eyes cruised over Shawn's six-pack. "You're at the barbershop all those hours; how do you find time to hit the gym?"

"I work out as soon as I get out of bed. No gym. No fancy equipment. I do push-ups…crunches. I get it in on my bedroom floor." As he bent to pull off his pants, his muscles, irresistibly visible, flexed and danced beneath his skin.

Her eyes slid over his toned body. She felt a pang in her stomach, imagining her and Shawn getting in a sensual workout on her bedroom floor. *Mmm*, she murmured inwardly as she pictured his throbbing erection, parting and penetrating her dripping sex.

The scant few sex partners she'd had since she and Shawn had parted ways possessed neither the finesse nor stamina to make her cum. Shawn had many bad traits, but lovemaking was not one of them. He was a patient and attentive lover who could deliver a hip-winding slow stroke that caused her body to rock and quiver so hard, she feared a seizure. Shawn's good-fucking dick had been her ruination, she remembered with a bittersweet smile.

"What's on your mind?" he asked, mouth aiming for hers.

Too turned on to respond, she closed her eyes and enjoyed the warmth of his kiss on her lips. His mouth held a sweet, chocolaty taste with a dash of tart, reminding her of a chocolate truffle with an added note of tangy lemon-ginger.

His delicious lips glided to her neck, nibbling at her flesh, and then licking her earlobe. She had no coherent words for him, and could only emit a series of purrs and soft moans.

His tongue found its way inside her ear, causing her legs to part as if an invisible string had pulled them apart. She felt her clit began to swell and took in a deep, shuddering breath.

"I need you, Shawn," she whispered as she lowered her body. "Fuck me. Right here." She patted the floor. Though she tried to control the coarseness of her voice, her bold demand came out raspy and broken.

Grunting while holding his dick, Shawn joined Vangie on the cold, laminate wood floor. His hand slipped between her legs as he dipped his finger into her heated moisture.

She gasped at his touch. Vangie realized that she was playing with fire, but she didn't care about consequences.

Shawn's finger suddenly abandoned her hot box. "Where's the remote?" he asked.

Perplexed, Vangie frowned. "What?"

"I wanna turn the TV on, you know, so Yuri won't hear us."

She pointed in the direction of the metal TV stand.

Shawn got up; a huge erection led him to the other side of the room.

Vangie couldn't help feeling a twinge of guilt. As Yuri's mother, she should have been more concerned than Shawn about Yuri overhearing them. She blamed her clouded judgment on the lengthy sex drought she'd been enduring.

She stared at Shawn's handsome profile as he aimed the remote. Then her eyes journeyed downward to his erection and his tightened nut sack. *Umph!*

Shawn selected a music station. Classic R&B.

He turned around and gazed at Vangie, who was sitting up, fingers racking through her hair.

"You look better than ever," he murmured, coming toward her.

Meanwhile, Lionel Ritchie's smooth sound crooned in the background. "*Hello! Is it me you're looking for?*" Under ordinary circumstances that song would have been a perfectly sweet greeting. But these were not ordinary conditions. Vangie was so worked up, her anxious eyes locked on Shawn. She had to fight an urge to run across the room and tackle him. Had to hold herself back from forcefully taking the dick.

So while Lionel Ritchie was singing a sweet melody, her pussy was belting out classic Marvin Gaye lyrics, "*Let's Get It On!*"

On the floor, Shawn climbed on top of her, separated the lips of her aching pussy and eased inside her opening, pushing between a passageway so narrow…so tight, it seemed like virgin territory.

Vangie's body reacted to the sweet invasion with squirms and jerks.

"Relax, Vangie. We gon' take it nice and slow."

Shawn covered her mouth with his. He ran his hands against the soft skin of her shoulders and back, his gentle caresses making her body tingle with desire.

The tender, slow fuck Shawn was delivering was driving Vangie over the edge. She wanted to be fucked hard. Without emotion. She wanted an exchange of raw desire. It had taken such a long time to get over Shawn, the last thing Vangie needed was to fall in love with him again.

"I want it rough!"

"No," he whispered.

"Yes! Pull my hair," she demanded breathlessly.

"Nah, that's not even me. I'm not tryna hurt you all like that."

"Come on, Shawn," she cajoled, believing that a little bit of pain would help keep things in perspective. Pain would remind her that she and Shawn would never be an official couple again. Being booty buddies was the most she could hope for. And that wasn't the kind of situation she wanted to be a part of for more than one night.

"Before you cum, I want you to turn me over and smack my ass!" she cried out savagely. Her contracting vaginal muscles gobbled up a few more inches of dick.

"No, I'm not into that." His mouth latched onto a nipple. His tongue swirled around the pearled flesh.

She cupped the back of his head, pressing his lips to her right breast. "Bite it," she hissed.

Shawn jerked his head away. "What kind of freak shit are you into?"

"I like it rough."

"Since when?" he asked, now pumping her pussy at a faster pace. Going in deeper, stretching out her walls, aroused by her request and no longer concerned about causing her pain.

"Stop asking so many questions. Tear this pussy up."

His dick strokes became lightning fast, creating streaks of fire. Vangie opened her legs wider, welcoming the burn.

He palmed her ass cheeks, and then squeezed the round mounds, pulling her closer as he pounded her pussy as though dispensing a harsh punishment.

"Oh, yes. Hurt my pussy, Shawn. You know that's how I like it."

"For real?"

"Uh-huh." She wrapped her legs around his back, inching upwards toward his shoulders, permitting ample access.

Shawn grunted and perspired as he deep stroked. Vangie matched his accelerated pace.

"That's how I like it, Shawn. Fuck me hard!" she yelled. She probably looked and sounded crazy. Her demands sounded over the top and demented even to her own ears. But she didn't care. She was out of control, and unable to stop herself.

Shawn slowed his stroke. "When you start acting like this?" he asked, frowning down at her face, clearly disapproving of her sudden and unaccountable lust for pain.

Hell if I know. Having no answer, Vangie went silent. She closed her eyes, bit down on her lip. She'd been sex-deprived for too long. Winding and writhing, her body invited him to ravage her.

Shawn ignored her demands, and began removing his hardness, inch by inch.

"Oh!" she gasped, feeling deprived. Dipping his head, he kissed her. Gently at first, and then more passionately with a deep open mouth kiss with his tongue boldly exploring her mouth.

"I never stopped loving you, Vangie," he admitted, his voice shaky and tortured, like a dying man making a final confession.

It was in her heart to share his sentiments, but she was afraid to expose feelings that would leave her vulnerable, set her up for heartache.

"This is about sex, Shawn. Nothing else," she told him firmly.

"But I miss you, baby. I miss us being together," Shawn murmured, now paying attention to her sensitive breasts, dispensing kisses to each hard-puckered nipple. "You still like to get your titties licked and sucked?"

"Uh-huh." Lost in the sensations, she briefly threw her head back, enjoying the tingle of his lips pulling at her pebbled flesh.

"I like sucking these titties," he growled, mouth widening, devouring her dark areola. He pushed her breasts together, sucking her right nipple and circling the other with the pad of a pussy-moistened fingertip.

"Stop it, Shawn." Vangie tried to rise, to pull away from the heat of kisses, but surrendered. Breathless and weakened by the abundant accumulation of molten heat that bubbled over and was sliding down her thighs, she surrendered as he nipped and licked on her dark pearls.

Shawn had her writhing on the edge of ecstasy.

"You ready for me?" he asked, gasping raggedly.

Vangie moaned in agreement. Shawn nudged her legs apart with his knees, and then sank between them, his hard erection sliding against the insides of her thighs that were streaked with honeyed arousal.

With long thrusts, he entered and reentered her, over and over, driving her back into the floor that was now warmed from their body heat.

Her body accepted him with a hunger. No longer concerned about the repercussions of having sex with her ex-man, Vangie grabbed his shoulders, threw her legs up and locked her ankles around his waist.

Shawn slowed his movement, and then stopped abruptly. Panicked, Vangie feared that he was on the verge of ejaculation. She didn't want him to cum…not while she was so close to getting an orgasm. She could feel the beginning of an orgasm vibrating through her system. "Hold on, Shawn. Wait, baby," she murmured desperately.

"I'm good, baby. I just wanna get deeper." Shawn untwined her legs from around his waist. With her thighs spread wide, he scooped her butt cheeks inside his palms, and pulled Vangie closer. From that angle, the glide of his dick soared upward, connecting with a part of her that had never been touched. An orgasm blossomed, sending spasms of pleasure reverberating though her body.

It was the longest and the most intense orgasm she'd ever experienced. She released gasps of excitement. Her body quivered as shockwaves jolted through her, causing her to react with wild excitement and violent convulsions. "Oh, shit! Shawn! What's happening to me?"

"Ride with it, baby," Shawn encouraged, shafting her with his hard throbbing dick.

Vangie heard a popping sound that seemed to emanate from within her vagina. The floodgates opened. "Oh, God!" she shouted, holding onto Shawn as bursts of fluid spurted from her vagina. *What the hell? I know I'm not pissing all over myself!*

Then all thoughts left her. Mindlessly, she became one with the raging orgasm that ripped through her.

"Did I hit that spot?" Shawn asked when Vangie's breathing calmed down.

She shrugged, unsure and slightly embarrassed.

"I must have hit something cuz you squirted out a big-ass nut." There was pride and incredulity in Shawn's voice.

I did? Overwhelmed by the lengthy and all-consuming orgasm, she couldn't speak, could only pant. She smiled to herself, relieved that the liquid heat that was sliding down her thighs was evidence of passion and not the result of a weak bladder.

Vangie had heard about women squirting, but thought it was a myth. "Squirted? I squirted?" she finally asked between ragged breaths.

"Yo, that was crazy," Shawn said, breathing heavily as he increased the tempo of his stroke. A few moments later, he verbalized his explosion with a thunderous groan.

Overcome with an unexpected rush of emotions, Vangie wrapped her arms around Shawn, holding his quaking body as he flooded her with his passion.

It was a beautiful moment of connectedness. Two people who'd been involved in years of conflict now clung to each other, allowing their natural capacity for love to overrule their disagreements of the past.

Shawn rolled off Vangie. Propped up on an elbow, he smiled at her. "That was awesome." Leaning down, he kissed her fully on the lips.

After the kiss, Vangie gazed at him. "What are we doing, Shawn?"

"Finishing what we started six years ago."

"But what if it doesn't work out? I don't want Yuri to suffer again—not for our mistakes."

"We're good, baby. I'm never going to neglect my son again. And I'm going spend the rest of my life making up for the way that I hurt you."

CHAPTER 16

Nivea came out of the shower and could not believe her eyes. Eric was standing inside their bedroom, his face troubled. In his hand, he held the handle of an infant carrier with his infant son bundled up inside.

Nivea tightened the bath towel around her body, and gawked disbelievingly at the baby. "What the hell do you think you're doing, Eric? I told you that I don't want that slut's baby inside my home."

"This is *our* home, and he's my son, too," he reminded her with an edge to his voice. He set the infant carrier on top of the bed.

Nivea waved her finger in the direction of the infant carrier, "He has to go! Take that baby back to his mother, right now!"

"I can't do that."

"Oh, yes you can!"

Eric wore a grave expression. "Dyeesha's not home. She bounced."

"Where'd she go?" Nivea folded her arms, furious that Dyeesha had managed to stir up more trouble in her life.

"I don't know where she's at." Eric blew out a gust of frustrated air and scratched his head. "Dyeesha's got issues, man. I keep calling her cell, but she ain't picking up."

"That's not my problem! You have to find her!" Nivea shouted.

Jolted by the volume of Nivea's voice, the baby began to cry and squirmed inside the blankets that covered him.

"It's all good, man. Daddy gotchu," Eric cooed to his son.

Nivea grimaced. Having Eric's child in her home put a sour taste in her mouth.

"Why you grilling my son?"

"I'm still traumatized over the fact that your son even exists." She rubbed her forehead. "It's really insensitive of you to bring your indiscretion to our home."

"What did you expect me to do with him...leave him outside on the steps?"

"Sarcasm isn't necessary." Using remarkable restraint, Nivea refrained from picking up a candleholder and beating the crap out of Eric.

"Take him to your mom's house," she suggested in a voice as quiet and calm as she could manage under the circumstances. Then she got loud. "Shit, why should your mom or anyone else have to put up with that baby? Doesn't he have a grandmother on his gutter side?"

"Man, cut out all that talk about his gutter side. All that name-calling ain't even necessary. You're being childish, Nivea."

"Oh, really? If I'm childish, then you're a nasty-ass, baby making, skanky, male ho!"

"Come on with that, Niv. You don't even mean that trash you talking."

"Hmph!" After a brief hesitation, she turned her back to Eric and sauntered inside the bathroom and closed the door. Unwilling to be caught butt naked if she and Eric got into a physical altercation, she removed the towel and put on a robe.

Nivea came out of the bathroom, wrapping the fluffy robe around her body.

"Are you going to take him to your mom's house?"

"My mother ain't like a regular mom-mom. She's still young and full of life."

"What about his other grandmother...the gutter one?"

Eric sighed at the snide comment. "Dyeesha's mom ain't right in the head."

"I'm not surprised that she has a nutjob for a mother. Well, I'm not getting stuck with this baby. Not for one damn minute!"

"Ain't nobody asking you to be stuck with my son. I'll take care of Little Junior."

"Little Junior? Is that what you call him?"

"That's his nickname."

"That's so ghetto."

"Man, I like his name."

"Whatever." Nivea stuck her hand on her hip. "Look, he's got to go. Seriously, Eric, I can't have that horrible woman's child in my home."

"He's my child, too! Damn, Nivea, you act like this is my son's fault."

"I'm not blaming the baby. I'm blaming you! It's your fault that I have to deal with the humiliating fact that you've fathered a child out of wedlock. I'm totally disgusted that you're trying to make me suffer for the mistake that you made. I am not lifting one finger to help you take care of your bastard child!"

"Stop calling him that."

"There wouldn't be any Little Damn Junior if you hadn't stuck your dick where it didn't belong."

"You're never gonna let me live this down, are you?"

She glowered at Eric. "I'm not riding for you on this bullshit." She shook her head emphatically.

"Come on, baby. Don't be like that."

"The minute I think that the situation is somewhat under control, you come at me with some new hood jinks." Nivea frowned at the baby. "I'd be a fool to allow you to drag me deeper and deeper into hood ratchetness."

"We can get through this together."

"I can't trust anything you say. I told you I didn't want that baby around me and the very next day…here he is! This situation has gone from bad to worse. Do you really think I'm going to be changing your little bastard's diapers?"

"My son ain't no bastard, so watch your fuckin' mouth," he bellowed.

"I guess what they say is true: lie down with dogs, and you end up with fleas. Everybody tried to warn me against marrying you, but I wouldn't listen. I gave you the benefit of the doubt. I've tried to upgrade you, but look at the thanks I get." She sneered at the baby. "There's no getting around it; I have to call off the wedding."

"You back on that again?"

"I can't do it, Eric. It's clear that the only thing you're bringing to the table is trouble and strife." She took a deep breath. "Seriously. You need to gather up your possessions. It's over. I need my space, so take your son back to the apartment and wait for his mother over there."

"You're putting me out?" Eric leaned to the side and stared at Nivea incredulously.

"Tell Dyeesha that I said congratulations. I'm withdrawing from the competition. She can have you."

"I work every day. I'm not broke."

"Your salary ain't shit," Nivea retorted.

"Why you wanna throw my salary up in my face?"

"Because I'm educated and sophisticated. I make six figures a year, and you had the nerve to cheat on me and make a baby with a trashy stripper."

"Ex-stripper," he corrected.

"Shut up!"

"We're supposed to be a team, Nivea. We should be tryna straighten out this mess together."

"I didn't sign up for this."

"After all the time I've put in with you—"

"You should have thought about that when you went out and made a baby. Don't try to act like a victim because I'm the one who was cheated on, betrayed, and beat up!"

"I didn't hit you. I'm the one that ended up with a head wound."

"You brought that on yourself."

"I was trying to be a stand-up guy. I was tryna take care of mine. But you know what...I'm getting sick of the way you keep going back and forth with this wedding. One minute it's on, and a second later, you're calling it off. So, fuck it then!"

"Yeah, and fuck you, too," Nivea shot back. "You and that tramp have brought me more drama in the past few days than I've experienced in my entire life. If you think I'm going to be losing sleep while that little bastard is screaming and crying—"

"Yo, watch your mouth!" Eric stomped over to the closet and swung open the double doors. Nivea observed as he yanked clothes off hangers and slung them onto the bed. Pairs of jeans, shirts, and sweaters were building into a tall pile next to the sleeping baby.

I'm not going to be able to live it down if I call off this wedding. I'm going to hear "I told you so" a million times. I don't know what to do. Eric is beneath contempt, but I can't let myself end up a pitiful old maid while my sister marries a damn doctor.

Nivea cleared her throat. "Listen, I don't want us to break up. But I can't allow you to bring your son over here every time his negligent mother feels like running the streets."

"Can't you be a little more understanding? The way you acting, I'm scared to leave you alone with my son. Real talk."

Nivea felt her face begin to twitch. "What are you saying?"

"I'm saying, it might be a good idea for me and Lil' Junior to go back to the apartment. I already experienced your violent side.

I couldn't forgive myself if I didn't protect my son." Eric sauntered over to the closet, pulled out a huge duffle bag and tossed it on the floor next to the bed.

"Do you think I'm capable of child abuse?" Nivea touched her chest, indignant.

"Yeah."

"That's crazy."

"What's crazy is the way you keep calling an innocent baby out of his name."

Nivea sighed. "Look, Eric, I said a lot of stuff that I didn't mean. I was angry. Now put your things back in the closet."

"I don't know, Niv. You said some harsh stuff about Lil' Junior."

"I'm sorry. I was upset."

"So, what we gon' do about him?" He glanced down at the baby.

"Take him to your mom. It won't kill her to watch her own grandson for a while."

"He's not my mom's responsibility."

He's not my goddamn responsibility either! Nivea stared off into space, trying to think of a solution. She looked up at Eric. "Where do you think Dyeesha is?"

"Who knows? She could be anywhere."

"Do you have the number of any of her friends? We should call the police. Abandoning a child is a crime."

"Not when the mother leaves him with his other parent. I'm not tryna start nothing with Dyeesha. I know she loves our son, but she has a wild streak."

"You sound delusional, Eric. A loving mother does not run off and abandon her child."

"She stormed out the crib after I told her that me and you were going through with our wedding. She cussed me out and said she'd be damn if I was going to saddle her down with a fatherless baby."

"Did she take any clothes with her?"

"No."

"If she didn't pack anything, obviously, she'll be back." Nivea paused for a moment, and then added, "She wouldn't really abandon her own baby, would she?" The last thing Nivea needed was to have to hide this baby from her family and friends for more than a few hours.

"Let's give her a chance to calm down. I'm sure she's going to come to her senses by tomorrow."

"Tomorrow! That baby can't stay here overnight."

"Why not? I'll change the diapers and make his bottles. You don't have to get your pretty little hands dirty," Eric said with a chuckle.

Nivea didn't see the humor.

The baby started crying again. Softly at first, and then he turned up the volume.

"What's all that fussing for?" Eric said lovingly, as he lifted his son out of the carrier.

Feeling trapped and helpless, Nivea walked out of the bedroom. In the kitchen, she reached for a bottle of vodka. Poured a shot, threw it back...straight with no chaser.

CHAPTER 17

N ivea did not lift a finger to help Eric with the baby, but she was exhausted from watching Eric warm formula, change diapers, and walk the floor with the baby that wouldn't stop crying. To no avail, he'd called Dyeesha's cell every half-hour. Each call went to voice mail.

By eleven that night, the little monster was finally knocked out. The child was wrapped in blankets and lying on Eric's side of the bed. Eric sat next to him, gazing down with love and pride in his eyes.

"Why don't you take him in the guestroom?" Nivea suggested.

Eric frowned. "Suppose he rolls off the bed?"

"I don't feel like arguing with you; I'm tired."

"Why you talking out the side of your neck?" he barked. "You know Lil' Junior's too young to sleep in a bed by hisself."

Nivea couldn't suppress her irritation. "It's starting to feel real crowded in here, so take your goddamn son in the guestroom!"

"Why!"

She waved a finger through the air. "Having that baby sleeping in my bed is where I draw the line, Eric. If you don't like it, you can join him."

Mumbling in discontent, Eric rearranged the blankets, tightening them securely before gathering up his son, and stomped out of the bedroom.

Fuck you! She snuggled under the down-filled comforter. She was relieved to have her bedroom to herself...grateful for the privacy. But after struggling to find a comfortable position, she realized that she missed the warmth of Eric's husky body lying next to her.

She tossed and turned some more, flung a pillow, and then sat up. *This is not fair. After everything I've done to accommodate Eric, I still wind up in bed by myself.* She questioned her sanity in allowing Eric to draw her into his drama-filled existence.

Being realistic, she'd be much better off without Eric. Letting him convince her to allow his baby to stay overnight was outrageous. It was absolutely degrading. She'd only gone along with the absurd request because she didn't want to give Eric any excuse to run back to that lowdown stripper. She'd put in too much time with Eric to start looking for a new man. Finding one who was ready to get married would be next to impossible.

The single status sucked. It was like a stigma. Being a single female at twenty-eight was disgraceful. In her subconscious mind, Nivea felt like she had a disease that could only be cured if somebody—anybody—put a ring on it.

❤ ❤ ❤

Though her mind chatter seemed to go on and on without cessation, at some point drowsiness seeped in between her troubled thoughts, pulling her in a peaceful slumber.

But something that sounded as explosive as a bomb detonation yanked Nivea from the serenity of sleep, had her out of bed and on her feet. Clutching her chest, mouth agape in fear, she ran out into the hallway. Had terrorists attacked her tranquil community?

Wearing only boxers, Eric came rushing out of the guestroom with the baby in his arms.

"What's going on, Eric? What was that noise?"

"I don't know. Something hit the front door." He passed her

the baby. "Here, hold Lil' Junior. Take him in the bedroom and close the door."

Nivea hesitated, unsure of what had caused the commotion. She didn't want to hold Little Junior or take him into her bedroom. But another boom—this one louder than the first—had Nivea screaming and running. Inside her bedroom, she followed Eric's suggestion, and turned the lock for extra protection.

Boom, boom! "Open da fuckin' door, Eric! Ain't nobody playing with yo' ass! Open da goddamn door!"

Recognizing the voice, Nivea gasped in shock and outrage. Though slurred, it was unmistakeably Dyeesha's ugly voice.

No that slut didn't have the nerve to bring her drunk, skank ass over here, kicking on my door like she's the one paying the bills! Nivea leapt from the bed. Carrying the baby, she hurried to the bedroom door. Vibrating with anger, she imagined herself inviting Dyeesha inside and showing the ghetto tramp what was really hood. Nivea was so revved up, she could feel her fingers itching to tear that red weave off the bitch's head.

She opened the bedroom door and could hear Eric yelling, "Go 'head, Dyeesha! You drunk…that's why you acting up! Go home and sleep the liquor off!"

That bitch is the one trespassing now. Standing on my porch, kicking and cussing and creating a scene. I got something for that drunken ass, Nivea thought as she rushed down the hallway.

"Open up the damn door before I blow this bitch off the hinges!" Dyeesha shouted. Her command was followed by the sound of locks being turned.

Eric opened the door and Dyeesha burst inside the living with sneakers on her feet, but for some reason, she was carrying a pair of thigh-high, shiny black boots in her hands. They were most likely the boots that she wore during her stripper routine.

Dyeesha proved to be crazier than Nivea had imagined. She

started swinging the boots through the air. Holding onto the shiny plastic end, she began wielding the boots like they were a set of nunchucks. Nivea began backing up, deciding it was best if Eric took over the situation. If anyone got clobbered with those boots, it needed to be Eric.

"Do something, Eric," Nivea said sharply.

"Why you got my son in your arms? You ain't his mother. Hand me my goddamn baby," Dyeesha demanded.

Static had Dyeesha's red weave sticking out all over her head. Drool trickled from the corners of her twisted lips. Nivea would have gladly handed over the child, but she didn't dare get too close to the boot-swinging enemy. "I don't want your baby," Nivea said with revulsion. She shot a glance at Eric, and noticed he was standing in the background as if helpless. "Do something, Eric. Call the police."

His brows drew together in a frown. "I can't call the cops on my baby mom." His voice came out low and weak.

Nivea gawked at Eric. *What a pussy!*

Wearing a maniacal smile, Dyeesha inched up a little closer. "First you try to steal my man, now you tryna play mommy to my son. You crossed the line, bitch. Now, hand me my son."

Take your little bastard, Nivea wanted to say, but she couldn't risk provoking drunk-ass Dyeesha. It occurred to Nivea that she could make a quicker getaway if she tossed the baby like a football toward his father. It would be on Eric if he missed the catch.

"Watch the way you swinging them boots, Dyeesha!" Eric bellowed. "I'ma fuck you up if you hurt my son."

What about me? Nivea scowled at Eric.

Dyeesha kept swinging, and deliberately smashed a lamp. The blast of noise made Nivea jump. The baby screamed with fright.

"Yo, what the fuck is your problem?" Grappling with Dyeesha,

Eric managed to confiscate one boot. Arms wrapped around her waist, he confined her, holding her in a steely grip.

Dyeesha twisted and lurched forward but couldn't escape Eric's grasp.

"Calm the fuck down, Dyeesha," he bellowed.

Trapped inside Eric's strong arms, she hissed at Nivea, "Give me my fuckin' baby!" Nivea noticed that Dyeesha seemed to be frothing at the mouth, and that her teeth were bared—like a vicious animal. "Oh, you like playing Mommy to my baby? Okay, alright, then." She gave a menacing chuckle.

Nivea cringed at the sound of that threatening chuckle. She'd obviously misjudged Dyeesha, thinking she could win a fight with her due to the hussy's undernourished appearance. Dyeesha had crazy working to her advantage, giving her the rage and most likely the strength of the mentally insane.

Nivea glared at Eric. "I'm calling the cops. You have exactly five seconds to get her out of here."

"I ain't going nowhere without my baby," Dyeesha insisted as she struggled with Eric.

"Stop clownin', girl. You can't take Lil' Junior nowhere in your condition," Eric responded brusquely. "And I can't let you get behind the wheel, either. You gon' wind up with the car wrapped around a tree."

Nivea raised an eyebrow at Eric. "What do you plan to do, Eric? Invite your jumpoff into my kitchen…sober her up with a pot of my gourmet coffee?" Nivea said sneeringly.

This is it. I'm really through with Eric. I'd rather stay single for the rest of my life than have go through eighteen years of this madness.

With a burst of unexpected energy, Dyeesha broke free from Eric's clutches. She used the heel of her stripper boot to bash Nivea in the head, staggering her.

Eric rushed over, but it was his son that he rescued. "Y'all acting all crazy; the baby could get hurt," Eric scolded, giving both Nivea and Dyeesha equally dirty looks. He stormed out of the living room with the infant in his arms.

Nivea's head was spinning, and she was stunned that Eric had left her to deal with Dyeesha, a scrawny but brutal opponent. While she tried to get her bearings, Dyeesha delivered a swift kick to her groin.

"Ugh!" Nivea grunted. Her face contorted in pain, she grabbed her crotch and bent over in agony. Next Dyeesha used her bony kneecap to jut Nivea in the chin, knocking her completely off her feet. Nivea went down, and Dyeesha leaped on top of her, pinning Nivea to the floor with fingernails embedded in her forearms, and teeth implanted in her shoulder.

Nivea shrieked in pain. "Eric! Get this bitch off me!"

CHAPTER 18

After getting Nivea's frantic phone call, Vangie threw on a heavy coat, a hat, earmuffs, scarf, gloves, and boots and rushed out into the cold night. She drove as fast as she could to Nivea's townhouse. She had no idea what was wrong with her girl, but Nivea was crying and begging her to come over.

It was a good thing that Shawn was over and could watch Yuri; otherwise she would have had to drag Yuri out in the middle of the night. Thinking about Shawn's reappearance in her life put a faint smile on Vangie's face.

Her smile faded when she arrived on Nivea's doorstep. She stared in puzzlement at the chinks on Nivea's beautiful red door. *What the hell?* Anxious, she jabbed the doorbell four times in quick succession.

Nivea opened the door. "I'm sorry you had to come out so late," she said weakly, her eyes bloodshot from crying.

"Don't worry about it," Vangie said, her breath forming into a small cloud of fog. Questioningly, she nodded her head toward the damaged door.

"Come on in, before you freeze to death," Nivea said without responding to Vangie's unspoken question.

"You really had me shook, so I got here as fast as I could. Seeing those gashes on your front door doesn't make me feel any better. What's the deal?"

"It's a long story."

Vangie nodded toward the smashed lamp. "That's not a good

sign, either. Will you please tell me what's going on, Niv? And where's Eric?"

Tears welled in Nivea's eyes at the mention of Eric's name. She wiped her eyes. "The wedding is off, Vangie. I can't marry Eric."

"You can't be serious. Your wedding is all you've been living for. Did you and Eric have a fight? Where is he? I saw his truck outside." Vangie's inquisitive eyes darted about as she looked for more signs of violence and mayhem. But aside from the broken lamp, Nivea's townhouse appeared to be in pristine condition.

"Eric is not the person we think he is," Nivea murmured.

Vangie knew Eric to be a gentle spirit, but maybe he'd finally gotten tired of Nivea bossing him around. Maybe he finally exploded. "Did Eric mess up the front door?" she gently prodded. Vangie nodded toward the shattered lamp on the floor. "Are you calling off the wedding because he…uh…snapped?"

"No, his baby mamma did," Nivea spat.

"His baby, what?"

"Eric has a four-month-old son. He got some skanky stripper pregnant."

Vangie gasped. "Eric has a baby?"

"That's right. The no-good bastard was leading a double life. He got a stripper pregnant and had her and the baby living in his old apartment. He's been lying to me regularly, pretending that he was working double shifts while he was shacking with the stripper."

Too stunned to speak, Vangie covered her mouth with her hand. All she could do was grimace and shake her head.

"This is between you and me, Vangie. Do not share this information with Harlow."

"Why not? After you announce that you're cancelling your wedding, the truth is bound to come out."

"I don't want Miss Priss all up in my business."

Vangie wrinkled her nose. "Why are you making digs at Harlow? She hasn't done anything to you and after the hard life she's had, growing up in foster care, she certainly doesn't deserve to be labelled Miss Priss."

"I know. But her life is so perfect now. She's going to marry a handsome, successful man. And she doesn't deserve him. I don't want to share my dirty laundry with her. Promise me you'll keep this to yourself, Vangie."

Vangie squirmed a little, and then gave in. "Okay. But what are you going to tell your parents? Are you going to tell your mom and dad the truth about your break-up?"

"Absolutely not! My mother would ridicule me for the rest of my life if she knew what Eric did to me. I'm going to make up a story…tell my parents that I finally came to my senses and realize that Eric isn't good enough for me."

"Okay, that sounds like a plan." Vangie eyed the shattered lamp. "So, what happened here? Did you break the lamp over Eric's head?" She caught a quick glimpse of something unidentifiable in Nivea's eyes. "And how did you get those little chinks in your door?"

There was that look again. *Shame!* She saw shame in Nivea's eyes as they shifted uneasily away from hers.

"The stripper fucked up my crib," Nivea admitted with her head lowered. She looked up and released a sigh, and then began telling Vangie the entire, sordid story from the day she had stopped by Eric's old apartment until tonight.

"That rat bastard," Vangie spat when Nivea concluded her awful story. Uttering sympathetic sounds, Vangie drew Nivea into a sisterly embrace.

"Ow." Nivea pulled away. "It hurts where she bit me."

"Do you want to go to the Emergency Room and get some shots? You don't know what kind of diseases that slut is carrying in her nasty mouth."

"No, I don't need a doctor. She didn't break the skin."

"Well, you can't let that smut get away with violent behavior. She needs to be held accountable for her actions. Damn, I can't believe that crazy bitch kicked you in the pussy. You sure everything's alright down there?" Vangie's eyes travelled down past Nivea's tummy area.

"It hurt like hell, but I'm not injured."

"Nivea, you really should press charges," Vangie said, her voice angry and indignant.

"I can't," Nivea whined.

"Why not?"

"Because…" She paused and let out a mournful sound. "It's all so sordid and embarrassing. I just want to forget that it happened. I want to move forward."

"That's crazy, Nivea. That loony toon chick maliciously assaulted you—scratched and bit you. And she kicked you all up in your vagina. That's not something you can easily forget." Vangie slid her cell phone out of her purse.

"Who are you calling?"

"Nobody, but I'm taking pictures for evidence, just in case you come to your senses." Vangie swivelled her head toward the toppled lamp. She walked over to it and began snapping pictures. "I can't believe Eric is such a punk ass. After that tramp broke in your crib, destroyed property, and attacked you, he drove her home!"

"He claimed that she was too drunk to drive."

"She wasn't too drunk to get here."

Vangie sucked her teeth. "Shit, his ass needs a beat down and he needs to get slapped with some criminal charges," she said as she clicked on the porch light and aimed the camera phone at the splintered door. "You need to have the police waiting on that ass when he comes to pick up his truck."

"I packed his clothes. He's out of my life. I just want to let it go."

"Why? Your fiancé made a fool out of you. His jumpoff tries to kill you and for all you know that kick in the coochie might ruin your chances of ever having kids."

"My reproductive organs are intact," Nivea said flatly.

"I'm shocked that Eric is so manipulative and heartless. That bastard had the nerve to coerce you into helping him babysit his child."

"I didn't actually babysit."

"Stop making excuses," Vangie grumbled in disgust. "Isn't that why the bitch went off on you...because you were holding her child?"

"Yeah, but—"

"Sounds like babysitting to me." Vangie shook her head wearily. "You're a good woman with a head on her shoulders and you have a great career. Eric threw it all away for a stripper."

Nivea bobbed her head. "I know.

"It seems to me that the more you let Eric get away with, the more emotionally abusive he became. You're such a strong woman. What happened to you, Nivea?"

"I don't know. I can't believe half the things that I've allowed since I found out about Eric's double life. I'm pathetic," Nivea said, sounding defeated.

Vangie flinched. "Don't say that. Look, I'm sorry. I should be uplifting your spirits; not making you feel worse."

"It's true, though. I'm really pathetic. I was so desperate for somebody to marry, that I settled for Eric, knowing that he was deficient in so many ways."

"We all make mistakes when it comes to love."

"I'm not even sure if I ever really loved Eric."

"No?"

"He was alright. I liked him enough to put up with all his short-comings because he was easy to get along with and he let me have my way. Or so I thought."

"Eric was bringing too much baggage with him. He actually did you a favor by showing his true colors before you tied the knot."

Nivea nodded.

"I still don't understand why you're letting that tramp get away with assault and battery. My God, you have her teeth marks on your shoulder. Where is the real Nivea, the one who fights back?"

"The stripper, the baby, the endless cussing and fighting…it's too much. All of this drama has me so beaten down, I feel grimy and drained. Seriously, Vangie all I really want is to reclaim my dignity. I need my self-respect back. I can't heal if I have to talk to the police, go to court, and relive these disgusting events. I want to forget that Eric and his secret family ever existed."

"Alright, Niv. Don't worry; your secret is safe with me. I'll back up whatever statement you make about the wedding. Okay, girl?"

"Okay," Nivea replied, her voice tearful.

Vangie didn't want Nivea to start crying, so she went for humor. "I guess it's safe to assume that you're gonna keep that rock that Eric put on your finger."

Nivea glanced down at her engagement ring. "Eric didn't give me this," she admitted. Tears welled in her eyes. "I put this on one of my credit cards. He was supposed to make payments, but he never made any. I guess he was too financially burdened from taking care of his *family*. Now how pathetic is that?"

"Damn!"

Nivea burst into tears. Her choking sobs echoed mournfully as Vangie rubbed her back, making comforting sounds.

CHAPTER 19

There really shouldn't be secrets in a marriage. But how can I tell Drake the truth about what happened to me? I don't want to see pity in his eyes, and I don't want to see revulsion. I just want him to love me for who I've become, despite all the odds that were stacked against me.

Harlow looked out the window of the plane, trying to find comfort in the fluffy white clouds, but the clouds didn't help.

Jody! Harlow screamed in her mind.

Pretty and shapely, Jody used to brag to her friends that she never paid for her get-high. "All I have to do is wait 'til after-hours, page Skeeter, and wait. He don't even hit me back. He knows what I'm beeping him for. Ten minutes later, Skeeter's outside my door, his pockets filled with the dope I need. I don't have to pay for shit," Jody had bragged.

Jody's friends murmured in awe.

Four-year-old Harlow had seen plenty of those tiny plastic bags. Sometimes Skeeter brought her mother little glass bottles that stored her get-high. Harlow was happy for her mother, satisfied in the fact that Jody was special enough to receive her get-high for free. And judging from the other women's admiring faces, Jody was indeed, an exceptional person. Looking up from her coloring book, Harlow sent her mother a smile, her eyes bright with love and pride.

I was only four years old when it all started, Harlow recalled, staring blankly at the clouds.

Grimacing at the bad memories that were resurfacing, Harlow desperately searched the blue sky, hoping its beauty would distract her from her torturous thoughts. But her mind kept reverting to the past.

By the time Harlow was six, Jody was strung out so bad, she'd sell anything for a rock...including her own daughter.

"Be quiet. Stop crying," Skeeter growled.

Jody coaxed her on the other side of her closed bedroom door. "It's gon' be okay, baby. It won't hurt that bad the next time. I need you to be brave."

The plane shook slightly, jolting Harlow back into the moment. Her eyes watered. She squeezed them shut, trapping the tears, refusing to allow them to fall. In a struggle to be strong, she banged the window, alarming the flight attendant.

"Everything okay, ma'am? There's nothing to be concerned about; it's just a little turbulence."

"You're right. It's only turbulence. Sorry for overreacting," Harlow said after composing herself.

CHAPTER 20

Shawn, Vangie, and Yuri browsed the lot filled with pine trees.

"There's a big one, Daddy!" Yuri exclaimed, pointing at a tall, skinny tree.

"Too scrawny. Keep looking. Find something with some bulk, son."

"What's bulk?"

Shawn stretched out his arms in explanation.

Yuri scrutinized the rows of tied-together trees. "There it is! That one has bulk," he said using the word he'd just acquired. He trotted over to a colossal tree.

Shawn smiled. "That's what I'm talking about, son."

"Can we get it, Daddy?"

"Maybe. Let's see how much this dude gon' try and beat us for," Shawn replied, switching from a smile to a stern face.

"Why would he beat us?" Yuri asked, looking perplexed as he tried to decipher his father's terminology.

"Shh. Lemme handle this," Shawn said in a lowered voice. "Hey, man," he called out to the tree salesman. "How much you want for this one?"

"That's seventy-five," the man replied, smiling as he approached.

"That's kinda steep, my man. You know that tree ain't worth all that."

The man looked up at the sky briefly. "I can let you have it for sixty-five."

"Nah, that ain't gon' work. You gotta do better than that. It's only a couple of days 'til Christmas. I know you not tryna get stuck with all these trees."

"Fifty-five dollars," the man conceded. "That's the best I can do."

"That'll work," Shawn said, thrusting his hand inside his pocket and pulling out cash. He glanced at Yuri and gave him a wink. "Mofos be out to get you," he told his son in a conspiratorial tone. "Don't ever accept the first offer."

Yuri nodded, brows furrowed.

There were important life lessons that Yuri needed, and learning how to haggle wasn't one of them. Shawn's advice was ridiculous, but harmless. Vangie laughed to herself, *It's not like he's instructing Yuri on how to roll a blunt.*

What mattered was that her son was getting an opportunity to have a man's perspective on life…something he desperately needed.

Yuri scampered alongside his father as Shawn and the tree seller transported the tree to the car. Yuri was practically dancing with joy as he watched the tree being hoisted and tied to the roof of Shawn's car.

It was freezing outside but Vangie felt warmed by her son's smile.

Vangie sat in the passenger seat while Shawn made sure that Yuri was situated in the back.

"Can we stop at McDonald's, Daddy?" Yuri asked while Shawn was looking over his shoulder, backing out of the lot.

"Don't you ever get tired of McDonald's?" Shawn asked, laughing.

"No!" Yuri giggled.

"Whatchu wanna eat, Vangie?" Shawn asked.

"Whatever you two decide is okay with me."

"Can I order a number four like you, Daddy?"

"That might be too much food for you, Yuri," Vangie intervened.

"No, it's not," Yuri whined.

"Cut out that whining, man. That's not cool. You can get your point across without all that extra stuff," Shawn scolded.

That's right, you tell him, Shawn!

Yuri cleared his throat, attempting to remove the whine from his voice. "Happy Meals are for babies; I want a number four like Daddy gets," Yuri said in an even tone.

"All right then, but you gotta promise to eat all your food," Shawn said.

"I promise!"

Feeling temporarily released from the binds of single mother-hood, Vangie was in a peaceful place. Something as minor as having Shawn take responsibility for getting Yuri strapped in his seat, and answering their son's numerous questions was a tremendous relief. Being a passenger instead of having to drive in treacherous weather was heavenly bliss. Vangie stared out the window. Consumed with love, she cherished the moment.

❤ ❤ ❤

Shawn, Vangie, and Yuri had spent a few hours decorating the tree. Now Yuri was in bed asleep, and Shawn was at Clean Cutz working overnight. Vangie had to work in the morning, but she wasn't ready to call it a night just yet. She sat on the sofa, sipping wine and staring at the beautifully decorated tree.

The Christmas tree was stunning with its red and silver ornaments. It looked designer-decorated, like it should have been featured in a magazine. And it was all because of Shawn. He wanted Yuri to have a memorable Christmas with a real tree instead of the artificial tree that Vangie pulled out of the storage bin year after year.

Her life was finally changing for the better. In addition to the money he'd given her at the beginning of the month, Shawn had been giving her portions of the tips he made at the shop. Vangie appreciated having extra cash. Shawn even kept Yuri's pockets filled with one-dollar bills and loose change. For the first time in years, Vangie was relaxed and without pressing everyday money worries.

Though she and Shawn hadn't become an official couple yet, he had started assuming responsibilities and was behaving like he was her man, so it wasn't unreasonable to start thinking in terms of a stable future together.

It was possible that wedding bells were on the horizon. She smiled, imagining her and Shawn jumping the broom.

Her cell suddenly buzzed. She glanced at the screen…a text from Shawn. He wanted her to take a picture of the tree and send it to his cell.

Shawn wants to show off our tree to his customers and the other barbers at the shop. Cell in hand, she walked toward the Christmas tree. With a surge of exhilaration, she began snapping away, getting shots of the tree from a variety of angles. She wished she could hear the reactions from the men in the barbershop, but since she couldn't, she began sending the pictures to her own family and friends, and added a caption: Merry Xmas from Vangie, Shawn, & Yuri.

But she was hesitant about sending a picture to Nivea. Niv was going through a hell of a rough patch; she probably wasn't feeling the holiday spirit.

Nivea never took my misery into consideration when she bragged about her salary and extravagant wedding plans. I should be allowed the pleasure of sending a picture of my Christmas tree. Vangie scrolled to Nivea's name, and hit SEND.

CHAPTER 21

Alone in her suite at The Four Seasons, Harlow snacked on the complimentary chocolates and pastries that were set at her beside. The sweet taste did not substitute her yearning for Drake. She missed him so much. She wanted to call him but knew that he needed space.

For the past few days, Harlow's telephone conversations with Drake had been brief and awkward. He was always pressed for time, rushing off the phone to attend a meeting, or some business function that required his presence. There was nothing new about Drake having to conduct business, but he knew that Harlow was anxious to learn what he'd done with those stones. It was completely out of character for him to avoid a topic that was so important.

She swallowed back a knot of suspicion. *Please don't be involved in this mess, Drake. Please.*

Closing her eyes, Harlow thought back to happier times, when she first met Drake.

Without any real job skills, Harlow had bounced around from one low-paying job to the next. When she applied for the receptionist position at Elite Luxury Car Rentals, she was hired on the spot, and told that the person she'd replaced had advanced to a sales position. Harlow loved the atmosphere at work. Being in an environment with beautiful exotic cars was uplifting, and she was determined to learn all that she could about sales. It was time to focus on a career. This was an opportunity to improve her life.

After a couple of days on the job, Harlow heard through snatches of conversations that the owner was a black man. He lived in New York and came to the Philadelphia dealership only a few times a month. She could tell from the reverence in the employee's voices that the boss was well-liked and respected. Photographs of Drake posing with athletes, businessmen, and politicians, adorned the walls. She heard that her boss was a sought-after bachelor who dated women on both coasts, but there were no rumors of hanky panky with any females on his staff.

When she was finally introduced to Drake, Harlow's heart did a somersault. She was prepared for his distinguished good looks, but she wasn't ready for the electrical jolt that coursed through her when he shook her hand. From the startled look in his eyes, she had a feeling that he'd felt the sensation, too. When Drake released her hand, he welcomed her to the company and wished her good luck. She thanked him, and then eased back into her seat. It was difficult standing while the earth was quivering beneath her feet.

After their initial meeting, Drake didn't seem to notice her at all. During his brief visit at the Philadelphia dealership, he was polite to Harlow, but he pretty much ignored her. In the course of a day, he rarely said more than "good morning" when he arrived and "good night" at the end of the workday.

I thought we made a connection. Guess I was wrong. What did I expect? I was told that he didn't mix business and pleasure. Besides, a distinguished man like Drake can pick and choose among hundreds of beautiful women: fashion models, successful businesswomen, celebrities. Why would he want to get chummy with a receptionist? I better stay in my lane before I get my feelings hurt.

After a few days, Drake returned to his life in New York. Harlow was relieved. Her schoolgirl crush had been a huge distraction.

Now she could get back to the business of being a super receptionist who would soon be promoted to sales.

A beautiful floral arrangement was delivered to the reception desk the next day. Harlow was told that corporate wanted to enhance the company's image by jazzing up the lobby area. Each week, a different eye-catching bouquet arrived. Harlow pretended that the flowers were sent to her personally—a gift from Drake. It was a harmless fantasy.

Months later, on a Friday after work, Harlow was pushing a BMW sedan that she got on loan from Elite. Getting an occasional free luxury rental for the weekend was one of the perks of her job. Tomorrow night, she and Vangie were going to hit the clubs in style. Vangie didn't have a babysitter, so they didn't have any plans for tonight, but Harlow was anxious to get to Vangie's apartment so she could show off her latest rental.

Needing gas, Harlow pulled into a Sunoco station. While pumping gas, she noticed that one of the back tires looked a little low. She hated fooling with air pumps. It was awkward and unladylike. Harlow wasn't in the mood for bending or squatting, but dealing with the air situation was preferable to having to call someone to change a flat.

Harlow drove over to the air pump and parked. She searched inside her purse for quarters, but found only nickels and dimes. Damn!

Almost as soon as Harlow armed the car and had started making her way to the cashier, a sleek dark car glided onto the lot—a Maserati Granturismo—not your average car. She glanced at the car with curiosity as the driver parked behind her car.

She could have fainted on the spot when Drake Morgan emerged from the Maserati.

"Need some help?" Drake asked, displaying a beautiful smile.

"Hi, Drake. My supervisor let me borrow the car for the weekend. I hope that's okay with you."

"It's cool. So what's the problem with the whip?"

"Well, the tire looks a little low. I was going inside to get some change for the air pump."

"Did you check the pressure?"

She looked surprised. "Should I have?"

"Let me help you out."

"Oh, that's okay," she said, trying to be considerate of the fact that her boss was wearing a suit, a crisp white shirt, and tie. He was looking too dapper to be crouched on the oily ground.

"I'm going to have to insist. That's one of my cars, and I don't want you damaging the tire."

"Right. Okay." Her face flushed with embarrassment.

"Unlock the door."

Harlow hit the keypad. Drake opened the driver's side door and read something on the side panel. He walked back to the Maserati and took something out of the glove compartment.

"This is a digital tire gauge. I hear that you're hoping to advance to a sales position, so you'll need to know the basics about cars," he said, sounding amused.

"Absolutely." Harlow felt so stupid, but she was relieved that Drake didn't seem irritated. In fact, he seemed to be in a very good mood. They'd never exchanged so many words, and it was thrilling to hear the rich timbre of his voice.

"Good thing I was driving past and noticed the Elite sticker on the vehicle," he said as he crouched and unscrewed the valve cap, and checked the pressure.

"Yes, it is," she agreed.

Drake stood up and put quarters inside the slot of the air pump. Pulling the hose, he squatted in front of the tire. Harlow gazed at him, admiring his take-charge attitude and his willingness to get his manicured hands dirty.

"All finished," he said as she replaced the hose on the air pump. "Did you take notes?" His smile was dazzling.

"Sort of," she said, nodding.

He lifted one brow. "You're quiet. You need the gift of gab to be in sales."

"I'm not usually quiet," she told him. "I'm a little flustered because I'm not accustomed to talking to you," she said, adding a little sass in her voice and posture.

"I guess I haven't been very friendly."

"You're a busy man. I understand."

"There was something about you…the day we met." He smiled. "Something strange happened."

Harlow recalled their handshake and the resulting electrical jolt. Looking into Drake's dark luminous eyes, she asked, "You felt it, too?"

"I felt something. I can't describe it. But whatever it was, it had me shook."

Time seemed to stand still. People meandered in and out of the mini-mart. Some stopped and gawked at the Maserati, but Harlow was barely aware of their presence. She only saw Drake.

"Do you have plans tonight?" His voice snapped her out of a trance-like zone.

"No." Her plans with Vangie could definitely wait.

"Do you like the flowers I've been sending you?"

Harlow's mouth fell open. "They were for me?"

He stroked his chin and nodded.

I knew it! I can't wait to tell Vangie.

"Are you in a hurry?"

"Not at all."

"Can I take you to dinner?"

"I'd love that." *Sorry, Vangie. I'll holla at you tomorrow.*

That first dinner led to more dinners, extravagant gifts, and romantic retreats. With Drake, every day was Valentine's Day. Before long, Harlow moved into Drake's lavish apartment in New York. Perhaps it was unwise to make Drake her life. She stopped working, dismissing the idea of a career. With Drake, she discovered that what she really wanted out of life was to be a wife and a good mother.

Back in the moment, Harlow checked her cell, hoping for a text from Drake. There was nothing. She was starting to fear that her Cinderella story would not have a fairy tale ending.

CHAPTER 22

Nivea was in bed. Miserably, she stared at the ceiling. Loneliness, stress, and worry cheated her of badly needed sleep. When her cell pinged, she grabbed it, expecting a desperate text from Eric. She brought the phone close to her face and clicked the button.

There was no message from Eric. Instead, she was frowning at an over-dressed Christmas tree, sent by Vangie, of all people. But it was the puzzling caption that put a dagger of jealousy in Nivea's heart. *Vangie, Shawn, and Yuri! What the hell?*

Irritated, Nivea immediately called Vangie. "What's going on, Vangie?"

"Hey, girl, that tree is something, isn't it?" Vangie said.

Nivea refused to throw her a compliment. "You were here yesterday, and you didn't mention anything about getting back with Shawn."

"It didn't seem appropriate, considering what you were going through."

"I'm still going through it. I think it's totally insensitive of you to hit me with this news at a time like this."

"What's wrong with sharing my good news, Niv? I never noticed your sensitivity to my financial situation when you were bragging about how much you make and how much you spend on your clothes and shit."

"I didn't know you had all that hidden animosity toward me. Well, I guess you picked the perfect time to kick me while I'm down."

"I'm not kicking you. I'm merely sharing my happiness. Did you expect me to keep Shawn and me a secret until you get over Eric?"

"I am over Eric!" Nivea shouted. "Look, Vangie. I wish I could say I'm happy for you, but I'm not. Shawn hurt you deeply, and you're a fool if you take him back."

"We're getting married. Yuri deserves both his parents," Vangie blurted.

Nivea gasped.

"Shawn is cutting hair at a shop, making so much money he's thinking about investing in the business, or opening his own shop."

"That's crazy. A month ago, you were crying the blues about having to ask Harlow to pay for Yuri's Christmas presents."

"Things have changed. Instead of lecturing me, you should be congratulating me. But I guess you're too selfish and full of yourself to share anyone else's joy."

"For years you've complained about what a terrible father Shawn is. I was there when you caught him with that other chick. I was standing by your side when he packed his things and callously walked out the door, leaving you to raise Yuri by yourself. And over the years I've witnessed you having to squeeze a dollar, trying to make ends meet. Every other month, you have to hide your car in the safety of my complex to keep it from getting repossessed. Why should I be happy that you've allowed Shawn to slither his way back into your life?"

"I'm busy, Nivea. I don't want to have this conversation with you." Abruptly, Vangie hung up, and Nivea rolled her eyes at the phone.

First her sister, now Vangie. Before long, Harlow would be getting married. *Everybody's getting married except me!* Wide awake, and without any hope of a peaceful night's sleep, Nivea threw off the covers and got out of bed. She slid her feet into slippers and shuffled off toward her kitchen, deciding that a stiff drink was most definitely in order.

♥ ♥ ♥

The next morning, Nivea stumbled inside her bathroom and cringed at her reflection in the mirror. Drinking hard liquor late at night had her hungover and looking haggard. Trying to get rid of the nasty taste in her mouth, she brushed her teeth and rinsed twice with Scope.

She glanced in the mirror again, hoping the elapse in time had improved her image, but she still looked like shit. She rubbed her bloodshot eyes. There seemed to be a sudden shift in the atmosphere. Nivea grabbed the edge of the sink and held on. As the world spun, her head throbbed at the same time.

This kind of sickness was a hefty price to pay for trying to drink her troubles away. Maybe she should stay in bed and take care of herself…skip her parents' annual Christmas Eve breakfast.

But who was she fooling? If she didn't show up, she'd never live it down. Her mother would call, and if Nivea didn't pick up, she'd leave venomous messages, hurtful voicemails that cut to the core. The truth definitely hurt, and Nivea couldn't bear to hear her mother's voice once again accusing her of being bitter and jealous of her sister, Courtney.

I have no reason to be envious of Courtney. I'm a successful pharmaceutical sales rep and she's an idiot-moron.

Behind the wheel of her car, Nivea drove cautiously, but sleet was gusting down, falling rapidly, creating treacherous driving conditions. The glare of the sun didn't help the situation. Nivea fumbled around in her handbag for her designer sunglasses. It seemed crazy to drive in such hazardous conditions to try to prove to her mother that she wasn't feeling bitter or jealous toward her sister.

Holding an armful of beautifully wrapped gifts, Nivea rang her parents' doorbell.

Her mother opened the door. Mrs. Westcott glanced at her wristwatch, and then at Nivea. "Merry Christmas, dear," she said with an edge.

"Merry Christmas, Mother. Sorry, I'm late," Nivea replied as she entered the foyer.

"Put the gifts under the tree." She waved her hand in the air distractedly and hurried toward the kitchen to bark at the caterers.

In the living room, Nivea placed her gifts under the eight-foot tall artificial tree. *If Vangie wanted to see a tree worth photographing, she should see this realistic-looking Denmark Fir.* The stunning, two-thousand-dollar tree was positioned between the baby grand piano and the elegant staircase. A chandelier hung near the top of the tree, casting a golden glow. It was a majestic sight, a picture worth taking. Nivea pulled out her cell. She had to stand back several feet to capture the entire tree and the presents.

She couldn't quite pinpoint why she felt so irritated by Vangie's newfound happiness. Nivea didn't like the idea of being the only single person among her family and friends. It was cruel of Vangie to announce her new status with a caption and an image of a tacky Christmas tree. Nivea felt compelled to put Vangie in her place by sending her the picturesque shot of her parents' elegant tree.

"Don't you look pretty, Nivea!" Nivea's father bounded into the living room, his arms outstretched. She quickly sent the image to Vangie and then set the cell phone on a nearby end table, freeing her hands to give her father a tight hug.

"Merry Christmas, Daddy," she murmured, her words slightly muffled by his wool sweater.

At fifty-two, her father was still a very handsome man. His salt-and-pepper-colored hair added to his distinguished look. He was a partner in a law firm, specializing in corporate accounts, but at home, his wife was the boss. Denise Westcott ruled with an iron fist, and her handsome husband dared not stray.

"Where's Eric?" her father asked.

"He had to work."

"Are you spending Christmas Day with Eric's family?"

"We're supposed to, but he may have to work. He's putting aside money for our honeymoon and his job pays double on holidays." Nivea felt like a blithering idiot, going on and on, weaving lies.

"Eric's a hard-working young man," her father said with a firm head nod, letting Nivea know that he didn't share her mother's disdain for laborers. He guided Nivea toward the dining room, his arm around her, his large hand gripping her shoulder. "If he has to work tomorrow, I want you to spend Christmas Day with your family."

"I will, Daddy." Guilty and upset with herself for lying to her father, her voice came out choked.

CHAPTER 23

"Hey, Niv!" Courtney called out brightly. She was perched on her boyfriend's lap, an arm draped around his neck.

A slight flush of annoyance warmed Nivea's face. *Get a hotel room!* Sitting on her boyfriend's lap at the dining room table was such inappropriate behavior, but Courtney could get away with murder and her parents would think it was adorable. Nivea groaned inwardly.

There was no denying her sister's beauty. Courtney was sickeningly stunning. While Nivea was covered in MAC makeup, Courtney only required lipgloss to enhance her looks. It was so unfair that Courtney got the soft features, satiny skin, and overall fabulous looks of their handsome father, while Nivea, who inherited her mother's pronounced chin, had to work so hard to look attractive.

"You remember Knox, don't you?" Courtney asked, beaming.

"Sure. Hi, Knox," Nivea mumbled, noting that Knox wore an argyle sweater vest, a yellow long-sleeved shirt, khakis, and a pair of L.L. Bean loafers. A real preppy-looking fucker. Though she needed something much stronger, she accepted the glass of eggnog that her father handed her and chugged it down. This was going to be a long and torturous Christmas Eve brunch.

"Good to see you again, Sis," Knox said cheerfully as he stroked the side of Courtney's neck.

I'm not your sister.

"Those two are real lovebirds," her father chimed in.

Nivea wanted to roar like an infuriated lion, but she forced a tight smile.

Her mother swept into the room. Carrying trays, the caterers stepped behind Mrs. Westcott.

She bestowed a bright smile upon Courtney and Knox. "Before we begin our meal, Knox has something to say."

With a look of surprise, Courtney gazed at Knox and then peered around the dining room. Knox kissed her on the cheek and then patted her hip. "Get up a minute, Courtney."

Giggling, and suspecting that something wonderful was about to happen, Courtney stood, glancing around in wide-eyed amazement.

Oh, God. This is an ambush. Had I known I was going to forced to witness some contrived marriage proposal bullshit that I'm definitely not in the mood to see, I would have stayed my ass at home!

Acting out of spite, Nivea asked, "I don't know what's going on, but it needs to wait until after brunch. I'm starving."

Mrs. Westcott gave Nivea an irritated glance, and then ignored her. "Knox," she said sweetly, "Go ahead, dear."

Knox nodded his assent. "Courtney," he began in a serious tone, "from the moment I saw your face, I realized that you were the woman I want to spend the rest of my life with…" He paused and reached inside his pocket and pulled out a velvet case.

Courtney yelped. She actually clapped her hands and jumped up and down. "Oh, my God, Knox! Oh, my God!"

That fake little bitch knew she was getting a ring!

Mrs. Westcott cleared her throat. Knox looked in her direction. Nivea watched her mother mouth the words and motion with her hand, "Down! On your knee!"

Being a good sport, Knox got down on one knee. Nivea wanted to vomit over the hypocrisy that was unfolding before her eyes. Her parents and Courtney all knew that Knox was going to propose today. It was vulgar and insulting to be forced to watch Courtney and the rest of her family pretend that this proposal was a god-damn surprise.

Revelling in all the attention she was getting, Courtney held out her hand and smiled joyously. Knox slid a hell of a rock on her finger. When Nivea noticed the size of the diamond, which appeared to be at least three carats, she felt her stomach lurch. She shot out of her chair and hurried from the dining room. Cheeks ballooning and a hand covering her mouth, she ran toward the powder room that was on the other side of the kitchen.

Nivea was on her knees, heaving into the toilet bowl when her mother opened the door. It felt like the whole world had turned against her and she was open to being comforted by her mother. Instead of seeing a mother's sympathetic face, she was met with a cold expression.

"You ruined Courtney's moment. How could you?" Mrs. Westcott said bitterly.

Nivea looked up at her mother. "I can't help if I'm sick. Do you think I planned it?"

"You've been pulling attention-getting shenanigans since the day your sister was born. I wouldn't put anything past you."

"I have a queasy stomach. I'm sick. If I wanted to intentionally ruin Courtney's moment, I would have stayed in my seat and spewed all over the table."

Lips drawn tight in anger, Mrs. Westcott waved her hand in the air. "Wipe your face. You look revolting," she snarled.

Wounded by her mother's sharp words, Nivea dropped her head. When she forced herself to look in the mirror, she was mortified to see traces of vomit at the corner of her mouth. She grabbed a tissue, hurriedly wiped her mouth, and then filled a Dixie cup with water.

"You need more than water. There's mouthwash in the medicine cabinet," her mother said, running her hand over her hair, clearly aggravated. "You are seven years older than your sister; it's not normal for an older sister to constantly compete with her baby sister. You need to see a shrink. I'm serious, Nivea. This sibling rivalry is really unhealthy."

"Mother, my stomach is upset. Why are you yelling at me when I'm obviously not feeling well?"

Mrs. Westcott sucked her teeth. "I hope you're not pregnant."

"That's ridiculous."

"You feel that it's acceptable to marry an uneducated laborer, so I wouldn't put it past you to walk down the aisle, heavy with child."

Nivea groaned. She wasn't pregnant nor was she walking down the aisle anytime soon. This conversation was disgusting.

"I'll tell you one thing, Nivea, if you're brazen enough to sashay down the aisle in God's house with a big belly, don't expect your father to escort you."

"I said, I'm not pregnant. I have more sense than to get knocked up."

"Stop using vile terminology. That thug you intend to marry is really starting to rub off on you. The way you speak, your lack of concern over punctuality—"

"Mother, I'm fine."

"No, you're not. Something is wrong you. What is it?" Her mother's eyes searched Nivea's face for the truth. Nivea looked away.

Everything's wrong, Mother. Eric cheated on me. He fucked a stripper and had a baby. But Nivea couldn't reveal the true source of her ailment without facing harsh ridicule. She looked down at her engagement ring. Compared to her sister's new bling, Nivea's ring looked like junk jewelry. Nivea sneered down at the meaningless piece of glitter on her finger, angry at the fact that she would have to keep up the payments if she intended to maintain good credit.

Nivea's life was joke, while Courtney's future seemed as bright as her new diamond. Nivea's stomach roiled again. She dropped to her knees, sticking her face back inside the toilet.

"Oh, for heaven's sake," Mrs. Westcott said in a voice filled with loathing. "If you're that sick, why'd you come here in the first place?" Her mother paused for a moment. "Don't return to the table. I want you to go home, Nivea. I can only pray that you haven't infected the rest of us with that nasty bug you've got." Her mother expelled a long sigh of disgust before closing the powder room door, leaving her daughter behind, groaning and retching her guts out.

CHAPTER 24

"Something smells funny." Yuri wrinkled his nose.

"I'm cooking collard greens," Vangie responded, busy peeling sweet potatoes.

"They stink."

"No, they don't. You're not used to the strong smell of collards."

"I'm not used to the smell of anything cooking." Yuri giggled.

"Oh, listen to you. You're starting to sound like your dad." She shook her head, smiling at her precocious child.

"Daddy says I need to eat more home-cooked meals if I expect to be strong enough to play football." Yuri pushed his sleeve up and flexed his muscle. "Look at the muscle I got from drinking two glasses of milk this morning." Teeth gritted, he strained to pump up the little knot in the middle of his arm.

"Wow! You are getting strong," Vangie said, indulging him. "If milk did that, imagine how big you'll get from eating collard greens and other vegetables."

"I like milk. But I don't like vegetables."

"What did Daddy tell you?"

"He said I have to start eating vegetables," Yuri mumbled.

"That's right. We've been eating nothing but junk food, but we're going to start eating healthier."

"Daddy, too?"

Holding back a wistful smile, Vangie nodded. "All of us."

"Does Daddy live with us now?"

"No. He still lives with Nana."

"How come he doesn't sleep at Nana's house? I always see him sleeping in your bed with you," Yuri added. "Are you and my Dad married?"

Vangie took a breath. "No, Yuri. We're not."

"Divorced?" He looked worried.

"No. We were never married."

Face scrunched in thought, Yuri scratched his head. "If Mommies and Daddies sleep in the same bed, doesn't that mean they're married?"

Vangie rubbed her forehead, thinking hard on how to respond. "Yuri, I don't have time to answer a million questions," she said, dodging his question. "Your dad bought a ton of food and I have to cook all of it by tomorrow, so give me a break, okay?"

Yuri didn't look happy and Vangie felt guilty. "Do you wanna help me cook? Want me to teach you how to use this potato peeler?" She held the kitchen tool up, waved it back and forth as if she were tempting him with a fun toy.

Yuri recoiled. "I don't wanna cook. I wanna play Smackdown vs. Raw."

"Okay, go ahead." Vangie was glad to get him out of her hair.

Yuri dashed out of the kitchen, and took off down the hallway. She could release a sigh of relief now that the interrogation was over. But Vangie felt troubled and unable to resume her culinary duties. Yuri's probing questions had really struck a nerve. She sat down at the kitchen table, and thought hard about her predicament. Sure, Shawn was back in their lives, but he hadn't proposed.

Tomorrow was Christmas and he hadn't asked her about her ring size, and hadn't taken her to look at any jewelry. She hoped that Shawn's idea of family life wasn't having a toothbrush in her bathroom, some clothes in her closet, throwing money her way, and sleeping in her bed when he chose to.

So far, Shawn was proving to be a good parent. Vangie didn't want to lose that, but she really preferred a husband to a hands-on baby daddy.

Deep in thought, Vangie sat down at the kitchen table. She had to figure out a way to get Shawn to put a ring on her finger. But she couldn't pressure him, or spring the idea on him suddenly. She had to be patient.

God, she wished she hadn't lied to Nivea. The lie had slipped out of her mouth in a moment of anger. Now instead of enjoying the fact that her little family was reunited and preparing to celebrate their first Christmas together, Vangie was staring at her bare ring finger, wishing Shawn loved her enough to put a ring on it.

❤ ❤ ❤

Vangie had always been hardworking. By the time she was nineteen, she'd been employed as a bank teller for over a year. She was driving a new Honda, had her own, modest, one-bedroom apartment, a closet filled with designer-labeled clothing from TJ Maxx and Marshall's. Possessing a fake ID, she was very active on the Philadelphia club scene.

Mature for her age, back then Vangie only became involved with men who were about their financial business. From ballers to married men, she'd had her share of love affairs gone wrong and way too much drama.

She met Shawn while she and Harlow were waiting in line to place their orders for cheesesteaks at a joint with the crazy name Gooey Looie's. Harlow had lived all over the city while in foster care and she was familiar with South Philly. Harlow had sworn up and down that Gooey Looie's cheesesteaks were bigger and better than Pats, Geno's, and Jim's. Vangie doubted it, and had only made the trip to the crazy-named place to prove Harlow wrong.

She ended up loving the melt-in-your-mouth huge cheesesteak. And she also fell in love with Shawn.

Shawn was there with one of his friends. While his friend flirted with Harlow and tried to get her number, Shawn stood in line, minding his business, not making any moves on Vangie. In fact, he acted as if he didn't even notice her.

Intrigued by his handsome face, athletic physique, and his short haircut with beautiful deep waves, she was challenged by his seeming lack of interest, and so Vangie made the first move.

"My girl's from around here in South Philly, and she swears these cheesesteaks are banging. What do you think? Are they really better than Jim's on South Street?"

Shawn scowled. "Jim's ain't got nothing on Gooey Looie's. We were feenin' so bad, we drove here from the northeast."

"Oh, okay. I live on Belmont Avenue in West," she said, mesmerized by his smooth, coffee-colored skin.

"You got a man?"

"Not at the moment."

His luscious lips formed into a smile. Then he took out his cell. He didn't have to say another word; Vangie took her cue and began rattling off her number.

If Vangie hadn't been so thrown off-guard by his cool demeanor and exceptionally good looks, if her judgment hadn't been clouded by the sex appeal that he oozed, she would have done a reference check and found out what was what with Shawn's money situation. Unfortunately, she fell hard for a dude who was living in his mom's basement, cutting hair to pay for weed, booze, and his gear. She fell deeply in love with someone who was living in the moment with no goals or future plans.

Her pregnancy came as shock. Abortion occurred to her, but she also saw the unexpected pregnancy as an opportunity to force Shawn to grow up and settle down. Throughout the entire nine months that she carried Yuri and during his first five months of life, Vangie's life was pure hell. Shawn rebelled against fatherhood and settling into a stable lifestyle by continuously lying and cheating.

It all came to a head when Nivea reported seeing Shawn's car parked near Drexel University, where Vangie was going to school.

Vangie ran out of her apartment carrying Yuri. She didn't have time to get his car seat. Holding her baby in her lap, Vangie rode with Nivea to Shawn's secret love nest.

They arrived at the spot and Vangie's heart stopped beating when she saw Shawn and a cute chick emerge from the house that Nivea had pointed out. With eyes that went blurry from shock and disbelief, she watched Shawn walking with another girl—a chick with a banging body. The girl's tummy was exposed, unmarred by childbirth.

Giving birth to Yuri had put a hurting on Vangie's young body. Her breasts sagged a little and her stomach would need surgery before she could ever flaunt it in public again. Her envy of that girl's body was enough to send daggers shooting out of Vangie's eyeballs.

Shawn had his arm draped around his jumpoff, lowering his head and kissing her cheek as they strolled toward his car.

Seeing Shawn all booed up with another woman sent Vangie into uncontrollable rage.

Vangie placed Yuri in Nivea's arms and yanked Nivea's bottle of Pepsi out of the cup holder. Shaking the bottle up and down, she ran toward Shawn and the chick. She unscrewed the cap and shot Shawn in the face with a blast of Pepsi. Momentarily blinded, he yelled and bent over, holding his face.

Vangie recapped the bottle and turned on the jumpoff chick. When the jumpoff saw Vangie shaking up the Pepsi, the girl turned around and tried to run back to her house. But motivated by jealousy and the desire for revenge, Vangie outran the competition. She caught the girl, grabbing her by the back of her collar before she could get to her front door.

The girl struggled and yelled for Shawn to help her, but Vangie yanked her into a headlock. With her free hand, she gave the Pepsi bottle a couple more furious shakes.

"No!" the jumpoff pleaded, but Vangie flicked the cap off and stuck her thumb into the opening of the soda bottle, fizzing the girl's perfect makeup job.

"Whatchu doing fucking around with my man, bitch?" Vangie hissed while spraying the chick's luxurious curly weave.

Vision restored, Shawn came running fast. With what seemed like unnatural strength, he unlocked Vangie's grip on the jumpoff. "Let her go, Vangie!"

"Is this where you've been spending your nights? Huh? You've been staying over here with that bitch instead of seeing about me and your son?"

"Take your ass home, Vangie."

"Or what? What are you going to do, Shawn? You gon' whip my ass in front of your son over some random slut?"

"Her name is Tanya and she ain't random. I thought you'd get the message. A normal person would take a hint." He leaned close to her face. "Check this out; Tanya is my new jawn. Now that you know, don't come over here starting no more shit. I'm with Tanya now. Accept it and move on."

Shawn's words hurt like a punch in the gut. "Wh...what about

Yuri?" she stammered. "You're just gonna walk away from your son for that tramp?"

"Trust and believe, I'ma take care of mine. But that don't mean I have to deal with your nutty ass. Take my son home, Vangie. What kind of mother would bring her child out in this hot sun while she goes berserk in public? You on some nut shit!" Grimacing, Shawn turned.

Vangie grabbed him.

Nivea intervened. "Come on, Vangie. Let him go. Any man that would do you like this is not worth it."

"Shawn!" Vangie screamed. "All those nights that I was sitting up waiting for you, you were over here with your bitch?"

"Vangie, you need to listen to your girlfriend, and take your monkey ass home!"

Vangie gasped. Shawn's words were degrading and contemptuous. Vangie threw the empty plastic bottle at Shawn, clunking him on the shoulder.

"You better get your nutty girlfriend," he told Nivea through gritted teeth. "She got one more time to throw some shit at me."

"Are you threatening me, Shawn?" Vangie lunged for him.

Holding Yuri, Nivea jumped in front of Vangie.

Shawn shook his head, giving Vangie a look of contempt. "I'm trying to figure out what I ever saw in you," he spewed, twisting his mouth in loathing. He snatched the door open, and went inside, slamming it shut in her face.

CHAPTER 25

Harlow would have loved for the trip down Memory Lane to have stopped at the part when she fell head over heels in love with Drake, but her mind was swiftly rewinding. Unable to stop the blast of cruel memories that began exploding in her mind, Harlow stretched out on the bed, grimacing at sights and sounds she wished she could forget.

1995

"What the hell is this?" Jody frowned at the letter from the school nurse. "You passed out on the playground?"

Eleven-year-old Harlow nodded.

"You alright, now?"

"Uh-huh."

"So why is that nurse trippin'? Why do I need to come up to the school because you were running around and got dizzy?"

"I wasn't running around."

"Well, what happened, then? People don't faint for no damn reason." Jody was acting anxious—twitching like she did when she wanted to get high. Harlow didn't want to get her more upset than she already was.

"I was talking with some of my girlfriends, and I got dizzy. I was trying to go sit down on the steps, and the next thing I knew, I was in the nurse's office. The nurse tried to call you."

"I don't have any minutes on my phone. I have to get some when I get my check."

"That's why you have to come to the school. She said she has to talk to you."

"That nurse can kiss my ass. I have better things to do than to be sitting up in your school. You probably got food poisoning from that garbage they serve in the cafeteria. Hmph, they better hope that I don't hire me a lawyer and file a lawsuit against the whole damn district." Jody popped some pills. "That nurse is working my nerves, trying to make me responsible for something that happened at school. You got sick on their watch, not mine!" Jody tossed the letter in the overflowing wastebin.

"Did you read the whole letter, Jody?"

"I read enough. I got shit to do tomorrow. I'm not breaking up my day to go talk shit with that nurse."

"She said I can't come back to school unless you sign me in."

"You're suspended?"

"I think so."

"For fainting? Are they fucking serious? I'm going up there tomorrow, and I'm cussing everybody out. The principal, the teacher, and that fucking nurse. Everybody!"

"Please don't embarrass me at school, Jody."

"I'm going up there to defend you!"

"The nurse was asking me all kinds of questions."

"Like what?"

"Like whether or not I'm sexually active, and when's the last time I had my period…stuff like that."

"Is that bitch crazy? What she tryna insinuate, that you're pregnant or something?"

Harlow shrugged, and then looked down guiltily at the floor.

"You better not be pregnant! There's no way you could be carrying a damn baby at eleven years old." Jody reached out and gripped Harlow's chin. Staring directly in her daughter's face, she hissed, "I taught you how to take care of yourself. You know what I'm talking about, don't you?"

Harlow swallowed. She blinked her eyes, and opened her mouth, but couldn't speak. "Uh…" she managed to say.

"Talk to me, girl. Did Skeeter pull out like he was supposed to?"

"Not all the time," Harlow said miserably.

"Damn! Why'd you let him shoot his load up inside you? I told both of y'all that you had to be careful."

"I tried to make him, but he won't listen to me. You were getting high and—"

"Oh, now it's my fault!" Jody twisted her face in anger. "Let me tell you something, you little bitch, if you let Skeeter knock you up, you better not be pointing your goddamn finger at me."

Harlow kept her mouth closed. Jody scared Harlow when she was mad; especially when she was mad and acting jumpy. Harlow inched away from her mother. She'd come to associate jerky movements with violence. Jody had a tendency to slap her face or knock her upside her head for no reason at all whenever she was feening.

"Answer me. Is it my fault?"

"No." Harlow didn't blame her mother; she blamed Skeeter. Jody had warned her that she'd get pregnant if Skeeter didn't pull out. Now there was the possibility that she could have a baby in her stomach. Harlow felt both excited and terrified by the possibility.

"I taught you right. I know I did. I did everything I could to keep this from happening," Jody said bitterly. "But you wanna know what's really burning me up?"

Harlow shrugged.

"I don't understand why I had to hear this mess from the school nurse? You should have been told me that Skeeter wasn't handling his business right. Shit, if you had pulled my coat, I could have got you the morning after pill, took care of the situation before it got out of hand."

Harlow wanted to ask Jody what a morning after pill was, but was afraid the question might rile her mother.

Harlow raised her head. "I'm sorry, Jody. I was scared to tell you. I knew you were gonna get mad at me."

Jody looked at her daughter with disdain. "You're hard-headed. Now it's on me." She pointed at herself. "If I don't take care of this shit, I'm gonna end up looking like an unfit mother. All you had to do was follow my goddamn instructions!" Jody yelled.

"He told me to keep it a secret. I didn't want Skeeter to get mad at me, either."

"Oh, really? You more worried about how Skeeter feels than your own mother?" Seething, Jody rolled her eyes and then popped two more pills. "Skeeter's locked up for twenty-six months, leaving me to deal with this mess by myself. When was your last period?" Jody snapped, glaring at her daughter.

Feeling a mixture of fear, guilt, and shame, Harlow responded in a whisper. "I don't know."

"What do you mean, you don't know? When was the last time you were on the rag?" Jody started pacing and rubbing her arm. "I have enough problems, Harlow. I swear to God, I don't need this shit right now! What about your titties?"

Harlow grimaced and folded her arms across her chest. "What about 'em?"

"Are they sore? Are they getting bigger?" Fury rose in Jody's voice.

"No!"

"If you're pregnant, I need to know how far along are you? Let's see, when did Skeeter get popped?" Jody mumbled to herself. She stared into space for a while. She finally broke out of her daze.

"Skeeter's been locked up for a couple of months; that means you have to be at least two months pregnant—maybe more. How long have you been getting dizzy?"

"About two weeks."

"Why didn't you come to me? Why does the school nurse have to be involved in our private business?" Jody said harshly.

"I don't know," Harlow said absently, her thoughts focused on the terrifying occasions when she'd gotten dizzy. She didn't know what was happening to her. The first time, she'd been on her way to the corner store. All of a sudden she felt woozy, afraid that she'd end up on the ground if she took another step; she leaned against a parked car, and waited until the dizziness stopped. It happened a few days later, during math class. This time she'd placed her head on her desk, but that worsened the sensation. Her desk seemed to whirl around like a carnival ride. Finally, she asked her teacher for a hall pass. Miraculously, she'd made to the girl's bathroom without fainting. Once inside, she'd lain on the floor, thinking it best to lie down before she fell down.

"Stop shrugging your shoulders. You gotta have some kind of answer for why you didn't come to me about this dizziness."

"I was scared. I thought I had a brain tumor. I thought I was dying."

"I wish you did have a brain tumor. Medical Assistance would pay to have that removed. But a pregnancy..." Jody shook her head. "They don't pay for an abortion, to remove babies."

Harlow didn't like the sound of the word "abortion" or the thought of having a baby removed. It sounded cruel and painful.

"Ain't no point in me racking my brain trying to figure this mess out. I guess I have to go spend my last little bit of money on a goddamn pregnancy test. If you're knocked up, I don't know where I'm gonna get the money for an abortion."

Jody threw on her jacket and slammed the door behind her.

Harlow had expected her life to get better after Skeeter had gotten locked up. It seemed that way at first. For the first time since she was a tiny girl, she'd been able to sleep through the night without rough hands pulling off the covers and tugging on her pajamas.

Other than the times she worried about the tumor in her head, she'd finally started feeling content, like she'd been given a new lease on life.

But not anymore. Now she had a new problem to worry about: pregnancy.

Jody had said that baby had to be removed. That made Harlow sad. She imagined a baby that was so small, it could fit inside of her cupped hand. What would happen to the poor little baby after it was taken out of her stomach?

Harlow closed her eyes and squeezed out burning tears.

CHAPTER 26

Like a leper, Nivea had been banished from her parents' home. Tears streamed down her face as she drove at a snail's pace. She wanted to talk to someone—not a psychiatrist as her mother had suggested; she needed a heart-to-heart with her best friend. Vangie was sensible, a good listener, and most of all, a forgiving person. Admittedly, lashing out at Vangie for getting back with Shawn was completely irrational. After all the nonsense she'd taken from Eric, she didn't have the right to judge Vangie or anyone else.

Vangie deserved an apology. She rifled through her handbag, searching for her cell. She stared at traffic through a veil of tears, sniffling as her hand groped around her wallet, makeup bag, sunglasses, mints…everything except her phone. *Oh, damn!* She'd left it on a side table after sending Vangie that boastful image of her parents' luxurious Christmas tree.

When Nivea got home, she picked up the phone in the kitchen, intending to call Vangie and apologize. She noticed a half-filled bottle of vodka in a corner of the granite counter. Instead of calling Vangie, she returned the phone to its base. The vodka was calling her.

Nivea had always been a social drinker, never one to indulge in drinking in solitude. But after the shock of Eric's indiscretion and after being assaulted by that chicken head, Dyeesha, vodka had become a silent companion. Its medicinal properties instantly numbed her pain.

An hour later she cracked open a fresh bottle and sat in her bedroom having a private party—drinking, arguing, crying, laughing, and singing in the dark.

The phone blared in the middle of an argument she was having with herself. She sleepily lifted her head and squinted at the caller ID. Private Caller. *You can kiss my ass, private damn caller!* The ringing stopped and then began again. This time the caller ID spelled Nivea's name. *Is this a prank?* The next episode of ringing identified her mother as the caller. *Fuck you!* Defiantly, Nivea gave the phone her middle finger, and then turned the bottle up to her lips. The phone rang without cessation. She glared at it. *Leave a fuckin' message, bitch!*

As if she possessed psychic abilities, her mother's voice filled Nivea's bedroom. "Nivea! Your sister is outside your house. She has your BlackBerry."

Oh, yeah! I forgot about my phone. Delighted to have her cell returned, she quickly staggered to the living room. The sash of her robe had loosened; the gaping front revealed her breasts. Too smashed to care about her appearance, and somewhat delighted to have an opportunity to offend her sister, Nivea swung the front door open. Her nipples peeked out, tightening into corkscrews when hit by the frigid air.

At first Nivea's vision seemed out of focus. It wasn't Courtney outside her door. Her argyle-sweater-wearing fiancé stood under the porch light, his preppy sweater covered by a heavy jacket.

Shocked, Knox took an audible breath and then immediately tore his eyes away from Nivea's bare breasts. Trying to give Nivea her dignity, he fixed his gaze on the mailbox, then the doormat, and then the wreath on her neighbor's door. His gaze finally settled on the BlackBerry in his hand. "Sorry to wake you," he mumbled, keeping his focus on the phone.

His discomfort amused Nivea. Emboldened by alcohol and feeling devilishly wanton, she giggled and ran a finger down her cleavage. From her peripheral vision, she could see Courtney waving at her from the passenger seat of the car. She regarded her sister with irritation, gave a curt wave, and then returned her attention to Knox. She moistened her lips.

Knox wouldn't look at her. "Courtney...she wanted..." Flustered, he gave up trying to be articulate and abruptly stuck the cell in Nivea's hand.

"Thanks," she said, wearing a lopsided, drunken smile.

"You're welcome. Uh...goodnight." He started backing up.

"Wait! How much do I owe you? I'll go get my wallet." Nivea's words were slurred.

Knox scowled. "You don't owe me anything." He sounded appalled.

"But I have to give you something." She leaned lazily against the doorframe, posing and smiling crookedly. She placed a clumsy hand on her hip. She'd never been much of a flirt, but with the vodka coursing through her system, she felt like the queen of seduction.

Warmed by liquor, Nivea was unfazed by the gust of wind that lifted the front of her short robe, revealing her private area.

Knox lowered his head and respectfully looked down at his boots. "H-have a good night," he said shakily. He looked up at her with fear, like he was facing a she-devil. Anxiously, he looked over his shoulder at his car, feet moving like he was ready to bolt.

"Why do you have to go? What's the problem? Don't you like the view?" Nivea patted her crotch and giggled. She was having a drunken good time at Knox's expense.

Courtney honked the horn twice.

"Wait a minute!" Nivea barked, frowning in the direction of

the idling car. Then she regarded Knox, her lips curled scornfully. "Your future wife is impatient. Bossy. Just like her mother."

Knox straightened his shoulders, a gesture that rejected the notion that he'd ever become a henpecked man. Standing tall, he gave Nivea a pitying look. "Cover yourself up." He nodded toward her open door. "Go inside before you get sick." He turned around and walked briskly toward the car.

Did I ask you for your medical advice? Punk-ass. She slammed the door and rejoined her liquid lover.

CHAPTER 27

Jody returned home late at night with her get-high buddy, Ronica. They both wore tense expressions, which made Harlow more jumpy and uneasy than usual.

Ronica came close and looked at Harlow. She shook her head. "You're only eleven years old. Do you realize you could get taken away from your mother over this?"

"Talking to her is not gonna do a damn bit of good," Jody said with a sneer. "Miss Fresh Pot acts like she don't even care."

"I care," Harlow said, ducking her head down. Her shame was tremendous, and she was having a hard time looking her mother in the eye.

"Don't seem like you give a damn to me. I took my time teaching you how to take care of yourself, and for what? Just to hear myself talk?" Jody shoved the pregnancy kit in Ronica's hands. "Take her in the bathroom, and give her the test. I'm feeling stressed, girl. I can't deal with it." She shook out more pills to calm her nerves.

Inside the bathroom, Harlow braced herself for the pregnancy test. She was expecting the pregnancy test to require a needle in her stomach or a thermometer in her vagina. She didn't have the foggiest idea of how the test was conducted.

"You gotta pee," Ronica said absently as she opened the box.

"Huh?"

"You gotta piss on the stick. That's how you take the test."

Harlow did as Ronica instructed. Minutes later, Ronica shrieked as though gleeful. Excitedly, she opened the bathroom door, and rushed out with the stick in her hand. "Look at this shit, Jody. It's positive. You're about to become a twenty-nine-year-old grandmother," Ronica said, laughing.

"The hell if I am," Jody hissed. Jody gave a hateful glare. "This lil' tramp is out to get me. But I'm not going for it."

"You're high off those pain killers, and now you're talking a bunch of mess," Ronica said. "Harlow ain't nothing but a child. How is a little girl out to get you? You're the one who allowed Skeeter to mess with her."

Jody twisted her neck around. "Whatchu tryna say, Ronica! You blaming me for her condition?"

"Well, you sound stupid, blaming Harlow for something you had her doing."

"I was looking out for her. Hmph! I'd rather my daughter make something off her poontang than to just give it away."

"All what you saying would make sense if Harlow actually got something out of it. But you can't bullshit me. You had Harlow hustling for you. If you gon' be mad at somebody, then you need to be mad at yourself and Skeeter."

"Skeeter's doing a bid. I won't be seeing his ass for a couple of years."

"Then you need to go see his main man, Thad. If you tell Thad what Skeeter did, I bet you could get some hush money to pay for an abortion. Thad would want to protect his man from some child molestation charges. You should check on that, Jody. Find out how much he's willing to pay for you to keep quiet."

"You crazy! Talking all out the side of your neck, Ronica. Do I look stupid? If go to Thad on some hush money shit, he'll shut my mouth forever. Me and Harlow will both end up tossed in the river with cement blocks tied to our feet."

Harlow shot her mother a look of horror. *Tossed in the river with cement blocks on our feet?* She didn't quite get the meaning, but it sounded deadly.

Jody stared at Harlow. "Thad's a spiteful motherfucker. Don't open your mouth about your situation to nobody. Do you understand me, girl?"

"Yes," Harlow said meekly.

Ronica shook her head. "Thad's man got your daughter knocked up, and it seems to me that Thad should make it right. He should step up to the plate and give you the money you need. Abortions ain't cheap."

"How much they cost now?" Jody asked, frowning. "I ain't had no abortion since before Harlow was born."

Ronica eyed Harlow as if tallying up the cost. "Young as she is, they'd probably have to put her to sleep. That costs a lot more than getting it done while you're awake."

"How much more?"

Ronica shrugged. "I don't know. You gotta call the clinic and find out."

Jody let out a loud sigh, and then dropped her head in her hands. "It's always something. I can't ever get ahead."

"Ain't that the truth," Ronica agreed, lighting up a cigarette.

"I don't have a choice. I can't let her start having babies this soon in life. I'm gonna have to figure out a way to get that money from somewhere."

"I know that's right. Girl, can you imagine being a twenty-nine-year-old grandmother?" Ronica fell out laughing.

"Fuck no!" Frowning, Jody scratched her head "Seriously though, Ronica, this has to stay between us. Don't be putting my business out on the streets."

"I don't run my mouth," Ronica said, offended.

"Okay, so we gonna keep this shit on the low. Meanwhile, Miss Fresh Pot has to stay home from school until this situation is done and over with. "Get out of my face, Harlow. Go watch TV or something."

Harlow skulked to the living room, but it was hard to enjoy watching cartoons on a TV screen that had gone fuzzy ever since the cable had gotten cut off, so Harlow listened to the exchange between her mother and Ronica.

"I'm getting nervous," Jody confided to Ronica. "The truancy people came by here today. I couldn't believe that they had the nerve to come here and bang on my door."

"What did they say?" Ronica's eyes twinkled with excitement.

"Girl, I didn't go anywhere near that door. Those assholes stuck a note in my mailbox." Jody shook her head. "I gotta get this girl straight so she can take her ass back to school. I need those motherfuckers to get off my back."

"What did the note say? Do you have to go to truancy court?"

"I don't know. I ripped that shit up into a million little pieces. I ain't trying to hear nothing that's gon' shatter my nerves any worse than they already are."

Ronica lit another cigarette.

"Let me borrow a smoke," Jody said, reaching out her hand and shaking her fingers impatiently.

Ronica screwed up her face. "This is my last one."

"Well, lemme catch it."

Ronica begrudgingly pulled the cigarette from between her lips and passed it to Jody.

Jody took a long drag off the cigarette. "I gotta figure something out," she said, her words emerging with a long stream of smoke.

"I heard that there's this old lady that knows how to get rid of babies. Backstreet abortions."

"What?" Jody screwed up her face.

"She takes care of people who can't come up with the money for a real doctor at the abortion clinic," Ronica told Jody.

"Oh! For real?" Jody said with interest. "What does she use? I hope she ain't dealing with coat hangers or no shit like that."

"I don't think so. But she does use some old school method from back in the day when they had to do at-home abortions. But I don't think she be getting down with no coat hangers. I mean, who would be desperate enough to let some old ho stick a coat hanger up their twat? It seems like it would be better to go ahead and deal with the pregnancy rather than let somebody jack you up with a coat hanger."

Harlow felt a sharp pang of apprehension. This abortion thing was sounding scarier by the second.

Jody looked down briefly as she mulled over Ronica's words. "I'm sure the old lady is up-to-date by now. Do you think she has that suction machine that they use at the clinic?"

Ronica reached for her cigarette. Jody handed it to her. Ronica took a couple of puffs. "I doubt if she has that kind of equipment. I think she be giving out some kind of pills. You know…something that gets them girls real sick with diarrhea."

"There you go, talking all out the side of your neck again."

"Why you say that?"

"How's diarrhea gonna stop a pregnancy? Can't nobody shit a baby out their ass!" Jody suddenly cut an evil eye at Harlow. The skin on the pad of the finger that she pointed was coarse and darkened from many years of flicking innumerable lighters to fire up her glass pipe. "I need that lil' bitch over there to have a period so she can pass a pregnancy test."

"Well, I don't know how the old lady does it, but I heard she makes it happen for way cheaper than what these expensive abortion clinics be charging people."

"So how can I get in touch with her?"

"I could ask around, but you said you don't want anybody getting all up in your business."

"I don't. When you ask around, don't put Harlow's name in it. Make sure you say that I'm the one who's knocked up."

"Okay, I'll put some feelers out there for you."

"And find out how much that old lady charges, so I can scrounge up some extra money."

"Maybe you should try to hook up with Thad. Now that Skeeter's upstate, you could use some help. Thad is running shit is this 'hood."

Jody sucked her teeth. "Thad thinks he's too cute for me."

"Well, maybe he'd pay you some attention if you fix yourself up like you used to. Start getting your hair and nails done."

Harlow craned her neck, taking in her mother from head to toe. Jody hardly ever got her hair done anymore. She kept a scarf tied around her head most of the time. Jody didn't have a crowd of girlfriends hanging around admiring her anymore. Ronica seemed to be Jody's last friend in the world.

"I ain't thinking about Thad. He's stingy. Everybody knows that he don't give up nothing. Not money or product. Besides, I heard he got pimping ways. And honey, I'm not hustling my ass nowhere for nobody. But it's all-good, though. I got my eye on somebody."

"Oh, yeah!" Ronica perked up. "Who? Someone working for Thad?"

Harlow knew Jody shared the bags she got from Skeeter with Ronica, so it would benefit Ronica if Jody got herself a new drug dealer boyfriend. But it would be Harlow who paid a hefty price. Harlow's heart sank, imagining another drug dealer slipping into her stuffy little bedroom.

"Nah, I'm through messing with corner boys. I'm getting me a working man. Somebody with a set income who can take care of me on a regular basis."

No more corner boys! Harlow relaxed and squinted at the TV screen, now only half-listening to her mother and Ronica.

"Meantime," Jody continued, "if worse come to worse, I'm gon' have to sell all my food stamps to pay for my bags."

"What about Harlow's situation. How you gon' pay for that?"

Hearing her name, Harlow swivelled her neck around.

Jody shrugged. "I don't know. Something's bound to come through."

Looking doubtful, Ronica nodded her head.

"Hey, Harlow!" Jody yelled.

Harlow yanked her head back around toward the blurry TV. "Yes," she said, eyes now glued to the screen as if she hadn't been eavesdropping.

"I need you to run to the Chinese store and get me a Pepsi and a couple of loosies."

"Miss Kim won't sell cigarettes to children."

"Fuck Miss Kim. You know what to do. Go to Mr. Kim. He'll hook you up."

"Ain't you scared those truancy people might catch Harlow out there?" Ronica asked.

"Nah, they done made their run around here today. They on the other side of town by now. Hurry up, Harlow. I need a cigarette."

CHAPTER 28

Startled by the ringing phone, Nivea awoke from a stupor and tried to prop herself up. The room began spinning. Dazed with sleep, she looked around in confusion. Through the narrowed slit of an eye, she glimpsed an empty bottle of vodka on her nightstand, and had an idea of why she felt so dizzy.

The ringing stopped.

Then Vangie's voice filled Nivea's bedroom. "Hi, Nivea. I guess you're still at your parents' house. Give me a call when you get in; I really need to talk to you." There was a pause. "Oh, yeah. I got the picture of your parents' Christmas tree. Breathtaking."

Even in her disoriented condition, Nivea could hear the forgiveness in Vangie's voice. Vangie never held a grudge, but Nivea was too intoxicated to talk. If Vangie knew that Nivea was sprawled across her bed, drunk as a skunk, she'd rush right over to take care of her. That's how Vangie was, a nurturer. Nivea was cognizant enough to realize that she didn't want to be seen in her current condition by Vangie or anyone else.

An unpleasant image popped in her mind. She groaned, vaguely recalling that she'd shown her boobs to her sister's fiancé. She wondered if Knox would tell Courtney. *Probably*. And knowing Courtney, she'd go screaming to their mother that Nivea was drunk and acting like a floozy.

Trying to get comfortable, Nivea flopped over on her stomach. Before plunging back into a coma-like sleep, she decided that if Courtney or her mother confronted her, she'd fake amnesia.

❤ ❤ ❤

Using the key that Vangie had given him, Shawn came home from the barbershop a little after three in the morning. With memories of the day that she and Shawn broke up still fresh in her mind, Vangie was preparing the Christmas feast, feeling hostile and oppressed.

"Hey, babe," he called from the living room.

"Hey," she said dryly. The memory of their break-up had set something off inside her. She was irritated and couldn't play it off like there was nothing wrong.

"The tree looks like it should be on a Christmas card," Shawn said from the living room. Vangie had wrapped Yuri's and Shawn's presents and they looked picture perfect beneath the tree. She could hear the crinkle of wrapping paper as Shawn was sliding her gift in with the others.

He came in the kitchen, smiling. "Santa left something under the tree for you."

She gave a tight smile, picturing a new bathrobe, a bottle of cologne, or a chain with a dangling heart. "How was work?" Vangie mumbled without looking up from the dough that she was rolling out on the kitchen table.

Shawn made a sound of frustration, ran a hand across her forehead. "Man, that joint was a zoo. Every time we got the place cleared out, here come ten more knuckleheads, wanting a cut."

"Why didn't you tell them the shop was closed for the night?"

"That young bull ain't turning down no money. I don't own the place; I just work there."

Vangie instantly thought about the other lie she'd told Nivea. She'd braggingly told her that Shawn was a co-owner of the barbershop. She gave a loud sigh.

Shawn pulled off his jacket and studied Vangie for a moment. "Something wrong?"

"No, just tired." She pointed toward the stove. "Turkey's in the oven. The macaroni and cheese is on top of the stove. The roast and everything else is in the fridge." Vangie looked down at the dough and frowned. "The sweet potato pie is the last thing I have to make."

Shawn studied her briefly. "You're working on that dough like you got skills."

Despite her agitated mood, Vangie smiled. "I called my grand-mother. She gave me all her recipes. I've been slaving since this morning, Shawn. Two kinds of meat and ten different sides. Why'd you buy so much stuff?"

"Excited, I guess. Happy to be spending Christmas with my family."

"The family you kicked to the curb for that Tanya girl?"

Shawn flinched. "Why'd you go there?"

"I'm just saying, if you did it once, what would stop you from doing it again?"

"That was five years ago. I was a young bull...still wet behind the ears. I'm a grown man now, and I don't have any doubt about what I want. Do you?" Shawn began moving closer to Vangie. "What's up? You having second thoughts about us?"

"It's just that everything's happening so fast. And today Yuri started asking me questions."

"What kind of questions?"

"He wanted to know if we were married."

Shawn laughed. "Inquisitive little guy. What did you tell him?"

Vangie shook her head. "I told him the truth. Then he asked if we were divorced. I guess he's wondering if you're only here for the holidays."

"The holidays! I'm going the distance," Shawn declared. "Is that why you got that nasty lil' attitude?"

"I guess so. I was feeling great until Yuri started questioning me about our status. His questions made something click in my head. It's not like it's just you and me. We have to consider our son. We need to have a reasonable response to his questions."

"You're right." Shawn looked at her intently. "I'll think of something while I'm in the shower." He started walking out of the kitchen, then stopped and turned around. "I'm real tired baby; let's go to bed. You can finish that pie in the morning, can't you?"

Vangie sighed. "I guess."

Shawn gave her a wink.

She gazed at him, prepared to return the affectionate gesture with a smile. Then realization descended on her. Shawn wanted her to hurry up so he could get a quickie before he drifted off to sleep.

I'm nothing more than a piece of ass to Shawn. After all the hell he put me through, I should be more than a bootie buddy. I need to start demanding some real security. I need a ring. A wedding ceremony. A legal document.

CHAPTER 29

"Having sex hurts a lot more than what I'm gonna do to you, so don't be scared. Try to relax," the woman named Miss Cakie told Harlow. Miss Cakie was tall and stout, though more solid than fat. She had chestnut-colored skin. There was an unhealthy film covering her eyeballs that made the color of her eyes indistinguishable. Steel grey locks hung to her shoulders. Her unpleasant face was moist with sweat. More perspiration gathered in the creases of her fleshy neck. Wet circles under the arms of her brown blouse announced sweaty armpits. Harlow cringed. The sight of the awful woman sent ripples of terror through her.

Harlow lay shivering and twitching atop the dining room table in Miss Cakie's dismal house in a section of North Philadelphia that was so devastated, it looked like a bomb had been dropped on it. This part of town was known as Beirut.

Harlow's cotton panties were tossed aside and hung off the edge of the table. There was a plastic tablecloth beneath her bare bottom. In that bizarre setting, her life in the hands of a scary-looking woman, Harlow tried to remain calm and to be still, while controlling the urge to scream in fear and outrage.

Harlow had two impulses. One was to plead for mercy and the other was to jump off the table and run. But neither would do her any good. Trying to take her mind off of her hopeless predicament, Harlow began to imagine that she was at the carnival that came to Parkside Avenue every summer. She thought about eating pink cotton candy and being at the top of the Ferris wheel. She would have preferred envisioning a wild roller coaster ride at Dorney Park or Great Adventure, but since she'd never been to either amusement park, the neighborhood carnival was all she could picture in her mind.

Miss Cakie patted Harlow's thighs, urging them open. Harlow's heart leapt in her chest. She locked her knees, straining to keep her legs closed so tightly they began to shake. She threw a fearful glance in her mother's direction.

Jody met her daughter's eyes and gave Harlow a hard look.

Having the illusion that her mother would have a sudden revelation, Harlow kept her thighs pressed together and silently pleaded with her eyes.

"Open your legs, Harlow. Miss Cakie gotta examine you," Jody said without emotion.

Realizing that her mother wasn't going to have a change of heart, Harlow's face crumpled. Tears began to spill. "Please, Jody," she called in a thin voice.

"Don't start no mess, girl. Do what Miss Cakie says," Jody said sternly. Her attention drifting away from her terrified daughter, Jody began to fidget with the clasp of her purse.

Miss Cakie's lips tightened in exasperation. "I don't have a whole lot of patience like I used to. Now I need one of y'all to help me out and hold this girl's legs open for me?"

"Harlow!" Jody snapped. "Stop making this harder than it needs to be. Open your damn legs. You wanna go back to school, don't you?"

With fear and great dread, Harlow unlocked her knees. Impatiently, Miss Cakie stretched her thighs apart. Harlow felt as helpless as she did each time Skeeter skulked into her bedroom.

She clenched her hands as Miss Cakie worked between her legs, sticking her long finger deep inside her vagina while pressing hard on her tummy, causing Harlow to grunt and writhe in indignation.

So far the abortion procedure didn't seem that much different from what Skeeter did to her. He always started off using his finger, twisting and digging around inside her. Harlow decided that the only thing different from Skeeter's night-time visits was that her mother was witnessing with her own eyes what was happening to her. Ronica, too. Ronica was watching closely, but her presence was not a comfort. Ronica was there as a spectator. And taking notes, Harlow suspected.

And there was another difference. Skeeter had a distinctive scent that was a combination of lust and his favorite cologne. Miss Cakie smelled sour, like dried-up sweat.

Miss Cakie finally withdrew her long, searching finger. Harlow released the breath she'd been holding.

"She's about eight weeks," Miss Cakie muttered. "I need the money before I do anything."

Jody looked up at Miss Cakie with tiredness in her eyes. "Okay." Jody already had the knot of money in her hand. She gave it to Miss Cakie. Miss Cakie counted it and then tucked the money inside a side pocket.

Then she caught a glimpse of the tools that Miss Cake had spread out on the table. There was a rubbery red tube, and a bowl filled with a thick, greyish liquid that gave off the smell of disinfectant. Next to the bowl was a funnel, the kind that Skeeter used to pour oil in his car.

Worrying about the safety of the substance in the bowl, Harlow sat up suddenly. "Jody, don't let this lady pour nothing in me," Harlow cried.

Openly aggravated, Miss Cakie sucked her teeth.

"Lay down, girl. Let Miss Cakie do what she gotta do." Jodie's voice was strained. Her eyes scanned the room anxiously, like she was looking for an escape route. She looked over at Ronica. "This is too much for me. I can't handle it. Do me a favor and sit with Harlow. I gotta get my head right."

"Okay, but save me something," Ronica answered, her eyes riveted to the illegal procedure.

"Can I use your bathroom, Miss Cakie?" Jody asked, fidgeting with her purse.

"Yeah, go ahead. Turn right at the top of the stairs."

Jody squeezed her daughter's shoulder, a gesture meant to provide reassurance. But all Harlow felt was fear. And abandonment.

"Don't leave me, Jody." Harlow was on the verge of tears.

"Calm down," Jody switched to a gentle tone that pleaded for Harlow to be cooperative. "Ronica's gonna stay with you. Ain't that right, Ronica?"

"Uh-huh," Ronica said absently while trying to memorize every step of the illegal procedure to memory.

Jody patted the side of Harlow's arm. "You'll be alright," she said and then padded quickly out of the dining room.

Harlow knew that once her mother got behind closed doors, she'd pull out that dirty, burned glass pipe from her purse. She wouldn't be rejoining her daughter anytime soon. Harlow was on her own.

She didn't want to get rid of her baby. She was young, but she was willing to learn how to take care of it. She needed Jody to take the time to teach her.

Jody had taught her how to deal with Skeeter. "When he gets on top of you, all you have to do is lie still and pretend you're somewhere else. Skeeter don't take long. He's real quick," Jody had said encouragingly.

Jody had also gone into lengthy detail about sperm and what it produced. She was adamant when she told Skeeter, "I'ma let you get with her, but only if you promise to pull out. I'ma be in deep shit if my child gets pregnant."

"Do I look crazy? I'm not trying to get your child or nobody else pregnant," Skeeter had said, sounding insulted.

Harlow wished Jody would come back downstairs and save her. She wished she could hear her mother say, "It's gonna be alright. We gon' get through this together." Those were the words she'd given Harlow after the first time she allowed Skeeter to have his way with her daughter.

Now she needed Jody to give her some tips on how to get through a pregnancy and care for the baby that Skeeter put in her stomach.

Maybe if her tummy was big and round, and if there were some obvious signs of pregnancy, perhaps Ms. Cakie and Jody would have second thoughts about removing it.

But the baby was invisible to Jody and the other two women. They didn't care about it.

Miss Cakie held the long tube taut between her hands and began to insert it inside Harlow. Ronica squeezed Harlow's hand. "It's gon' be alright, Harlow. Miss Cakie's gonna get you fixed up so you can go back to school."

Harlow tensed. This woman was not a doctor and she didn't believe that she was in capable hands. She tried to breathe calmly, but she couldn't help from gasping and panting. And trembling.

"You're gonna have to keep still, now, so I can get this tube into your cervix."

"My what?" Harlow asked, her voice shaky.

"Keep still!" Miss Cakie said with annoyance.

"Relax, honey," Ronica said, stroking Harlow's hair. Though Harlow was grateful for Ronica's kindness, she would have preferred if Ronica told Miss Cakie to stop.

Agonizing seconds crept by. Unable to distract herself with her carnival fantasy, Harlow thought about being back in school. Having an abundance of school uniforms, lots of shoes and sharp boots. And a lot of cute jewelry from Claire's at the mall. She imagined being so special that she became the teacher's pet. But none of her imaginings were working. She was painfully aware that it was taking forever for Miss Cakie to get that red tube inside her.

"Whew, it's hot as hell in here." Miss Cakie mopped her brow. With the back of her hand, she wiped perspiration from her neck.

"What's the problem?" Ronica asked.

"Tube keeps bending. Can't get it in. Get me a hanger from inside the closet." Miss Cakie pointed to the small living room.

Alarmed, Harlow sat up. She definitely didn't like the direction this abortion was going in.

"What do you need a hanger for?" Ronica inquired.

Miss Cakie clucked her tongue. "I'm not sticking it inside the girl. I have to put the hanger inside the tube to keep it straight."

"Oh!" Ronica said and went to the living room. A moment later, she returned with a wire hanger. Harlow noticed excitement dancing in Ronica's eyes and realized that she'd lost Ronica's compassion. Ronica had resumed being an enthused spectator. Harlow felt alone and more terrified than ever.

No longer fumbling, Miss Cakie guided the tube inside Harlow. The foreign object went well beyond the known boundaries of her vagina. It seemed to be inside her stomach. The tubing didn't exactly hurt, but it was extremely comfortable. She wanted Miss Cakie to hurry up and take it out of her.

With slow and calm motions, Miss Cakie attached the funnel thing to the end of the tube. "Hand me that," she mumbled to Ronica, referring to the bowl of gook.

"What's that supposed to do?" Ronica asked. Harlow could tell that Ronica was asking to be nosey, not because she was concerned for Harlow's safety.

"Stops the fetus from growing."

What's a fetus? Harlow had no idea. She imagined that a fetus must be that wiggly-looking cord thing that she saw on the Discovery Channel when the station showed a program about giving birth.

Ronica removed her soothing hand from Harlow's hand and moseyed next to Miss Cakie. "What is that stuff? Smells like some kind of soap."

Miss Cakie snorted. "I don't give out my secrets."

Miss Cakie poured the solution into the funnel. Harlow gritted her teeth, expecting to feel a horrible sting or a burning sensation, but she didn't feel anything.

After the bowl was emptied, Miss Cakie slowly withdrew the tube.

Harlow's thighs were sticky with the substance from the bowl. Skeeter often left her in that exact condition when he exited her room.

"Go on upstairs to the bathroom and clean yourself up. There's some washcloths in the bathroom cabinet," Miss Cakie mumbled as she began to pick up the objects from the table.

Harlow sat up and looked around. "Where's the baby you took out?" she asked, hoping she could hold the little miniature thing.

"Ain't gon' be no baby. You're gon' have some big ol' clumps of blood. That's about it. But it's gon' take a day or so for that to happen. Now, go on and clean yourself up."

Harlow swung her legs over the side of the table and hopped down.

"Don't forget your panties," the woman said, nodding her head toward the chair in which the panties had fallen.

"When you get home, I want you to move some furniture around. Stay active. Jump some rope outside." Miss Cakie turned her attention to Ronica. "Do children still jump rope?"

Ronica shrugged. "Do y'all jump rope, Harlow?"

"Sometimes," Harlow mumbled.

"They having sex at such a young age, I can't even imagine kids running and playing like they did back in my day." Miss Cakie shook her head.

Harlow was an outcast at school. She didn't get invited to jump rope very often, and therefore wasn't very good at it. She hadn't always been a social piranha. Back in the first and second grade, back when Jody used to comb her hair and had kept her clothes up-to-date and clean and ironed, Harlow had been treated like a normal child at school. But the past few years had been tough. As Jody's drug habit escalated, Harlow's social status plummeted. Harlow was often the butt of cruel jokes. She never fought back. She'd been picked on for so long and with such consistency, she had begun to believe that she was all the low down names the kids called her.

In Harlow's mind, her life would change when she became an adult, when she could get away from Jody and her addiction.

She fantasized about being married with children. Two boys and a girl. She and her family would live in a beautiful home. Her fantasy family were happy and loving, like on TV. Her husband would wear a suit and tie, not loose clothing with pockets filled with bags of crack and weed.

CHAPTER 30

At four in the morning, Nivea could no longer ignore her full bladder. She stumbled out of bed and flopped down on the cushioned toilet seat, releasing what seemed like an everlasting stream of urine. Her head hurt, and her heart ached. *Is tomorrow a work day?* Feeling panicked, she wondered how she could possibly perform the responsibilities of her job. Then she remembered that it was the wee hours of Christmas morning and that she'd taken a week off for the holidays. She breathed a huge sigh of relief.

Washing her hands, she peered at her reflection and saw a puffy face with smeared mascara around her eyes. She tore off the flimsy short robe and tossed it in the clothes hamper. Rather than dwell on her awful appearance, she stepped into the shower.

Blissfully, she stood under the showerhead while jets of hot water pummelled her skin. As worrisome thoughts began to creep in her mind, she began lathering. She couldn't keep up the pretense much longer, but she couldn't figure out how to break the news to her family that she'd called off the wedding. Though her mother would be relieved that she wouldn't have to claim a common laborer as her son-in-law, she would still find a way to make Nivea feel inadequate for being single.

After drying off, she pulled on a fluffy robe. She was alert now and sober enough to realize that if she didn't stop guzzling bottles of vodka, her life would soon spiral out of control. Eric had never deserved her in the first place and she'd be damned if she'd let him and his chicken head, baby mama drive her to a state of perpetual drunkenness.

The doorbell rang and Nivea jumped out of her skin. Someone was pressing on the bell repeatedly, acting desperate to get inside.

It had to be Eric! He'd taken all his personal belongings, and there was absolutely no reason for him to be ringing her bell, harassing her. That bastard had a lot of nerve, bothering her early Christmas morning. If he thought he could buy his way back into her life with some cheap piece of jewelry, he was out of his mind.

Indignation sent her rushing toward the front door. Prepared to use maximum force, she picked up a brass candlestick from the mantle in the living room. *I'm bashing Eric upside his stupid head for putting me though this trauma.*

Prepared to curse out Eric, Nivea swung the door open. And like déjà vu, there stood her sister's fiancé...again. She stared at Knox in disbelief, recalling her lewd antics earlier that night.

"What do you want?" she asked irritably. Knox was an unpleasant reminder that her drinking was getting out control.

"Hey, Sis. I'm sorry for dropping by this hour of the morning, but I was in the area and I wanted to check up on you. You seemed kind of messed up when I left." He peered at her questioningly.

"As you can see, I'm fine," Nivea said sullenly. "Look, stop calling me Sis. We're not related." Nivea moved to close the door.

"I apologize. I'm really concerned about you. Are you alone?"

"That's none of your business."

"We need to talk." His tone was serious.

She scowled. "About what?"

"About your behavior."

This boy is letting his future foot doctor status go to his head. He's acting like he's about to become a damn psychiatrist or something. So what if I flashed some boobage? I was drunk. Sue me!

"Are you nuts? It's after four in the morning. If you want to talk to somebody, you better go talk to your fiancée. Get with Courtney about her goddamn behavior."

"You got it all wrong."

"What are you talking about?"

"I *like* your behavior. Since I left here, I can't get you out of my mind. The thoughts I'm having…" He paused and shook his head. "Every time I think about tonight, I feel like I'm going crazy. You're real sexy, Nivea. I think we're on the same wavelength."

Should I be insulted? She blinked at him, perplexed.

A teasing grin spread over his face. With his features in full focus, she had to admit that Knox was a good-looking young man. But he was clearly was up to no good. She looked at the candleholder in her hand, wondering if she should use it on him.

"I can't stay long," he added. "I just want to find out if that thing tastes as good as it looked."

Feeling tempted, a spasm of nerves went through her. Instead of ordering her sister's fiancé to get off her porch, Nivea pulled the door open. Oddly, his crude language was getting to her. Had her all creamy between her legs. And the idea of fucking around behind her sister's back was extremely appealing.

Knox came inside, bringing with him a rush of cold air.

He didn't try to smooth talk his way inside Nivea's bedroom. He didn't lead her over to the couch. He didn't even take off his jacket or his knit cap. Breathing hard like he'd run a race, Knox backed Nivea into a corner. His hunger was palpable as he crouched down before her, ripping open her robe. His cold hands gripped her thighs as he pressed his face almost reverently against her crotch.

Unable to control her lust, Nivea didn't question this act of betrayal. Wordlessly, she spread her legs for her sister's fiancé, a man she'd only spoken a few words to over brunch…a man who was virtually a stranger.

His tongue made contact. He used the tip to separate her labia, delicately, like he was gently spreading silk curtains. "Mmm. You got that good-good," he uttered in a strangled voice.

"Oh, God," she replied, her legs beginning to shake uncontrollably. She widened her stance, trying to give him complete access to all the pussy he could eat.

Holding Nivea by the hips, Knox lowered her down to the floor. He rolled onto his back.

You know what I want, don't you?" he asked, his voice roughened like he was ready to get violent.

"What?" she questioned breathlessly.

"I want you to ride my face."

"Ride what?" Bewildered, Nivea blinked a couple of times.

"Get on my face. I want you to squirt cum all over my face and in my mouth."

A sudden heatwave overtook her. She wiped a trail of perspiration from her neck. This nasty-talking pervert was bringing out something savage in her. She couldn't blame it on the alcohol. No, something else had her going. She was jealous of her sister, and was happy for the opportunity to hurt her. She was angry with Eric and wanted revenge. The stickiness between her legs was accumulating. Announcing its need, her ravenous pussy began to make loud, demanding, wet sounds.

With Knox's head sandwiched between her thighs, Nivea gyrated against his soft lips. She lifted up slightly. Using two fingers of each hand, she stretched her pussy wide open, accepting the stiffened tongue he inserted. She rotated her hips; her pussy clenching his tongue like it was an erect dick.

Nivea had never thought of herself as being a freak, but the savage sounds that tore from her throat made her wonder about herself.

But there was no time for self-analysis. Knox's puckered lips began to tug on her clit, affecting raw nerve endings, making her writhe and lose her rhythm. Awash in delicious sensations, she emitted a long moaning whimper. She could feel an intense orgasm travelling through her. On the brink of ecstasy, she froze, incapable of moving.

As if her passion had taken on a different flavor, Knox grunted, opening his mouth wider as he awaited his pleasure.

Thighs locked around her future brother-in-law's face, Nivea exploded.

CHAPTER 31

Yuri had entirely too many presents. Vangie was trying to keep up with Yuri, snapping pictures as fast as Yuri could open them.

"Slow down, Yuri. You're tearing into your presents and then tossing them aside. You're barely looking at any of the presents from Aunt Harlow, and Daddy and me."

"Yes, I am," Yuri responded, snatching a big red bow off an oblong box and tossing it into the chaos of wrapping paper and ribbons.

Shawn patted Vangie's thigh. "He has his own way of doing things."

"We're not filling this living room up with unappreciated toys next year," Vangie whispered in a pissed-off tone.

"Lighten up, baby. It's Christmas. Let him have fun." Shawn squinted at Vangie as if trying to figure out why her mood had gone sour.

It was their first Christmas together as a family, a momentous occasion that should have brought her joy, but Vangie's mind was preoccupied. Trying to spot a puffy, ring-shaped boxed, her eyes darted among the gifts beneath the tree.

This is ridiculous; I'm acting like a child. At that moment, she decided to stop pouting and to count her blessings. Her greatest gift was having her family together. Yuri was definitely behaving better now that his father was in his life.

Besides, Shawn had spent so much money on Yuri, he probably couldn't afford to buy her a ring, even if he wanted to. And there was another holiday to look forward to. Valentine's Day was only a month and a half away.

Feeling much better, she picked up a box with Shawn's name on it. "This is for you, sweetheart."

Smiling, Shawn gently shook the box. "What is it?"

Yuri stopped ravaging his presents. "Open it, Daddy!"

"Nah, ladies before gentlemen," Shawn said. He stood up and went behind the tree and retrieved a beautifully wrapped present topped off with a big pink bow that had been hidden from sight.

Vangie's heart sank when she saw the size of her gift. Any hopes for a ring were now shattered. She mentally prepared herself for lingerie. With an awkward smile, she handled the box, gauging the heaviness. *It's not a ring*, she thought unhappily. *But it's the thought the counts*, she reminded herself.

"Open it, baby," Shawn prodded.

Vangie was afraid to open it, fearful that she'd grimace. Vangie ran her fingernail beneath the strip of adhesive tape, and slowly peeled the gift wrap away from the box. *Shawn knows that I want to get married, so why is he looking at me with such a satisfied smile? I hope I can pretend to be thrilled about whatever is inside this box.*

Her heart sank when she saw the Victoria's Secret lettering on the outside of the box. Vangie looked at Shawn, a strained smile in place. Beneath the tissue paper were a gorgeous red lace garter slip, a colorful array of garters, push-up bras and thongs. And several pairs of thigh-high stockings. One of the bra and thong sets was covered in crystal pieces. She picked up each piece of lingerie, peeking around for her hidden diamond ring. But there was no ring inside the box. "Thank you, Shawn. Everything's beautiful." Vangie leaned in and gave Shawn a quick, half-hearted kiss.

"You gon' model some of that for me tonight?" he said in a husky whisper.

I'm nothing but a sex object to this man. She laughed, but she wanted to cry.

"Open your present, Shawn," Vangie said, trying to sound enthusiastic.

"Not yet. I wanna see that pretty smile get bigger," Shawn said confidently.

She felt a little leap of excitement. Vangie's heart picked up speed. *He got me a ring!*

"Hey, son, can you stop unwrapping gifts long enough to get your mom's other present from under the tree."

"The one I got her?" Yuri asked.

Vangie was instantly deflated, but pretended to be happy. "You got me a present, Yuri?"

"Uh-huh. Daddy helped me pick it out," Yuri said proudly. His face was alit with joy as he presented Vangie with a gift wrapped with shiny red paper. Vangie could feel the corners of her mouth twitching as she struggled to keep the forced smile on her face.

There was no point in delaying disappointment. She ripped off the wrapping paper from the box, flipped off the lid and stared forlornly at a Louis Vuitton bag. A fifteen-hundred-dollar bag that any woman would have been thrilled to receive. But the money Shawn had spent on the designer gift was money wasted. She wanted a ring, not a handbag.

She forced out a gasp of surprise. "Oh, Yuri. It's beautiful!"

"You like it, Mommy?"

"I love it, sweetheart. Thank you. I'm going to treasure this bag forever," she said, cupping his face.

"Your turn, Daddy." Yuri watched his father with happy anticipation.

Like his son, Shawn didn't waste any time tearing off the paper and getting to his gift.

"I needed these," Shawn said, holding up a shiny pair of clippers.

"I picked them out, Daddy!"

"And your head is gonna be the first head I cut with these."

Silently sulking, Vangie snapped another picture as father and son shared a moment.

"This is from me," she said, sticking a white envelope in Shawn's hand.

Shawn pulled out two Eagles tickets, eyed them closely, and let out a loud boom of pleasure. "Baby! Yo, how'd you get these good seats?"

"That's my secret," she said, picking up the camera. With the camera in front of her face, she hid her immense discontent as Shawn posed, holding up the Eagles tickets that Harlow had made possible.

CHAPTER 32

1995

Eating a bowl of cereal, Harlow sat on the couch watching a cartoon that was out of focus.

Scratching her head, Jody stumbled into the living room. "Good morning. How you feeling, baby?" Jody asked in a pleasant voice.

Harlow gave her mother an odd look. Jody's tone was too cheerful to be normal; especially at eight o'clock in the morning.

Jody sat next to Harlow, and stroked her daughter's hair. "You okay?"

Harlow inched away from her mother. "Yeah."

"Bleeding yet?"

"No."

"Not even spotting?"

Spotting? What's that? Harlow turned up her nose and shook her head.

"What about cramps?" Jody looked hopeful.

"I said, I feel fine."

"Well, it's been three days. How long did Miss Cakie say it's supposed to take?"

Harlow didn't have an answer. Miss Cakie had told her to expect clumps of blood, and Harlow wasn't looking forward to that.

"Did you follow her instructions?"

Harlow shrugged.

Growing agitated, Jody sighed. "Look, I gave that old bitch a lot of damn money, and something needs to be happening right about now. Didn't she tell you to move around…to be active?"

"I guess."

Jody looked at Harlow, blinking impatiently. "You guess? What exactly did Miss Cakie tell you to do?"

"She told me to jump rope." There was an edge in Harlow's voice.

"Then jump some damn rope."

Harlow rolled her eyes. "I don't to go school anymore, so how am I supposed to jump rope?"

Jody gritted her teeth and took a deep breath. "I'm not in the mood for your shit, so don't work my nerves. You don't need a rope. Just do some jumping jacks, something like that."

"Jumping what?"

"It's an exercise. Don't y'all do exercises in gym class?"

"We play basketball sometimes, but we usually do freestyle dancing or we watch a movie with a sports theme. I don't know anything about that back-in-the-day stuff you're talking," Harlow said with a sneer.

"You better watch your mouth. I'm not one of your lil' girl-friends; I'm your goddamn mother."

"Well, act like one," Harlow mumbled. Harlow was starting to see Jody in a different light. Her mother was as skinny as a twig, and always looked a hot mess. She wasn't the scary, imposing figure she'd always seemed to be. Her mother was a pitiful, drugged-out wreck.

"I'ma slap the shit outta you, girl." Jody's voice trembled with anger.

Daring her with her eyes, Harlow boldly looked her mother up and down, and then stared in her face.

"See, you starting to act like you think you're grown. Ever since you had that goddamn procedure you've been showing your ass.

I'm not having it." Jody reached into the pocket of her robe and pulled out a pack of Newports.

"I'm bored, Jody. There's nothing to do all day. I wanna go back to school."

Jody lit a cigarette and blew smoke in Harlow's face. "Well, you can't go back until you drop that load."

Scowling, Harlow fanned the cigarette smoke away from her face. "Why not?"

"Because I said so."

"This house is starting to feel like a prison."

"Ain't nothing I can do about that. Do what Miss Cakie told you to do and you'll be back in school." She blew more smoke in Harlow's direction.

CHAPTER 33

Nivea put the finishing touches on her makeup. She stood in front of the full-length mirror in her bedroom and smiled, surprisingly impressed by her own reflection.

She looked amazing in her Christmas outfit. Skin-tight black sequined spandex pants, a sexy pair of knee-high leather boots, and a stretchy sheer top that clung to her curves, showing off a flat tummy and tiny waistline. Those few pounds that she'd dropped while she was dealing with Eric's drama were all in the right places.

Her confidence was back. She felt vivacious and sexy.

There were no twinkling lights surrounding her windows, no wreath on her front door, and no Christmas tree. There was nothing that suggested that Nivea was feeling the Christmas spirit, except Mariah Carey's carols that played softly in the background.

Lights were dimmed and every room was illuminated with the soft glow of a scented candle.

As she spritzed her wrist with a new fragrance that smelled divine, it occurred to her to that inserting a dab of powdered sugar inside her coochie would be a good treat for Knox, her good pussy-eating, secret lover.

She shook her head, imagining her sensitive pussy having a bad reaction to powdered sugar or anything foreign. She couldn't even switch brands of bath gels without getting an annoying itch between her legs.

I don't need any damn sugar up in my twat. The way Knox was lapping it up last night, my juices must be as sweet as honey.

The doorbell chimed. Nivea gave herself one last look in the mirror. She and Knox had been texting all day, and his visit was no surprise. He had slipped away from her parents' house and out of Courtney's clutches. He was outside Nivea's door, ready to sample something tastier than Nivea's family's Christmas dinner.

It was obvious that Courtney didn't know what to do with her freak of a fiancé.

But Nivea did and her plans were now in motion. Knox not only had an experienced tongue, the cute future doctor was holding like a damn horse, and had the stamina of a stallion.

Knox wouldn't be sniffing between Nivea's legs if her sister was on top of her sex game.

Sorry, Courtney, but you're too young and dumb to be married to a doctor. Even if he is only a foot doctor, I'm much more deserving.

Grinning, she opened the door for Knox. No khakis or Argyle. He looked extra sexy in jeans and a Polo thermal pullover beneath his jacket. He was carrying a bottle of Ketel One vodka. A red bow decorated the bottle. *How sweet.*

But Courtney came up behind him, her arms filled with presents. Nivea's smile vanished. *What is she doing here?*

"Merry Christmas!" Courtney exclaimed and pranced inside. "Mother wanted me to bring these gifts for you and Eric!"

Sending a menacing glance at Knox, Nivea rolled her eyes at the gifts.

Oblivious to Nivea's distress, Courtney set the cheerfully wrapped gifts on the coffee table. She sniffed the air. "Mmm. It smells good in here. And you look great, Sis. What's up? You and Eric going somewhere?"

"Yeah, I'm waiting for him to get off work." Nivea was becoming a skilled liar. She shot another furious glance at Knox. Wordlessly, he handed her the vodka. Eyes cast downward; he refused to meet her gaze.

Courtney pulled off her coat. "Make yourself comfortable, honey," she said to Knox. "We might as well keep Niv company until Eric gets home."

"No, no. You don't have to stay. I'm fine," Nivea said in protest.

"We have a lot to talk about," Courtney said, practically singing the words as she held up her ring finger and held it in front of Nivea's face. "You ran out of the house yesterday without getting a good look."

At the sight of Courtney's rock, Nivea flinched and recoiled like a vampire being tortured with a crucifix. "Um, yeah. It's really… um…beautiful, Courtney," Nivea stammered. She cut an eye at Knox. He averted her gaze.

"Look how clear it is," Courtney bragged, holding her hand out at arm's length as she admired her diamond.

"Where's your ring?" Courtney asked, noticing Nivea's bare finger.

"I'm cleaning it. It's soaking," Nivea quickly responded.

"Oh! How often do you have to clean it? Like once a week or something?"

"Depends."

"On what?"

What a dolt! "It's up to you, Courtney. I clean my ring whenever it looks dull."

"Good to know," Courtney said with a firm head nod. "What time is Eric getting home? I wanted us engaged couples to make a toast together. We should all celebrate love!"

Ugh! My sister is stupid and revolting. "Why don't we make this toast another time? I really have to finish getting ready," Nivea said, hoping Courtney would take a hint, and realize that she wasn't welcome.

"Oh, we'll toast without Eric. I'll get the glasses," Courtney said and dashed to Nivea's kitchen.

Alone with Knox, Nivea narrowed her eyes and folded her arms firmly in front of her. "What the fuck?"

"I tried to slip out without her, but she insisted on coming."

"Why didn't you warn me? How could you spring her on me like this?"

"I'm sorry," he said. "I tried to text you, but she was sticking to me like she had some sort of sixth sense."

"Bullshit! You've been sending me texts all day. It's hard to believe that you couldn't have slipped to the bathroom or somewhere private to let me know that my sister was coming with you."

Before Knox could respond, Courtney was back in the living room, carrying three tumblers that clinked together. She set them down. Knox twisted the cap off the vodka he'd brought and filled each glass.

Courtney downed her drink. "Ah!" she said and smacked her lips together. "Mother told me that you and Eric decided to push your date up. That's great because Knox and I have decided that we want a June wedding. Guess where?"

"Where?" Nivea said dryly.

"OMG! Are you ready this?" Courtney said excitedly.

"Not really," Nivea muttered.

"On the freakin' beach! I'm having a beach wedding!"

Needing something for her nerves, Nivea threw back her drink and grimaced. "The beach?" She questioned Knox with her eyes.

Knox cleared his throat. "I love snorkelling; it's a hobby of mine. Courtney thinks a beach wedding and a snorkelling party afterward would be a great idea."

Courtney sat next to Knox. "We're getting married in the Bahamas!"

Nivea couldn't remove the grimace off her face. "What does Mother think about your beach wedding idea?"

"She doesn't like it. That's why I need you to back me up."

"I'm not getting involved." Nivea had heard quite enough of Courtney's stupid wedding plans. "Courtney, you can't even swim. It's a ridiculous idea and I'm backing up Mother."

"Aw, Niv!" Courtney whined.

"Listen, I have to finish getting ready—"

Courtney refilled the glasses. "Come on, party pooper. Have another one. You look great. Besides, we downed the first drink without making our toast." Courtney held her glass in the air. "Here's to Nivea and Eric's little civil ceremony." She swallowed her drink with one large gulp and refilled her glass. "And here's a giant toast to my big, friggin' beach wedding!" Courtney laughed uproariously.

Courtney was getting as sarcastic as their mother. Nivea turned her second drink up to her lips and threw it back.

Courtney smiled at Nivea. "See, all it took was some booze to loosen you up." She looked at Knox. "Take your jacket off, sweetheart. We're going to do shots until Eric gets home."

Pulling his arms out of his jacket sleeves, Knox gave Nivea a sneaky wink. Nivea wanted to bitch slap him.

"At the beginning of my ceremony, I'm going to be wearing my gown. I've been looking at an awesome Vera Wang gown."

"You have Vera Wang money?"

"Yup! Daddy is going to let me spend all of my college fund on the wedding. Who needs college when you're married to a doctor?" She elbowed Knox and beamed. He smiled back.

Nivea was ready to physically toss her gloating sister out of her house. If it weren't for the fact that Knox had revealed that Nivea's pussy was addictive and he could no longer go through with marrying her sister, Nivea wouldn't have been able to stomach Courtney's bragging.

"My gown is going to have some secret snaps and right after the preacher marries us, I'm going to rip it off. I'll be stripped down to a bikini. My body is going to be ripped. I had a feeling that Knox was going to pop the question soon, so about a month ago, I started working out at the gym twice a day."

Behaving as if she were a hyperactive adult who needed a strong dose of Ritalin, Courtney jumped up from the couch, and moved around the coffee table. Taking center stage, she stood in the middle of the living room and pulled up her top, showing off her abs. "I'm looking good already!" Courtney turned from side to side. "Check out those side abs, Niv! I'm going to look so freakin' amazing by June. OMG, my wedding is going to be so awesome. I want the entire wedding party to strip as soon as the ceremony is over. No one can be in my wedding if they're not in shape. Everybody is going to look super hot. People are going to be talking about this wedding for…for like, forever!"

While Courtney was preoccupied with herself, Knox snuck a feel. When his hand snaked its way to Nivea's hip, her immediate reaction was to swat his hand away in indignation, but she didn't. Instead, she moved closer, allowing his hand to sneakily roam.

"Your ass looks good in those pants," he whispered.

"I put them on for you," she said softly.

"You look delicious." He licked his lips.

Nivea turned her attention to her sister. "Courtney, your beach wedding idea might work. I want to hear all about it, but I can't keep drinking this vodka straight. Here, take this bottle and go whip up some cocktails."

"We're gonna have cocktails? Oh, goodie! What do you want me to make?" Courtney was really so cute, it was sickening.

"Surprise me," Nivea said. "There's orange juice in the fridge. Peach Schnapps and grenadine on the counter. Be imaginative."

"Okay!" Courtney dashed from the room, happy to oblige as long as she could have her sister's undivided attention.

"And while you're at it, fill up the ice bucket with some ice cubes!" Nivea yelled.

"Will do!" Courtney called happily from the kitchen.

Nivea turned to Knox, cupped his face and kissed him on the lips. Gave him tongue. He gave it back. A warm glow began to spread through her body. Her heart pounded in her chest. It was extremely thrilling to share a stolen moment with her sister's fiancé.

Keeping an ear out for Courtney, Nivea broke the kiss. "I want you to get Courtney out of here," she said with quiet menace.

"I will. Meantime, can I make it up to you?"

"How?"

"Let me suck your pussy...Courtney's in the kitchen."

It was an absurd suggestion. But the way her pussy began to tighten up, Nivea realized that she was aroused by the freakiness of Knox's proposition. Nivea released a soft moan. The sexual tension between them overwhelmed her. Made her feel light-headed, caused her body to go weak.

Knox was bringing out a kinky side that she'd never known she possessed.

She tried to process how she could get her pants down and receive a tonguing with her sister in the next room. The thoughts that were skittering around her mind halted when Knox suddenly dropped to his knees. Sitting on his haunches with his back against the coffee table, he grabbed Nivea's ass, pulling her legs apart and aiming her crotch toward his face.

Nivea made a small, wordless exclamation when Knox's tongue touched the damp patch of her arousal. His tongue slid up and down the seam of her crotch. Pleasure fluttered in her stomach. She moaned softly, her body writhing to the rhythm of his tongue stroke.

His wet tongue slid up and down the copious flow of her juices that dampened the crotch of her pants.

Holding onto the swell of her hips, Knox cupped his mouth over her pussy and alternated sucking and nibbling on her pussy lips. His low groans vibrated against her pussy, and Nivea couldn't stifle tiny whimpers of pleasure that escaped her throat.

Still in the kitchen, Courtney rambled on, having a one-sided conversation about her wedding.

As Knox brought her to feverish heights, she could only comprehend snatches of Courtney's monologue. Nivea heard her sister say something about all of her friends being so jealous. She heard the words, snorkelling, musicians, sand, and tight abs. The sound of Courtney's voice was terribly annoying.

I can't concentrate! I wish my sister would shut the fuck up. But Nivea was being unreasonable and she knew it. She needed to hear Courtney's running dialogue to know her sister's position.

Somehow Knox's lips found their way to her clit. He got a grip and managed to suck the swollen nub through the fabric. The sucking sensation was unbearably intense. Nivea went rigid. The beginning of a powerful orgasm rocked her as it travelled through her body. Pleasure throbbed down her neck and through her chest. There was tingling in her that went from her fingertips and down to her toes. Nivea groped for a throw pillow. Finding one, she used it to cover her face, muffling her moans.

"OMG! You guys are gonna love this!" Courtney gushed as she returned to the living room, carrying a tray of some greenish concoction. "It tastes like melon and—" Courtney gasped. "What's wrong with you, Niv? Are you sick?"

Recovering from a powerful orgasm, Nivea was collapsed on the sofa, her eyes closed dreamily. Nivea cracked an eye open. "No, I'm good," Nivea said. She straightened up, brushed her hair from her face. "I must have dozed off. What did you make, Courtney?"

"I made Jolly Ranchers." Courtney stared at Nivea. "Why are you breathing funny? Are you sure that you're okay?"

"I'm fine," Nivea said, her eyelids fluttering, a pleasant smile on her lips.

Sitting next to Nivea, Knox arranged his hands in his lap. Wearing a poker face, he sat perfectly erect. The only telltale sign that he'd been involved in hanky panky was the light sheen from Nivea's juices that covered his lips.

Courtney frowned. "What's that on your mouth, Knox?"

Knox licked his lips. "Too much ChapStick."

CHAPTER 34

1995

Harlow's pregnancy stubbornly refused to terminate. Though Jody estimated that Harlow was in her fourth month of pregnancy, she still held on to the hope that the baby would soon abort. Refusing to return Jody's payment, Miss Cakie had told Jody to be patient and wait for Harlow to experience severe cramping.

Harlow had been kept out of school for over sixty days, and the truancy officers had been making routine visits, leaving citations with court dates circled in red.

Hiding out from the truancy officers, Jody and Harlow moved out of the apartment, and were hiding out at Ronica's house. After a couple of days, Jody got antsy. "I gotta go find us a new place to live. You stay put right here; don't be mouthing off at Ronica. You hear me?"

Ronica was a functioning addict. She usually waited until the weekend to light up her pipe. She went to work, paid her bills, and even kept food in the fridge and snacks on hand. She didn't have a working telephone, but she had cable channels, so staying at Ronica's was kind of nice for Harlow, like being on a mini-vacation.

Another good thing about being at Ronica's place was that Harlow didn't have to respond to Jody's constant questions about cramping. "You cramping yet?" Jody asked her a million times a day. Harlow would shake her head no. "Pass any blood clots?" her mother would ask next. The words "blood clots" would make

Harlow grimace and vigorously shake her head. At that point, Jody would start firing off rounds of cuss words, some directed at Miss Cakie for beating her out of her money, and others directed at Harlow for getting knocked up in the first place.

Harlow was scared to tell Jody about the little kicks she'd been experiencing—real light and fluttery sensations, like butterfly wings spreading inside her tummy. The fetus that Jody was hoping would pass through Harlow in the form of blood clots was growing and making its presence known to Harlow with kicks and the unmistakable swelling in her lower abdomen.

Her hand inside a bag of Cheetos, eyes glued to *The Jerry Springer Show*, Harlow was so deeply engrossed that she hardly noticed the tightening in the pit of her stomach. The next time it happened, the pain was sharper, causing her facial muscles to tense. She closed up the Cheetos bag, thinking the cheese snack might be upsetting her stomach.

The cramps grew worse, and Harlow paced the living room. When the cramping turned into unrelenting, vicious spikes of pain that shot from her stomach to her shoulders and then cruelly twisting down to her toes, Harlow thought she might be dying of food poisoning.

Wincing in agony, she checked out the expiration date on the Cheetos, and then she checked the date on the milk she'd had with her cereal. Nothing had expired. *What's wrong with me?* she wondered, hunched over and gripping the back of a kitchen chair, as unbearable pain ripped through her young body.

There were four rooms in Ronica's one-story house. Each time Harlow felt the pulsing vibration that announced the beginning of another body-gripping spasm, her legs would go into action. The pain was propelling her to sprint from room to room, but her legs refused to cooperate. Crippling pain made her movement sluggish and stumbling. There was no rationale for her desire to stay in constant motion, but her body seemed unwilling to stand still or sit quietly while what felt like a giant, torturous fist, twisted her guts, brutalizing her insides.

Groaning, she staggered inside the bedroom. She was struck by a shaft of pain so excruciating, she was thrown off balance. She caught hold of the metal bed frame, creating a racket as she shook it forcefully while releasing anguished cries.

The moment she was released from the agony, she hurried to the living room, only to be seized again by monstrous pain. This time, she kicked the wooden legs of the coffee table, trying to do anything that might help her fight off the agonizing torture. She kicked and kicked until she collapsed. Teeth gnashing, she rolled helplessly around on the floor.

She dared not roam the neighborhood looking for help. Skeeter's friends would put cement blocks on her feet and throw her in the river. Hours passed. Harlow didn't think her suffering could get any worse, but the pain grew stronger. The darkening sky told her that Ronica should be home from work soon. She'd know what to do.

She kept watching the door, desperate for Ronica to help her. The angry stabs of contractions grew more violent by the minute. Suddenly there was great pressure on her bladder. The cramping subsided but an unnaturally strong urge to urinate had her straining and squeezing her legs together. Tightening her muscles, Harlow awkwardly yanked her panties down, kicking them off as she rushed to the bathroom. The toilet was only a few feet from the doorway, but she had to pee so badly, she doubted if she could make it. Feeling ashamed and utterly helpless, she unclenched her vaginal muscles, expecting the hot splash of urine to hit her thighs and splatter the floor.

But what emerged from her, crashing from her vagina and dangling between her legs was so shocking, she sank to the floor. With her back propped against the bathtub, her thighs splayed wide apart, she gawked at the tiny baby that was no bigger than a doll, lying on the cold bathroom floor. Carefully, she picked up the slimy creature, and examined it. It was balled up tightly, eyes closed, lips sealed. Silent. Unmoving.

Wake up, wake up! She grabbed a towel from the rack above her head. She wrapped the towel around the little baby, trying to warm the fetus that was attached to her by what appeared to be a long slimy rope.

Desperate to give the child life, she pushed up her knit top, and held the face of the silent fetus to the immature buds that protruded from her chest. The baby remained still and silent. Harlow looked at the baby's face, hoping to see its eyes flicker open, yearning for its mouth to pucker in response. *Wake up!* She thought that if she had full womanly breasts, perhaps the stiff baby would be more inclined to open its mouth.

Cradling the unmoving child, she rocked and rocked, humming a made-up lullaby, doing what she hoped might bring out the gurgling sound of contentment or even a squall of distress. The sweet tune she hummed eventually became a tuneless, mournful sound.

Rocking back and forth at a rapid pace, eleven-year-old Harlow clutched the fetus to her chest, and finally gave into long choking sobs.

She didn't know that Ronica had come home until she heard her footsteps hurrying down the hall. "Oh, shit," Ronica gasped, looking in horror from the expelled placenta to Harlow's grief stricken face.

"It won't wake up." Harlow cried. Unsteadily, she came to her feet. "Can you go buy my baby some milk and a bottle?"

Ronica grimaced at the unmoving fetus. "You had a miscarriage."

Harlow didn't know what the word "miscarriage" meant, but she could hear the revulsion in Ronica's tone.

Backing up, Harlow tightened her arms protectively around the unmoving child.

In a swift, savage motion, Ronica snatched the towel-wrapped baby from Harlow's arms and bolted.

Screaming in outrage, Harlow chased Ronica. But she wasn't fast enough. The next sound she heard was the slamming door. And then Ronica's jangling keys outside the apartment as she locked Harlow in.

CHAPTER 35

There was an expression Vangie's grandmother used to say: act like a lady in public and a whore in the bedroom, or something like that. The expression should have been, cook and clean like a house slave and act like a slut between the sheets. Vangie laughed to herself. However the saying went, she was determined to get her ring by any means necessary—fuck, suck, cook, clean, and prance around the house dressed like a hooker.

She sauntered into the bedroom wearing the lingerie that Shawn had bought her for Christmas. A push-up bra, a garter, thigh-high stockings, a thong, and a pair of stilettos for a special hookerish effect.

Shawn was lying in bed watching TV. A gleam shone in his eyes when he saw Vangie wearing the lingerie he'd given her. "That shit looks good on you," he said, looking her up and down. His eyes settled on her breasts. "Damn shame that it's about to come right off. Come over here, girl. Lemme holla at you."

Feeling confident and pleased with herself, Vangie sashayed over to the bed, but didn't get in. She took the remote, but managed to dodge Shawn's reaching arms. She aimed the remote and switched the TV to a music channel.

"I'm not getting in bed with you. You gotta pay for this," she said tauntingly as she swayed her body to the music.

"Whatchu mean? I dropped a bundle on the Louie bag."

"Get some dollars, Shawn. I don't dance for free." Seductively, she fondled her breasts, rubbing a thumb teasingly over her nipples.

"Alright," Shawn agreed, eager to role play.

Sitting on the side of the bed with a wad of money, Shawn motioned for Vangie to come closer. She danced over to him. He stuck a five-dollar bill in her stocking.

"You can do better than that," she asked breathily.

"That's more than they get in clubs."

"Oh, you've been spending money on strippers?"

"Who me? Hell, no," he said protesting and frowning excessively. "I heard about it, though."

"Oh, you only heard about it," she said doubtfully. "Never paid a stripper to dance for you?"

"No, this is my first time," he said with a chuckle.

"Well, you're in for a treat."

"Is that right?"

She turned around, bent over, and shook her ass. He grabbed her cheeks.

"Bouncer!" she yelled.

"Yo, why you tryna get me kicked out?"

"Watch your hands. You don't know me like that."

They both laughed. Then Vangie took the game to the next level. Her right hand wandered downward. Her fingers curled, pulling the fabric to the side, showing Shawn her pussy.

"Come here, baby; let me kiss it."

"Not yet. I gotta make sure you get your money's worth."

"I'm good. You can have all of this." Shawn threw a shower of bills at Vangie, making it rain. The money floated to the floor.

"I like the way you tip."

"I like the way you look. Now get your ass in this bed."

But Vangie didn't move toward the bed. She remained standing, her hips swaying gently. Her middle finger found its way to the lips of her pussy, and slipped inside. Wet sounds echoed as her finger slid in and out.

Rubbing his dick, Shawn watched with fascination as Vangie masturbated.

Unwilling to be merely a spectator, Shawn gripped Vangie's butt cheeks, pulling her closer. His face positioned at her crotch, he began licking her creamy finger each time it emerged from her pussy.

"Come on, baby. My shit is bricked up. I'm ready to fuck."

Vangie inserted her cream-covered finger inside Shawn's mouth. His lips puckered around it as he sucked it hungrily.

With her stilettos on, Vangie crawled up on the bed. On all fours, she crawled to the bottom of the bed and starting with Shawn's toes, she licked and sucked her way up to his thighs.

He reached for her, attempting to pull her on top of him, but Vangie resisted. She kissed and licked his thighs until they parted. Situating herself between his legs, her ass high up in the air and her breasts pressed against the mattress, she stroked his balls. Holding and then briefly squeezing and tugging them gently before licking the flesh of his nut sac.

Vangie worked her way up to his rigid dick, slowly licking, her tongue covering every raised vein and contour from the base to the smooth crown. She pulled his hard length inside her mouth. Her tongue swirled against flesh, while her lips tugged, urging Shawn to thrust deeply inside the warmth of her mouth. His dick began to stretch and swell until the head was pushing into her throat. Tears stung her eyes as his hard thrusts threatened to choke her. She began to gag but she kept on going, taking in five, six, seven inches of dick. She could feel his balls tightening inside her palm. Another inch and she was at the base of his dick, her nose pressing into the hair that surrounded his genitals.

"Feels good. Suck it, baby," he whispered hoarsely, as his fingers curled into her hair, gripping it tightly, and then pulling her tresses.

Driven to the edge, Shawn seemed close to the brink of ejaculation. His dick became warm and pulsed against Vangie's tongue. His thrusts were urgent. Pumping in and out, Shawn was striving to release a splash of hot cum.

With her tongue, she pushed his steely erection out of her mouth.

"Aw, baby," he groaned in disappointment.

"Let's make it last."

"I can't. You got me going. Let me bust. I can get it up again."

"No, we're doing this my way."

"Oh, you're in charge now?"

"That's right." She climbed on top of Shawn.

"So you just gon' take the dick?"

"It's mine, isn't it?"

"Damn right," he said, lying back in surrender.

CHAPTER 36

Jody had a new boyfriend. Another corner boy. He was about seven years younger than Jody. His name was Smoke. He was nice to Jody and Harlow. Very generous. He personally went to the cable, gas, and electric companies to pay Jody's bills. Since Jody was on Section Eight, it would raise a red flag if someone other than her took the rent money to the rental office, so Smoke bought money orders and dutifully mailed the payment the first of every month.

Things were starting to look up for Harlow. She was back in school—a new school. Jody didn't feel like answering a lot of questions about Harlow's extended absence so she used a phoney address and enrolled Harlow in school in Upper Darby, which was outside of the Philadelphia School district.

Smoke bought Harlow new clothes and lots of school supplies, and he made sure that she had lunch money, and a weekly supply of tokens to ride public transportation back and forth to school.

Wearing clean and up-to-date clothes had improved Harlow's self-image. She was no longer the girl who was pointed at—snubbed and ridiculed.

She was finally happy. Except when she thought about her dead baby. It bothered her that she'd never found out whether she'd had a boy or a girl. The baby's legs had been clenched together so tightly, she hadn't been able to pull them apart to find out its gender.

Harlow had one eye on the TV, and the other on the dress she was ironing for school, and her mind was on her baby. Her little girl. In her heart, she believed that the baby was female. Ronica could have verified the sex of the child, but she told Harlow that she'd had a miscarriage and that the sex didn't matter.

Months had gone by since the ordeal of going through labor and giving birth, but she was left with a sad and hollow feeling that crept up on her when she least expected it. Like now. Solemnly, she ran the iron over the cotton fabric of her school dress.

But she was snapped out of depression when Jody suddenly banged on the front. "Open up, Harlow. I lost my keys!"

Harlow's face knotted up into a frown. Jody had left her keys at the crack house again, and Harlow refused to rush through her ironing for her irresponsible mother.

Jody knocked again, hard and urgently. "Open the goddamn door!"

"Wait a minute!" Harlow snapped. Being openly disrespectful toward her addict mother had become the norm for Harlow. Deliberately irking Jody, Harlow continued ironing her dress.

"I ain't got time for your bullshit, Harlow. Unlock this fucking door!"

Rolling her eyes and grumbling under her breath, Harlow made a slow tread toward the front door. She wished her mother would get herself together before she lost Smoke to another woman. She'd heard Ronica warning Jody. "A good man like Smoke ain't gon' take your triflin' ways but for so long. You better get it together and stop stealing his money and smoking up his shit."

Harlow feared that if Jody lost Smoke, they'd end up ragged and dirt poor again. She was filled with resentment toward her mother. Feeling angrier than usual, she unhinged the chain and cracked open the door. Lips poked out, she was set to greet her mother with a disdainful glare.

Jody burst through the door looking like a wild woman. Dismissing Harlow's hostile expression, Jody pushed her daughter aside. "Did the cops or anybody come around here?"

"No!" Harlow turned her nose up at her bedraggled mother. Appearance-wise, Jody had good days and bad. Sometimes she could pull off looking normal, and on rare occasions she looked really pretty. But tonight, with her eyes bugged out and shifting from side to side, and with a dirty bandana tied around her head, Jody looked like the stereotypical, neighborhood crackhead.

"We outta here," Jody announced.

Harlow eyed Jody with disdain and then jutted out her tiny hip, placing a hand on it. "You trippin', Jody. I'm not going anywhere with you."

"Move your ass, Harlow. Grab a trash bag and throw your clothes in it. We gotta be out with the quickness!"

Having picked up on her mother's attitude and mannerisms, the eleven-year-old reared back in indignation. "*We* aint gotta do nothing," she said with her top lip turned up. "If you wanna leave, then go! Ain't nobody stoppin' you. I'm staying here with Smoke." Harlow's voice was ridiculing, but she would use a much more respectful tone when she asked Smoke if he would adopt her. Realistically, he probably wasn't in a position to legally adopt her, but he'd take care of her and make sure she was alright. Smoke was nice like that.

With a desperate look in her eyes, Jody shoved past Harlow and stalked out of the living room. Looking over her shoulder, she said, "This ain't no game. I'm serious. We're in some deep shit."

Harlow felt a sudden sense of panic. Something was really wrong. She followed Jody's frantic footsteps. Inside the kitchen,

Jody began opening drawers and cabinets, as she muttered incoherently.

Hustling off to the unknown with Jody was like the blind leading the blind, and Harlow was troubled by the prospect. She'd feel like she was in capable hands if Smoke was driving them to wherever they were going. "Is Smoke waiting outside for us?"

Jody shuddered and then gave a long sigh.

"Where's Smoke?" No longer bold and brazen, Harlow's voice was shaky.

"He's dead."

Harlow's eyebrows shot upward. "Dead? No! He can't be."

Jody nodded, her face contorted in despair. "Yes, he is. Ronica's dead, too. Everybody's dead."

Everybody? Jody wasn't making sense. Maybe there was hope that she was so high out of her head that she was talking trash. "How did *everybody* die?"

"Somebody threw one of those cocktail bombs through a window, and everybody that was buying or selling drugs inside the spot is dead."

The *spot* was the crack house where Smoke did business. It was the place where Ronica and Jody smoked their dope. Harlow's stomach dropped.

"I made it out a back window, right before the place went up in flames."

Harlow covered her mouth in shock and disbelief. "Smoke is dead?"

"Yeah, baby. He's gone." Jody's voice dropped to a low, mournful tone.

"How can you be sure?" Harlow held on to the hope that Jody was confused. In the short time she'd known Smoke, he'd become her guardian angel. To society, Smoke was nothing more than a lowlife criminal, but he'd treated Harlow with more kindness than her own mother.

"They're all dead, Harlow. I'm the only one that made it out of there. Now get your shit together," Jody said impatiently. "We gotta get out before the cops come 'round, tryna get some answers outta me."

Harlow folded her arms across her chest. "Let's wait for the police. They might have some information. Smoke could still be alive."

"He's dead! Now get your shit and let's go!"

Harlow began to choke up. Whimpering and crying, she said, "We can't leave Smoke. He was so nice, Jody. We should go to the hospital and sit with him or something. We can't just leave him."

Jody gave Harlow a hard look. "Ain't no more Smoke. That nigga blew up with the house. He went, poof! Now what part of that don't you understand?" Jody started moving fast, rushing from room to room, flinging clothes and household items inside plastic bags.

"If you want all those nice outfits Smoke bought you, you better grip 'em up. I'm not gon' be here when the cops or the drug boys show up."

"Why would the drug boys come here?" she asked with apprehension.

Jody's eyes slid guiltily away from Harlow's face. "For you," she mumbled.

"For me? What for?"

Jody shook her head like she wished she didn't have to give Harlow an answer. "Skeeter might come for you. He's the one who blew up the place."

Apprehension was replaced with cold terror. Harlow covered

her mouth in horror at the mention of her tormentor's name. "B—but Skeeter's in jail," she said, her eyes stretched wide with incredulity.

"They let him out. He found out that me and Smoke been kicking it together and he wanted revenge. Now hurry up, Harlow. We gotta get out of here. Do you want Skeeter to come 'round here and snatch you up?"

"No!" Harlow's face went pale.

"Well, come on then. Let's go. Skeeter has it in his head that he owns you."

"Why does he think that?"

"His nut ass claims I sold you, but that's some bullshit. Come on, Harlow; we gotta roll!"

Leaving with only the clothes on her back, Harlow trotted out of the apartment, clutching her mother's arm.

CHAPTER 37

After work, Vangie stopped in the office at Yuri's day care center. "How are you, Ms. Connelly," she said to the owner. Ms. Connelly was a stern woman who charged ridiculously high rates when parents were late picking up their kids. And she charged a twenty-dollar late fee when day care payments were not paid on time.

Ms. Connelly looked up from the paperwork on her desk, and pulled off her reading glasses. "What can I do for you, Vangie?"

Vangie had extra money now but she didn't want to waste it on a stupid late fee. "I wanted to talk to you about the late fee. Listen, with the holidays and everything, my whole schedule is off. Yuri's father has been dropping him off in the morning and I honestly forgot to tell him to take care of the bill. Do I have to pay that extra charge?"

Ms. Connelly scanned the papers on her desk, and then looked up. "Yuri's day care bill is paid in full. In fact, it's paid for the next two weeks."

"Oh! Shawn didn't mention it." Yuri's day care bill had never been paid in advance before. Her money situation had improved drastically, yet she was only slightly happy.

"It's good to see a hands-on father. That breed is becoming obsolete," Ms. Connelly said.

"Yeah, Yuri's dad is back in his life. So far, so good." Vangie sounded pessimistic.

"Yuri appears to be benefiting. He's a much better behaved

child. I didn't know what had brought about the change, but I know now that he's modelling his father's behavior. Young boys need a strong male figure in their lives."

"Yeah, you're right," Vangie said dryly. "Okay, well…have a good evening, Ms. Connelly."

"Good night, Vangie. Oh, by the way, that's a real nice bag you're carrying."

Vangie glanced at her Louis Vuitton bag. "This is my Christmas gift from Yuri and his dad."

Ms. Connelly looked at Vangie with curiosity. "It seems you like that beautiful bag out of obligation; like it's a homemade gift glued together by Yuri and his father." Ms. Connelly chuckled. "I'll gladly take it off your hands."

Vangie smiled sadly and waved goodnight. She wished she could explain her somber mood to herself. Though she wasn't getting money like Harlow, her money concerns had subsided. Shawn's participation in Yuri's life was a dream come true. He told Vangie that he loved her morning, noon, and night. He sent her loving texts throughout the day, letting her know that she was constantly on his mind. He called her whenever he had a break, telling her barbershop gossip, or sharing the latest outrageous shenanigans on *Maury*, *The Steve Wilkos Show*, or even *Judge Judy*. Barbers watched TV all day long while cutting hair.

With so much loving attention from Shawn, and the break from financial stress, Vangie would have been in heaven a few months ago. But it was too little, too late. She wanted more. She wanted a commitment from Shawn. Nothing short of marriage would do.

She was living a lie. Pretending to be the happy hooker in the bedroom while agonizing inside. Shawn was torturing her. She loved him with all her heart, had never stopped, but she was definitely starting to resent him. *Selfish motherfucker! Giving me what he wanted me to have for Christmas. I want a fucking ring and he knows it. Just fucking marry me, Shawn,* she grumbled to herself as she walked Yuri to her car.

"Can we stop at McDonald's?" Yuri asked.

"No!" Vangie yelled. "We have a ton of leftover food in the fridge and you're asking me about McDonald's? Boy, you're about as unreasonable as your father," she snapped.

"Huh? My Daddy likes KFC better than McDonald's."

"He liked McDonald's a long time ago, before you were born. He wanted it all the time," Vangie lied. That crack she'd made about Yuri being as bad as Shawn had sort of slipped out. Vangie didn't mean to complain about Shawn in front of Yuri. Now that Yuri was happy and secure in his father's love, she never wanted to portray Shawn in an unflattering light ever again.

She clearly wasn't concealing her resentment toward Shawn very well. In the future, she'd have to keep her thoughts to herself and monitor what came out of her mouth with regard to Shawn.

In Yuri's mind, their new family life was perfect. The last thing Vangie wanted to do was burst Yuri's little bubble of familial happiness.

❤ ❤ ❤

"Hey, baby. I'm stuck here at the shop. Can't leave anytime soon," Shawn said over the phone.

"Why not?" Vangie couldn't hide her disappointment. She had finally gotten Yuri to bed and she was gearing up to work some more sex magic on Shawn.

"It's crazy in here. Crowded as shit. Looks like I'm going to be cutting hair all night."

She glanced at the racy red thong and bra set that was laid out on the bed. And this time she'd planned to wear stretchy boots to enhance her sex appeal and seduce Shawn into proposing marriage.

"You don't have to rush around in the morning. I'll take Yuri to school. Okay, baby?"

"Okay," she mumbled.

"Love you."

"I love you, too," she said in a solemn tone.

"Why do you sound so sad?"

"I had something planned."

"Oh, yeah? Does it involve sexy lingerie?"

"Uh-huh."

"Damn! Which bra you got on?"

"I was gonna put on the red one."

"Mmm. You look good in red. Put it on for me. Take a picture and send it."

"No way!"

"Why not? Come on, Vangie. I need to see those big titties to help me get through the night."

"Nuh-uh. I don't want my half-nekkid ass splashed all over the Internet."

"How would that happen? You think you got celebrity status?" Shawn said, laughing.

"No, but a person doesn't have to famous to become an Internet sensation. I'm just saying…I can't risk having my boobage being seen by anyone except you."

"I'll be kissing on that boobage as soon as I get home."

"I miss you," she said, sounding sad and disappointed.

"I miss you, too. Yo, a customer just sat in my chair. I gotta go."

"Okay."

"Cheer up, baby. I'm getting this money. For us. You dig?"

"I know. I'll see you in the morning."

After she and Shawn hung up, Vangie put the lingerie back inside the drawer. Her efforts thwarted, she crawled into bed with her mouth drooped downward.

With nothing else to do, she clicked on a recorded episode of *My Big Friggin' Wedding*. *Where do they find these couples?* she wondered. None of the loud-mouth women seemed to be marriage material. All of the future husbands were losers or punks who took all kinds of crap off horrible and undeserving women. The show was irking her and making her angrier with Shawn, so she switched to *Amazing Wedding Cakes*. This show that featured civilized couples and the creation of fabulous wedding cakes was fun to watch. Vangie plumped up her pillows, getting comfy. Soon after the opening credits, she nodded off to sleep.

But she was awakened by an intrusion of the worst kind.

Shawn was behind her, hands cinching her waist. Slobbering on the back of her neck, breathing hard as he pumped dick into her.

She hated it when he took the pussy without permission. It felt like rape. Fucking a sleeping woman was perverted, and similar to necrophilia.

Vangie squinted at the bedside clock. Four-ten in the morning. She groaned in discontent. A mere month ago, Vangie used masturbation as her only sexual outlet. Now she had the perfect man—her gorgeous baby daddy, and yet she was miserable.

It was okay when she initiated sex because she had a motive. But when Shawn came home acting like a pussy bandit, she felt demeaned and aggravated. She'd probably have a totally different outlook if she and Shawn were legally bound. Pussy thievery in the wee hours of the morning wouldn't seem like such a heinous crime if they were married.

"You woke, baby?" Shawn said in a husky voice.

She grunted in anger, but Shawn didn't pick up on her irritated tone.

"Mmm, your pussy is real juicy, baby. Were you dreaming about me?"

She groaned again, a sound of distress.

Thinking that she was enjoying the sneak attack, Shawn grabbed her titties and squeezed them as he thrust deeper, growling like an animal. "Knowing I'm coming home to all this good pussy, keeps me going while I'm at work." He nipped her on the shoulder.

"Ow!" *Damn, now he's biting me. Acting like a dog in heat.*

"Sorry, baby. I can't help myself. You got that gushy goody. Makes me lose control."

Gushy goody! Shawn, you need to shut the fuck up. If my shit's so damn good, then how come you won't marry me!

"Love this pussy!" Shawn exclaimed as he escalated the tempo of his stroke.

Can we get this over with? Shawn was behaving in such a primitive manner, Vangie was disgusted. There was nothing loving or sexy about his guttural moans and desperate penile thrusts. Less than two weeks ago, she was madly in love with Shawn, but now all she could think about was how hurt she was by his unwillingness to make an honest woman of her. How angry she was by his stubborn refusal to marry her. She was filled with so much resentment, it seemed that every word out of Shawn's mouth was beginning to irk her.

If it weren't for the fact that she needed to stay on his good side, Vangie would have snatched away from Shawn and ordered him to buy a blow-up doll for his nasty needs. What the hell did he think she was—a human hole for his cum deposits? *Motherfucker thinks he can come home and smash every time his dick gets hard.*

Yearning to conclude the vulgar interaction, Vangie began faking enjoyment. Winding her hips and whispering his name as she clenched her pussy muscles tightly around his girth.

Shawn shuddered as he exploded.

Vangie rolled her eyes. *Now I have to take another damn shower. Shit!*

CHAPTER 38

1995

Harlow and Jody had been hiding out in South Philly for the past two weeks, living in a dump with an old man named Mr. Calvin. Mr. Calvin had kidney problems, diabetes, and only one leg. He called Jody his lil' chippy. Harlow didn't know what a chippy was, but from the look in his happy look in his eyes and the way he tried to pull Jody onto his lap even though he was sitting in a wheelchair, Harlow could tell that Mr. Calvin thought Jody was his girlfriend. But Harlow knew better. Jody was only using the sickly old man in exchange for drugs and a roof over their heads.

Harlow's dreary lifestyle consisted of eating, sleeping, watching TV all day, and peeking out of windows every time the doorbell rang, afraid that Skeeter had found her.

Mr. Calvin was on dialysis and was away from the house for seven to eight hours daily. Though the old man lived in a dump, he seemed to have plenty of money. He allowed Harlow to order anything she wanted from the neighborhood deli: cheesesteak, turkey hoagie, wing dings, pizza. The sky was the limit. And she could have any kind of dessert that the deli carried: cherry cheesecake, lemon meringue pie, Chocolate Tastykakes. He gave Jody so much money, she was smoking crack around the clock.

The way Jody explained it, she had to smoke more than usual to take her mind off the fire.

Harlow was miserable at Mr. Calvin's house. She missed Smoke, but thinking about Smoke was almost as painful as thinking about her baby. Harlow wore a sad expression that seemed permanently etched on her face. So many bad things had happened to her, she doubted if she'd ever have a reason to smile. Then she thought about school, and that gave her hope.

"I want to go back to my school," she said to her mother.

"It's too risky," her mother said.

"I'll be careful."

"Stop pestering me. I'll put you back in school after I find us our own place. Somewhere outside of Philly."

"When is that gonna be?"

"Soon."

"How soon?"

"You're getting on my damn nerves, Harlow." Jody stuck a cigarette in her mouth.

"You're getting on my damn nerves, too," Harlow retorted, twisting neck.

"You're not grown. You better watch your smart-ass mouth," Jody said, puffing hard on the cigarette.

Lips pursed, Harlow held up her middle finger.

Jody lurched toward her, one scrawny fist balled up. "I'ma pop you upside your head."

Harlow gave her mother a belligerent look. "I dare you. Touch me and I'ma knock you on your ass." Harlow's resentment toward her mother had escalated to new heights. Jody was gaunt and starting to look slightly stooped. Harlow was sure she could whip her mother's ass if she had to.

"If you ever raise your hand to me, I'ma call the cops and let them put you away." Seeing the quick glimpse of fear that lit her daughter's eyes, Jody went on in a taunting manner. "How many asses do you think you can whip inside a detention center? I guarantee that you won't be able to do shit with those big, manly girls. You ain't got nothing for those hardcore lil' bitches up in them kiddy jails."

Harlow heaved a sigh and then whined, "All I do is sit around in this raggedy house. I'm bored, Jody. And I miss going to school. I finally had some friends…and the teachers were really nice, too."

"I can't send you back to that school. So drop it!"

"Why not?"

"People in our 'hood knew that you were taking the bus to Upper Darby. Don't you think Skeeter has that info by now?"

Scared and defeated, Harlow dropped her head.

"If he finds out where you are, he'll storm your classroom and march you out at gunpoint?"

"You're scaring me, Jody!" Harlow squealed.

"Well, it's the truth. Don't underestimate Skeeter. If he wants to get you, there won't be anything the teacher, the principal, or nobody else can do about it."

After leaving that terrifying image in Harlow's mind, Jody settled herself on the living room couch where she openly lit and puffed on her crack pipe. She used to hole up in her bedroom or stay locked up in the bathroom for hours. But not anymore. Ever since the fire, Jody acted like she didn't care who saw her sparking up her pipe.

Disgusted with her life, Harlow trudged to the kitchen. She was thinking about how much she despised her mother as she put a half-eaten cheesesteak in the microwave. While it heated, she decided that when Mr. Calvin came home from dialysis, she'd ask him to order her a PlayStation from one of those shopping channels he loved to watch. Or maybe she'd ask him to buy her a computer. Playing around online would allow for some sort of communication with the outside world.

She was starting to feel a little bit better about her predicament, and then she heard Jody making strange, gurgling sounds.

A mixture of fear and guilt sent Harlow running from the kitchen to the living room. Jody sat crookedly with her head pressed into the back of the rumpled couch. Froth seeped from the corners of her mouth. Eyes wild with disbelief, Jody grabbed at her own neck with both hands. It looked to Harlow like her mother was trying to strangle herself.

"What's wrong, Jody!" Harlow shouted. She pulled at her mother's fingers, trying to peel them away from her neck, hoping to give her mother some relief, a chance to catch her breath. Face contorted in a horrific grimace, Jody kept struggling, her hands gripping her neck.

"Be still, Jody. Move your hands." Frantic, Harlow fought to pry her mother's strangling hands away. She left scratch marks on her mother's wrists and arms during the skirmish.

The look of shock suddenly left her mother's bulging eyes, leaving them blank and unfocused.

Giving up in her struggle against death, Jody's hands fell away from her throat and hung limp at her sides. A gush of bubbly saliva that looked like soap suds spilled down her chin. Jody released a strangled gasp and slumped to the side.

"Oh, God!" Harlow screamed. She had one eye on her mother and the other eye of the blackened pipe on the floor. She grabbed her mother by her frail shoulders and shook her. She pounded on her back. "Take a deep breath, Jody. Try to breathe." She had to call an ambulance and get her mother some help. She looked around helplessly and chewed on her bottom lip. The telephone was upstairs in Mr. Calvin's room. Jody was dying, and she was scared to leave her side.

So she screamed. "Somebody, help me! My mother needs help!"

What should I do? On TV, people saved lives by blowing air into the dying person's mouth. Intending to revive her, she puckered her lips over Jody's saliva-smeared mouth and blew her breath into her mother's mouth.

"Come on, Jody, breathe," she frantically urged her mother.

Jody's eyes rolled into the back of her head. Convulsing, her mouth gaped open, a torrent of the sudsy substance flooded out.

"I'm sorry about what I said. Jody, please don't die. I wouldn't ever hit you. I swear. I was talking trash." It occurred to Harlow to call Ronica and ask her how to do CPR, but then she remembered that Ronica had burned up in the fire.

"I don't know what to do!" Harlow wailed. "Help me!"

Jody released a long sigh. That disconcerting expulsion of air was the last sound that Jody ever made.

CHAPTER 39

Harlow rose early. She pulled back the drapes in her hotel room and gazed at the snow-covered streets. People with shoulders hunched from the cold hurried along the Parkway. Everyone seemed to be in such a great rush to get somewhere. It was so different from St. Croix where people went about their day at a leisurely pace.

She yearned for Drake. She'd spent Christmas Day alone and sequestered in her suite, reminiscing about her sad life and praying that she and Drake could move forward together.

He called to wish her a merry Christmas, and apologized for not being with her. She lied, telling him that she was spending the holiday with Vangie's family. Relieved that she wouldn't be alone, Drake rushed off the phone. Why didn't he have time to talk? Surely, he and Talib weren't bogged down in business on Christmas Day.

All Drake had to do was let Talib know that one of his men was dealing with blood diamonds. He had the evidence to prove it. So why was Drake lingering on the island?

Drake knew more than he was admitting, and Harlow had an ominous feeling that their relationship was hopelessly broken. Her suspicious thoughts went from Drake being with another woman to him being deeply involved in diamond smuggling.

Cabin fever was getting to her, so she sent a text to Vangie, letting her know she was in town. She invited Vangie and Nivea to join her for dinner.

Then she had a sudden thought. Taking a deep breath, she picked up the hotel phone and called for a car. There was something she needed to do. Something she'd been avoiding for a very long time.

❤ ❤ ❤

Alone in the snow-covered cemetery, Harlow brushed a gloved hand against the letters that were etched in the granite grave marker. Her mother's remains had been in an unmarked plot for sixteen years, and Harlow felt a great sense of relief now that she'd finally honored Jody's memory. She'd bought the marker soon after she'd started enjoying Drake's wealth, but she'd never visited the grave—had never had the emotional strength, until today.

The only thing Harlow had ever told Drake or her friends about her was that she'd died young. Without any known relatives, Harlow had been sent to foster care.

With that sad and vague description of her childhood, friends didn't pry. They could surmise that her life hadn't been easy. She'd shared only snippets of her life with her best friend, Vangie. Mostly, she shared memories of her living in a group home. She could never tell Vangie or anyone else the complete truth—that she'd survived atrocities that no child should ever suffer.

If purging was necessary to heal, then Harlow would be forever wounded. Her heart twisted at the thought of having to bear her soul. She couldn't do it. One of the worst memories was losing her baby—that poor little infant that never had a chance.

"Merry Christmas, Jody," she whispered, her throat tightening as she tried to erase the memories of so many Christmases without a tree, toys, or even a Christmas dinner. Most Christmases, Harlow was home alone or hustling to pay for Jody's drugs.

Unable to stop the flow of tears, she raised gloved hands to her face and cried. Deep sobs from her soul.

When the tears finally stopped, she stood. She pulled off a glove and touched the top of the cold marker. "I forgive you, Jody," she whispered. "If you made it to heaven, and I really hope you did, please kiss my baby for me." Harlow gasped in anguish, tears rolling down her face. "I love my baby. Tell her that she's always in my heart. I'll never stop loving her."

CHAPTER 40

Vangie called Nivea. "Harlow's in town. She's staying at the Four Seasons, and she invited us to dinner tonight."

Nivea sighed. "I don't go running when Miss Priss snaps her fingers. I have a date tonight."

"You met someone new?"

"Sure did. And he's hot."

"I'm happy for you. What's his name, and where'd you meet him?"

"Uh, I'd rather not divulge any information about my man."

"Why not?"

"I think it's best to keep my business to myself."

"Nivea! You're talking to me. You can trust me."

"Don't take it personally, Vangie."

"Okay, whatever works for you. So, are you saying that you won't be joining Harlow and me?"

Nivea let out a long groan. "What time? Maybe I can rearrange my schedule."

"Well, I told her that I had to pick up Yuri, but then Shawn agreed to get him—"

"Get to the point, Vangie. Do I really need to hear every aspect of your domestic life? What time should I meet you and Harlow?"

"Are you okay, Nivea? You're sounding rather testy."

"I'm great. But I'm losing my tolerance for bullshit."

"Bullshit! I was merely trying to tell you that with Shawn helping out, I could go to the hotel straight from work."

"You're trying to rub your new relationship in my face. I would expect a little more sensitivity from a true friend."

"I wasn't rubbing anything in your face, but I'm not going to argue with you. Believe what you want. If you want to meet us for dinner, we'll see you at six-thirty in the hotel's dining room."

"I hate hotel food," Nivea said irritably.

It was Vangie's turn to sigh.

❤ ❤ ❤

"I can't believe the dude that parked my car tried to hit on me. I should report his ass to management. I bet he wouldn't have come at me like that if I were a white woman. Black dudes are always taking liberties with sisters. It doesn't matter how well-dressed or educated we are, they still think they're entitled."

"Was he hot?" Vangie asked, trying to lessen the tension.

"Hell no! He was all pimply-faced and scrawny. Had a mouth full of bad teeth."

"Wow! He was that bad?" Vangie added.

"Yes! His teeth were all separated and crooked like an old-ass picket fence."

Both Vangie and Harlow laughed.

"You're as funny as ever," Harlow said. "Good to see you, Niv. How are you?"

"I'll be better after I have a stiff drink," Nivea replied, refusing to acknowledge how nice Harlow looked and she refused to look at Harlow's left hand. Nivea couldn't come to terms with Harlow living the good life. It was infuriating. Harlow had barely made it out of high school. She never attempted to build a career. How does a fucking receptionist latch on to such a rare commodity as a rich, handsome, single black man?

"We're having mojitos," Vangie said.

Nivea wrinkled her nose. "I don't want that girly shit. I want vodka—straight."

Vangie and Harlow exchanged confused looks.

Nivea scanned the menu and told the waitress, "I'm sure that everything on this menu tastes like crap, so just give me whatever they're having."

The waitress blinked, offended by Nivea's rude comment. "Do you want the grilled salmon or the Philly cheesesteak?"

"Surprise me. But bring me a drink right away."

"Would you like to see the drink menu?" the waitress asked.

"No. A double shot of Absolut."

"Mixed with…?"

"Straight," Vangie blurted before Nivea had a chance to be rude.

After the waitress scurried away, Nivea leaned forward. "So let's discuss the elephant in the room." She held up her bare left hand. "Eric made a baby with some skanky stripper. As you can imagine, it got ugly. We broke up. My parents don't know yet, and I don't know when I'm going to tell them."

"Oh, Nivea. I'm so sorry. That's horrible!" Harlow said.

"Stop playing dumb, Harlow. I know Vangie couldn't keep that juicy tidbit to herself."

"Actually, she didn't tell me anything," Harlow remarked.

"Mmm-hmm," Nivea murmured doubtfully.

"I didn't," Vangie said. "I've been too busy bringing Harlow up to date about my own life. About Shawn and what a good father he's being to Yuri. How he's paying most of the bills and has finally stepped up to the plate."

Nivea rolled her eyes at Vangie and then finally turned her attention to Harlow's left hand. "Your ring is gorgeous," she said. "Some people don't require an engagement ring, you know." She cut an eye at Vangie. "Some people are so happy to have a man around, they'll accept shacking up with the very man who ruined their life in the first place. Umph, umph, umph." She stared at Vangie, mouth turned down in disgust. "You should be ashamed, handing out keys to Shawn when he never even paid any child support. Pitiful!"

Vangie leaned toward Nivea. "If you have a problem with me, just say it. Your comments are vicious and I'm starting to get pissed off."

Nivea ignored Vangie. Though she resented Harlow's large diamond, Nivea wanted to irk Vangie. "Drake has excellent taste. And you've obviously overcome your impoverished childhood."

"I guess I have," Harlow said, refusing to let Nivea get to her.

The waitress placed Nivea's drink in front of her. She downed it in an instant. "Can I get another?"

"Certainly." The waitress hurried away.

"Go easy, Nivea. You have to drive," Harlow reminded her.

"I have other options. I can afford a cab. Or a limo. You're not the only person with money, you know."

"I wasn't suggesting—"

Vangie patted Harlow's hand, silently letting her know that it wasn't worth her time to argue with Nivea.

"I can afford a lot of shit. And the money I do have, I earned. You won't catch me depending on a man." This time her derogatory comment was aimed at Harlow.

Vangie and Harlow gawked in surprise at Nivea's nonstop insults. More amused than angry, Vangie smiled and shook her head.

"Anyway, I wanted to tell you about my revved-up sex life," Vangie said, directing her conversation to Harlow.

"Oh boy. I'm not sure I'm ready to hear this," Harlow said, blushing.

"Well, you would think Shawn just met me. He can't get enough. I go to work walking all crazy from all the sex I'm getting. I swear

I must have gold between my legs because no matter how many times he smashes, he still wants more. Seriously, I can't make it through the night without Shawn easing up behind me and trying to steal some pussy while I'm asleep."

"Considering the fact that you were depending on an assortment of sex toys for your pleasure, you should be pretty thrilled about Shawn's ravenous sex drive," Harlow said, laughing.

Nivea received her second drink, took a swig. "I guess Shawn has been away so long that the old pussy that he got sick of five years ago has started to feel like new pussy." Nivea laughed loud and inappropriately.

Speechless, Harlow and Vangie exchanged shocked, wide-eyed looks.

Nivea gave a feigned innocent shrug. "I'm just sayin'…"

Fed up with Nivea, Vangie let her breath out slowly. "Why are you being so obnoxious? What's wrong with you?"

"Nothing's wrong with me. You can't stand hearing the truth."

"You keep throwing slurs; it's obvious that you have a problem with me. So spit it out. What's up, Nivea?"

"I hate seeing you go down a path of destruction. Shawn is no good and you know it. Don't forget, I was with you and Yuri when he dumped you for that little hoochie five years ago. I witnessed his ignorant ass publicly dumping you with no consideration for his infant son."

Embarrassment flashed across Vangie's face, and then her expression hardened. "Did I make slurs when you announced that you were marrying that box-lifting, big-bellied bum? No, I didn't. I never said an unkind word about your mismatched relationship," she retorted, gesturing with her hand in a confrontational manner.

"Well, it's obvious that you had your nose turned up, but unlike me, you weren't woman enough to speak your mind."

"I don't go around making cutting remarks and deliberately trying to hurt feelings. And I especially wouldn't try to hurt someone that I consider to be a close friend." Vangie rolled her eyes at Nivea.

Harlow nodded her head. "Nivea, you're really not yourself tonight. You've been making sarcastic and snide comments from the moment you sat down. What's going on with you? Are you on your period or something?"

"Oh, that's really original." Nivea pulled her cell out of her handbag, glanced down, smiled and began texting. Finishing her message, she looked up. "Listen, I wish I could stay longer. But I have things to do." Nivea flung a twenty on the table. "That should cover my drinks. You can send back that nasty-ass food I ordered."

Harlow waved her hand. "Keep your money, Niv. This is my treat."

"Great," Nivea muttered, picking up her money.

"Drive carefully," Vangie said in a tone that contradicted her words.

"Don't worry about me, chica. The person you need to be concerned about is that no-good baby daddy you allowed to come back into your life."

Nostrils flaring, Vangie rose from her seat. "I'ma fuck you up, Nivea. Say another word."

"Calm down, Vangie," Harlow soothed. Vangie flopped down in her seat.

"Good advice, Harlow, because ya girl was about to get a blast of pepper spray."

With those words, Nivea threw on her coat and sashayed out of the restaurant.

CHAPTER 41

Vangie shook her head. "I swear I was on the verge of punching Nivea right in her sarcastic mouth."

"I'm glad you restrained yourself. Nivea's going through something. She's always had a bitchy side, but her behavior tonight was deplorable."

"I don't know if our friendship can survive whatever she's going through. That bitch is acting like she's lost her damn mind. I believe she really would have pulled out some pepper spray and used it on me. Nivea needs to get some help."

"She is acting a little off. And she's particularly furious with you, Vangie. I wonder why?"

"Jealous."

"Because you got back with Shawn?"

"Obviously. But she's also upset about you."

"Me? What's my crime?"

"You rocking that big-ass, flawless ring. Drake is rich, handsome, and devoted to you. Look, she pretty much admitted that she was jealous of you when I told her that Drake got down on his knee and proposed to you."

"What did she say?"

"I can't quote her verbatim, but to sum it up, she thinks you've gotten stuck-up since you got with Drake. She thinks that you're a lazy gold digger."

Harlow became briefly pensive. "I didn't know she resented me."

"Now you know." Vangie waved her hand dismissively. "Girl,

she's been upset with you since the day she met you. She's still irked over the fact that you didn't have to pay any fees to that fancy summer camp where we all met."

"I was a charity case. She should have felt sorry for me."

"I was a charity case, too," Vangie said. "My mom got me in that camp because she worked as an administrative assistant to someone on the board. I don't know why Nivea thought I deserved to be there more than you."

Harlow's eyes turned sad; she looked down at the table.

"Girl, Nivea has issues. Nivea is more like her siditty mother than she realizes."

"I wonder why she started hanging in the hood with you back when we were teens. Why didn't she stay in her tree-lined, sub-urban neighborhood?"

"Because all her friends in the 'burbs were corny. She turned her nose up at poor people, but she was still attracted to the ghetto fabulous lifestyle we were living. Niv was so wild while we were growing up, I'm surprised she was able to settle herself down long enough to get an education."

Harlow nodded.

Feeling relaxed, Vangie kept talking. "Nivea loves money, and she knew she couldn't mooch off her parents the way her sister does. But Niv is still rebellious as hell. Her parents expected her to marry a doctor, but she chose Eric. See what I mean? Nivea is still defiant as hell."

"Yeah, I hear what you're saying, but I'm still a little confused. After all these years of us being friends, are you saying that Nivea has never really liked me?"

Vangie shook her head. "She's always referred to you as *my friend* because I'm the one that invited you to join us at our lunch table at summer camp."

"Wow. I'm shocked. I didn't realize that she dislikes me."

"Girl, do you care? Nivea was always jealous of your looks."

"Nivea's pretty."

"She's not a natural beauty like you."

"I could have been jealous of her cushy lifestyle, but I wasn't. She had it all: clothes, big house, professional parents. Nivea had the best of everything. Why would she resent the fact that I got an opportunity to go to an upscale summer camp?"

"She's selfish." Vangie cut her eye at Harlow's ring. "Girl, judging by that chunk of ice you're rocking, your social worker knew her stuff. Mingling with the upper class taught you some valuable lessons."

"You know I'm not with Drake for his money."

"Just kidding. For real though, I'd be happy if Shawn gave me an engagement ring with a diamond chip."

"Give him time. You two haven't been back together that long, Vangie."

"I'm trying to be patient." Vangie looked sad, but then her expression turned into a smirk. "Since Nivea showed her ass tonight, I don't feel like I should have to keep her dirty little secret."

Harlow leaned forward, interested.

"Guess what she told me?"

"I'm scared to ask."

"She paid for her own engagement ring and pretended that Eric bought it. She has to continue making all the payments, too."

Harlow looked stunned.

"It's true. And it seems that ever since she found out that Eric went out and got that stripper pregnant, Nivea has not been in her right mind."

"I'm shocked that Eric would do something like that. I thought he was too afraid of Nivea to run around."

"Hmph. Nivea thought she had him by the balls, too. Girl, his baby mama came over Nivea's crib and whooped her ass."

"Whaaat!"

"Uh-huh. Eric brought the baby over to Niv's house. The dancer found out and went ballistic. Kicked the door in. Attacked Nivea. Biting, kicking, and scratching. She fucked Nivea up."

"Did Nivea press charges?"

"No."

"What did she do about it?"

Vangie snickered. "She went out and bought that pepper spray that she's so eager to use," Vangie said, laughing.

Harlow put a hand over her mouth, shoulders jerking as she laughed along with Vangie.

Vangie's chuckles trailed off. She shook her head. "On a serious note, though. Eric and that stripper did a job on Nivea. I think she's at a real low point. She took a beat down for a dude who cheated on her and made a baby. Nivea was so embarrassed, she didn't want anyone to find out about it. Not her job and especially not her mother. She knew her mother would say, when you lay down with dogs, you wind up with a pack of fleas."

Harlow started laughing. "Vangie, you're killing me with your crazy twist on idioms."

"I'm serious. Nivea's ass is irritable because she's been itching and scratching from that flea infestation that Eric left behind."

CHAPTER 42

Knox had texted her three times, wanting to know where she was and what was taking her so long. She shouldn't have allowed Vangie to talk her into joining her and Harlow for dinner. One look at Harlow's hand and Nivea knew she'd made a huge mistake. There wasn't a chance in hell that she was going to sit around while Harlow gloated and flaunted her bling.

Obliging Knox and his oral fetish was more exciting than breaking bread with two boring bitches.

Being with Knox was sexually fulfilling and emotionally stimulating. Every time he ate her box out, it seemed that he became a little more attached. If feeding Courtney's fiancé pussy was a way to interfere with their wedding plans, then Nivea would be sure to give him a coochie snack every day.

Nivea laughed to herself as she recalled the perplexed look on her sister's face when she came into the living room carrying a tray of cocktails.

Knox had just finished slurping between Nivea's legs, giving her a toe-curling, heart-pumping orgasm. Courtney came in while Nivea was in recovery mode, breathing hard, eyes closed in ecstasy.

Courtney thought Nivea was sick. What a dummy. The only information swimming around in her empty head was the location of designer outlets and the number of abdominal exercises required to get abs of steel. Courtney was losing her man to her older sister and she had only her own clueless self to blame.

Courtney's wedding was not going to happen. There wasn't going to be a beach wedding or any other kind of ceremony. Her mother had been right; Nivea was bitter. She was very, very bitter. And she had every reason to be. How many low blows could one woman deal with in less than a month?

She'd been trying to deal with the shock of Eric fathering a son with a stripper when her mother dropped the news of Courtney's upcoming nuptials...to a future doctor. Soon after that, she received the unwelcome news that Harlow had gotten a ring from her super rich and uber handsome boyfriend. Now Vangie, a woman who hadn't had any dick in a couple of years, was suddenly cohabitating with her child's father and was looking forward to a ring and a wedding ceremony.

Nivea heard the beep of her cell and smiled. Knowing it was most likely another urgent text from Knox, her face lit with a huge smile.

She couldn't check his message yet; she had to wait until she reached a red light. Philly cops were serious about giving out tickets to people they caught texting or even looking at their cell phones while driving. *Be patient, boo boo; I'm getting to you as quickly as I can.*

Only ten minutes away from Knox's apartment, Nivea pressed impatiently on the gas pedal. As the car accelerated, she began to feel a rush of excitement.

A few blocks from Knox's street, Nivea finally came to a red light. Feeling self-satisfied, she pulled out her cell. The first part of Eric's text was in bold letters: COURTNEY'S HERE. I'll catch up with you 2morrow.

Nivea banged her hand against the steering wheel. *Are you serious, Knox?* How dare he do this to her again? It was the second time he'd allowed Courtney to interfere with their plans. She wasn't sure how much longer she could keep up the pretense.

Something had to be done. If she continued to allow herself to play second position, it would be hard as hell to get out of that spot.

In turmoil and deep thought, Nivea didn't notice the red light had turned green. A car horn honked impatiently behind Nivea. Forced to keep driving, she approached Knox's apartment building. Seeing her sister's car enraged her. Her first impulse was to ram into Courtney's little Volkswagen, but she couldn't risk damaging her company-owned car.

Feeling depressed and lonely, she called Eric. Maybe they could patch up their relationship. Get back on track. Together they could figure out a way to keep the stripper and the baby out of their lives.

She drove past Knox's apartment and then pulled to the curb and called Eric.

"Hello." The familiar sound of Eric voice tugged at her heart.

"I miss you, Eric. We need to talk."

"Uh...it's not a good time right now."

"Are you at work?" Eric had always claimed to work doubles and swing shifts, and Nivea had never been able to keep with his work schedule.

"Yeah, I'm at work. I can call you back in a few minutes." He spoke softly, guardedly.

"I'm ready to forgive you. Ready to try to work with you to resolve our problems."

"That's cool," Eric said indifferently.

Nivea was a little confused by his lack of enthusiasm. The last time she'd spoken to Eric, he'd been begging and pleading for her to give him another chance.

Maybe she needed to be a little more direct. "Why don't we

get together? I'm on my way home. I want you to come by when you get off? I need to suck that dick, baby. It's been a long time." Nivea smiled smugly, waiting to hear Eric's raspy voice, telling her that he was dropping everything and would rush right over.

Instead she heard, "You ain't sucking shit, you nasty trick!" Dyeesha shrieked, her ugly voice piercing Nivea's eardrum.

Oh, my God! He's not at work. Eric is such a damn liar.

"You better stop harassing my husband."

"Your what?" Nivea squeaked.

"My muthafuckin' husband, bitch. Me and Eric are married."

"Put Eric back on the phone." Nivea refused to believe what this chicken head was saying. It couldn't be true.

"Hello." Eric sounded sheepish.

"Is it true?"

"Yeah, it's true. We tied the knot."

"Why, Eric? Why would you do this to me?"

"Yo, Niv. You gon' have to stop calling me all the time like this."

"What the hell are you talking about? You've been calling me and leaving a bunch of sad, pathetic messages on my damn phone."

"I'm just saying, yo...you gon' have to respect my marriage."

"Tell her that she needs to respect your wife!" Dyeesha yelled in the background.

"That's right, Niv. You have to respect my wife." Eric paused for effect, and then his voice dropped ominously, "Or it's gon' be something."

"It's going to be what? I know you're not threatening me after you let that stripper attack me in my own home."

"She ain't no stripper. That's all in the past. Yo, I ain't gotta explain nothing to you. Delete my number!"

Nivea pressed a button and ended the call. Eric's threat, the fact that he'd gotten married, it was all too much to bear. Steaming with rage, she needed to hit something, to break something, so she banged her BlackBerry against her dashboard. Yearning to hear the satisfying sound of the phone cracking open, she banged it over and over until her energy was drained. But the sturdy BlackBerry remained intact.

CHAPTER 43

Sharing time with Harlow had been fun—just like old times, but as they laughed, gossiped and brought each other up-to-date, Vangie couldn't get rid of the nagging pang, the horrible sinking feeling in the pit of her stomach every time she glimpsed Harlow's big-ass, clear-as-hell diamond ring. That ring was the most beautiful thing Vangie had ever seen—tangible evidence of Drake's love for Harlow.

Unfortunately, Vangie's panic level was rising. She couldn't wait much longer for Shawn to commit.

Vangie arrived home after ten. The apartment was cozy, warm, and quiet. Coat folded over her arm, she crossed the living room to the closet, trying to decide if it was wise to disrupt the peace in her household.

Undecided, she checked on Yuri. Snuggled beneath his yellow SpongeBob quilt, Yuri was sound asleep. She noticed a book on the nightstand. Shawn had read Yuri a bedtime story. Wearing a faint smile, she clicked off the light in Yuri's room. Closing her son's bedroom door, she reconsidered confronting Shawn. Maybe she should leave things alone for now. It might be unwise to upset the balance.

But she couldn't let it go. She was miserable playing wifey, sick of holding her breath, waiting for Shawn to pop the question. If she didn't speak her mind, it would be Valentine's Day before she knew it. If she didn't hurry up and let Shawn know how strongly she felt about marriage, instead of a ring, her Valentine's gift would be a box of chocolates and some more sleazy underwear.

Inside her bedroom, she stole a glance at Shawn's profile. *Goddamn, he's fine, even while he's asleep.* She let out a breath of excitement and turned the dimmer to low. She began to orchestrate a plan as she undressed in semi-darkness. She'd seduce Shawn, soften his resolve with some amazing sex.

He loved being awakened with his dick in her mouth. In the middle of sucking him off, she'd stop and tell him how much she loved him and then casually mention that they should get married.

She didn't need a big wedding. She didn't have time for all that. There was a Justice of the Peace in nearby Upper Darby. They could get married there, and Vangie would be as happy as a bride who'd been indulged with a platinum wedding.

Imagining being carried over the threshold of her small apartment, Vangie giggled. Her tinkling laughter woke Shawn. "Hey, baby. How long you been home?" he asked.

"Not long," she said, peeling off her panties.

"Damn, look at this!" He nudged his chin down toward the tented bedspread. "You got my dick programmed. Soon as you show a little bit of pussy, my dick gets hard as shit." Shawn started rubbing on his erection. "Get in bed. Let me get a quickie." Shawn wrinkled his face, expressing the urgency of his desire.

Vangie's plan of prolonged seduction was being replaced with a damn quickie. Her face felt enflamed by the heat of sudden fury. "Why don't you just buy yourself a blow-up doll? That's all you really need," she spat.

"Dag. Why you gotta come at me like that? What's wrong?"

"I'm tired of being treated like a sex object."

"Your naked ass turns your man on; why is that a problem?"

"I need to be more than convenient pussy, Shawn. I want to get married. But every time I bring up the subject, you turn cold, like getting married is a disease or a crime."

"Come here, baby. Sit down," Shawn said, his face composed, his voice filled with patience. "Let me talk to you."

Shawn sat up, revealing his bare chest. His taut, muscular upper body was a mouth-watering sight. Shawn was hot, there was no doubt about that, but Vangie couldn't allow herself to be distracted by his physical attractiveness.

Pouting, Vangie flopped down of the edge of the bed. "What do you want talk about?"

"Listen, we don't need a damn piece of paper to hold us together."

"I do," she said, touching her chest for emphasis. "I need to be validated, Shawn. We were already shacked up before Yuri was born. It didn't work out. Don't you see that our son needs the stability of married parents?"

"Let's get this out in open..." he paused for a beat. "I don't believe in marriage."

She gave him a furious glance. "Why not? Marriage is something that civilized people do to honor their relationship."

"I don't agree with that. To me, being married is some ole, played-out shit. Marriages don't work out like they used to."

"It can work when two people are committed to making it work. But this isn't just about us, Shawn. We have to think about Yuri. He didn't ask to come into this world. He deserves two parents who are—"

Shawn interrupted her with the wave of his hand. "I already had a talk with Yuri, and I explained my position. Yuri's all right with the situation."

Vangie gave Shawn a long, indignant look. "Oh really? You took it upon yourself to give our son a one-sided perspective on marriage. What were you thinking, Shawn? We should have talked to Yuri together."

Shawn shook his head, adamantly. "After you told me that Yuri had asked whether or not we were married, I had a big boy conversation with him. Isn't that what you wanted me to do?"

"I didn't want you to give him your twisted viewpoint."

"My way of thinking is real."

"You're not exactly an expert on the subject of marriage," Vangie said with a sneer.

"I know plenty of married people. And the ones I know are all miserable. They don't seem to make it past five or six years."

"Don't you even care about what I want?" Vangie said, sulking.

"I've been cutting hair for over ten years. I hear the way men talk. I know how they think and I know how they feel about women."

"So you formed your opinion over barbershop talk?" Vangie looked like she wanted to kill Shawn.

"I'm trying to tell you that just because somebody is married, it don't mean they're happy. All the married men I know are still on the hunt. When they get their shave and fresh Caesar cut, they're hooking up their appearance so they can go out and pull a new jumpoff. Most of 'em already have a couple of chicks on the side, but they need a break from jumpoff number one because she's in his ear harassing him about leaving his wife, and jumpoff number two is complaining about being a booty call. These dudes wanna smash something brand new. And the wife at home…" Shawn paused and twisted his lips to the side. "Ain't nothing sexy about her anymore. She's like a sister or a cousin. Somebody he don't even like anymore, but a piece of paper has him shackled to her."

"Those people sound immature and disgusting. We don't have

to end up like that, Shawn. Those men you're referring to don't have any respect for themselves or their marriages."

"Some of them are thugs and considered immoral. But a lot of 'em are considered to be upstanding citizens. Professional dudes. Churchgoers and what not. "

"Obviously, they're fronting," Vangie said, shaking her head. "Shawn, we don't have to be like them. I'm willing to put in the work to make our marriage last."

"I'm putting in the work right now. I'm doing my part to make sure that our relationship is meaningful and can last beyond a few years. What am I doing wrong, Vangie?" he asked, gesturing with his hands, causing the muscles in his arms to flex.

Vangie looked away from his sculpted physique, as if staring at his hot body would mesmerize her and persuade her to fold. "You won't put a ring on my finger. That's what you're doing wrong."

Shawn scowled at her, and even with his face frowned up, he was still a gorgeous sight. "So you believe that a ring equals love?"

Vangie nodded.

"It doesn't matter that I work hard for our family? I don't get points for coming home putting in time with my son, for showing my love instead of speaking empty words?"

"Everything you're doing means a lot. But I need to be validated as a woman. I deserve to be your wife. You owe me for all the years that I was a struggling, single parent. You owe me for the humiliating way you broke up with me and left me with an infant to care for."

"I'm not here with you because I owe you something. If it was about what I owed you, I'd drop off money and keep it moving." Shawn flung off the covers. Vangie got out of the way as he angrily swung his legs over the side of the bed. Sitting on the edge of the bed, Shawn bent over and held his head with both hands.

He appeared anguished, but Vangie stood over him, her arms folded across her chest, unrelenting.

He finally looked up, his expression pained. "I come straight home to you after a twelve-, thirteen-hour-day at the shop. I would be putting in even more hours if it weren't for the fact that I want to put in quality time with you and my son. I've been balancing my time here and at work as best I can."

"I know, Shawn, but—"

"But nothing! Hear me out before you start running your mouth about marriage."

Vangie sighed.

"I give you most of the money I make. Not because I have to. I do it because I want to. It makes me feel good. It feels good to know that my family is straight."

"Shawn, where is this conversation going?"

He sighed. "If I have to sign a contract in order to be with you, everything is going to change."

"It doesn't have to. You've convinced yourself that marriage will change our relationship."

"I thought I was making you happy."

"You treat me like a sex object. Always wanting pussy on demand. Like tonight. I planned on making love to you, but you started stroking your dick, expecting me to jump on it and get you off real quick."

"Don't I satisfy you?"

She shrugged. "I guess."

He reared back in shock. "You guess! Whatchu saying? You've been faking orgasms?"

"Sometimes," she said guiltily.

"Why?"

"To get it over with."

Shawn winced. "Damn, it's like that?"

"It's hard to enjoy sex when I'm always so angry and frustrated with you. I feel so betrayed."

Shawn stood up. "This is the kind of bullshit that I was trying to avoid. Look at us; we're at each other's throats like we're enemies."

"Well, I feel like you expect me to act like a wife without the benefit of a marriage license. I feel like you only want sex from me because you don't think I'm good enough to marry."

"If it was only about sex, I'd be smashing everything that walked past the shop. For real, though. Women are constantly throwing pussy at me, but I know how to turn shit down."

"Bitches be coming in the shop, and giving you their numbers?" Vangie shouted, enraged.

"Every day," he said with a firm head nod. "But I just keep on clipping; I don't pay them chicks any mind. In my opinion, that's what love is about. Keeping my priorities in order. Not letting random pussy distract me."

"Shawn, if your feelings for me are that strong, can't you give in this one time? Please."

"I don't believe in it. Marriage is a messed-up institution. I can't change my beliefs, and I guess it's not fair for me to expect you to change yours."

"In the eyes of God, we're living in sin," she said, grasping at straws.

"Man, get off of that living in sin crap. You don't even go to church."

"So what! I still believe in obeying the Word of God!"

"If you're going to obey God's laws, then start obeying all of them. Don't pick one that happens to suit your taste."

"I've made mistakes, but I'm not going to willingly choose to live in sin."

"You shouldn't even be bringing God into this discussion. You only want to get married so you can brag about it to your friends." Shawn started making steps toward the bedroom closet.

"What are you doing?"

"Getting ready to pack my shit."

"Why?"

"I never intended to hurt you, but that's what I'm doing. I can hear the pain in your voice."

She wrapped her arms around his waist. "Don't leave, Shawn. Let's discuss this like two responsible adults."

"I'm getting a headache. I have to be to work early in the morning. I don't need this kind of aggravation. I don't want to be arguing about this every night." Shawn disengaged her hands.

"Well, what am I supposed to tell Yuri?"

"I'll talk to him. Nothing can change the bond between me and my son."

"But he expects you to be here when he wakes up tomorrow. What am I going to tell him?" Panicked, Vangie wanted to go back in time, start back to when she walked into her peaceful living room.

"I'll give Yuri a call tomorrow night. And I'll see if I can make some time to pick him up this weekend."

"Shawn, don't leave. Can't we work this out? We don't have to talk about marriage right now."

He looked at her with sorrow in his eyes, and then shook his head. "There's nothing to work out. You're faking orgasms to get sex over with, like I'm a pervert or a sex fiend. I was happy, and didn't know that you were miserable. I feel like everything we were building was based on a lie. Nah, we don't have anything to work out, except a visitation schedule for me and my son."

"You can't leave!" she yelled as she watched Shawn filling a duffle bag with his clothes. "We can't give up." She paused. "For Yuri's sake."

"You want me to fake it like we're happy for Yuri's sake?" He shook his head. "I'm not going to do that."

"I love you, Shawn. My feelings are real."

"We don't have the same definition of what's fake and what's real."

Vangie's mind was flooded with desperate thoughts as she watched Shawn snatching up his personal possessions. No amount of begging and pleading stopped him. Finally, he tossed his keys on the dresser, and exited the bedroom.

CHAPTER 44

I n the privacy of her suite, Harlow was once again consumed with suspicion. She couldn't shake the nagging feeling that Drake wasn't as innocent as he pretended to be.

She gazed at her ring, and became momentarily entranced by its brilliant shine, but the thought that this glowing symbol of love might be tainted with someone's blood snapped her back to reality. Frowning in repugnance, she twisted the ring off her finger and firmly set it on the nightstand.

What would she do if she discovered that Drake had lied to her? Would she call off the wedding? Refuse to ever see him again? She shook her head, trying to coax her mind away from the disturbing thoughts that plagued her.

She clicked on the TV, searching for mindless entertainment, but couldn't concentrate; her thoughts kept returning to Drake. Despite her troublesome doubts, her love for him remained. Being away from him for so long had her shaky and anxious, like she was detoxing from a potent drug.

The doorbell chimed, startling Harlow. Assuming that room service was at the door with more complimentary sweets, she sighed deeply as she crossed the room. It would take more than an attractively arranged tray of gourmet goodies to lift her spirits.

She looked through the peephole and shrieked with joy. There was a large and delicious-looking mocha treat right outside her door.

Hastily, she unchained the lock. "Drake!"

Drake came inside the room, dropped his overnight bag on the floor. Harlow fell into his arms. "I missed you so much," he whispered.

"Don't talk," she said breathlessly, and then covered his mouth with hers. Below, her hands struggled with his belt.

There was a trail of clothes that went from the door to the bedroom. Later, lying in Drake's arms, feeling his arms wrapped tightly around her, Harlow wished that the moment could last forever. But it couldn't.

"I've been so scared," she said, her hand smoothing the hair on his chest. "I've braced myself to expect the worst."

"What do you mean?" He sat up and turned his head to glance at her. At that moment, he noticed the ring on the nightstand. Drake looked confusedly at her bare hand. "What's going on, Harlow?"

She sat up. "We have to talk, Drake. There's so much going on in my head. I feel so uncertain—"

Frowning, he gazed at her. "Do you doubt my love?"

"No." She paused and took in a deep breath. "But I have doubt about the story you gave me...about the stones I discovered."

"I wouldn't lie to you, Harlow. I told you the truth." Drake got out of the bed, walked naked over to the table and poured himself a drink. He picked his boxers off the floor, stepped into them and sat in a chair across from the bed.

"Did Talib confront the security guy—did he fire him? What happened?"

Drake inhaled a deep breath. "What I have to tell you is going to sound crazy—"

"Drake, please. No fantastic stories; I need the simple truth. I need to know why a total stranger would give you those diamonds. Was he trying to strike some kind of deal with you? Did he want you to help him smuggle them?"

"No. I'm not corrupt. I earn an honest living. You should know that."

Harlow anxiously searched Drake's face. "I want to trust you, Drake. You don't know how badly I want to believe you. It's breaking my heart that I'm filled with so much mistrust and confusion."

"Do you really think I'm that callous?" his voice came out harshly, his handsome features contorting. "Do you think that I'd risk everything that I've built to be a part of a smuggling ring?" He shook his head. "The situation that I unwittingly became involved in was not that elaborate. There were no clandestine meetings, no great master plan. There was only one individual involved in this..." His voice trailed off. He closed his eyes as though forcing away a horrible image.

"Talk to me," Harlow whispered, scooting over to the edge of the bed.

Drake released a breath. "The guard who slipped Alphonso those stones...his name is Jimoh. He comes from an impoverished, war-torn country in Africa. Most of his family members either work or have worked in the diamond mines—"

"And you know the guard's back story because?" Harlow prodded.

Drake lowered his head. "Because I was responsible for getting that man beaten unmercifully," he said, sounding pained.

Open-mouthed, Harlow gawked at Drake. "What?"

"I took the stones to Talib, accusing him of using his man to get me involved in the corrupt diamond trade. The surprised look on Talib's face told me that he didn't know what I was talking about. I showed him the stones." Drake paused and with closed eyes, he lowered his head as if shamefully reliving a horror.

"Go on, Drake," Harlow prompted.

"Talib wanted to know which man had given Alphonso the

stones. Alphonso pointed the man out." Drake sighed. "The beating that man took…it went on for several days. It was barbaric."

Feeling sickened, she grimaced. "Why didn't you step in and tell Talib that we're civilized people?"

"Are we civilized?"

Harlow's upbringing had been anything but civilized, but she nodded her head. "I'd like to believe that we are," she said softly.

"A lot of heinous crimes are committed by so-called civilized people, but when you're face-to-face with the ugly side of human nature, and listening to the sounds of a man being tortured—"

"Talib *tortured* his guard…and you just stood by and watched!"

"Hear me out."

Harlow made a strangled noise. "Oh, my God, this is appalling. I can't believe that you—"

"I need you to listen!" Drake's voice boomed with hurt and irritation.

It was rare for Drake to be upset with her. Responding to the pain in his voice, Harlow went from snippy to contrite. "Sorry," she murmured. She looked up at Drake, giving him her undivided attention.

"In Africa, diamonds can be the difference between life and death," Drake continued, now speaking in a soft, measured tone. "There's wicked corruption in the diamond trade. Those poor miners are exploited—it's practically slave labor. And here's the worst of it…if a guard suspects a worker of swallowing a stone—"

Harlow flinched. *The miners swallow diamonds?* Without speaking, she held up a hand, gesturing for Drake to explain.

Drake nodded grimly. "Some very desperate workers actually swallow diamonds to sneak them out of the mine. But many are falsely accused, and an accusation alone can cost a man his life. Being accused can get a man eviscerated."

She sucked in a sharp breath. "I don't understand."

"I mean that a miner that is merely suspected of swallowing even the tiniest rock, is often slaughtered right there on the spot. Jimoh was a miner before being hired to work for Talib. Many of his family members still work in the diamond mines. One of his cousins had been swallowing diamonds and collecting the stones in hopes of making enough money to escape the brutality of his country."

Harlow groaned, and shook her head.

"It took months for Jimoh's cousin to accumulate the stones, but he soon discovered that exchanging them for currency wasn't as easy as he'd hoped."

Still shaking her head, Harlow frowned. "Are you referring to those filthy stones that ended up in our bathroom in St. Croix?"

Drake nodded.

Those nasty stones travelled from someone's bowels and into the palm of my hand. Ugh! She covered her mouth, cringing at the memory. But an instant later, she felt guilty for being petty and shallow.

"The cousin realized that once Jimoh began working for Talib, he'd be mingling with people who had money and means, and so he gave Jimoh the rocks. Jimoh turned to Alphonso, asking for a fair price."

"And what's a fair price for those disgusting-looking stones?" She couldn't keep the grimace off her face as she imagined their grimy appearance.

"That's the shame of it all. What's a diamond anyway? It's just a damn rock like any other rock, right? Crude-looking stones that don't look like shit until they are polished and cut into facets. So for all intents and purposes, a diamond's value should be no more than an ordinary pebble. But our society...our culture has made the diamond a symbol of status and wealth."

"I don't understand why Talib tortured the guard."

"Being associated with diamond smuggling could have brought danger to Talib and his family. His methods were brutal, but eventually he arrived at the truth."

"How bad off is Jimoh?" Though she'd never met the man, Harlow felt enormous sympathy for him.

"Badly bruised, but he'll survive. No broken bones. No missing fingers or limbs."

"Thank God," she murmured. "What happened to the stones?"

"As far as I know, they were thrown in the ocean."

As relief washed over Harlow, she became pensive. This was the perfect opportunity to tell Drake the truth about her past—the whole story—not just the parts that she was comfortable divulging. She looked at him. "I have something to tell you," she said, nervously rubbing the skin around her bare ring finger.

"I'm a step ahead of you." He walked over to the nightstand and picked up Harlow's engagement ring. "After hearing Jimoh's story, I can't help feeling that every diamond from Africa has a germ of crime in it. Tomorrow, we're going to find you another ring. I could buy you a lab-created, synthetic diamond. Or a colored, conflict-free diamond from the mines of Australia," Drake said thoughtfully.

Harlow opened her mouth to protest, to confide what was really on her mind, but she choked on the words. "I don't need any kind of diamond," she finally said. "A diamond doesn't validate our relationship, engagement, or marriage. The only thing that matters is our commitment to each other."

Drake sat next to her. He wrapped his arms around Harlow, hugging her close. "I'm lucky to have you. And I'm going to spend the rest of my life showing you how much I love you."

Harlow buried her face in Drake's broad chest. She yearned to unburden her heart, but couldn't risk seeing the look in his eyes change from love to loathing. Inside his powerful arms, she was protected and cherished. She couldn't tell her secrets. After a lifetime of being damaged and broken, Harlow was finally loved. She couldn't risk losing Drake.

CHAPTER 45

Dealing with a fierce hangover while trudging around in bad weather from one doctor's office to the next was messed up! But Nivea's sales were down, and she had to do something about that. Her personal life was a disaster but she wasn't going to stand by and watch her stellar career go down the toilet. Hangover or not, it was time to get her numbers back up.

She felt like shit, but it didn't show. The bags under her eyes were hidden by expensive concealer. A clip-on weave hid hair that hadn't seen her stylist in weeks. She was rocking a Prada business suit that was classy, elegant, and sexy. Looking like she was on top of her game, Nivea glided into Dr. Sandburg's office.

"Good morning, Dr. Sandburg. How did your patients like the samples that I left last month?"

"No one asked me to write a prescription," the balding doctor replied.

"Did you tell your patients about the loyalty program my company offers? After six purchases, the seventh prescription is free." She'd mentioned this new incentive last month and yet her sales were still crappy.

"Yes, I've made them aware of that. But the general feeling seems to be, why buy the name brand when you can get the generic much cheaper?" the doctor said, chuckling.

"I see," Nivea muttered. "Can't you suggest that the brand I'm representing is superior to the generic?"

"That would be unethical."

It was unethical for Dr. Sandburg to insist that she give him a personal supply of painkillers. The doctor had become addicted to the freebies he should have been giving his patients. "How are you doing?" she asked, raising a brow.

"Business is great."

"I was referring to your personal situation. You know, being that you're middle-aged and all, I would imagine that it's unpleasant having to contend with ED."

The doctor face flushed with embarrassment. "I'm offended."

She touched her chest. "I'm genuinely concerned."

"I take medication for that."

"Yeah, but it's a shame to have to wait a half-hour for your dick to cooperate."

Dr. Sandburg gasped, and then gave her a condemning glare. "Young lady! I thought I was dealing with a professional, but you're crass, uncouth, and—"

"My company has a new get-hard-quick drug. In less than five minutes you can be packing wood. Whatcha think, Doc? You wanna give my medication a try?" She poked around in her briefcase and then pulled out a packet of pills. "Here. You'll be amazed at how fast this little pill works."

"I don't want to try it at the moment. I'm working. Leave me some samples—"

"No more samples for you until you start writing some prescriptions for my drugs."

"I can't force my patients to take your pharmaceuticals."

"After you experiment with me, you can push my drugs with a clear conscience."

"What do you mean?" he asked, backing away from Nivea.

"And I can't keep giving you free stuff without any compensation. After you test your hard-on with me, you'll be able to report to your patients. You can tell them how quickly you obtained a stiff dick. With your word of mouth promotion, all your patients suffering from limp dick syndrome should switch to my company's brand. Do we have a deal?"

Dr. Sandburg wiped his forehead. "I don't know. It seems immoral."

Life had taught Nivea that men had no control over their dicks. They'd fuck whatever was in front of them with no compunction. Impatient with the doctor, Nivea said, "I've noticed how you look at me...always undressing me with your eyes—"

He looked offended. "I do not!"

"Oh, yes you do. And today I'm going to make your sick fantasies come true." She slid down the zipper of her smartly tailored slacks.

Dr. Sandburg's face turned crimson. "Oh, my! Are you actually trying to—?"

"Uh-huh. I'm real horny, Doc. Take one of those pills so you can give me what I want." She pulled her trousers down, showing off red satin panties.

"You want to do it here? Right now...in my office?" He sounded appalled.

Nivea winked. "Lock the door."

"It only takes five minutes, you say?" he asked, popping a pill out of the packet. His face took on a raw excitement, and then he washed the pill down with water. Hurriedly, he locked the door.

"How's your head game, Doc?"

He gave her a startled look. "My what?" he asked in a voice pitched higher than normal.

Nivea stepped out of her pants and hoisted herself up on the examining table. She slid off her panties, kicked them to the floor. Her mouth curled in amusement after ridding herself of the confining red fabric. "Come on over here and eat some of this." She ran a manicured finger up and down her silken slit.

Dr. Sandburg was pulled like a magnet toward the thatch of dark pubic hair between Nivea's legs. "I don't engage in these kinds of activities," he murmured as he lowered his face to her crotch.

"Today is a good time to start." She brushed her hand down the side of his face. "Taste it, Doc. Keep yourself occupied while we're waiting for that pill to kick in."

Tentatively, he dabbed around her pussy lips with the tip of his tongue. As the juices of Nivea's arousal began to spill, the doctor began lapping and moaning. "Mmm. Ah. Oh, yes. This is good, but I'm not sure if I should—"

"Shh!" Nivea patted the bald spot on the top of his head. "It's ill-mannered to talk with your mouth full."

Dr. Sandburg did not have Knox's tongue skills, but Nivea was determined to get something out of the encounter. Holding the doctor's neck in a vise grip, while mashing the end of his nose into her clit, she let out a moan of appreciation as she obtained a modest orgasm.

❤ ❤ ❤

After leaving Dr. Sandburg's office, Nivea had the bright idea to check on another account. She didn't have an appointment, but since she was in the area, it couldn't hurt to stop by and see if she could work her magic again.

Dr. Joseph, a thirty-something, entirely too cute for his own good, and totally egotistical physician, was always too busy to listen to Nivea's eighty second sales pitch. He acted like he was doing her a huge favor by allowing her to leave samples.

I bet that arrogant bastard will want to hear what I have to say today.

Tapping his pen impatiently, Dr. Joseph sat behind his desk. "What do you have for me, Ms. Westcott?"

Sitting across from the doctor, Nivea cut to the chase. "I've been leaving you samples for months. I need you to start writing prescriptions for my drugs."

"Ms. Westcott, I don't appreciate your strong-arm tactics."

Her eyes roamed leisurely over his chest. Dr. Joseph was the full package. Handsome, successful, and as fit as an athlete. His broad chest and bulky arms were apparent beneath his lab coat. Nivea could imagine how hot he was going to look when she stripped his ass down to his birthday suit. She smiled alluringly. "Do you realize that I have a crush on you?"

He didn't blink. "That's completely understandable. Most of my female patients experience similar feelings—"

Sucking her teeth, Nivea interrupted him. "I'm not one of your patients." She came out of her coat and leaned forward. "I drove over here with one hand stuffed inside my panties," she said in a hushed, sexy tone.

"I see." He maintained a serious expression, and gave a professional head nod, as if her murmurings were of a clinical nature.

"My pussy is still hot. It's all wet and puffy from fingering myself while imagining the things I want to do to you," Nivea whispered.

Dr. Joseph's shoulders rose as he inhaled a large breath of air. "What exactly do you want to do to me?" He dropped the pen and swiped his fingers across his forehead.

Nivea could see the spark of arousal dancing in his eyes. "You have a boner, don't you, Dr. Joseph?" she remarked knowingly.

"Uh…not exactly."

While the doctor stammered a denial, Nivea rose from the

chair and made her way to the other side of the desk. Gazing at his lap, she noticed a moderate bulge that stiffened to an urgent salute in a matter of seconds. Satisfied with the results, Nivea went down to her knees.

"Ms. Westcott, what do you think you're doing?" Dr. Joseph croaked.

"Call me Nivea," she said as she roughly unbuckled his belt.

No longer protesting, Dr. Joseph helped Nivea get to his dick. He lifted up from his seat, and speedily unzipped his pants.

Nivea reached into the opening of his briefs and sheaved his erection inside her warm fist. Dr. Joseph had more than a mouthful of manly length. It was the kind of dick that was created for sucking. Not overly big, the right amount of girth for a dick-sucking experience that didn't involve stretching her mouth to the point of gaping discomfort.

Nivea yanked his pants down. Dr. Joseph's body tensed when she licked his pre-cum-covered glans. With her fingernails pressed into the flesh of his cheeks, she persuaded him to feed her another few inches of penile skin.

Breathing like a freight train, Dr. Joseph pumped his hard-on in and out of Nivea's mouth, hard and fast, and without any discernable rhythm.

Unable to control the head she was giving, Nivea accidentally nicked Dr. Joseph's dick. With both canine teeth.

"Jesus!" Dr. Joseph yelped.

Nivea stopped sucking. Dr. Joseph pulled out. Blood smeared both sides of his shaft. "What the fuck! I think you broke a blood vessel in my cock!"

"Sorry. But you were ramming it in my mouth so fast, I couldn't—"

"Shit! Look at this!" He glared at her, palming his discolored and sagging rod.

"Wow," Nivea said, noticing that his dick was turning a sort of purplish color.

"I thought you knew what you were doing. But you don't! I need medical care."

"You're a doctor. Can't you patch it up?" Nivea said in a placating tone.

"What the hell am I going to tell my wife?"

"That your dick got caught in your zipper?"

"On both sides?" he shrieked in exasperation.

Out of ideas, Nivea threw up her hands.

"Get out! And take your samples with you!" Dr. Joseph yelled. Cradling his injured dick, he limped toward a cabinet and grabbed a first aid kit.

CHAPTER 46

The sheets were cold. Seeking the warmth of Shawn's body heat, Vangie rolled over. Alarmed, she reached for Shawn but found only an empty space. Waking up alone was a jolt to her system.

Yuri was going to freak out when she told him that his father was gone. She flinched, wondering if she'd made the right decision. Maybe she should have waited a few more months before hitting Shawn with an ultimatum. What difference did it make how long she waited? Shawn was adamant about staying single and she was just as adamant about legalizing their union.

Padding down the hall to wake Yuri, she assured herself that she'd done the right thing. It hurt like hell, but Vangie was determined to stand by her principles.

She paused at the threshold of Yuri's room, and regarded her sleeping child with worried eyes. *Poor little guy. He has no idea that his world has been shattered. It was Shawn's decision to leave, so I'm going to let him deliver the heartbreaking news to Yuri.*

She bent over and kissed her son's cheek. "Time to get up, sweetheart," she said in a sugary tone that showed no trace of despair.

Yuri wriggled beneath the covers, and launched into expressions of aggravation. He never grumbled or showed any type of attitude when his father woke him in the morning. He jumped right out of bed like a little man.

"Get up!" She used a stern voice, pulling the covers off of him.

"It's cold."

"You'll be warm in a minute."

"Aw, Mom," he whined as Vangie steered him to the bathroom. "Where's Daddy?"

She let her breath out slowly. "He left for work already. Daddy had to open the shop."

"Aw, man. I like riding with Daddy."

"Too bad. Now wash up and brush your teeth." Vangie sounded a lot tougher than she felt. She dreaded having to deal with Yuri's terrible morning attitude on a regular basis.

❤ ❤ ❤

The evening routine was madness. Vangie had to pay the day care bill, an expense that Shawn would have handled had he taken Yuri to the day care center this morning. Yuri was in the back seat squirming around and trying to avoid putting on his seatbelt, and he was whining for her to stop at McDonald's. In the blink of an eye, she'd become a struggling single parent again.

When her cell chimed, Vangie rolled her eyes at Shawn's name and handed it to Yuri. "It's your father," she said with an attitude.

"Hi, Daddy! We're on our way to McDonald's. Do you want us to get you a number three?"

At the light, Vangie turned around and caught a glimpse of Yuri's expression changing from joy to confusion.

"Daddy said he's not coming home anymore." His tone of voice accused her of chasing his father away.

Disgusted, Vangie reached for the phone. "Give me the phone, Yuri."

"This is not the way to handle this situation, Shawn," she spat. "You should have come to the apartment and talked to Yuri in person."

"It's crowded at the shop. I can't get away right now," Shawn explained.

From the backseat, Yuri started crying.

"Do you hear your son? Do you hear what I have to deal with? Thanks a lot, Shawn."

"I told you last night that I was going to call him. If you wanted me to talk to him in person, why didn't you say so?"

"I was distressed last night. I couldn't make any rational decisions."

"I'll stop by tomorrow."

"What time?"

"I'm not sure."

"Look, you don't get to drop through whenever it suits you. If you want to see Yuri, then make a damn appointment."

She clicked the red button and tossed her cell back in her purse.

"Why'd you hang up?" Yuri asked tearfully. "I wasn't finished talking to my Daddy."

"You'll see him soon."

"When?"

"I don't know."

"He'd come back home if you stopped hollering at him. You made my Daddy leave me."

"That's not true. Your father moved out because he and I don't agree on a very important issue...marriage. He wants to stay single and I want to be married. I have principles, Yuri. You'll understand when you're older."

"Daddy told me that you didn't need a piece of paper to be married."

"Oh, really? Don't listen to everything your father tells you. A man and a woman who have a child together should be married. I was young when I had you. I shouldn't have put the horse before the cart," she said, misusing the old expression.

"You put a horse before what?" Yuri said with a baffled look in his eyes.

"A woman should be married before she has a baby," Vangie explained. "But now that I'm older and wiser, I refuse to be shacking with your father indefinitely. I need a ring on my finger."

"Is Daddy ever coming back?" Yuri asked, unconcerned about his mother's marital woes.

"No, he's not."

"But I want him to come back!"

"I can't force your father to come back," Vangie said in a voice that was flat and dispirited.

Yuri wailed while Vangie placed their order at McDonald's drive-thru. He cried for the duration of the drive home. By the time they got to their apartment, he moped around, refusing to eat his Happy Meal, and speaking to Vangie in sullen tones. The boy was treating her like she was a she-devil and acting like his father was some sort of martyred saint.

CHAPTER 47

Feeling good about herself for the first time in quite a while, Nivea pulled into the parking space in front of her townhouse. Thanks to the grounds crew that worked at her complex, her private parking spot was cleanly shovelled and salted. The sun had set and the temperature had plummeted. The unending bitter cold didn't affect her mood this evening.

Her mint green bra, hastily removed by a nimble-fingered physician, peeked from her briefcase. Nivea smiled in gloating satisfaction at the memory of the day's conquests.

Though she'd struck out with Dr. Joseph, the other male doctors she'd paid special visits were enthusiastic about doing business with her. After sampling her personal goods, they'd all promised to increase their amount of monthly prescription writing.

Sure, she'd had to stoop to whorish tactics to get what she wanted, but her method for success would remain her own dirty little secret. She'd done what she had to do to secure her top sales position. And she'd had fun in the process.

Now she had to get her personal life in order. If Nivea didn't tie the knot before her sister's wedding, she'd be considered the family failure.

But she had absolutely no prospects. No way to make a husband materialize.

Knox! Nivea shook her head. She'd really been into him, but he'd turned out to be a huge disappointment. She hadn't realized until last night how totally attached Knox was to her ditzy sister.

Maybe she'd have better luck trying to work her magic on one of the doctors on her client list. On second thought, why bother? They all were wearing wedding bands, and she simply didn't have the time or patience to break up a marriage.

Inside her house, she went straight to her bedroom and changed from her work clothes into a flannel nightgown. With no man in her life, she could dress for comfort. She finished the frumpy look with a pair of unattractive wool slipper socks.

Hungry, Nivea plodded to the kitchen and was hit with a horrible odor. A dead mouse trapped in the walls? She grimaced at the thought. Then she eyed the trash bin with suspicion and lifted the lid. *Oh, Gawd!* There was a half-filled container of Chinese food…chicken broccoli that she'd tossed three or four days ago. The broccoli was rancid, funking up the whole house.

Filled with disgust, Nivea yanked out the green plastic bag, and secured it with a tight knot. She threw her big faux fur coat over her nightgown. She hated having to take the trash out. Times like this she wished the hardworking crew who took care of the grounds around her complex would handle some household chores, too.

The frigid cold had her pacing quickly to the Dumpster, which was situated in a semi-private spot behind visitors' parking. A cold and sharp wind smacked against her back. Yearning for the warmth of her house, Nivea quickly flung the trash bag. It thumped heavily into the Dumpster.

Just as she was about to turn around, she noticed a looming shadow. Her muscles tensed and she instantly felt the sudden sensation of warmth.

Someone had crept up behind her, blocking the whipping wind. She sucked in a frightened breath.

Large hands pressed her against the Dumpster, preventing her from moving.

"Oh, my God!"

"Shh!" The utterance was husky and male.

"Please don't hurt me," she squeaked, trying to twist around and face her attacker.

"Be quiet!" the voice said in a whispered shout, forcibly holding her in place.

With the side of her face pressed against the cold Dumpster, Nivea shivered as the assailant yanked up her coat and flannel gown. He pushed against her bare backside, grinding and murmuring hoarsely, "You like it dirty, don't you?"

She couldn't speak. She shook her head, denying the accusation. She didn't like it dirty! At least not like this, not outside in the cold…next to a trash Dumpster. Nivea trembled with fear and indignation.

From behind, he shoved a hand between her thighs, his four fingers journeying purposefully toward the slit of her vagina. His middle finger took on an unexpected tenderness when it reached its destination, burrowing into the sticky heat that had accumulated into a thick puddle of lust.

His finger delved deeper. A flood of passion swept through Nivea; she acknowledged that something dark and carnal had been awakened inside her.

The stranger withdrew his finger from her warm depth. Mounting her from behind, he replaced his finger with the swollen tip of his dick.

Like an apprehended criminal, Nivea widened her stance, arms outstretched, palms pressed against the metal surface of the trash bin. Inexplicably, she wanted every inch of this stranger's pulsing flesh. She briefly wondered if she were being fucked by one of the Hispanic workers who shoveled snow and kept the grounds neat and clean.

His dick probe was harsh and unrelenting as it searched for her hidden treasure.

With each thrust of his heated shaft, he pulled her hair. "You like it dirty?" he demanded in a coarse voice, spoken close to her ear. The attacker wore a ski mask; Nivea could feel the rough fabric scraping against her neck and the side of her face.

"Tell me! Do you like it dirty, bitch?" he whispered in a voice that was so strangled with lust, there was no discernible accent.

"Yes," she finally admitted after giving up on trying to detect an accent or place the voice. This ski-masked, night-fucker was bringing out her depraved side.

She moved in concert with the masked man, shoving back as she willingly accepted the hot and meaty dick that filled her. Nivea moaned and scratched at the metal trash bin, her pussy clenching around the base of the stranger's dick as it pounded violently.

Then his strokes slowed, leisurely searching until her sweet spot was found.

"Ahh," Nivea cried out as she tumbled to the edge of ecstasy. She went limp, murmuring and moaning with her head and torso drooping downward.

The stranger wrapped his arms around her waist, pulling her inert body to him, as he hammered hard. Nivea's pussy made squishy noises. "That girl juice feels nice and nasty on my dick," he groaned.

Too spent to talk or move, Nivea smiled in perverted satisfaction.

"Damn, you look sexy taking out the trash…" His voice trailed off as he groaned and released a titanic explosion.

The stranger's voice sounded suddenly familiar. Nivea whipped around and grabbed at the ski mask.

"Knox!"

"Miss me?" he asked, wearing a crooked smile. Before she could speak, he started turning her around.

"You crazy bastard! What the hell is wrong with you?" She raised her fist to hit him.

He caught her fist. "Chill out."

"How could you do something like that to me? I was terrified."

Knox looked stunned. "I thought you enjoyed getting freaky and living out your fantasies."

"Getting raped is not one of my fantasies."

"The way you were slamming that pussy back at me, seemed like you were into it."

Nivea opened her mouth to protest.

"Shh!" Knox said. "Feel my dick; I need some." He pressed hand against his hardness. "Ooo, come on, baby. Bend over for me. Let me get up in it one more time."

She looked around nervously, wondering if any of her neighbor's had witnessed the whorish exhibition. "Let's go in the house, Knox. It's cold out here."

"I can warm you up." His dick pulsed inside her hand. He nudged Nivea into the side of the Dumpster.

"Someone might be watching, Knox," she murmured.

"Let 'em watch," he replied, pushing his dick inside her creamy warmth. "Don't you like being watched?"

Sopping wet and writhing with desire, Nivea responded with a shuddering whimper.

CHAPTER 48

Being alone on New Year's Eve felt like crap. Yuri was with his father, and Vangie had no one to celebrate with. She'd planned on spending New Year's Eve with Harlow, but Drake came to town unexpectedly, and Vangie couldn't blame Harlow for dropping their plans to spend a quiet evening with her man.

So here she was, absolutely alone, guzzling cheap champagne, and gazing at the TV and waiting for the ball to drop at Times Square. When the clock struck midnight, Vangie felt panicked. She didn't like bringing the New Year in by herself. It was ridiculous for her and Shawn to be apart. Ridiculous!

She thought about the way Shawn made love to her. Pictured his hot chocolate body, and she wanted him more than ever. It seemed unfathomable that while they were together, she had become annoyed by his sexual advances.

After another glass of champagne, Vangie became emboldened. She called Shawn, pressing his number quickly, before she lost her nerve.

"Yeah," Shawn answered gruffly.

"Is Yuri awake? I wanted to wish him a Happy New Year." Despite being tipsy, her voice came out in a steady and even.

"Nah, Yuri's out cold."

"I was thinking about you, you know…thinking about us. Maybe we acted too hastily. I miss you, Shawn," she admitted timidly.

Shawn didn't say anything. The silence on the other end of the phone was deafening, causing Vangie to instantly regret calling Shawn. "Are you there?"

"Yeah, I'm here," he replied dryly.

"Well, say something."

"Nothing to say. I spoke my peace. You spoke yours. We don't see eye-to-eye. No point in beating a dead horse."

In desperation, Vangie swallowed her pride. "I really want to try and work things out. Why don't you and Yuri come to the apartment tomorrow?" Nervously, she cleared her throat. "I'll fix dinner," she said with forced joviality. "I want to start the year off right."

Once again, Shawn went mute, and Vangie felt compelled to fill the silence. "I'm willing to work with you, Shawn. You know, compromise," she rambled. She heard herself agreeing to compromise, but she knew in her heart that she hadn't changed her viewpoint on marriage. But she intended to change Shawn's. Once she got him back in her clutches.

"Nah, I'm good."

"What do you mean, you're good?"

Shawn paused for a long moment. "I'm good!" he insisted. "I've already moved on."

"Meaning?" A blaze of hot jealousy had her nostrils flared and her chest heaving up and down.

"I'm with somebody," he said emphatically.

"Already!" she screeched, losing her cool. That she'd been so quickly replaced left her feeling cheap, undesirable, and insignificant. "You're such a fucking whore, Shawn. Always have been. I don't know why I let you back in my life. How can you hook with a new bitch in a matter of fucking days?"

"You finished cussing me out? Got it all out your system?" Shawn said calmly.

Vangie detected a trace of smugness in his tone that she found absolutely infuriating. "I didn't get a damn thing out of my system. I'm just getting started." She grabbed the flute and downed the rest of the champagne.

"Vangie," Shawn said in a tone that was tinged with pity. "You sound like you've had too much to drink. Why don't you call it a night and get some rest?"

"Why don't you bite my ass?" she snarled.

"Aye, look. I don't have time for this. I'm hanging up."

"Don't you fucking hang up on me, Shawn."

"Happy New Year," he added and then hung up.

Hurt feelings took a back seat to furious indignation. And the desire for revenge. With one eye narrowed, Vangie shook her head, envisioning the many ways she planned to make Shawn's life a living hell.

CHAPTER 49

Tickets to the 12 Midnight New Year's Eve bash at the Crystal Tea Room were hard to come by. Expecting to ring in the New Year with Eric, Nivea had bought six months in advance. The party was advertised as a night to remember. So far, it was a night she hoped to forget. Here she was, inside the grand ballroom with its hand-carved columns and crystal chandeliers that acted as a backdrop to the gala event.

Mixed in with over twelve-hundred revellers atop the old Wanamaker building, Nivea was dressed to impress, wearing a stunning black sequinned mini-dress. Instead of flaunting her long shapely legs, she shrank in the background, fidgety and ill-at-ease as she waited impatiently for Knox to join her.

Knox swore that he was going to make it to the gala event. He said that he told Courtney that his study schedule was too intense for him to party that night, and she'd agreed to go out with friends while he stayed home and studied.

Hanging out at one of the specialty bars, Nivea craned her neck, looking for Knox. She was starting to feel panicky and wished he'd hurry up. She'd asked him to pick her up so they could arrive together, but he'd claimed that it was more convenient to meet her here.

He was supposed to arrive at nine, but it was now ten o'clock, goddamnit! *Where is he?*

She pulled out her BlackBerry for the zillionth time and texted Knox. It seemed as though every happy couple that came up to the bar looked at her pityingly. Their sympathetic looks were driving her to drink. "Another vodka," she said to the bartender, slamming down her empty plastic cup.

Feeling conspicuous, she walked away from the bar and meandered over to one of the numerous buffet tables. There was a bountiful display of attractive cuisine, but she didn't have an appetite. Needing to occupy her time, she inched along the long buffet line, allowing smiling servers to plop food on her plate.

Trying to stay occupied, Nivea had made numerous trips to the ladies room and she was getting disgusted, feeling hatred for Knox and all mankind.

By eleven o'clock, Nivea was blind with anger as she imagined Knox and Courtney enjoying drinks and celebrating together. She wondered what ploy Courtney had used to get Knox to sacrifice his studies. She downed another drink. Needing a refill, she approached the bar for another.

"You might wanna lay off the hard stuff for a while," the well-meaning bartender suggested.

"You might wanna fuck off," she said sneeringly and then staggered over to another bar that was a few feet away. She was surrounded by over a thousand people, but they were all total strangers. Nivea had never felt so alone, or more in need of a friend.

"Absolut," she said, making sure that she didn't slur the word. If this bartender tried to cut her off, there was a strong possibility that she would get rowdy.

He offered her a friendly smile, which she interpreted as flirtation. She looked him over and decided she liked what she saw: medium height, the angles of his face were nice, and his eyes were a luminous baby blue. Though skinnier than she preferred, he had a certain male sensuality that stirred something inside her.

"Happy New Year," she said seductively.

"Same to you," he replied with another friendly smile. "How come you're not wearing a party hat?"

Nivea shrugged. "Didn't want to ruin my 'do." She fluttered her eyelashes, and patted her hair enticingly.

The bartender looked at her with a baffled expression. He gave Nivea her drink and then beckoned forward the next patron in line.

Nivea moved out of the way, but lingered to the side. Giving the bartender a furtive glance, she decided that his lean physique was actually kind of sexy. He was a cute white boy. Blond spiked hair. Two earrings glittered in his lobes. Visible tats on his neck, and probably more hidden beneath the suit he was wearing. Urban, with a touch of thug—like his name should have been Slim Shady.

When the crowd thinned, Nivea approached again. "Do you take breaks?"

"Not if I can help it."

"How do you relieve yourself? Is there a urinal behind the bar?" she wisecracked, which brought a chuckle out of Slim Shady.

"I'm working for tips, so I try to hang back here as long as I can," he said, laughing. His laughter held a rich, masculine sound, which aroused Nivea.

She'd noticed that there were only ones and fives in his tip cup. She checked her BlackBerry one last time to see if Knox had texted her, but there wasn't one word from the lying creep.

Frugal by nature, Nivea hated to part with her money, but desperate times…She slid two fifties from her wallet and pushed them in the cup. "Why don't you take a break?"

Taken aback, he asked, "What are you getting at?"

"I'm trying to have a good time with you, and I don't mind

paying." She smiled alluringly. Nivea was the kind of drunk whose mood could switch from mean to amorous in seconds. Right now, she desired the attention of a man. And any man would do under the circumstances. Somewhere in the back of her mind, she considered it ominous to bring in the New Year alone. And she wanted to get even with Knox.

"I guess I could use a smoke."

"Ready when you are," she said.

"Why don't you wait for me over there by the exit sign?" he said, pointing.

"Sure, but don't keep me waiting too long."

Leaning against a column, Nivea checked her messages. Nothing! She felt justified in luring the bartender to…Hell if she knew where she was going to lure him. Her car? She shrugged, deciding to play it by ear.

Nivea's mind wandered back to Knox. Clearly, it was time to move on.

While absorbed in thought, she felt a hand touch her shoulder. "This way," the bartender whispered, steering her down a corridor, away from the noisy crowd.

"Where're we going?"

"The break room."

"I guess that's better than the backseat of my car."

The bartender smiled and kept moving. He definitely had some swag, his long legs moving in a confident glide.

The break room was a dreary place. Small and stuffy. There were only a couple of uncomfortable looking chairs, and a scratched-up wooden table.

Nivea disregarded the appearance of the room and turned her gaze on the bartender. "Do you have a name, Slim Shady?"

He chuckled at the nickname. "You can call me Slim."

He didn't ask her name, and Nivea didn't volunteer the information. Her tongue felt too thick and lazy to take on the task of forming any more words, so she used her eyes to talk dirty.

Acknowledging that he understood her language, the bartender moved in closely, trapping her in a corner as he groped her body. Breathing fast and hard, he slid his hand under her dress. "You got some pussy for me?" he whispered fiercely, forcing his tongue between her teeth before she could answer.

Nivea was excited by the way Slim Shady was taking control. His kiss was fiery. His hands moved urgently over her body. He pulled the stretchy fabric of her dress down past her shoulders, and expertly removed her bra. He cupped her breasts in his palms as if weighing them, and then clenched each nipple between his thumb and forefinger, rolling until the flesh swelled into an aching knot.

She dropped her head back, moaning as Slim drew a plump nipple in his mouth. Nivea wrapped her hands around him, pulling him so close, her breast smashed against his face. Slim worked on the right breast and then the left. Nivea groaned in delight as he sucked and savaged her nipples like they were ripened fruit.

"I don't have a lot of time," he whispered. "Suck my dick and then I'll take care of you."

Slim undid his pants, and let them fall around his ankles. His body was like a canvas, tight and taut and splattered with beautiful body art. Nivea caressed the tattoos, wishing she had enough time to outline each tat with the tip of her tongue. "Get on it," he said in a rumbling voice.

She shivered with excitement, and sank to her knees. She couldn't resist stroking the blond hair that curled above his groin. She fondled his dick, enjoying the warmth and the heaviness of his thick erection. Fingernails digging into his hipbone, she pulled him into her mouth, taking him as deeply as she could.

"Make me cum," he demanded.

She didn't want him to cum, but his dick felt so good inside her mouth, tasted so juicy and flavourful, like she was sucking on brined meat. She sucked hard, her tongue swirling against his hot and sensitive flesh.

Slim gripped a handful of her hair, keeping her head in place as he pumped dick inside her mouth, delivering long strokes that made her eyes water. Impaled by the dick that was embedded in her throat, Nivea could no longer work her jaws or pucker her lips around his juicy meat. With her mouth wide open, and her eyes bulged, Nivea was helpless to stop him from mercilessly driving dick down her throat.

With an agonized cry, Slim discharged a blast of salty, masculine flavor that overflowed, spilling out the sides of Nivea's mouth.

Before she could swallow, catch her breath, or wipe her mouth, Slim was clumsily guiding her to a lumpy chair. Walking with pants around his ankles took away some of his swagger. But as soon as he sat down and positioned Nivea onto his saliva-slick pole, he was back in control.

The door opened suddenly. Nivea jumped. "Oh, that's Ryan. He came to join in. I hope that's okay with you."

Nivea's head jerked in the direction of the door. Sauntering into the room was the bartender who'd cut off her vodka. Her mouth curled in anger, and almost yelled for him to get the fuck out. But he stepped behind her, reached around and grabbed her breasts, squeezing them gently until Nivea purred.

"This is so freaky," she said breathlessly.

"Let Ryan get some of this," Slim suggested.

Nivea nodded. She gasped as Ryan's hand went lower, his fingertip lightly stroking her extended clit while Slim, groaning and undulating, filled up the plush depths of her pussy lining.

"It's your turn, Ryan," Slim said, taking panting breaths.

Nivea felt herself being lifted from Slim's softening manhood. Gasping for breath, Slim rose from the chair.

Ryan unzipped and pulled down his pants. Pants hanging over his waist, he took Slim's place in the chair. Ryan jostled her about, reversing her position.

Nivea closed her eyes in ecstasy as Ryan, taking his firm dick in hand, inserted it between her slick folds. It gave her a rush to feel his length pushing inside walls that were soaked with another man's lust.

Ryan groaned as he thrust deeply, sloshing through cum-sodden territory.

What they were doing was depraved. It was animalistic. Nivea cried out, loving every second of the wanton debauchery. She squeezed her own breasts and pinched her nipples as she pushed back, her hips circling wildly. Squishy sounds from her pussy echoed loudly, taking Nivea to an extreme level of decadent pleasure.

She couldn't hold back the squeals of passion. As if pulled by a mating call, Slim appeared before her. His eyelids heavy, his mouth slack, he placed the heel of one hand on Nivea's forehead, the other hand held his throbbing dick. He parted her lips with the smooth, hot crown.

There was a dick in her mouth and another in her pussy. Getting fucked by two hot white boys was truly amazing. A roaring sound in her ears and tingling flesh announced that an orgasm was near. Her climax coincided with fireworks and an explosion of champagne bottles popping off.

It was the best New Year's Eve ever!

CHAPTER 50

The disheveled woman waited in the shadows. She staked out the hoity toity restaurant from a distance. Fidgety and impatient, she craned her neck to see if any patrons had come out. *It's cold as a bitch out here. I hope I don't have to be waiting past midnight.*

Her irritation increased as she imagined the prosperous diners. *Rich people get on my goddamn nerves. They don't care about nobody but their own greedy selves. Bitches and bastards in there chattin' and chillin', thinking about what they gon' eat for dessert while I'm out here freezin' my ass off. Those fools need to eat their food and go celebrate New Year's Eve somewhere that has a DJ and a dance floor. Taking their time, eating all slow. I got money to make. Goddamn! Come on, y'all!*

A sudden gust of wind sent a chill straight to her bones. Angrily, she gave her coat a hard yank, pulling it tightly around her chubby body. She felt the thread loosening on the only button that was left on her ragged coat.

"Shit!" she muttered as she ripped off the useless button and tossed it over her shoulder in disgust. She paced impatiently, her scarred hands holding the shabby coat together. She clutched a worn Bible to her chest. Her ratty wig, which always seemed askew, served as a hat, keeping her keloid-scarred scalp warm. With her eyes fixed on the entrance, she was prepared to shuffle up to the first prospect that exited the upscale restaurant.

Collecting donations for her ministry was hard work. It took patience and cunning. And good common sense. It wasn't in people's nature to tithe simply because it was the right thing to do. She had to play on their emotions and sensibilities to get donations for her ministry. And she had to select the right locations, targeting establishments with a predominately white clientele.

The woman didn't bother to hang around establishments that catered to black people. Experience had taught her that black people didn't feel the same kind of pity and subconscious guilt that white people did. When Caucasians saw her dark, disfigured face, they generally felt pity, guilt, and disgust. These feelings motivated them to dig into their pockets to relieve their discomfort—handing over a crisp twenty to make her go away.

"Thank you, Jesus. Oh, bless your merciful heart!" she'd shout with passion, holding her Bible up to the heavens. At this point in her routine, her contributors would extend a painful smile and then briskly walk away.

But high-falootin' black folks didn't feel anything but embarrassment when she waddled up to them. When she approached well-to-do blacks, they would stiffen, look straight ahead, and pretend like she wasn't there, often muttering in anger as if her shabby presence was a disgrace to the race. Black folks were way too damn good at iggin' her, so she didn't waste her time trying to collect donations from them.

The woman had been doing quite well at this new restaurant she'd stumbled upon. The only problem was that management had chased her off, preventing her from posting up directly in front of their high-end establishment.

Pacing to keep warm, the woman stepped on the button that she'd discarded. She studied the button, and had half a mind to pick it up and put it in her pocket. She could sew it on her coat later. *Oh, the hell with that. I'll get me a couple of safety pins to keep this coat closed.* She kicked the worrisome button out of her sight. She glimpsed movement from the corner of her eye, and looked up. A couple had exited the restaurant. The woman was adjusting the scarf around her neck.

As hastily as she could, the shabby woman hot-footed toward the brightly lit restaurant.

It was difficult running with bad feet. *Oh, lawd. I done slipped up. Fuckin' with that button might have caused me to miss some money.*

She quickened her shuffling steps and then abruptly halted. She sucked her teeth in disgust when she realized that the well-dressed couple was black. *I'm having some fucked-up luck tonight. Them high-falutin' Negroes aint gon' give me the time of day.*

The affluent pair stood beneath the overhead light waiting for the valet to bring their car.

The haggard woman felt irrational loathing for the couple who were cuddled together. She viewed them as selfish people who'd never known one day of despair. Instead of slinking back into the shadows she took a moment to glare at them, her mouth turned down in disdain.

Look at 'em, all hugged up and happy. I guess the world must be their oyster. Black motherfuckers get on my nerves. Acting like they better than somebody. Noses all turned up in the air like they shit don't stink like everybody else's. I'm out here in this cold, holding God's Word in my hand, and they all snuggled together tryna pretend like they don't see me standing right here, patting my foot, and waiting for an offering for my ministry. They got a lot of nerve, tryna igg me. I can't stand fake-ass niggas!

The overhead lighting suddenly illuminated the well-heeled woman's face. The woman with the Bible let out a tiny sound of surprise. *I know her! Well, I'll be damned! I know that bitch!*

Eyes narrowed, she took a few tentative steps forward. Then

she moved quicker, closing in on the couple. *Management can try to run me off if they want to…they better kiss my ass. I got me a live one right there, and I'ma get me some goddamn money!*

❤ ❤ ❤

Waiting for their car, Harlow stood outside the restaurant, cuddling next to Drake. She noticed the woman's silhouette, and curiously lifted her head from Drake's shoulder.

A bedraggled woman came into view. "I'm collecting donations for my ministry. Any offerings are kindly appreciated," the scruffy woman said, wearing a smile that lacked warmth or sincerity.

"Oh, yeah?" Drake said, whipping his coat open as he reached inside his pants pocket. "What's the name of your church, ma'am?" Drake asked, making polite small talk.

"Well, it's my personal ministry. I'm an ordained minister, and I'm out here tryna get some funding to open a church."

"I see," Drake said absently as he peeled bills from a large wad.

Harlow gazed at the beggar woman as she stuffed Drake's money inside the pocket of her grungy coat. The woman had a horrible disfigurement on the left side of her face. But there was something oddly familiar about her. Nervously, Harlow shifted her eyes away.

Instead of moving on, the woman inched closer to Harlow, and said, "You look nice and cozy bundled up in all that nice mink." The woman's voice was filled with hostility.

It was on the tip of Harlow's tongue to inform the so-called minister that her coat was faux fur, but before she could get the words out, the woman spoke again. "Don't I know you?" The woman's voice was chilled, her words sounding like an accusation.

Harlow smiled uncertainly, and then shook her head. "No, I don't know you."

Through eyes filled with cunning and calculation, the woman squinted at Harlow, sizing her up from head to toe. "Yeah, I know you." She clenched her chin, pretending to try to place Harlow's face, and then she pointed an ash-encrusted finger at Harlow. "Hey, wait a minute. Ain't you Jody's child?"

Harlow gasped, but didn't reply. She couldn't. Hearing her mother's name...being tied to her past...constricted her throat and held her paralysed with cold, numbing terror. *Who is this woman? And what does she know about me?*

With great relief, Harlow saw the valet pull up with their black Mercedes. "Our car's here, Drake. Let's go." Harlow tugged on Drake's arm. She didn't know this frightening woman and certainly didn't want to know her.

"Your name's Harlow, ain't it?" The woman chortled. "Looks like you done pretty good for yourself." She paused. "All things considered."

With wide-eyed amazement, Harlow regarded the woman. A sick feeling filled her chest. She could feel the color draining from her face.

Noticing Harlow's look of distress, Drake's attention sharpened. "Hey, what's this about?" he asked the shabby vagrant.

The woman kept her attention focused on Harlow. "I'm Ronica," she stated proudly, twisting her disfigured face into a horrific facsimile of a smile. "Remember me?" Her wide grin displayed chipped and uneven, grayish-colored teeth.

As if seeing a ghost, Harlow reeled back in horror. *Oh, my God! This can't be happening.* Ronica had died in the fire, and the dead don't rise. But there Ronica was, about fifty pounds heavier, and wearing an ugly smirk as she looked Harlow in the eye. One side of her face was charred and thick with scar tissue, but it was Ronica, and she was very much alive.

Harlow suddenly had trouble finding words. She closed her eyes, wishing Ronica away.

"I know you ain't forget about me, did you, Harlow?" Ronica asked, easing forward, eyes narrowed into slits, shoulders hunched against the cold wind, one hand grasping the Bible, the other clutching together her buttonless coat.

Ronica had once been rather skinny. She was pudgy now and barely recognizable with her burned face.

"I said, I don't know you," Harlow snarled, turning her back. There was no law that forced her to have to admit to knowing someone from her terrible past. Pulling Drake along, Harlow took a few steps toward the waiting car.

Ronica hobbled closely behind Harlow, her damaged face twisted in contempt. "Oh, you don't know me now, huh? But I sure do know you." Ronica's eyes subtly shifted to Drake and back to Harlow. "And I remember your dead baby, too. I had to wrestle that thing out your arms…after you had that abortion. 'Member that? You was rocking and singing a lullaby to a corpse."

Harlow froze, momentarily paralyzed. She released her grasp on Drake's sleeve as her knees began to buckle. She managed to straighten up, and shakily progressed toward the car.

Waddling as quickly as the burned soles of her feet allowed, Ronica caught up to Harlow. She pinched the sleeve of Harlow's coat. "Don't run from the truth. I'm holding God's Word! Atone for your sins." With one charred hand, she maintained a grip on Harlow, and with the other she held up the Bible, raising it toward the dark and mournful sky. "I ask You to have mercy on this selfish and wicked girl, Dear Lord." Ronica swayed from side to side as if imbued with the spirit of the Holy Ghost.

Drake stepped forward. "Are you crazy? Take your hands off her."

Harlow tugged away from Ronica and hung onto Drake. "Get me out of here!" Her voice came in the high-pitched tone of a frightened child.

Drake put a protective arm around Harlow. "Take your hustle somewhere else," he hissed between clenched teeth.

But Ronica would not be deterred. "You got a lot of nerve, tryna snub me, Harlow. I'm the one that helped you while your momma was getting high inside her bedroom. I got rid of that dead baby for you." She paused, letting her words sink in as she eyed Harlow resentfully. "Yup, I sure did take care of that problem. And this is the thanks I get? If it hadn't been for me, you probably woulda been sittin' there rockin' that dead thing 'til it got funky and turned rotten."

Rattled by that horrific memory, Harlow grimaced and covered her mouth. She could feel the vibration of the scream that was trapped in her throat.

Satisfied with Harlow's reaction, Ronica grinned manically, and then shuffled off into the gloom of the night.

"Baby," Drake said. "Are you okay?" With concern in his eyes, he reached for Harlow and pulled her into his arms.

The sound that Harlow finally emitted was a low, guttural cry. She wrenched free from Drake, shoved him aside, and then broke into a full run.

CHAPTER 51

Impulsively, Harlow fled without a plan or any particular destination. Sprinting in heels on ice-encrusted pavement was absurd and challenging. Though she was slipping and sliding, her instincts told her to keep moving, to run from her sordid past. But it didn't take long for Drake to catch up with her. Crazed and irrational, she fought Drake like he was an attacker in the night. Snarling and growling like something wild, she kicked at him, swung her arms, and tried to claw him with her fingernails.

"Stop it, Harlow. What's wrong with you?" Having no choice, Drake jerked Harlow roughly, and then subdued her with a bear hug from behind. But Harlow still struggled, screaming like she was being viciously maimed.

Mouth stretched wide, she released ear-piercing screams that she'd bottled up inside for most of her life. "Let go of me!" she screamed in the way she'd wanted to scream when she was a little girl who was forced to keep her mouth shut while being violated.

"Harlow, it's gonna be alright. Calm down, baby," Drake cajoled.

"Don't touch me!" She struggled savagely, delivering back-kicks, and wielding blows with balled fists held over her head.

She screamed, releasing the rage that had been reduced to a squeaky whimper when Ronica took her baby away. She screamed and screamed against the betrayal of a mother who should have protected her but had instead rented out her tiny body like it was a seedy hotel room.

Taking notice of the tussling pair, motorists began slowing down. "People are looking at us, baby," Drake whispered in a calm tone.

"I don't care!" she shrieked, her face sculpted in fury. "Get the hell off of me! Leave me alone!" Her next scream was like a siren, loud and long, but Drake's steely embrace tightened.

He whispered directly in her ear. "You're gonna get me locked up tonight. If that's what you want, so be it, but I'm not letting you go."

Harlow's gut-wrenching screams began to soften into inconsolable sobs. Depleted, her body sagged, and then she collapsed to her knees. Holding her tight, Drake dropped with her, his body cushioning her fall.

On the cold concrete, Drake cradled Harlow. "Baby, what's this all about? Who was that woman?"

"She was…" Harlow didn't finish the sentence. She sniffled and wiped tears from her face. "My life was so fucked up, Drake. Horrible things happened to me," she said weakly.

"Did you get hurt when you were in foster care?"

"No," she said in squeaky whimper. Of course Drake would assume that anything awful that happened to her would have been done while in the custody of virtual strangers. But that wasn't the case. An image of Jody formed in her mind and tears streamed down her face.

"Baby, come on. Get up. We can talk about this in the hotel." Drake moved her out of his arms and stood. He reached for her hand, and pulled her to her feet.

"We're gonna get through this. I'm your man, Harlow. I love you and I'm going to protect you." His face became hard. "Nobody's ever gonna hurt you again."

Harlow was grateful for his pledge of devotion, but she wondered if Drake could live up to his promise once he knew the whole story. It didn't matter anymore. The weight of her dark secret was too heavy to carry any longer. It was time to release it, and let the chips fall where they may.

❤ ❤ ❤

Drake was careful not to bombard Harlow with questions. They both removed their soiled, and in Drake's case, torn clothing, without conversation.

When Harlow came out of the shower, there was a pot of tea waiting in the sitting room. Barefoot and dressed in a T-shirt and jeans, Drake appeared comfortable and relaxed with his laptop in front of him. "I ordered tea for you. Thought you might want something soothing." He raised his glass. "I'm warming up with bourbon." His mouth smiled, but his eyes were sad.

"Thanks," Harlow said, turning her back as she poured tea. With her back to Drake, she took sips and slowly gathered her thoughts.

After a few minutes, she felt brave enough to confess. She set the cup down and perched herself on the ottoman facing Drake. He closed the laptop and placed it on a table, his eyes studying her face.

Instead of pushing away the dreadful recollections, Harlow allowed the memories to take shape and form. "To support her drug habit, my mother let her dealer violate me." Her words came out tentative and shaky. "It all started when I was only about four years old." She took a shuddering breath. Drake closed his hand lovingly around hers, and then the story that she'd never uttered to another living soul began spilling from her lips.

Throughout the telling, she noticed Drake flinching and

cringing, his free hand tightening into a fist, but Harlow ignored his reactions. Pressing onward, she gave uncensored details of the horror story that was her childhood.

"Damn," he murmured when Harlow concluded, revealing that she'd secretly purchased a headstone for her mother's grave and had made a clandestine visit to the cemetery. "You didn't have to go through that alone."

"I should have told you about my miserable childhood a long time ago, but I didn't want you to look at me like I was damaged goods."

"I would have understood. None of that was your—"

She gestured for him to let her finish. "I couldn't change my past, and so I mastered the ability to present myself as a self-assured person. I'm such a fraud," she said bitterly. "Inside, I feel tainted and worthless."

Drake groaned, but he didn't interrupt.

"I kept telling myself that with you I could finally let go of the past. Get married; have the family I never had. But I was wrong to think I could erase the past."

"I heard you out. Now it's my turn to speak. First of all, I love you. More than anything. Secondly, you're not a fraud, and pretending that you were okay was a coping mechanism. You didn't have any other tools to work with. You've kept these secrets long enough; now it's time to seek help from a professional."

"I know," she said in choked voice.

"I'm right here with, Harlow. I'm not going anywhere."

CHAPTER 52

On New Year's Day, Vangie went to her mom's apartment for dinner. Her mom and her new boyfriend, Mr. Harold, had already eaten and were watching football. They both were wearing Eagles jerseys. Mr. Harold was stretching the hell out of his jersey. His gut looked like he'd swallowed a watermelon.

Her mother was sitting on the edge of the couch as if she really cared what the Eagles were doing. Vangie knew that her mother had no interest in sports; she was fronting for Mr. Harold.

"Make yourself a plate, baby," her mother said, sounding distracted. "There's plenty of food left. Cabbage, black-eyed peas, ham hocks, cornbread—"

"Touchdown!" Mr. Harold shouted, cutting her mother off. Her mother joined, whooping and hollering like she gave a damn.

Being a third wheel at her mom's house was the pits. Vangie lost her appetite. "I didn't plan on staying," Vangie said when the noise level decreased in the living room. "Yuri is with Shawn, so I'm gonna fix my plate to go," Vangie called from the kitchen.

"That's nice," her mother responded, disinterested.

Vangie filled plastic containers with enough food to feed her and Yuri for several days. "See you later, Mom," she said as she headed for the door.

Sitting up under Mr. Harold and grinning like a lovestruck teenager, her mother waved goodbye.

❤ ❤ ❤

Denise Westcott wouldn't have dreamed of serving southern-oriented food on New Year's Day. Her version of a good luck meal was lobster tails, stuffed mushrooms, soft shell crabs, angel hair pasta with shrimp scampi, broccoli and cheddar quiche, arugula salad with vinaigrette, and twelve-grain dinner rolls.

There was tension at the Westcotts' dining table, and no one knew the cause except Nivea and Knox.

"Most black people eat black-eyed peas and chitterlings for New Year's dinner," Nivea remarked with an edge as she observed the seafood spread that her mother set out.

"We're not most black people and I thank God for that," Denise Westcott retorted. "We can afford the best, so why would I serve my family pig intestines or any other type of slave food?"

"It's tradition. A way for African-Americans to stay in touch with our roots," Nivea said sullenly.

"We don't need reminders of that that tragic chapter in American history."

"Now, now," Mr. Westcott intervened. "It's time to raise our glasses in a toast to a healthy and prosperous New Year."

Nivea ignored her father and turned hard eyes on her mother. "Don't you ever get tired of the burden of being the black bourgeoisie?"

"I don't make any apologies for being well off. Nothing was handed to your father and me. We earned—"

"Yes, I've heard that spiel a thousand times. With your high standards, it surprises me that you don't have higher expectations for your youngest child? How do you account for her lack of education, ambition, and drive?"

"Me!" Courtney shot a bewildered look at Nivea. "What are

you talking about? I'm marrying a doctor," Courtney said in defense.

"Right. You're *marrying* a doctor." Nivea took her focus off Courtney and gave Knox a fierce stare.

"Are you okay, Nivea?" her father inquired.

"I'm fine. Let's toast to prosperity." Smiling contemptuously, Nivea raised her goblet.

Courtney noticed Nivea's hand. "Hey, where's your ring?"

"Took it off."

"Why?" Courtney asked, looking at her parents questioningly.

Nivea set her goblet down. "I called off my wedding. I don't want to talk about it."

Mrs. Westcott stared at her daughter with disapproval.

"I'm sure you had very good reasons," Mr. Westcott ventured to say.

"OMG! I'm going to be married first," Courtney said excitedly. "I mean, seriously…OMG! You'll be my spinster sister." Courtney covered her mouth to stifle giggles.

Nivea glared at Knox, blaming him for her predicament and for the insult from Courtney. Being made fun of by her younger sister was the height of humiliation.

Brows arched and spreading his hands in a gesture of bafflement, Knox looked at Mr. and Mrs. Westcott.

Knox's phoney display of innocence had Nivea seething. She picked up her goblet and splashed red wine in Knox's smug face.

"Why'd you do that?" Courtney shouted. Cloth napkins in hand, she rushed to her fiancé's rescue and anxiously dabbed his face and blotted wine from his shirt.

"What on earth is wrong with you?" Mrs. Westcott demanded. "That kind of behavior is not tolerated in this household. I'm afraid I'm going to have to ask you—"

Feeling satisfied, Nivea grabbed her purse. "Save your breath, Mother. I'm leaving."

❤ ❤ ❤

Nine o'clock that night, Vangie unleashed all her rage on Shawn when he brought Yuri home.

"Hi, Mommy!" Yuri said happily. "It was so fun at Daddy's."

"Get ready for bed, Yuri," Vangie said firmly. Yuri didn't give her any back talk. He could tell that she meant business.

She turned her attention to Shawn. "You have a lot of nerve, bringing him home this late at night. It's way past his bedtime."

Shawn rolled his eyes toward the ceiling. "Stop acting childish. You just want to start some shit." Shaking his head, he reached in his pocket and pulled out some money. "This is for the day care."

Vangie counted the money and turned up her nose. "Oh, it's like that, now?"

"Like what?"

"Being a cheapskate now that you've you moved on." She made air quotes when she said, moved on.

Shawn sighed. "What's the problem?"

"You're not going to be handing me random amounts of money when the mood hits you. You're making a killing at the shop. I need regular child support that I can count on."

"How much do you want?"

"Four hundred a week."

"That's bullshit. I don't make that kind of money."

"Whatever," she said nonchalantly while holding the door open.

Shawn paused in the doorway. "We don't have to be enemies."

She made a cackling sound of laughter. "We damn sure can't be friends."

CHAPTER 53

Early in the morning, Nivea's cell pinged. **Sorry about yesterday. Can I make it up?** The text message from Knox ended with a sad face.

Fuck no! Propped up in bed, Nivea's fingers were poised to respond with a scathing message. Then the doorbell rang. It dinged and donged over and over with urgency. *Knox!*

It occurred to her to call the police and report that Knox was stalking her, but Nivea didn't pick up the phone. She hurried inside her bathroom and washed her face and rinsed her morning mouth with a capful of Scope. She told herself she wanted to look presentable when she slapped Knox's face and cursed him out.

She pulled the door open. Looking contrite, Knox was holding a steaming cup of Starbucks and a bag of croissants. "I thought you might want to wake up to your favorite coffee."

Nivea took the coffee, but sucked her teeth to express her disdain.

"Look, I know you're pissed with me—"

"You're beneath contempt," she snarled.

"You're right. My behavior wasn't very noble."

"You didn't open your mouth in my defense."

"I know," he said regretfully. "I hated the way your mom was talking to you. It took all my willpower not to leave right behind you yesterday."

"Why didn't you, punk ass?" she spat.

He shrugged helplessly. "For appearances, I guess. I had to take Courtney's feelings into account."

"Courtney will survive; she has my parents to wipe her tears. I'm the victim here, Knox. You're fucking me and planning a wedding with my sister!"

"I have to be cautious with Courtney's emotions; she's very sensitive."

"Bullshit! She's a spoiled brat."

"I have to let her down gently."

"How gently? While you're bullshitting, my mother and Courtney are planning a wedding."

"It's not Courtney's fault that I fell in love with you."

Nivea's lips were parted in preparation of firing off a round of stinging insults but she instantly clamped her mouth shut. Feeling herself turning to mush, she thought, *Aw, he loves me.*

"I'm not going to marry Courtney. You know that. I can understand your being upset with your mother, but don't take it out on me. I told you that I'm going to break off my engagement with your sister, but I have to do it in the least painful way."

"Any way you do it is going to be painful, but she'll get over it."

"This situation I'm in is driving me nuts. Can we please drop the subject for now?"

Nivea sighed. She walked over to the sofa, sat down and began taking careful sips of the hot coffee. Knox ambled over with the bag of croissants. He sat next to Nivea and took a croissant out of the bag. Holding it between his thumb and index finger, he guided the pastry to Nivea's mouth. "Take a bite."

As if helpless to deny him, she opened her mouth. Knox eased the soft dough between her lips, sliding it in and out of her mouth. "Show me how you suck a dick." His voice was coarse.

Spontaneous, Nivea sucked the warm pastry until it was soggy. Knox quickly retrieved another. "Lie down, Niv." As if under his freaky spell, Nivea reclined. He eased her knees apart. "Open that pussy up for me."

Nivea doubted if she'd get a good fuck from a damn pastry, but she stretched her pussy open until it was gaping, determined to do whatever it took to stop her sister's wedding.

❤ ❤ ❤

Vangie called in sick at her job. After dropping Yuri off at school, she pointed her car toward the expressway. Vangie mentally prepared herself to have to wait in long lines at Family Court, but getting back at Shawn would be worth a wait.

Now that he was working in a barbershop and no longer cutting hair in his mom's basement, she had proof that he was earning an income. It was time to hit him up for all the back money he owed her. He was making a nice living now, but he spent it as fast as he made it. It wasn't likely that Shawn had access to all the thousands of dollars that he owed in arrearages.

Vangie was not usually a vindictive person, but Shawn deserved to be punished for wasting her time and playing her. He knew the whole time that they were playing house that Vangie expected him to put a ring on her finger. She smiled a malicious smile. *I'm going to be laughing my ass off when they handcuff that slime ball and lock his ass up for back child support!*

"How long will it take for him to get served with these papers?" Vangie asked the clerk.

"Not long," the hard-faced woman answered without bothering to look up.

❤ ❤ ❤

A week later, Shawn was bellowing into the phone. "What's this shit?"

He got the papers! Yes! Vangie pumped her fist and did a quick little dance, and then calmly said, "It's time to pay up all that back child support."

"What about everything I've been doing lately? All the money I've been giving you? Doesn't that matter?"

"Too little, too late. See you in court, Shawn." She hung up. Shawn called right back.

"Go 'head and play your little girl games. I just want to remind you that I'm picking Yuri up Friday night, so have him ready, please."

"Nah, I don't think so."

"Whatchu mean?"

"Yuri needs to spend some time with his grandmother. I guess you can see him next weekend."

"You don't run shit, Vangie. Yuri's my son, too."

"All of a sudden, he's your son, too. But couldn't anybody find your ass when he was a baby. You didn't want to be bothered when he was wearing diapers and going through the potty training phase. I had to deal with Yuri on my own for five long years."

"I'm tired of you throwing that up in my face, Vangie." Shawn blew out a hard breath. "You know what...fuck it. I'm not gon' let you put me through this. I'm getting a lawyer."

"What the hell do you think a lawyer can do for you? Can a lawyer make those thousands of dollars in arrearages disappear?"

"No, but a lawyer can make sure I have joint custody. I'm not going to keep listening to your mouth...and I'm not going to kiss your ass in order to see my son."

"Whatever," she said blithely. "See you in court, Shawn." Vangie had a satisfied smile on her face when she hung up.

Yuri walked into the living room, looking worried. "Were you talking to my daddy?"

"Stop being so nosey, Yuri."

"I heard you cussing, and then I heard you say my daddy's name. I know you were talking to him."

"And…"

"Is he picking me up this weekend?"

"No, he's not."

"Aw, man. Why not?" Yuri's whined annoyingly.

"I have made plans for us."

Yuri frowned excessively. "I want to be with my daddy at the barbershop."

"Well, get over it. Missing one visit with your father isn't the end of the world."

"I don't want to be stuck with you this weekend!" Yuri said defiantly.

"We'll have fun, Yuri."

"Doing what?"

Vangie shrugged. "I'll think of something."

"I have fun when my daddy takes me with him to Miss Eva's house. Miss Eva has two puppies, and—"

"Do you mean to tell me your father has been taking you over that bitch's house?"

Looking both startled and guilty, Yuri shrugged.

"Oh, that's the end of your weekend visits. I'll be damned if Shawn is going to drag you around while he's chasing ass."

Yuri looked afraid; tears began to fill his eyes. It wasn't often that he heard his mother use foul language.

"That's it!" Vangie waved her hand with finality. "You won't be spending another damn weekend with Shawn. You can cry all you want to, Yuri. I don't care. I'm not letting your father expose you to every stank ho that crosses his path."

Yuri stubbornly folded his arms. He gave his mother a hateful long stare. "You piss me off!"

Vangie leapt from the sofa. "Boy, are you crazy, talking to me like that? Do you want me to spank that butt?"

"It's illegal to spank kids! I'm telling my daddy if you hit me."

"Tell your daddy!" Vangie yelled as she grabbed Yuri by the arm, smacking his backside with the palm of her hand.

CHAPTER 54

Grumpily, Vangie emptied her purse of metal objects and deposited the items in the requisite plastic bin. Then she tossed her purse in another bin. Ironically, Vangie and Shawn's court date was on Valentine's Day, but instead of opening gifts, she was opening her coat and sliding it off, putting it through the metal detector. Ugh! All this searching was such a violation.

Vangie rolled her eyes when Shawn strolled inside the courtroom with his attorney at his side. Instead of looking sheepish like he should have, Shawn wore a smug expression, like *he* was the one seeking justice. His attorney was a woman! An experienced-looking, hard-as-nails, Hispanic attorney. Vangie sent the female attorney a hateful glare. That heifa should have been ashamed of herself for representing a deadbeat dad. But Shawn's lawyer didn't seem to be the least bit ashamed. She appeared feisty and aggressive, like she was ready to rumble.

It hadn't occurred to Vangie to obtain legal representation. Hell, the petitioner in a child support case didn't need a lawyer, did she? She looked around the courtroom nervously. Fuck it. She was her own mouthpiece, and she had a lot to say. Additionally, there was a ton of court documentation to back up her claims.

When a black female judge entered the courtroom, Vangie relaxed. *Shawn's ass is going down!*

Vangie and Shawn stood in front of the judge, and Vangie

hardly got an opportunity to talk about Shawn being wilfully in contempt of his child support order before his pit bull of an attorney said something about a Motion to Modify and started waving a document around.

"He can't modify the money he owes me," Vangie blurted, knowing nothing about legal terminology. "He owes me five years of back—" The judge banged her gavel, shutting Vangie's tirade down.

Shawn's attorney continued calmly, "My client is fully prepared to pay the back support, but he'd like to modify his future payments."

The female pit bull presented the judge with some paperwork, which the judge looked over with a pair of glasses perched on the end of her nose.

"And the change of circumstances is?" the judge asked the pit bull.

"My client has his son in his custody every weekend."

"Is that true, Ms. Samuels?"

"Well, yeah," Vangie said hesitantly. "He usually picks our son up on Friday and takes him to school on Monday morning, but—"

"Fine," the judge said, cutting Vangie off for the second time. "You two need to think about your son's well-being and work this out. Get the joint custody papers in order," the judge said in a scolding tone. Then she sent Vangie a particularly scathing look and said, "A mother should work along with a father who wants to participate in his son's life."

Why's she acting like I'm the criminal here? Vangie wondered.

"After you work out the custody arrangements, I want to see proof of income from both parents, as well as tax statements for the past two years," the judge said, postponing the case.

Shawn had gotten a reprieve, but once the judge saw evidence of Vangie's paltry little salary, Shawn's trifling butt was going to have to hand over a huge lump sum of money…or go straight to jail!

Not wanting to seem like an unreasonable, angry black woman and desiring to get on the judge's good side, Vangie rode the elevator to another section of the Family Court building and grudgingly signed papers that allowed Shawn joint custody of Yuri. The custody order stipulated that Shawn was to pick Yuri up at six o'clock Friday evening and return him to his elementary school at eight-fifteen on Monday morning.

Outside the courthouse, it was biting cold and the hawk was out. The wind was so strong, it was rattling stops signs and blowing off hats.

Still, outdoor flower vendors were set up and racking up sales. In this cold and punishing weather, men stood in long lines to purchase a bouquet for their sweethearts. Vangie felt the sting of envy and averted her gaze, hunching up her shoulders as she hustled off to her car. She wondered what Shawn was getting his new girlfriend? Most likely, Miss Eva would be getting a pair of hooker heels and a very large bag from Victoria's Secret.

* * *

After a month of therapy, Harlow and her psychiatrist had only scratched the surface, but Harlow left her therapist's Eighth Avenue office with a great sense of accomplishment. Before getting treatment, she'd tried to suppress the painful memories. Now that she had finally begun to face her demons, she realized that there was no quick fix and no convenient pill that would instantly heal her emotional scars. She expected to be in therapy for several years. And that was okay with her.

When she exited the building, Drake was waiting outside. Drake was pure magnificence wearing a black cashmere coat, suit and tie, and dark shades. He was leaning against one of his cars—a Bentley—and holding an extra large bouquet of roses. "Happy Valentine's Day," he greeted.

"Oh, Drake, what a nice surprise. I don't have your gift with me; it's at the apartment."

"You're the only gift I need," he replied, giving her a quick kiss and then handing her the bouquet.

"Thanks, honey," she said as he opened the door for her. Living in New York with Drake was better than ever. Drake had been giving Alphonso more responsibility than usual so that he and Harlow could lead a more settled lifestyle.

"Did the session go okay?" Drake inquired, though he wasn't prying.

"Yes, but healing is a slow process."

Drake nodded.

"I like Dr. Thomas," Harlow went on, her tone upbeat. "I'm really comfortable with him."

"Really glad to hear that, baby." Drake's expression turned to serious as he merged into the aggressive New York City traffic. When he stopped at a traffic light, he retrieved a Tiffany's box from his pocket. The box was tied with a single white ribbon. "Hope you like it."

Inside the box was a cushion-cut pink sapphire ring, set in platinum. There was a paving of smaller pink sapphires extending halfway around the band.

"It's beautiful, Drake. And I love pink! You have incredible taste," Harlow said, sliding the ring out of the box and holding it up admiringly.

"I did my research," Drake told her. "At one time pink sapphires were rare. Sapphires come in the palest yellow to the deepest green, but pink is considered a romantic color used to demonstrate love." He smiled and shrugged. "And I love you. So, I'm asking you for the second time, will you marry me?"

"Of course, I will," Harlow exclaimed.

Car horns honked behind them, but Drake ignored the irritated drivers. He took the ring from the velvet case and slid it on Harlow's finger.

❤ ❤ ❤

Nivea ripped open the red shiny package and then gawked at the black leather strap with a white ball situated in the center. "What the hell is this?"

Knox grinned. "It's a gag ball. But the ball isn't rubber; it's a candy jawbreaker."

Nivea gave him a look of loathing. "You asked me to rush over here during the middle of my work day for this shit? Is this your idea of a Valentine's present... a goddamn candy gag ball?"

Knox lifted it out of the black box. "Sweets for my sweet," he teased. "It's one of my fantasies. You promised you'd be my fantasy valentine."

"Yeah, I thought we'd get into something kinky after dinner and drinks at a nice restaurant."

"Not tonight. Maybe tomorrow."

"Why not tonight?"

"You know...Courtney expects me to spend Valentine's Day with her."

"And what did you get Courtney, a set of fluffy handcuffs?"

Knox bent over laughing as if Nivea's words were hilarious. "No, I got her something romantic. Your sister's into traditional romance. She doesn't get me. She's not a freak like you."

"And that's the problem, Knox. I don't want to remain your

freak in the sheets. Every time we get together, it's another smash and dash situation. You keep telling me that you're going to tell Courtney that it's over; meanwhile, she's busy picking out her wedding gown. When are you going to tell her? I don't want to see my sister publicly humiliated on the day of her wedding. You need to tell Courtney before she racks up more unnecessary expenses!"

"I know. I'm going to tell her. After dinner, tonight."

Finally! Nivea breathed a sigh of relief. Knox slipped over to the closet and pulled out another gift-wrapped package. Nivea beamed as she tore off the paper, then her smile vanished. "Fluffy handcuffs," she said, her nose turned up in disdain. "What kind of bullshit gifts are these?"

"Damn, I love it when you get mad. Get naked, baby. This is going to be so much fun. You trust me, don't you?"

"I guess," she mumbled. "I thought you'd at least have a romantic lunch waiting for me."

"Are you serious? You're not even the romantic type and you know it."

Nivea didn't know what to say. She wasn't all that romantic, but still…

"Knox, I'm supposed to be working. Why can't we play this game later tonight?"

"I'll be with Courtney tonight."

"We can get together after you have dinner with my sister. I'm sure you'll want to be with me after you go through that emotional scene with her."

"Probably. We'll see." He gave Nivea a leering look. "Strip out of that business suit. I wanna suck on those big, luscious titties."

Nivea felt a warm rush between her legs. Her pussy had betrayed her yet again. She began flinging clothes off her body. And in a matter of minutes, Nivea was naked with a candy gag ball in her mouth, hands cuffed behind her back.

In that position of total surrender, Knox sucked her breast while Nivea, revved up with passion, sucked hard on the candy ball. When he lowered himself to the floor and began to feast on her legs, Nivea came so hard and with such wild abandon, she thought she might have broken a tooth when she began biting and gnawing on the jawbreaker that was inserted into her mouth.

CHAPTER 55

Inside the bridal shop, Nivea sat on the settee next to her mother. "What do you think?" her mother asked.

"I don't like it," Nivea mumbled. She was feeling dazed after watching Courtney twirl about in one frightful bridal gown after another.

"She's tried on three gowns. Can you be more specific?" Mrs. Westcott said snippily.

"I don't like any of them. They're all tacky. And her wedding concept is juvenile and tasteless."

Mrs. Westcott looked defeated. "You're right, Nivea. Your sister has gone from that outrageous beach theme to this ridiculous princess theme. Don't young people believe in traditional weddings anymore?"

Nivea shrugged indifferently. *There's not going to be a wedding, so don't worry about it!* Nivea wanted to say, but restrained herself. "She's calling it a fairy tale wedding, not princess," Nivea corrected with a smirk.

"Try to talk to your sister; give her some advice."

"Courtney doesn't listen to me," Nivea said. "You raised her to be a brat; now you have to deal with it."

"Now is not the time for, I told you so. Our family is going to be a public disgrace if Courtney insists upon this ridiculous, princess wedding."

Courtney came twirling out of the dressing room, looking like a black Cinderella in her off-shoulder, silver renaissance dress. "Do I look like a princess?"

You look like a retard! "Yes, you're breathtaking," Nivea said, looking down at a text message from Knox: Tonight is the night.

Courtney spun around again, and squealed in delight. "I want this one, Mother. Knox is going to love it!"

Don't bet on it! Knox didn't want to ruin your Valentine's Day dinner, but he's gonna make a bombshell announcement tonight!

❤ ❤ ❤

Back in court, Vangie sent Shawn and his attorney a confident look. She had all her records together. It was judgment day for Shawn, and Vangie was eager to see him getting handcuffed. His latest ho would undoubtedly come up with some bail money for him, but it would give Vangie a spark of joy to see him being carted off to jail.

While Shawn's attorney talked legal gibberish, Vangie sat back relaxed, waiting for the judge to order him to pay up now! Vangie's ears perked up when she heard the pit bull saying something about her client was the custodial parent.

Vangie waved her hand vigorously.

"You'll get an opportunity to speak, Ms. Presswood," the judge said to Vangie.

"Mr. Davis has his son from Friday until Monday and therefore is eligible for child support."

"Eligible for what!" Vangie shouted. She forgot about waiting for her turn to speak.

"The papers in front of me indicate that you and Mr. Davis share joint custody of the minor child. Is this true?" the judge asked Vangie.

"Yes, but I'm the custodial parent."

"Does Mr. Davis have the child from Friday until Monday?"

"Yes, but…"

"Mr. Davis is looking for work, your honor. But until he has steady employment, he's going to need support from the petitioner."

Vangie gasped. "Your honor…this is ridiculous. He owes me money from five years ago. How in the world can you listen to this woman talking about I should be paying *him* child support? I can barely make ends meet—"

"If the child is in your custody for only three days out of the week, it is only fair that Mr. Davis is compensated."

"I'm the one who wakes up with our son every morning, and gets him ready for school. I'm the one who has to wash his clothes, make sure his homework is done, and I'm the one who prepares all his meals. I have to take time off from work for his doctor's appointments…me! Not his part-time, videogame playing, take him to the movies every once in a while, father!" Vangie shouted, outraged.

"Sorry, Ms. Presswood, you tell a compelling story, but I have to rule in the favor of the respondent." The judge banged her gavel.

Shawn hugged his attorney. In a state of shock, Vangie sat without moving.

Tears fell from her eyes throughout the drive home. *A man isn't supposed to get child support. Oh, dear God, how can they let him do this to me?*

CHAPTER 56

Knox swallowed two aspirin. "My head is killing me. I feel horrible for what I did to Courtney."

Nivea could see the hurt in his eyes. Though personally elated that Knox had finally dumped her pesky sister, Nivea was compelled to show some human compassion. "Breaking up with someone is never easy." *Yay for pussy power!* Who could blame Knox for wanting to be with her instead of her dolt of a sister? According to Knox, Courtney thought that doggy style was being kinky. *Dumb bitch!*

"Courtney was outraged," Knox went on, his expression incredulous. "She pulled a knife on me—tried to stab me. I had to wrestle with her to get the weapon out of her hands!"

"Whaaat!" Nivea was stunned. "That doesn't sound like Courtney at all."

"Would I make something like that up?" Knox's tone was reproachful.

"No, you wouldn't," Nivea said carefully. "I'm just saying, that kind of behavior from Courtney…it's really surprising."

Knox sat on the edge of Nivea's bed, holding his head with his hand. "She kept crying about her perfect wedding dress. God, this is so awful. I don't know how I'm going to live it down. Your parents are going to hate me."

"Honey, don't worry; I'll put in for a job transfer. We can move away together…to the West Coast or somewhere."

"That's not going to work for me. I'm supposed to set up practice in this area. My family's church is supposed to pitch in, and now I've scandalized the church." Anguished, he dropped his head, shaking it as though he'd made a terrible mistake.

"I know the church is planning to contribute financially, but I'll think of a way to get your practice started. I'm in the medical field, you know," Nivea said proudly as she rubbed Knox's smooth face.

He pulled away from her touch. "You sell pharmaceuticals; you're not a physician," Knox said sullenly.

Ow! "I was only tyring to help."

Knox grimaced as if hit by a strong stomach pain. "That aspirin you gave me is making me sick to my stomach."

Fed up with Knox's griping and whining, Nivea said firmly, "What's done is done. You can't beat yourself up forever. Put this behind you so we can move forward. Please!" she said with much aggravation. "Now, I realize that it would be tacky to broadcast our relationship, and so for Courtney's sake, I think it best if we keep our affair a secret for a while."

"You're right," he agreed, seemingly relieved that Nivea had taken charge of the sordid mess they were in.

Damn, I really won! I've finally come out on top, Nivea congratulated herself. Feeling self-satisfied, she slipped over to the dresser and secretly turned off her cell and then sneakily unplugged the house phone. She didn't want to hear her mother's hysteria tonight. She'd listen and make the appropriate sounds of regret tomorrow. Right now she had to comfort her man and work out her own wedding plans. She wanted a big wedding, but that wouldn't be possible with all the controversy surrounding her nuptials. *I refuse to have a tacky Vegas wedding. I'll figure something out.*

Nivea kissed Knox, lightly. He hugged her tight, whispering, "I took a leap of faith. I'm putting my trust in you. Don't hurt me, baby."

She was touched by his willingness to be vulnerable. "Oh, Knox. I'd never hurt you. I love you. I'm going to be a good wife. You'll see." He pressed his face against her bosom, tears rolling down his face. "Knox! Baby, it's gonna be alright. I swear. You won't regret your decision. I'm the right woman for you. You made a wise choice," Nivea said.

"I hope so," he uttered.

"Have some faith in me, Knox."

"I want to. I feel like shit, ruining Courtney's life."

"Shh. Take your mind off Courtney. Think about me."

Overcome with emotion, Knox wept openly. Feeling almost maternal, Nivea soothed him with loving kisses, and gentle caresses.

Feeling like the dominant partner, she undressed the sobbing Knox, delivering kisses to his smooth naked body, trying to calm him. She fondled his balls and stroked his dick, but it remained soft and Knox continued to sob, distraught.

Oh, my God. I don't know what to do.

"Talk to me, Knox. I'm here for you. Tell what I can do to make it better."

He began moving his lips, but no sounds emerged. "Knox!"

Shaking his head, he bit down on his lips, mumbling in-coherently.

Taking matters in her hands, Nivea pulled off her panties. She propped Knox's head up with a pillow and straddled his face. "Is this what you want?" She positioned her pussy over his face, thighs clamping his ears. "Tell me what you want, and I'll—"

He didn't answer. He didn't have to. He cut off Nivea's words with a frantic kiss to the lips of her pussy. His tongue darted and played against her clit. Separating her satiny folds, his tongue plunged into her thickened honey. Knox feasted between her legs, lapping the outpouring of moisture, his tongue rolling in slow undulating waves, provoking Nivea to frenzied jerks of passion.

"That was fantastic," Knox said, sitting up, wiping his lips with the back of his hand.

"I know. You make me cum harder than any man I've ever been with." She kissed him again, and stared at his face. "I'm so happy, Knox."

"I'm happy, too."

"I like it when you sleep nude. I may want something else later on tonight," she teased, caressing his girth that had awakened.

"I can't stay tonight. I have to go." He sat up and began searching under the covers for his underwear.

"Why can't you stay?"

"I have to get some rest. You know Courtney's moving into my apartment early tomorrow morning."

Her ears had to be deceiving her. All she could do was grimace and hold up her hands questioningly.

"Courtney's sick of living with your parents. She's moving in."

"B-but you broke up with Courtney." Nivea's voice was weak and tearful.

Knox looked at Nivea as if she'd sprouted another head. "You can't be serious. I thought we were role-playing. All these months, you've been telling me that you love the way I keeping coming up with fantasises; you said you enjoy the way I can come up with a variety of scenarios." Squinting at Nivea, Knox shook his head.

"You're joking! You gotta be fucking kidding me!" Nivea watched in shock as Knox quickly dressed. Hysteria rising, she grabbed the first thing she saw...the bedside lamp. It was a beautiful piece with a crystal base, and though she hated to damage it, she needed to use it as a weapon. Holding the lamp by its neck, she swung it like she was wielding a baseball bat, aiming for Knox's head. He ducked and was struck on his back, but the blow wasn't as severe as Nivea intended.

Knox gave her a hard shove, knocking her across the room. "Hold up, Nivea. I'm not sure what we're doing. Do you want me to get rough with you? Is this one of your fantasies?"

Nivea clutched her stomach; tears ran down her face. "I'm about to vomit. I swear to God, I'm about to throw up. I can't believe I let you play me again, motherfucker. "

Knox raced to the safety of the doorway. "I'll call you in a couple days to see if you're feeling better, okay? Better yet, call me when you're back in the mood for something freaky."

"Get out, you sick bastard! I hate you!" Nivea screamed.

❤ ❤ ❤

Vangie went to the post office to pick up a registered letter. Registered letters never contain good news, so she braced herself as she accepted the envelope from the postal clerk. With trembling hands, she tore open the envelope and the words she read made her eyes burn. A total of two hundred and sixty-five dollars would be coming out of her biweekly paychecks.

That's over five hundred a month. What the fuck! The system is fucked up, anytime they help a no-good man screw over a hardworking mother. How can something like this be happening to me? Tears of anger streamed down Vangie's face as she drove to pick Yuri up from the after-school childcare. She wiped her tears and held it together until she and Yuri were back in the car.

"Strap up your seat belt," Vangie said in a tearful voice.

"What's wrong, Mommy?"

"Your father is trying to rob me."

"Why? My daddy has a lot of money."

"I know. But he gets it under the table."

"His money's not under the table; it's in his pocket," Yuri said innocently.

Infuriated, Vangie pulled out her cell and called Shawn. "I hope you're happy, you lying bastard. You should be ashamed of yourself, motherfucker! Stealing the little bit of money I make. How am I supposed to keep a roof over your son's head?"

"Mommy!" Yuri yelled from the backseat.

"Shut up, Yuri!" Vangie shouted.

"Cussing and carrying on in front of my son is not cool," Shawn said.

"Fuck you!"

"Don't make me haul you back into court for full custody."

"You and your scheming attorney are trying to ruin my life! I fucking hate you!" she screamed at the top of her lungs.

"Naw, you don't hate me…you hate yourself because your scheming backfired. I take care of my son. Yeah, I owe you back money, and in time you would have gotten it. You know that. But you wanted revenge…how do you like the taste?"

"You're not going to get away with this shit, Shawn. You're wrong and you know it."

"Whatever, man." Shawn hung up on Vangie.

Sniffling sounds from the backseat drew Vangie's attention. "What's wrong with you, Yuri?" she asked irritably.

"I don't like it when you cuss at my daddy."

"Your father is stealing my hard-earned money and you're shedding tears over him?"

Yuri cried louder.

Oh, dear God, what am I going to do? Feeling like the entire world was against her, Vangie put the car into drive and pulled out of the parking spot.

CHAPTER 57

Summer

The Lowery Castle was a beautiful venue that sat majestically above a tree-lined drive, surrounded by acres of lush green lawns, and meandering streams. The picturesque grounds, along with glorious blue sky and sunshine were the perfect backdrop for an outdoor ceremony. Every aspect of the wedding was planned and executed in detail. From the Rolls Royce Phantom the couple arrived in, to the hundreds of beautiful floral arrangements, the three-course meal of steak and chicken, the four-tier wedding cake, dessert station, and the premier wedding photographer.

Courtney and Knox's big day was set to be a platinum affair by anyone's standards.

Denise Westcott sat in the front row, beaming with pride. She had to bribe Courtney with the promise of a down payment on her dream home to persuade her to drop the tacky fairy tale theme and embrace a traditional wedding. House or no house, Courtney would not give up her castle. Acknowledging the beauty and splendor of the venue, Mrs. Westcott approved wholeheartedly.

Amidst four other bridesmaids, the groomsmen, and the groom, Nivea stood seething. She cut an eye at Knox, trying to silently inform him that there was still time to back out of this horrible charade.

But Knox stared straight ahead, deliberately ignoring her as he smiled at the lovely little flower girl who approached, purposefully tossing petals from a basket.

"I hate you." She mouthed the words at Knox, but his eyes were focused on Courtney, who had entered through a dreamy, gauze and floral-decorated arch. Wearing a breathtaking off-white, satin, strapless beaded gown, Courtney was stunning as she floated down the aisle, escorted by her father.

While the guests rose and applauded Courtney's entrance, Nivea was breathing fire and trembling with rage. *This is a travesty. Knox doesn't love Courtney; he should be marrying me!*

For Nivea, it was pure torture listening to Courtney and Knox exchanging long-winded, honey-dripped vows. *Lies, lies, lies*, Nivea shouted in her mind.

When the time came for Knox to put the ring on Courtney's finger, the best man took on a frightened look, and began fumbling inside his pocket. *Yay! He forgot the ring! No ring; no marriage*, Nivea told herself as she held her breath, hoping for a miracle.

But the ring was soon produced. Knox gazed lovingly at Courtney and placed the ring on her finger. "I now pronounce you man and wife," the preacher announced.

Knox gathered Courtney in his arms and kissed her with un-bridled passion. Sickened by the gratuitous spectacle, Nivea gagged and heaved, emitting a gush of multi-colored vomit that splattered Courtney's pristine wedding gown.

The entire wedding party, including the pastor, jumped out of the line of fire, as Nivea continued heaving and retching.

"Get this bullshit off of me," Courtney shrieked. "This can't be happening. Not on my wedding day! Oh, God, this is not happen-inggggggggg!"

The guests erupted in stunned gasps, their hands covering

their mouths as they gaped at the sight of Courtney's befouled wedding dress.

His face twisted in disgust, Knox attempted to soothe and calm Courtney, but was careful not to get too close.

Determined to bring some order to the chaotic situation, Mrs. Westcott rose from her seat, snatching the satiny fabric that decorated the back of her chair.

Glowering as she passed Nivea, Mrs. Westcott raced to Courtney's aid.

Using the satin fabric, she tried wiping the vomit that oozed thickly down Courtney's designer gown, but she quickly gave up. Mrs. Westcott grabbed Courtney by the hand. "Come on, baby. Mother's going to get you out of this disgusting dress."

Pushing past the pastor, she took a moment to glower at Nivea. "Get out of my sight, Nivea! You're a damned disgrace, spewing your guts out on your sister's wedding day!"

"I didn't get sick on purpose," Nivea cried, standing bowed and clutching her stomach, as if expecting another explosion.

"Couldn't you have excused yourself?" Mrs. Westcott snapped, wheeling away, tugging along her hysterical younger daughter.

"No, I couldn't excuse myself!" Nivea yelled in a voice that was loud enough for all the guests to hear. "Unfortunately, this baby that I'm carrying doesn't care that it's his father's wedding day!"

Mrs. Westcott froze. A hush went over the astonished guests.

"What did you say?" Courtney demanded, her bewildered gaze roving back and forth from Nivea to Knox.

Eyes wide, Knox shook his head, palms held heavenward.

"Don't play dumb, Knox," Nivea said snidely. "Don't you think it's time to tell your little bride about our secret love affair?"

Guests murmured excitedly. Mrs. Westcott fanned herself. Courtney's face crumpled with pain and humiliation.

"I think I'm going to faint," Courtney whimpered.

"Your sister is a liar," Mrs. Westcott hissed. "Get out of here, Nivea. Right now! Get out before I have you physically removed."

"Don't worry, I'm leaving." Nivea turned to Knox. "This isn't over, Knox. You don't fuck me over me and get to have a fairy tale ending."

CHAPTER 58

Harlow was in town with Drake and Vangie couldn't wait to share her good news.

Vangie and Harlow were seated inside the crowded Copabanna Restaurant on Fortieth Street. The place was jam-packed with noisy college students and tourists.

"I know you like to dine at five-star eateries, but we're on my dime," Vangie informed, laughing. "By the way, your ring is nice, but I still don't understand why you traded in your big bling."

"I like this ring better," Harlow said, and then quickly changed the subject. "And as far as eating at here at Copa's…Vangie, you know I still get down with their buffalo wings. And where else can I get a big ass container of Spanish Fries? So what's your news?"

"I don't have to pay Shawn another dime," Vangie announced, grinning.

"For real?"

Vangie nodded.

"I knew Shawn would come to his senses and do the right thing."

"Hmph. Shawn didn't do the right thing. I did."

"Explain…"

"Well, I knew that there had to be a way for me to prove that Shawn had income. I just couldn't see myself paying him all that money until Yuri's eighteen."

"Umph." Harlow shook her head.

"So I did some online research and I found countless cases of women paying men child support. Reading all of the information was so helpful to me, and let me know that I wasn't alone and that there were solutions."

The waiter interrupted to take their order.

"I'll have Southern-style crab cakes and buffalo wings," Vangie said.

Harlow gave the menu one last glance. "Chicken fingers for me and Spanish fries. Oh yeah, and I'll have a raspberry margarita with a sugar rim."

"That sounds good. Make that two raspberry margaritas," Vangie added.

"Okay, so what did you do?" Harlow asked after the waiter walked away.

"I hired a private investigator. I got his name off the Internet and called him immediately."

"Seriously?"

"Hell, yeah. His name is Mr. Mansfield. He wanted a hundred and twenty-five an hour, but once he heard my story, he cut me a big break."

Harlow peered at Vangie. "Okay…"

"Well, I called him, and I was like, 'I need to prove that my baby daddy is earning an income. Can you get me some evidence that I can take to court with me?'"

Harlow giggled. "You got right to the point, huh?"

"I couldn't afford to be playing around. Can you imagine going to work every day to pay some nucca to spend some time with his own son?"

"No. That's horrible. I'm shocked that Shawn would do you like that."

"Shawn's been watching too much TV. All this K-Fed, Halle Berry baby daddy bullshit done put ideas in his head. But I ain't got it like Britney and Halle; I had to handle my business. So I met with Mr. Mansfield and gave him a picture of Shawn. I gave him Shawn's address, his job location, and told him what kind of vehicle he drives."

"Vangie, that's so impressive."

The waiter returned. He set their margaritas in front of them and promised to be right back with the appetizers.

"Girl, I was desperate. I didn't have a choice. I couldn't go down like that. After I paid Mr. Mansfield a deposit, he called me a week later, asking if I had the balance."

"Did you have the rest of the money?"

"No, but I borrowed it from my mother. As promised, Mr. Mansfield delivered. He handed me a manila envelope filled with pictures of Shawn inside the barbershop with the clippers in his hand, cutting one head after another. Mr. Mansfield even had pictures of Shawn accepting payment from his customers."

"This is an incredible story."

"Yeah, well, I took that incredible story, along with the glaring evidence, right down to Family Court. I didn't even have a lawyer, but I figured out how to file a motion of newly discovered evidence. Girl, you couldn't tell me that I wasn't a powerful attorney. You should have seen me attaching that damning evidence to the paperwork. A month later, I was back in court. Shawn and his pit bull lawyer looked so dumb, trying to act shocked over the pictures, like they couldn't understand how Shawn had ended up with those clippers in his hands."

Laughing hard, Harlow almost choked on her drink.

"The judge ruled in my favor! Case muthafuckin' closed!" Vangie held up her hand and Harlow slapped it.

"So, Shawn is paying you child support now?"

"Uh-huh. I got six thousand toward his arrearages. And more to come. That's why we're sitting here celebrating!"

"All right, girl!"

Vangie's expression changed. "But on a sad note..."

"Oh, God."

"Nivea had a complete meltdown at her sister's wedding."

"What do mean?"

"I wasn't there, but from what I've been told, Nivea projectile vomited all over Courtney's hand-beaded wedding dress—"

Harlow looked aghast. "Are you kidding?"

Vangie shook her head. "And that's not the worst of it."

Harlow covered her mouth and then removed it. "What else?"

"Nivea's pregnant. And guess who she's accusing of being the father."

"I'm scared to ask. She's been running around screwing everything that moves, like she's on some kind of sex vendetta. Who's the father—Eric?"

"According to Nivea, it's Courtney's new husband."

"Aw, that's cold. Why would Nivea try to ruin that young couple's happiness? Is she really that mean-spirited and jealous-hearted? Or just plain crazy?"

Vangie shrugged. "It's possible that she's certifiably crazy. Her parents had to have her three-o-two'd right after the wedding because she kept harassing Courtney and Knox while they were on their honeymoon."

"Nivea flipped out like that?"

"Couldn't you tell something was going on with her when we all had dinner together at The Four Seasons?"

"In retrospect, yeah." Harlow leaned forward. "Is she really pregnant?"

"I don't know. I guess we'll have to wait until we hear Nivea's side of the story."

"Can we visit her?"

"No visitors. I hope they don't have our girl locked up in a padded cell."

"Poor Nivea."

"I know, right? Who would have thought that Niv would end up like this? She had the professional parents, went to the best schools…It just goes to show you that things aren't always the way they appear. To be honest, I think Nivea started slowly losing it after she and Eric broke up."

Harlow shook her head, feeling more grateful than ever that she was getting help for her problems.

CHAPTER 59

Autumn

Some girls grow up dreaming of their wedding day, but for Harlow, every day of her young life had been a struggle for survival. Back then, imagining that a day like today was remotely possible hadn't entered her mind.

But here she was, holding a cascading bouquet and standing next to Drake at the altar.

It was an intimate evening ceremony at a posh Philadelphia restaurant. The atmosphere was romantic, warm, and inviting. The twenty guests were close friends and family.

Having no blood relatives, Harlow regarded Vangie as family. And today was the opportune time to set her girl up with Drake's right-hand man, Alphonso. She hoped they'd find in each other the kind of connection that she and Drake had.

Nivea was also in attendance and she seemed like her old self. Five months pregnant, and uncertain of the paternity of her child, Nivea appeared to be coping with the dilemma.

The minister began, "Friends and family, we are gathered together to celebrate the wedding of Harlow and Drake." Throughout the speech, Harlow tried to pay rapt attention to each word that was spoken. Drake was making it difficult for her to concentrate, showering her with a continuous smile and admiring glances.

He became attentive when the minister addressed him: "Will you take Harlow to be your lawful-wedded wife, love her, honor, and keep her in sickness and in health, forsaking all others until death do you part?"

"I do," Drake answered.

Harlow was addressed next. And in a voice that trembled with emotion, she said, "I do."

Concluding the ceremony, the minister asserted, "I now pronounce you husband and wife! You may kiss your bride."

As Drake kissed Harlow, her teardrops dampened his face. "Why are you crying?"

Smiling through her tears, she whispered, "Because I'm so happy."

In a booming voice, the minister proclaimed, "Ladies and gentlemen, I give you Mr. and Mrs. Drake Morgan."

The reception immediately followed. Drake took Harlow in his arms and glided her across the dance floor. They clung passionately to each as if they'd never let go.

When the music ended, Alphonso approached. Bowing slightly, he extended his hand. "May I have this dance, Mrs. Morgan?"

Harlow giggled and blushed at her new name, but she declined. "All my dances are for Drake. Tonight and forever," she added. "Ask my girlfriend, Vangie, to dance." She pointed to Vangie. "She's been dying to meet you."

Alphonso gave Vangie an approving glance. Smiling slightly, he said, "I can do that. Your girlfriend's real cute."

Harlow signaled Vangie with a thumbs-up.

When Alphonso walked away, Drake put his arm around Harlow's waist. Drawing her close, he whispered in her ear, "We have a flight to catch, Mrs. Morgan."

"I can't believe we're actually married. In a way, I regret that we planned a honeymoon in Paris."

He furrowed his brow. "Why do you say that?"

Harlow shrugged. "I hate leaving. I want this perfect moment to last forever."

❤ ❤ ❤

Leaving their guests behind, partying, Harlow and Drake stepped outside into the cool evening breeze. Stars glittered in the sky as though purposely sharing their sparkle in celebration of the couple's union.

"It's a beautiful night," Drake murmured.

Harlow looked toward the sky and sighed blissfully. "It's magical."

He grasped her hand, escorting her toward the limo that was parked at the far end of the block.

Hand in hand, they strolled down Broad Street, taking in the sights of beautiful downtown Philadelphia at night. Seemingly out of nowhere, there was a rush of violent movement, jostling the newlyweds. The surprising collision threw Harlow off balance, but Drake's quick reflexes kept her steady and on her feet.

"You ain't shit, just like your no-good mother," croaked a horribly familiar voice.

Harlow gawked in surprise when she recognized Ronica's snarling, disfigured face.

"You and you mother owe me for all I did for y'all. Jody's the reason that my body got all burned up. But that bitch is dead, so you owe me double."

"Yo!" Drake held up a hand as if his hand alone could halt the offensive barrage. Brazenly, Ronica pushed his arms aside, and stepped in closer. In one hand, she held a tattered Bible, and in the other she brandished a rusted jackknife, fully extended.

"Pay up, Harlow, before I start spreading your business. I know you don't want that. Hmph! You think you're all important now that you grown; well, I know what kind of gutter tramp you really are."

"Shut your fucking mouth and get that knife away from my wife!" Drake grabbed for the knife, but Ronica was quick, slicing the soft flesh of his palm. Blood spurted.

Harlow gasped, unaware that Drake was now reaching for his gun.

And before Harlow realized that she'd moved, she had rushed forward, forcibly pushing the knife-wielding attacker away from her husband.

Ronica was shoved so hard, she stumbled off the curve and into Broad Street. Her Bible skidded into traffic, and Ronica fell flat on her behind. Possessing uncanny agility, she sprang quickly to her hobbled feet. No longer contemplating blackmail or extortion, her crazed thoughts were now focused on bloodshed. "Both of y'all bitches 'bout to die now."

Bringing herself to a full stand, Ronica took one menacing step forward. A split-second later, she was airborne.

Harlow covered her mouth. Holding back a scream, she witnessed her ragged tormentor catapult, as if launched into the sky.

The SEPTA bus driver pressed on the brakes, causing them to screech and wail. But it was too late; Ronica had already been hit. The driver ran off the bus. "She came out of nowhere!" he shouted out loud, and then gaped at the broken body that lay splattered on the asphalt.

With his necktie serving as a bandage on his wounded hand, Drake guided Harlow forward. "Come on, baby, keep walking. Don't even look over there." His expression was hard and intense. His voice sounded cold, and unnatural.

"B-but, I—"

"What are you worrying about her for? That bitch got hers,"

he said in a voice that was chilling. "Now get in the limo; we're going to Paris."

The glint in Drake's eyes was terrifying; he had a look that Harlow had never seen before. "Drake, I don't..." Harlow couldn't stop trembling.

Drake touched her face with his good hand, and spoke in a gentle tone. "It's over, Harlow. She won't be coming at you anymore. I love you, Harlow, and I'll never let anyone hurt you," he said as if explaining something that she didn't understand. "Get in the limo, baby."

Harlow got in. Drake slid in beside her.

"We're going to the airport," Drake told the driver.

Harlow searched Drake's face, looking for a hint of the ruthless person she'd seen only seconds before. But the look was gone and she was gazing into her husband's warm, beautiful eyes. Resting her head on his shoulder, she softly asked, "Don't you think a doctor should take a look at your hand?"

"Nah, that ain't nothing. Couple of Band-Aids, and I'll be all right."

Drake cracked a sudden smile and kissed the top of Harlow's head. "I'm good, baby. Tonight is the beginning of the rest of our lives."

ABOUT THE AUTHOR

Allison Hobbs burst on the literary scene with the release of her highly successful, debut novel, *Pandora's Box* in 2003. *Riveting! Graphic! Edgy!* Those are just a few words that describe the responses to Allison Hobbs' writing style. Allison Hobbs is known for her sexy scenarios and memorable characters. She takes erotica to another level but always interjects humor throughout.

A prolific writer, Allison is the author of fifteen novels and novellas, including *Stealing Candy and Lipstick Hustla.*

Allison has been nominated three times for The Annual African American Literary Awards show for Best Erotic Author.

Visit Allison online: www.allisonhobbs.com, www.facebook.com/allisonhobbs, www.twitter.com/allisonhobbs

Praise for Allison Hobbs

"The only woman on the planet freakier than me!"
—ZANE, *New York Times* bestselling author and co-executive producer of Cinemax's *Zane's Sex Chronicles*

"Allison Hobbs delivers a witty, insightful, and sexy treat that grabs your attention from the very first page and keeps it."
—MARY MONROE, Bestselling Author of *God Don't Like Ugly*

BE SURE TO CHECK OUT ALLISON HOBBS' NEXT
RED HOT RELEASE

SCANDALICIOUS

By Allison Hobbs
Coming Soon from Strebor Books

CHAPTER 1

He cupped her ass cheeks, tugging her closer, until his dick was embedded to the hilt. Gritting his teeth and squeezing his eyes shut tightly, he forced back the load that swelled his shaft.

She squirmed beneath him, urging him. Her moans were almost too much to bear. "You're so fucking beautiful." His voice was a low growl. After all these years, his wife's beauty still astonished him. Drove him mad. He pulled back a little, and then deepened his stroke. Going hard. Disregarding self control.

Getting a grip, he shook his head. He wasn't ready to disconnect. He wanted to be with her—like this—for as long as he could.

Desperately, his lips found hers. He put some tongue into the kiss, taking his mind off the juicy pussy that enveloped his dick. He stopped his stroke and lay motionless. Further movement would cause a premature eruption.

His mouth moved downward. He buried his face in her breasts, brushing his cheeks against the softness of her satiny skin. Licking, tasting. Lips hungrily surrounding the aching tips.

Overcome by her womanly softness, his dick throbbed, straining for release. She felt so good—so wet and creamy. It took every ounce of his willpower to maintain his self control.

He wanted to stay inside her forever, but with a soft groan, he withdrew himself. Palms pressed against the mattress, he slithered downward until he was kissing her thighs. Forcing her to spread her legs in helpless invitation.

His tongue slashed between her thick folds, and thrust toward the tiny entrance to her sex. Inside her walls, he daringly explored the moist and softly padded confines. Her pussy clenched and spasmed around his gliding tongue.

"This is good pussy, baby. So sweet," he uttered, as his finger toggled her clit, creating friction that made her moan in unbearable pleasure. He knew her body well. Could feel the pulse of a budding orgasm.

She writhed violently. Soft moans escalated to shouts of pleasure. Her chest rose and fell. Her body bucked wildly. She cursed. She prayed. And then her womb spasmed in grateful release.

It was his turn now. Sweat soaked her skin as he repositioned her languid body, pulling her to unsteady knees. He wanted to mount her…fuck her doggy style. One hand flat against her back, the other holding a dick that was heavy as a boulder. He steered his swollen length into her, gently at first.

Good pussy, he thought as he thrust with a pounding force. Driving himself deeply until he spurted his seed and collapsed. Drenched with perspiration, his chest molded to the curve of her back.

Good pussy motivated men to achieve their dreams. Good pussy was the reward for working your way through school and obtaining a college degree; it was the prize for earning a good living and enduring the challenges and pressures that come with a successful career. Good pussy was constantly on his mind. But keeping this pussy happy was becoming an impossible task.

Chevonne shifted. "You're smothering me, honey. Get up," she said with a grunt.

Lincoln opened his eyes. He was back in his bedroom, ejected from paradise. He closed his eyes again, unwilling to return to the reality of his life.

A career in peril. A dying marriage. An unhappy wife.

CHAPTER 2

An hour before dawn, Solay was out of bed, dressed, and ready to take on the new day. Situated beneath her modest apartment was her cupcake bakery, called Scandalicious. Only six months old, Solay's store-front business had taken off like a rocket. Known for their eye-catching appearance and scandalously delicious flavor, Solay's cupcakes were all the rage.

Keeping costs down, she offered limited selections with racy names like, Double Chocolate Decadence (chocolate cake and frosting), Sinful Seduction (rich red velvet cake with cream cheese frosting), and Passionate Kiss (moist vanilla bean cake topped with hot pink butter cream).

Solay also offered gourmet cupcakes as special orders.

She walked swiftly past floor lamps with fringed shades, chaise longues, and bistro-style chairs and tables. The provocative product names and the seductive ambiance of her shop added to the allure of Scandalicious.

Feeling a twinge of dissatisfaction, Solay stopped suddenly and looked around the small dining area. Her place was absolutely beautiful, but she needed more space. The wrought-iron tables and chairs were crammed together, not nearly enough seating to accommodate her growing clientele.

An unfamiliar sweet and spicy scent wafted from the kitchen. Holding a clipboard, Solay strolled behind the empty display case and pushed open the door to the kitchen with her hip. Her baking assistant, Mariama, was hunched over a butcher block table, chopping ginger root—of all things! Her work station was cluttered with oranges, lemon peelings, ginger root, a vast assortment of spices, and expensive-looking cellophane bags filled with gourmet caramel.

Solay scanned the odd assemblage of ingredients, and scowled at her baking assistant. "What's going on? What're you baking, Mari?" Solay tried to keep an even tone, but the quaver in her voice indicated that she was livid.

"I've been working on some new flavor profiles," Mariama said, her voice low and confident as she carefully sliced oranges. "We discussed adding a new addition to the menu, so I came up with an orange ginger cupcake, with a couple of twists." Mariama gave Solay a conspiratorial wink, and then jumped up and pulled a tray of cupcakes from the oven.

Solay felt anger settling around her, infuriated by the gall of Mariama. Oblivious, Mariama chattered happily about her concoction. "I'll use our signature butter cream frosting, but it's gonna be kick-ass when I mix in some tangy orange and lemon zest, and then top it with a caramel drizzle. There's gonna be a caramelized orange slice, adding extra flair and drama. I'm gonna call my creation, the Screamin' Orgasm." Mariama giggled. "The family-friendly version will simply be called, The Screamin' O."

Solay's jaw became unhinged. *Breathe, Solay. Count to ten before you go off on this heifer.*

"I thought it would be real cool if we featured each of my creations on the chalkboard as Mari's Delectable Special." Mariama beamed with pride.

A violation of this magnitude warranted an extended period of gasping in shock and gaping in disbelief. But time was ticking, and Solay didn't have that luxury. Momentarily stunned into silence, she pointed at the clock on the wall.

"I lost track of time, but when you see how popular my gourmet cupcakes will be, you'll understand that it was well worth the time invested."

"Business opens in a few hours," Solay exploded.

Sulking, Mariama grudgingly rose from the butcher block table. "I'll start mixing up the red velvet batter while the Screaming O's are cooling off."

"That display case is empty! It should be at least half-filled with trays of red velvet, chocolate, *and* vanilla cupcakes. What would possess you to waste precious time, experimenting with new flavor profiles?"

Mariama pinched her lips together and gave Solay a piercing look of irritation. "I'm not experimenting. I'm a trained pastry chef and—"

"You're a pasty school dropout," Solay reminded her. "You have a lot of gall referring to yourself as a pastry chef. Furthermore, I run this business...not you! How dare you take the liberty of ordering a bunch of expensive items without my permission?"

"Well, we talked about improving the menu," Mariama said weakly.

"We discussed *enhancing* the menu. My menu does not require improvement," Solay clarified as she set down the clipboard and huffily tied on a full-length apron, and began grabbing eggs, cream, and butter from the fridge.

Mariama touched the tops of her freshly baked cupcakes, and began scooping them out of the twelve compartments. "Wanna taste one?"

Solay frowned. "No, I don't. At seven-thirty, customers are going to come stampeding through the door. You're wasting time, Mari. No, start hustling. I wanna see tons of velvet coming out of the oven."

Mariama looked st her fragrant creations and gave a loud sigh. "What do you want me to do—trash the Screaming O's?"

"I don't care what you do with that ginger crap. Eat them for lunch, give them to homeless...I don't care what you do with them." Solay looked at her clipboard. "I came downstairs to tell you that I have a huge special order. One hundred cupcakes for a bridal shower. I planned on personally working on the order for most of the morning But now that I have to pitch in and help you, I don't know how I'm going to get it all done."

Solay was piping frosting onto a batch of chocolate cupcakes when the old-fashioned bell ding-donged above the front door.

"Morning, ladies," Vidal called with a musical lilt to his voice. Vidal worked the cash register, took phone orders, ran errands, and did a little bit of everything, except bake.

"Vidal! I need you in the kitchen," Solay yelled.

Fashion savvy, Vidal was looking particularly dapper in a cotton twill driving cap atop neck-length hair that was highlighted and coiffed by a stylist. Dark gray tailored trousers fit his lean body to a tee. His cherry gingham checked shirt was coordinated with a dark cardigan sweater and a bold gray plaid scarf was knotted around his neck.

He owned more shoes than both Solay and Mariama. He possessed oodles of accessories to complete his look: belts, ties, cuff links, hats, scarves, pocket squares, sunglasses, brooches, and earrings. You name the trinket, and Vidal not only owned it, he wore it well. It was a mystery to Solay how the man maintained such a stylish wardrobe with the meager paycheck he earned from the bakery.

Peering through tinted shades, and clenching his chin as he appraised the women's aprons that were dusted with flour and splashed with frosting and other unidentifiable stains, Vidal quipped, "Y'all look like hell. What's been going on back here—a cupcake war?"

"There's no time for humor," Solay chastised. "We have a situation, and I need you mixing batter—"

"Nuh-uh," he protested, shaking his bouncy hair. He waved a manicured finger, "I don't know anything about stirring up batter, chile." He scowled excessively, as if he'd been asked to kill, pluck, and cut up a chicken. "I can't work back here with my Dolce & Gabbana pants on," he said, folding his arms.

"This is a crisis, and I'm not going to argue with you, Vidal," Solay informed with a penetrating stare.

Vidal folded his arms. "You should have warned me. Had I known that you expected me to get all dusty, I would have thrown on something raggedy—something cheap and Old Navy-ish."

Solay was unfazed. "Grab an apron, Vidal, and get to work on the vanilla cupcakes."

"Solay, I can't be back here in this stuffy kitchen with all these ovens going. I'm a people pleaser; that's why I work the front."

Solay held up her hand. "You're whatever I need you to be, Vidal. Now get into an apron. Follow the recipe; don't get creative." She pointed to the recipes posted on the wall. "I have an important client that I have to focus on. I'll be damned if I'm going to lose business because Mari decided that she wanted to get fancy today."

A look passed between Vidal and Mariama.

"I'll be working in my apartment for a few hours. Call upstairs if you need me."

Vidal folded his arms and grumbled under his breath.

"Listen, I want this problem rectified. If that case isn't filled up by the time customers begin arriving, both of you can start looking for work elsewhere!" Solay grabbed her clipboard, wheeled around. She banged open the kitchen door with her shoulder.

"Oh, my Gawd, what's Miss Thang's problem?" Vidal inquired in a voice raised in exasperation.

"Dick! She needs to get laid," Mari said with a snort. "If Solay wants to rectify something, she should start by ending her sex drought. Some good dick would put a smile on her face, and we wouldn't have to deal with her being so mean and cranky all the time."

Solay heard Mariama's bitchy remarks, and felt offended. *I'm not mean and cranky! I'm a businesswoman. My schedule is too demanding to put up with the emotional attachments that surface when you hop into bed with a sex partner.*

CHAPTER 3

A delicious aroma filled Solay's small kitchen. In the privacy and serenity of her personal space, she sifted, poured, measured, and stirred, until she'd whipped up one hundred stunning cupcakes. The task could have been completed much quicker if she'd used the industrial equipment downstairs, but there was too much tension in that kitchen.

Mission accomplished, admired the pretty little masterpieces that she'd created. The cupcakes were frosted with French Vanilla butter cream that was piped into the shape of a rose, sprinkled with shimmering, edible pearls, and then dressed in silver cupcake linings. The assemblage of white rose cupcakes looked like a huge and elegant bridal bouquet.

As she began the task of carefully packaging them—twenty five cupcakes per each oblong box, she thought about Mariama's snide comment, and wondered if it were true? She shook her head. How could she be sexually frustrated with a drawer filled with a vast selection of sex toys?

But there was something to be said about the human touch. But where could she find the kind of intimacy she desired? She had neither the time nor inclination to go club hopping or cruising local bars. Besides, experience had taught her that the men who frequented meat market environments were the bottom of the barrel, not even worth a sleazy one-night stand.

Solay wanted sex—on her terms. Having to check in with anyone with a text message or a phone call to keep them from feeling insecure was asking to much of her. Women were accused of being clingy and needy, but from Solay's experiences, men were the ones that needed to be reassured with text messages and phone calls. Men were the ones calling her and asking, "How was your day?"

"Busy as hell!" she'd reply, allowing the stress to ring loud and clear in her voice.

"I was thinking about you."

"Oh, that's nice," she'd say, with uncomfortable laughter.

"Were you thinking about me?" the one-night stand would ask, totally testing her patience.

Hell, fucking no! she'd scream in her head, and then dryly respond, "Uh-huh."

At the point when the amorous caller began to hint that he was interested in seeing her again, Solay would have already labeled him a nuisance, and her fingers would begin rapidly tapping, as she deleted him from her contact list.

Call her selfish, but it was what it was. Solay was married to her business, and had scant little time for an extra-marital affair.

Everything about Scandalicious screamed sex, from the intimate French bistro décor to the provocatively sexy names of her cupcakes, and now Solay was feeling like she was somewhat of a fraud, running a sex-themed business when she wasn't getting any action.

There had to be a way to get the sex she desired without the complications of a relationship. After a few minutes of pondering her options, she went online. Wearing a naughty smile, she googled the phrase, "rent a dick." Her smile broadened when numerous possibilities popped on the screen.

She clicked on Rent-A-Man Escort Service. A variety of muscle-bound hunks represented the available offerings of that service. Solay was pretty sure that the beautiful images on the website were merely stock photos and not part of the actual selection. Undeterred, she perused the site, and learned that she had the option of hiring a man by the hour or renting his services for the night.

An hour's worth of no-strings-attached sex was all she needed to improve her attitude, and give her some of her swag back. Wheeling and dealing in the business world, required her to exude confidence and sex appeal.

Credit card in hand, she called and boldly requested a one-hour date, making it clear that she didn't need a dinner date, and she wasn't going to a business affair…all she wanted from her hired man was to be escorted straight to her bed!

* * *

As she swept through the dining area, Solay noticed that the place was jam-packed. Not one available seat. And there was a mob of people waiting at the counter. Business was good.

Vidal was entertaining the customers, joking and making quips as usual, enjoying the spotlight, and working the front as if it were his personal stage. Vidal had survived the kitchen war and had emerged without any noticeable battle scars. His appearance was as impeccable as always.

"Here you go. A dozen Passionate Kisses," Vidal said to a female customer. "I threw in a free Screaming Orgasm to complete your sinful night." Vidal said giving the patron conspiratorial wink. The customers who were in line waiting for their orders were not impatient. Thoroughly charmed by Vidal, the customers were completely entertained while waiting.

"What's the Screaming Orgasm?" someone in the line asked.

"Check out the menu." Vidal pointed to the chalkboard menu that hung on the wall behind him.

Solay's eyes wandered upward. Mari's Delectable Special: Screaming Orgasm (orange/ginger cupcake with Tangy orange butter cream frosting) $5.00 each

Solay was appalled at Mariama's willfulness, and intended to put her on a one-day suspension. Her thoughts were interrupted when she heard the next customer's request.

"I'll have a dozen cupcakes," said a woman carrying a briefcase and dressed in a conservative business suit. "I want four red velvet, four double chocolate, and four vanilla," she said, carefully avoiding the provocative cupcake names.

"Do you want the free Screaming O?" Vidal asked, his eyes gleaming with mischief as he put the business woman on blast.

"Sure, I'll try it," she said, lashes lowering in embarrassment, face flushing red.

Helping out in the front, Solay began packaging the woman's order.

"We'll have a half dozen Screaming O's," said two giggly college girls.

"Coming right up!" Vidal disappeared into the kitchen and then came right back, carrying a tray of six gorgeous. There were murmurings of "Wow," and "Oooh" as the customers glimpsed the pastel orange-colored delights. The caramelized orange slice embellishments gave the cupcakes an award-winning look . "Folks, we're down to the last half dozen of Screaming O's."

The customers released a collective groan. The two college girls clapped their hands as if they'd won a prize as they shelled over thirty dollars, plus tax.

While helping out in the front, Solay witnessed numerous customers who had gotten the free cupcake, returning to buy more.

"Those Screaming O's went like hot cakes," Vidal told a customer. "We'll have more tomorrow."

"No we won't," Solay's disagreed. "We'll be back to our regular menu tomorrow."

"You must not like money," Vidal muttered under his breath.

Solay let the comment slide. Vidal had no idea how expensive and time consuming it was for Mariama to create those cupcakes. She'd have to hire more help if she kept those Screaming O's on the menu.

By closing time, Solay had gotten over her anger and realized that she'd be only hurting herself if she put Mariama on suspension for even a day.

"Goodnight, ladies, it's been fun, " Vidal said, after tying his dramatic, fringed scarf around his neck. Before leaving, he bent and reached under the counter behind bags and cupcake boxes. "Voila!" He pulled out a single cupcake he'd carefully stashed behind the counter.

"Ooo, you're such a sneak," Mariama said, laughing.

"You're the Picasso of pastry," he said, eyeing the cupcake with admiration.

Flattered, Mari smiled, "Thank you, Vidal."

"I had to have at least one screaming orgasm after all that foreplay I put in today!" Vidal twirled around and headed for the door.

After Vidal left, Solay and Mariama cleaned up the kitchen. "In the future, you need to ask permission before you tamper with the menu. Nothing should be on that chalkboard or baked in my ovens with my explicit permission."

"But we discussed it…"

"Yes, we had a conversation, but nothing was finalized. Your cupcakes were a huge success, but I don't see how I can afford to allow you to bake anything other than the items on the menu."

"I can come in an hour earlier. Or stay a few hours later…you know, and start making up the batter for the next day."

"Why would you put yourself through that? I can't raise your pay."

"I'm bored doing the same thing every day. I need more creative expression."

"Well, that's something you'll have to do your own time. Seriously, Mari. I can't afford to buy those ingredients…even at five dollars a pop, I won't break even."

"Okay," Mariama said shrugging off the rebuff, but Solay could see the hurt in her eyes.

Solay patted Mariama's arm. "When I get a bigger shop, I'll add one of your concoctions to the menu, okay?"

"Sure," Mariama said dryly, and then turned her back and continued to briskly sweep flour from the floor.